The Whistle-Blower Onslaught

The Whistle-Blower Onslaught

David P. Warren

Chapter 1

December 16, 2015

My name is Scott Phillip Winslow. I live in Thousand Oaks, California, one of the many suburban areas within the Greater Los Angeles area, with my gorgeous wife, Lisa, and two amazing kids. I am a partner in a small law firm called Simmons and Winslow, in a practice that emphasizes employment litigation. My life has been pretty darn good, I must admit. At least until now—when changes in my world will soon come at me like a tsunami.

On Saturday morning, just nine days before Christmas, the chain of events that will change everything begins. I am perilously perched on the same rickety stepladder I had vowed to replace each year, for the past three years. I stand on the top step, which is plainly marked "do not stand," in an effort to reach the ragged hooks on the eves of our overpriced, suburban home with a string of Christmas lights. I am sweating, even though it is only sixty-five degrees outside, in keeping with my tendency to work too fast and too hard during what should have been a relaxing Saturday morning.

In truth, the kids had been asking me about our Christmas lights, or "Santa's wights," as Katy calls them with her adorable lisp and in her most serious tone, since Thanksgiving. I am feeling guilty about how long it's taken me to put them up. You should know that Katy is a force of nature. She is five years old, going on thirty-five. She has big blue eyes and blonde, wavy hair that flips just above her shoulders, where she carries the weight of the world. On no topic is Katy without an opinion. She knows how everything should be, and she makes it her business to see things happen as they should.

The end of my decorating procrastination came at the breakfast table just two hours ago, where I have been *had* so many times by the huckster disguised as my little girl and her "born cool" older brother, Joey, while my wife, Lisa, barely suppresses her laughter.

This morning's destruction of my plans to return to the office began with Katy's emergence for breakfast with the sad expression of a child whose hamster had just died. She sat silently pushing her fork at the pancakes on her plate, but eating nothing. Lisa and I exchanged perplexed gazes and then set about prompting her to share.

Through big, sad blue eyes, after brushing away a solitary tear, Katy confided, "This will be the first year that Santa's not coming on Christmas, that's what."

"What?" Lisa asked incredulously. "Why would you think that? Santa wouldn't miss us."

Katy shook her head in wide, slow motions, wholly unconvinced. "Santa's wights," she said. That lisp kills me. She furrowed her brow. "How is he supposed to land the sleigh?" I could already see my trip to the office becoming less likely.

Sometimes I hate how precocious she is.

"If we don't have a lit runway for the reindeer, there will be no presents on Christmas morning and no one to eat the cookies and drink the milk we leave on the fireplace on Christmas night," she said, pointing dramatically to the hearth for effect. Then she looked directly at me and said, "Daddy, I know how busy you are being a liar, but we need to have them on the house before *The Wizard of Oz* comes on Monday, because that's when Christmas really begins."

Seasons measured in TV events, I thought to myself, wondering what I might do to avoid having her extract the inevitable promise that I put the lights up now. A liar, for those outside our family, is a lawyer. It's both adorable and slanderous, and anyone who hears Katy refer to my profession requests that she do it again and again, grinning at me all the while.

Joey sat back in his chair with an expression that meant he was about to jump in, then said, "Yeah."

"Yeah?" I asked. "Yeah what?"

"She has a good point," he urged in his worldly seven-year-old manner.

"She does, huh?" I asked.

"Yeah. You can't dis Santa, then expect him to bring us all the stuff we want." The jet-black hair that Joey got from no one I know extended in all directions, with a few of the longer strands falling across his forehead into his right eye. His hair would remain a mess until we made him comb it after breakfast. He sat back in his chair, the man with all the answers, and waited while this gem was digested by his parents.

"Dis Santa?" I asked.

"Right," Joey urged with conviction. "He knows everything, so you can't fool the dude."

At this piece of wisdom from her big brother, Katy was nodding supportively. She is always impressed by the insights of her older brother. I looked over at Lisa for some support, but she was busy smothering a grin and silently enjoying watching me swim against the tide.

I frowned at Joey. "You can't fool the dude? Who taught you to talk like that?" He shrugged, having no time to waste on silly questions.

I looked from Joey to Katy. "Okay, you guys, we'll get the lights up," I offered, surrendering to this extemporaneous conspiracy.

Joey nodded with satisfaction, and Katy beamed. "Thank you, Daddy," she said and blew me a kiss. She reflected for a moment, and then said, "When?"

Once they have you on the ropes, they show no mercy. "This morning," I said, in total surrender. By the combination of Katy's face, and Joey's logic, I was had. I looked over at Lisa, whose blue eyes were alight with amusement. After ten years of marriage, the last several of which have been characterized by two kids constantly within earshot, we have developed a means of nonverbal communication that would make a porpoise jealous. She also knows that my Achilles heel is virtually anything that means a lot to the kids. I gave her a smile, acknowledging my predicament, while suddenly distracted by how great she looked. Those gorgeous blue eyes that she passed to both kids draw me in every time I look at her. Her blonde, shoulder-length hair and a slightly upturned nose evoke something between elegance and aristocracy, and her easygoing and practical manner helps keep me in check when I get too caught up in a crisis of the moment. Having been snared in a breakfast table trap and seeing no way out, I canceled my plans to go into the office in favor of putting up too many Christmas lights and adding to the energy crisis.

I walked over and whispered to Lisa, "I'm so glad you were having fun instead of bailing me out. You thoroughly enjoyed watching me squirm."

She put her arms around my neck and gave me a kiss. She smiled wryly and said, "You might also want to build a control tower, so Santa can get the proper landing clearances."

"I'm glad you're amused," I said. I started toward the garage, then turned back and added, "I'll deal with you later."

"Great. I'll put a good ravaging on my calendar," she said, then turned responsively to Katy's call for help with finding her shoes.

I went out to the garage, thinking that if I got this done fast enough, I could still get into the office for a couple of hours to finish jury instructions and my trial brief for the sexual harassment case set to start in two weeks. I found myself wondering how I would explain the case to Katy when she asked about it, and she would—she always asked about my trials. What I couldn't say was that the middle manager in a large company had spent two years asking his secretary about her sex life and favorite positions, and grabbing and rubbing against her whenever she bent over to file a document. I needed a more G-rated version of those events.

Once the work of putting up the lights begins, it proves to be as frustrating as ever. Burned out bulbs, blown fuses, and hooks that readily come off the house are among the highlights. And that has been my morning until right now.

Bernie Jacobs, my good friend and next-door neighbor, suddenly appears at the bottom of the ladder and looks up at me, a smug grin on his face. "Looks like you're working awfully hard at that," he offers with amusement. "You know, if you'd just convert, you wouldn't have to do all this stuff. I think everyone on this cul-de-sac should be Jewish. You guys and the McFaddens are the only holdouts."

I frown and say, "Maybe, but it's all I can do to prepare for one big day. If I had as many as you do to worry about, I'd never stay current."

"Not to worry," he says, "Katy would make you a chart."

I can't help but chuckle. He has her pegged. "She would," I offer, "in twelve colors, with footnotes." I point to the ground beneath the ladder. "Pass me that hammer," I ask.

He hands up the hammer. Bernie says, "Don't forget you and Lisa are coming over for drinks and dinner tonight."

I take the hammer and whack at a protruding nail, immediately bending it and causing it to drop to the ground. "Shit," I blurt out, staring downward at the grass that had swallowed up the fallen nail.

"Eloquent, counselor," Bernie muses. "Very articulate."

"Shut up and go start the barbecue. And get working on the mai tais. We'll be over in about six hours. I plan to be hungry and thirsty."

"Okay, I'll do it. It'll take that long to get your steak sufficiently well done to have that shoe leather consistency you strive for." I chuckle and glance down at Bernie.

His expression had become more solemn. "Actually," he offers, "there's another reason I came over."

"You want to apologize for four years of bad jokes and insults, right?"

"The thought never occurred to me," he says, sounding reflective. "Now that it has," he pauses a moment, then he adds, "no." He is grinning again.

"What then?" I ask, feeling as impatient as I probably sound.

"A good friend of mine came by this morning. His name is Kevin Walters, and he's got some big problems that are right up your alley."

I look down at Bernie, and there was no trace of humor in his expression. I climb down the ladder to make conversation easier. "And he needs to talk to me this morning?"

"If you can find the time." He pauses a moment and then adds, "It's important."

I nod. "What's the situation?" I ask, inviting a conversation that I had no time to have.

"Kevin is senior vice president with Consolidated Energy, or at least he was. The president of the company called him in and fired him on Thursday."

"For what reason?" I ask, now thoroughly off task and sucked into the scenario. It was an occupational hazard for an employment lawyer.

"Performance," is what he was told.

"And he disagrees with that conclusion, I take it?" I think briefly about my full calendar, and then say, "Maybe I can meet with him sometime this week."

Something caught Bernie's attention. He is looking over my shoulder toward his house. "Here he is now," Bernie says, gesturing for someone to join us.

My immediate response is an unspoken, *Oh shit,* at the thought of one more item on the morning's calendar. I turn around and see a tall, slender man of about sixty moving toward us. He wears wire rimmed glasses and has a full head of meticulously combed white hair. There are slight crow's feet at the corner of his eyes, and his features are sharp. He also wears a serious expression.

Walters joins us on the lawn and introduces himself with a deep voice that clearly enunciates, "I'm sorry to trouble you, Mr. Winslow. I know that you're a busy man and that this is your day off."

"It's okay," I say, somewhat disingenuously. "You want to come in and talk in my study?"

Walters nods. "Yes, if you're sure this is a good time."

Bernie says, "I'll leave you two to speak."

Walters shakes his hand. "Thanks for being a good friend, Bernie."

Bernie waves him off and turns toward home. "I'll see you and Lisa later," he calls out to me without looking back.

I nod to the back of him, and then lead Walters inside. I introduce him to Lisa, who greets him with a warm smile and an offer of coffee that he declines. As I lead the way into my study, Lisa asks that we let her know if we need anything.

My walnut desk is angled in the far corner of the room, while two armchairs separated by a small lamp table face the red brick fireplace on the wall closest to the door. Some evenings, when the kids are tucked in, between calls for water, retucking after bathroom trips and the comforting after the occasional nightmare, Lisa and I read by the fire in the warmth of each other's company.

I close the door and gesture to the closest armchair. I grab a yellow legal pad from my desk and sit down in the other chair. "How can I help, Kevin?"

"I don't know if you can, or for that matter if anyone can." He draws a breath, and then says, "I worked for Consolidated for twenty-seven years. As I'm sure you know, it is a huge international conglomerate. I was senior vice president of administration for the past seven years, reporting directly to the president and CEO, Michael Constantine. Before that, I was a regional vice president for the Central United States. I've been promoted seven times during my career—the whole fast track thing."

He pauses, and I sense that he was working to suppress emotion. "Anyway, Constantine called me in Thursday, flustered like I have never seen him, and tells me it's not working, and we need to part company. I knew instantly that it was because of my complaints about mine conditions that had gone unremedied, but part of me still couldn't believe it. Mike and I had been close for a lot of years, and I never thought ... "

He lets the sentence trail off, and then continues. "I told him that lives were put at risk by some of these conditions, and money can't be the reason not to protect employees. I'll never forget the anger in his eyes. Then he said he didn't know what I was talking about, and the company just needed a ... what were his words, yeah, 'a change in its top policy-making team.' I looked into his eyes and saw a flash of anger before he looked away. We sat in an awkward silence for a few minutes, while I tried to put all the pieces together. Then I told him I couldn't believe he could do this after all our years together."

Walters sits back in his chair and shakes his head as he relives the moment, then says, "He just looked at me and said that Human Resources would contact me to discuss my severance. Then I got up and walked out."

I am taking copious notes on my yellow pad, and looking up at Walters intermittently as I write. "Did Human Resources contact you?" I ask.

He replies, "Yes. Someone I had never spoken to before gave me a call and sent me the packet. The deal was that they give me a year's salary and medical, then I take early retirement, and I sign a release of any claims against the company." I could see anger on Walters's face. He pauses a moment, suppresses whatever it was, and speaks calmly. "I was about to take the package and retire, but the sons of bitches called me into a meeting and threatened me."

"Threatened you how?" I ask, thoroughly engrossed and having forgotten about my time crunch.

"With Alan Larson, one of the in-house lawyers, sitting there, the HR guy tells me that an officer of my rank could be prevented from working for a competitor, or sued for any proprietary information disclosed. I told him that I would disclose nothing proprietary, so he needn't worry." Walters sits back in his chair and reflects. "He told me that it goes a little deeper than that. That if I were to talk to any more outsiders, that they would construe my actions as disloyal, and act accordingly."

"What did you say?" I ask, already considering how all of this might play to a jury.

"I said, 'I get it.' Then I took the release they had given me, tore it into pieces, and let it fall to the floor. Sounds a little overly dramatic now, but I was pissed. I told them that they can keep their money, and they could construe my actions any way they liked. Then I said that I would do whatever it takes to see that no one else was hurt by the company's failure to protect them. At that point, I stood up and walked out of the room to complete silence."

"How long ago was this meeting?" I ask.

"Last Thursday, at two o'clock."

"Have you spoken to any company representative since then?"

He shakes his head. "No, although I have had five messages on my answering machine, two of which are from Constantine. Each of them assures me that they want me to have my severance and hope I haven't misconstrued what they had said. The bastards."

I take a moment to catch up on my notes, and then ask, "You said you knew instantly what it was about—when he fired you. What did you mean by that?"

"My complaints about dangerous conditions and violations that were not remedied were also not well-received. My complaints as well as some of the violations had to do with the conditions and safety of the shafts in the mine: inadequate ventilation and inadequate safety equipment. It was an old operation, and engineering inspections had shown rebuilding of the shafts were needed for the past year. The cure would have cost twenty million in engineering and construction costs, and would have shut down operations for at least four weeks, which is about another several million in revenue. So you can see what it would cost the company to comply."

As Walters draws a breath. I see the lines in his forehead deepen and his color turn ashen. The sincerity and the pain were evident in his face.

He forces himself to continue. "I had ordered correction of these violations, and it wasn't done. When I confronted the manager who failed to do it, he told me that Constantine had ordered him not to proceed with my instructions. I took the matter to Michael, who admitted that my orders had been ..." He pauses and his eyes narrow. "I even remember the term he used so dismissively. My orders had been 'set aside' because it was not a good time for the company to spend that much money. I had to swallow my anger to get the words out. I told him that we were risking lives. His response was that the engineers overstated the problem, and we would address it in due course. That was when the chasm between us opened up. I told him I could not accept that resolution; that something needed to be done now, not after a disaster. Michael stared at me silently for the longest time, and then he said that he would handle the matter from that point forward. I just walked out in silence and disbelief, knowing that there was no way back from this for me or him.

"I went to my office, and I called the mining inspector from Easton County, who told me that he had received a letter from the company two weeks ago stating that they were in the process of correcting the violations the county issued. I told him that the company was not correcting these violations, and we continued to operate at full strength. He told me he had been called to an emergency meeting in Richmond, but would be at the mine with a team within forty-eight hours, and that I should say nothing inside the company until then. I agreed. Seventeen hours later, before he and his team got there, we had a collapse at the site, and one worker died, and three were seriously injured."

"Holy shit," I say, incredulously.

"It gets worse. I also think that records were manipulated."

"Why do you think so?"

"Because violations that preexisted the disaster were no longer there. It's like they disappeared from the records."

"Unbelievable," I say. "That's the Wheeling collapse I heard about on the news?"

"One and the same," Walters says. "And you probably also saw reports showing everything was first-rate at that site."

"Yeah, the company was almost immediately vindicated. I was surprised how quickly."

"Right. The reporting said this was a great facility, and no violations were found to have caused the explosion. The whole thing was smoke and mirrors, but it was brilliant, and Constantine somehow got it done like that." Walters snaps his fingers to drive home the point.

I nod, reflect, and then ask, "So did this fellow from Easton County—you don't happen to know his name, do you?"

"I do," he said. "It's Miller. Carl Miller."

"Did he ever show up at the real site?"

"One day later. I met with him and told him that the conditions had not been corrected. He told me he was going back to the office to get the lawyers involved. He was angry, and he was talking injunctions and major fines. He shook my hand and left."

"Did he do it?" I ask, thinking that the fines, or even a report, would help us establish that the site had problems.

Walters pursed his lips and furrowed his brow. "No," he says, wonder in his voice. "Two days later, when I had heard nothing, I called him. They told me he no longer worked for the county. After I was fired, I spent a couple of days trying to track him, but I just hit a brick wall. No one seems to know where he is."

I stop writing for the first time in twenty minutes and exercise my cramping hand. "That's an incredible story," I offer. "Based upon what you've told me, I think you can bring a lawsuit for wrongful termination in violation of whistle-blower statute and wrongful termination in violation of public policy, which protects employees from retaliation for the reporting of conduct by the company that was contrary to law and public policy. If you win, you can recover economic losses, such as salary and benefit losses, and emotional distress damages. If a jury believes that the employer acted maliciously, punitive damages to punish the employer's misconduct for profit."

Walters regards me for a moment, and then says, "I understand, but I want you to know that this is not about money for me. This company has been my life for over twenty-seven years. I would have been satisfied to walk away, even though I don't think I should have been fired.

I'm okay for money, and I'll get by however this suit comes out. I just can't let the company trade lives for money and then cover it up."

That was the moment when I knew that I would represent Kevin Walters.

He takes off his glasses and rubs his eyes, and then replaces them. He looks at me with concern, and a certain vulnerability that gave him a very human, credible quality. My assessment isn't simply an evaluation of jury potential; I really like the man. "I'm told that you're good at what you do. Will you help me?" he asks, getting to the bottom line.

I momentarily ignore the ultimate question, instead posing one of my own. "What about reports prepared by Carl Miller? Have you attempted to get those?"

He nods, his expression a combination of perplexed and uncomfortable. "I did. The county says that they have no record of what he wrote or the letter I wrote; no notes, nothing." He was quiet, and then says, "I'm sure that everyone you talk to sees conspiracies around every corner, but I know what this company can do. What Constantine lacks in humanity, he tries to compensate for in IQ points."

I say, "I think you're a credible guy, and that's important to my assessment of whether I represent someone." I lean back in my chair, and add, "But, to be frank, my concern is how we prove any of this to a jury, especially in the face of disappearing evidence. If we can't turn up any critical documents, the company will do their best to pass you off as a sour grapes case; fired and looking for revenge." Walters silently considers this. I add, "Give me twenty-four hours to review and consider, and I'll get back to you."

"Fair enough," he says, and we both stand. He adds, "You should also know that they will fight us with everything they've got. And they've got amazing resources."

I nod. That fact was not disconcerting to me, because this was the story of my life. In representing an employee against a major corporation, it doesn't take long to become fully indoctrinated to large defense firms aiming to paper you to death; staffing a case with a partner, to make the big decisions; a senior associate, to handle most of the work on the case; and a new associate, to spend countless hours in researching obscure questions, preparing interrogatories and requests to produce documents, and whatever else rolls downhill. "I understand," I say. "I regularly tangle with members of the Fortune 500, and they never make the job easy."

We walk through the front door and then stop on the driveway to shake hands and say good-bye. "I like you, Scott," Walters tells me. "You seem like a good guy, and I'd be comfortable having you represent me. I hope you decide that you can take the case. In any event, thanks for taking time from your family to talk to me."

I had already decided that I would represent him, and I'm still not sure why I didn't tell him then. Instead I smile, extend a hand, and say, "It has been a pleasure to meet you, Kevin. I will call you tomorrow."

As I watch him walk toward the gray Tesla parked in front of Bernie's house, I evaluate the conversation. I believe what he said, and he seemed like a guy who was screwed over by his decision to do what was right rather than what was profitable or expedient. It was courageous, and I respected it. I take satisfaction in my work as a fighter for the underdog. The image of the little David whose rights have been trampled by the all-powerful Goliath is an image I like to convey to juries, who are often employees who don't like one of their own to be victimized by an entity much more powerful than themselves. And employees bringing an action are underdogs. The big company has all of the information, controls many of the personnel, and often has limitless resources at its disposal.

As I consider Kevin Walters, it occurs to me that he is the real thing. I already know that I want the case, and I will take it on unless Bernie reveals something sinister about the man, or I learn that he is a refugee from a state mental institution, both of which I doubt. As I consider all of this, I have no idea what the decision to represent Kevin Walters is going to do to me and my family life.

After saying good-bye to Kevin Walters, I turn back toward the house to see Katy standing on the lawn, looking up at the few lights so far in place with her hand on her hip. I suppress a giggle as I watch her shaking her head in displeasure. What a ball-buster she is. "Daddy, are you still going to have time to do this before *The Wizard of Oz*? Maybe I can get you some coffee to help you."

Apparently, my little girl thinks that caffeine is the only answer to my limited progress. "I'll get it done, sweetie," I say, reassuringly. "Don't you worry." I have visions of me outside on the rickety old ladder at midnight. She gives me a wide smile, and the idea of being on that ladder at midnight doesn't seem so bad. Clearly, little girls have way too much influence over their daddies.

Chapter 2

At 5:00 p.m., Lisa and I sit in Bernie and Kathy Jacobs' backyard watching the orange-infused clouds reach across the western sky. The four of us sit in a circle talking while Joe and Katy watch the movie *A Christmas Story* for the twentieth time. They know this movie so well that they periodically recite dialogue before it is spoken. Katy and Joey are both fascinated by Ralphie's obsession with a Red Ryder BB gun and are amused by his father's obsession with a bizarre lamp in the shape of a woman's leg that he won.

"It's getting cold," Kathy urges. "Let's go in."

"You and Lisa go ahead," Bernie says. "Scott and I will be in as soon as I pull the steaks off the barbecue. As a matter of fact, they may be done now."

I walk with Bernie to the barbecue as Lisa and Kathy move into the house. He grabs a plate and reaches for the meat with tongs. I frown. "If you aren't going to cook it, at least give it a tan before you pull it."

Bernie shakes his head. "Not everyone wants beef jerky for dinner. Don't worry, though, I put yours on right after we spoke this morning."

We laugh as he pulls three steaks off and turned the fourth. "So, how did it go with Kevin Walters?" he asks.

"Good. I like the guy."

Bernie nods. "Do you think you can help him?"

"I think I'm going to try, although I haven't committed yet." Bernie continues watching the grill. "How do you know him?" I ask.

"Consolidated Energy acquired Lincoln Energy out of Nebraska last year. One of about ten competitors they gobbled up. I brokered the deal, and Kevin and his team negotiated the acquisition from inside. The deal went on for a few months, and I had a number of meetings with Kevin. Smart guy and a good negotiator. When it was all done, I considered him a friend."

I nod. "How did you learn that they had fired him?"

"I ran into him at a ball game a couple of days ago and he told me he wasn't with Consolidated anymore. I pried what had happened out of him—couldn't believe it. Then I told him to call Robin Hood of the legal profession."

"That's me?" I ask.

"Sure. You take money from asshole rich guys and redistribute it to the people they fuck over, right?

"Certainly an eloquent way of putting it," I say. "But doesn't it sound a little more like Karl Marx? Each according to his need—that kind of socialist philosophy?"

"Maybe, but isn't Robin Hood a socialist for that reason?"

"I don't know, but I have to admit that I like the Robin Hood image."

"Yeah," Bernie says. "Me, too. Put it on your business card or something."

"Right. Maybe with a picture of me in tights?" I add.

"Awesome. I'll pass them out at the next Chamber mixer for you." Then he adds, "I hope you can do him some good. I really like the guy."

"He makes a good first impression."

"Second and third are even better," Bernie says as he pulled the last steak off the fire. "Well, let's eat while you analyze before all this gets cold."

Joey and Katy eat hotdogs hurriedly, so they can get back to the *Christmas Story* movie. Katy's dog was just a bun and a dog. No condiments in sight. Joey's dog was overflowing with ketchup, which could be followed across the plate and onto the table.

"Hey you guys, this is not a race. Take your time and digest a little bit," I say.

"Dad, we need to get back to the movie," Katy says, as if this were obvious. I suppress a smile.

"We have the movie recorded. It will wait for you."

"Yeah, Dad," Joey says through a mouthful of hotdog. "But it's at a really good part. A kid is about to get his tongue stuck on a pole."

Lisa smiles. "That is a good part." Then she adds, "Careful, Joe," and mops the table in front of him with a napkin to gather the escaping ketchup.

He grunts an okay and takes another bite.

Bernie looks at Lisa and then at me. "I hope you guys are still planning on joining us to celebrate our anniversary next Friday."

"We are," Lisa said. "We wouldn't miss it."

Bernie looks over at Kathy. "I am a lucky man," he says.

"Even after twelve years?" Kathy asks.

"More than ever."

"It's getting pretty romantic," Katy says, looking up from her hot-dog.

The room bursts into laughter. "Yes it is, sweetie," Bernie says. "We'll try to keep that under control."

"Thank you," Katy says, turning back to her show.

After a moment, Kathy turns to Lisa. "I don't think we ever heard how you guys met."

Lisa looks over at me and shakes her head. "Scott is such an asshole," Lisa says, mouthing the expletive silently because of the smaller ears in the area.

Kathy wore a look that was half amusement and half surprise. "What?"

Lisa says, "All right, let me tell you about our first meeting, and you'll see why we almost never happened. Scott and I both went to a party with friends. We saw each other across a large room and smiled at each other. I asked who he was, and I was told his name. I'm also told he is a great guy."

"Sounds good, so far," Bernie says.

"Yeah, but then he walked over to me and said, "Hi, how are you?"

I said, "I'm fine. And then he said, get this, 'Do we belong together, or is it just wishful thinking on your part?' "

Kathy and Bernie laugh hard. "Damn," Bernie says. He looks at me and says, "You really are an asshole. I'm surprised the two of you ever got off the ground."

"We almost didn't." Lisa says. "I groaned and said, 'What a creep.' I was turning to walk away when Scott started to laugh hysterically. I stared at him, a little confused, and then it hit me that this was a bizarre joke. I just looked at him. "I'm sorry, he said. "I just wanted to make an impression. I told him that it was obvious that he didn't care if it was a good one."

"Don't you love it," I say. "That's when I knew that I had to get to know this woman."

"And in spite of that start, she let you?" Kathy asks.

I nod. "Remarkable, isn't it? I had to work hard to overcome that first impression, but within a year she liked me."

"And most of the time I still do," Lisa adds.

"See," I say, "she also takes care of herself pretty damned well."

Bernie pours more wine, and we talk until we realize it is almost ten o'clock. We pick up our little girl, who had fallen asleep during the second running of the movie, and tell Joe it is time to go home. We hug our friends, and they walk us to the front yard. We thank them, and, as we walk toward home, I find myself contemplating Kevin Walters. I am intrigued and thinking about his case. Oddly, as I think about Kevin's case I have an inexplicable feeling of foreboding.

* * *

Two days later, at 10:00 a.m., I meet with Kevin Walters to discuss my final decision on whether I will take his case. When I take a case, I study what my new client did for a living before being terminated, demoted, harassed, or discriminated against. That way I can sound like I know what I'm talking about when I argue with a defense lawyer about whether my client graced the planet with brilliance never before witnessed in his industry. They, in turn, respond that he or she was a complete idiot, who lasted as long as he or she did only out of unparalleled levels of corporate benevolence. The truth, of course, is usually somewhere between the polar extremities I and my adversaries seek out, but we cannot accept that reality. There is simply no percentage in arguing mediocrity to a jury.

This process of identifying a client's virtues is what I engage in this afternoon, and I'm feeling pretty good about what I see. Kevin Walters sits across the conference room table in my office, waiting patiently while I review a neatly organized file documenting his history with Consolidated Energy that he brought along. He has documents revealing raises, promotions, performance evaluations commendations, policies, and other documents that chronicle over twenty-seven years of employment history, most of it spent climbing to great heights before the fall. I am considering how I will use these documents to prove my client is the good guy in this fight. After about fifteen minutes of silent review, I tear my eyes from the files long enough to look up at Walters and say, "I notice that the evaluations stopped about ten years ago."

He nods, and then offers, "When you get to vice president, the company stops that paperwork."

"Because?" I ask.

He raises an eyebrow in a manner that conveys careful consideration of the question, "Because no one has time for that stuff anymore. If you're doing well, you'll know it. If not, you're history." He has a direct and sincere style that I like and, more importantly, that a jury will like.

I nod, and then reply, "And Consolidated will say that's what happened to Kevin Walters. He wasn't doing well, so he's gone." I wave several of the performance evaluations in the air for effect. "Can you hear the argument? Walters's performance got progressively worse after these stopped." I wait for his response.

"I'm not too worried about that," he says with confidence, then falls silent.

"Enlighten me," I say.

He smiles. "You do this a lot, don't you?"

"At least," I reply, returning the grin.

His expression becomes more serious, and he speaks with confidence. "I think they will have a hard time refuting that every year, my performance bonus exceeded that of the other two division vice presidents. I also have several awards and congratulatory memos—more "attaboys" at home. There's a second file and some wall-sized certificates and awards that I didn't bring to this meeting."

Time for my eyebrows to reach for the sky. "Any of them directly from Constantine?

"Most of them," he says softly.

"Any during the last five years?" I ask.

"A number of them."

"Guard them with your life until you get them in here. That may well be what gets us past the bullshit that they will likely offer about your history of plummeting performance."

"Sure," Walters says. "I'll have them here tomorrow."

At that moment my assistant, Donna, knocks on the partially open conference room door, and then sticks her head in the door and announces that Mrs. Walters is here. Donna is thirty-five years old, about five feet five, and has short-length blonde hair and a wry grin. Her large brown eyes are warm and quickly make human connections. She has natural warmth that makes clients love her and opposing attorneys try to steal her after visits to my office for depositions. Fortunately for me, she always turns them down. She has been my paralegal for six years, and she is fiercely loyal.

Walters says, "I'd like my wife to meet you, if you have a few more minutes."

"Sure," I tell him. I look to Donna. "Ask her to come back to the conference room, okay?"

"Shall do," Donna says, and disappears down the hallway toward the front of the office. A few moments later, Donna escorts a woman I am guessing is about sixty into the room. She wears her short, graying hair up and has an elegant way about her. The impressive overall effect is Priscilla Presley meets Helen Mirren.

"Hi, sweetheart," Walters says, standing. "This is Scott Winslow. Scott, this is my wife, Julia."

"Mr. Winslow," she says, and we shake hands.

"Call me Scott, please," I say. "Won't you have a seat?"

I pull back a chair, and Julia Walters sits, puts her purse on the table, and glances around the room, considering her surroundings. The focus of the room is the conference room table, which seats twelve. The room's accessories include a glass cabinet on the far wall, a granite countertop and cupboards on the other side of the room, and an impressionistic Monet painting of the French countryside. Mrs. Walters takes it all in quickly in a way that suggests that the room is speaking to her and says, "I've never been much for lawsuits." The comment is delivered with a calm, friendly smile. A single comment that takes in the surroundings and my whole world, but in a way that sounds informative, rather than judgmental.

I am assessing whether to be amused by her dismissive review of my livelihood, and I'm still not sure when I say, "That seems like a healthy perspective. No one wants litigation that isn't necessary."

Walters interjects, "I was just getting ready to sign a retainer agreement with Scott. I want him to represent me in connection with the wrongful termination lawsuit."

She nods. "Scott," she says, focusing her attention on me, "let me tell you where I stand on all this. I don't think that my husband should pursue this case. We have nothing to prove. Kevin has done well, and we will be fine financially." She pauses and takes her husband's hand. She gives him a smile and adds, "Consolidated's dismissal of my husband was their mistake, and does not reflect negatively on a man who has done great things for them for over twenty-seven years. As much as I'd like to kick Michael Constantine in the balls, I think it is in our best interests to let go of all this."

The way she speaks in elegant tones of kicking someone in the balls makes me grin widely, and I instantly like her, too. I force a more serious expression onto my face. "I understand," I say. "I agree that whether to pursue a lawsuit is a serious decision, and as I've told

Kevin, if his heart is not entirely in it, he should pass. I would encourage you to take some time to discuss whether you want to do this if you'd like."

She seems momentarily pleased with this advice.

Walters leans forward and takes his wife's hands in his. "I appreciate all you've said, dear," he says without hesitation, "but I have not changed my mind about this." He turns his attention my way, and says, "Julia is correct, we can get by without additional money, but I am not doing this for money. I'm doing it because I care about this company and the way it behaves. One person died and others were injured, because it was financially expedient to keep operating an unsafe facility. Worse yet is the continued possibility of additional injury. Consolidated owes its employees much more, and so do I. If there's any way I can help the families of workers, and help Consolidated atone, I'm not going to sit on the sidelines and enjoy forced retirement."

I look at Julia Walters. "Do you want more time to discuss this with your husband?"

Walters flashes his wife a look that slowly becomes a knowing smile.

Julia Walters then shakes her head and says, "No, he's ready to go," in a tone that conveys acceptance, if not agreement. She grins at her husband in reluctant acquiescence, and then turns back to me. "So, if we are going to do this, let's use the legal process to kick these bastards in the balls."

I explain contingency fees to Walters, who already knows exactly what I'm talking about. He signs retainer forms, and I give him copies and shake hands with my newest client. I think he's a straight shooter, and I like the man. Many times since that day I have relived that meeting, wondering how different the world would have been if we had never signed those papers.

Employment litigation is the business I and my law partner, Bill Simmons, love or hate, depending upon how crazy life is and how many places we have to be, on any given day. Bill and I met in the employment litigation department of Fulbright and Barnes, a monster firm of three hundred lawyers that consumes new lawyers at a frightening rate, sucking the life out of them by having them work twelve to fourteen hours a day, six days a week, and only eight more on the seventh day, it being the day of rest, until they quit or expire.

Bill and I arrived at the firm the same year, and hit it off immediately, with a shared appreciation for our situation. As we saw it, this was a place to learn, and leave behind. The Thirteenth Amendment, while it abolished slavery for most folks, simply didn't seem to apply in large law firms, so we were slaves to be used at will by partners, who had no concern about the fact that we were working a hundred hours a week before receiving their latest assignment. That was the life of the new lawyer at the big firm until used up and burned out. Then the firm simply gets new ones. We spent our time defending the biggest of companies and insurance companies against the claims of employees and former employees who had allegedly been harassed, discriminated against, or in some other fashion thrown under the corporate bus.

The partnership carrot was used to keep associates performing at impossible levels for as long as possible, until they had to come to grips with statistics; only one in seven would have a shot at a partnership, and not until after nine or ten years of what we referred to as shoveling shit against the tide.

After five years at the firm, Bill and I both knew that this was not the life that we wanted and that we had done all the shoveling we wanted to do. We also had a secret that would have been very unpopular if revealed—we had a propensity for the other side, a desire to represent David against the corporate Goliath. We would have been drawn, quartered, and then fired, had we dared to mention that we wanted to represent these employees that were the casualties of our corporate clients.

Bill and I saved money, as our expenses weren't high at the time, and the firm never gave us enough time off to spend the money we made. After five years of involuntary servitude, we announced our departure from the firm to supervising partners, who considered us to be disloyal ingrates who had effectively stolen all the training we had received by not staying until the firm decided otherwise or we expired.

The master hates to give the slave his freedom. We were amused by the overreaction, but could have cared less. We had given the firm all the energy we were going to, and we were ready to go.

Bill won the coin toss, so we went into business together as Simmons and Winslow, nine years ago. Ever since, we have been working even harder, but with one big difference—now we work for us, and we are not supporting the big firm, with its million-dollar-a-year partners, and its $500,000 a year retirees. Life looked and felt a whole lot better from day one. It didn't matter that we had to pay the bills or that we didn't know what we would make month to month. We were doing what we really wanted to do, and we would never look back.

Chapter 3

January 4, 2016

It's three o'clock in the afternoon, and it's over eighty degrees as I run through the parking lot toward Department 15 of the Superior Court, where I will wait for Judge Roy Carswell to conduct a settlement conference, so that he can eliminate the sexual harassment case I am to start next week from his calendar. Not because he cares about my case, but because he has three trials set the same day and wants to eliminate all of them and go fishing. Judge Carswell has been on the bench since my ancestors were small children. He was appointed by a governor who hates lawyers, for the purpose of abusing lawyers, and he has never disappointed. The entire bar has railed against Judge Carswell, in an attempt to cause his ouster, but to no avail. He is politically wired in and will probably outlast us all.

I walk into the courtroom and check in with the clerk, a dark-haired woman in her thirties, who shows me a half-smile and a dimple. She has an unruffled air, as she tells me that the judge will be with us soon. "Soon" is a legal term meaning when Carswell is ready, whether ten minutes or two hours has passed. I see my opposing counsel sitting in the courtroom with a young man that I have never seen before, who looks like he doesn't quite fit the suit he wears. This would be the insurance adjuster I have never seen before. I give Doug Ferguson, my opposing counsel, a nod, which he returns almost imperceptibly, and then I walk out into the hall to look for my client. She is walking toward me. Linda Darnell is a very attractive woman in her early thirties. We met in my office last week to prepare for this conference and discuss our settlement position. Now she is waving vigorously, and has something important to say. Her excitement will have to do with the settlement dollars we discussed. Either she wants more money to sufficiently compensate for the injury inflicted, or she wants to accept less, and be done with it. In this case, I'm betting that it's the latter, because Linda has been stressed out by the litigation process, and does not want any contact with the harasser, who causes her nightmares. It doesn't take long to get confirmation that my guess is correct.

"Scott, how are you?" she asks, extending a hand.

I shake the hand. "I'm good, Linda. How are you feeling?"

"Well," she says hesitantly, "I've been better."

"What is it?" I ask, having a pretty good idea what comes next.

"Stressed," she says, glancing at the floor. She looks back at me. "I really want to get this over with—I mean the case," she offers, softly. I wait, sensing more is coming, and I don't have to wait long. "If we can settle it today, I'd be willing to take less than we talked about. If it's okay with you."

I smile and nod acknowledgment. She's a nice lady and appropriately nervous in this environment. "I understand. Let's see what kind of a settlement we can persuade these guys to put on the table. At the end of the day, I'll be with you whatever you choose to do."

She smiles softly and takes a breath. Like all whose lives are about to be evaluated and judged by strangers, whether judge or jury, she carries a substantial weight on her shoulders.

I check my watch. "We better get back in the courtroom," I say, and we start moving back down the hallway. We walk into the courtroom and sit down. There are pads and pencils in the jury box, from which I conclude that Judge Carswell is presently in trial, and has given the jury the afternoon off while he harasses others with the misfortune to have been assigned to his courtroom.

There is an annoying buzzing noise, and the clerk picks up her telephone. She mumbles and then nods in our direction. She cradles the phone. "The judge will see counsel in Darnell v. Kingston Brokerage Services now," she announces, then returns her attention to the documents on her desk.

I stand and walk toward the judge's chambers, where I am joined by Doug Ferguson and the young suit. Being closest to the door, I knock. "Come in, counsel," the gravel-like voice of Carswell bellows, uninvitingly.

We walk in, and the judge gestures to the two chairs in front of his desk. I take the first and let Doug figure out where to put his insurance adjuster, who happily keeps his distance from Carswell by taking a seat on a black leather couch behind us.

"Afternoon, Your Honor," I offer, extending a hand. "Scott Winslow for Ms. Darnell."

"Yes," he says, quickly shaking my hand and then looking over at my opponent. "You must be Mr. Ferguson."

"Yes, sir," Ferguson says, and the judge shakes his hand. "Pleasure to see you, Your Honor," Ferguson says with a wide smile. It's convincing—almost as if he means it.

Carswell says, "Right," in a way that suggests he doesn't believe it for a minute. I don't either. No one could be glad to see Carswell. "Who do we have here?" he asks, having collected a business card from the clerk, and already well aware of the answer.

"This is Derrick Olson from Underwriters' Insurance, Your Honor," Ferguson offers. Olson offers a hand. "Hello, Your Honor," he says nervously. The judge takes and shakes the hand. "Hello, Mr. Olson," Carswell says, then leans back in his chair. He pauses, and then says, "I've read the briefs. What else do you want to tell me?"

He looks at me. "I believe that we've laid out the chronology of the conduct in our brief, Your Honor. In summary, the harassment was undertaken by a supervisor, continued for almost two years, and involved both verbal harassment and repeated groping and physical touching."

Ferguson is wide-eyed, and looks offended. "Your Honor, we dispute almost all of the alleged conduct."

"Of course you do," Carswell says, rolling his eyes. "I don't think I've ever seen a harassment case when the defense didn't deny most or all of it." At this point I'm amused.

Carswell interlocks his hands and says, "All right, Mr. Ferguson, let me speak to Mr. Windsor for a moment."

This is probably not a good sign. He wants to pound on me first, which likely means that he wants to talk me down from my settlement demand before he works on getting money from the defense. This suits Ferguson fine, and he almost runs from the room followed closely by the young suit. They close the door behind them.

Carswell leans closer and grins. "So, Mr. Winslow, what do you really want?"

"Well, Your Honor," I say with a practiced thoughtful look, "two more associates and two weeks in the Bahamas would be great. Can you help me?" I smile at my humor, but Carswell does not look amused. A not so good sign, but I've been doing this too long to care—except for the fact that he will be my trial judge in this case. There is complete silence, so I attempt to get us back on track. "We have some flexibility in the demand, Your Honor, but I believe that this case is worth every nickel of the two hundred thousand we're asking."

I lean back and wait a moment. Now he starts to smile. "You know, Mr. Winslow, I've been in the business world a long time. In the real world, sometimes people have to put up with a little playful behavior once in a while. He glances down at the paper on his desk and says, 'There's just not too much that is worthy of big numbers here.' "

I'm considering my response, so I can leave out the things that will most surely piss him off. "This is not just a verbal harassment case, Your Honor. This guy was grabbing Ms. Darnell's breasts and buttocks, and promising her good reviews if she would put out. I wouldn't want to work with that going on, and I don't think that anyone on the jury would either."

Carswell waves me off and says, "I'm not suggesting your case isn't worth something. I just think you're way over the top here." He leans toward me, as if about to share a secret. "You know, if I can get you forty thousand on this case, I really think you ought to take it and run."

Take it and run; like a thief in the night, I'm trying to find a tactful way of responding, but every possibility eludes me, so I say what I am thinking. "I think that if I took it and ran, I would have to stop at the pay phones outside and call my malpractice carrier." His eyes open wide. Maybe I could have been more tactful.

Now that I've told him his assessment of my case is malpractice, he's pissed, and it shows on his face. "All right, Mr. Winslow. I try to do what I can to keep cases that should settle off my trial calendar, but if the parties won't be reasonable, there's nothing more I can do." This confirms his old school approach and his lack of any real mediation skill.

He shakes his head. "Send Mr. Ferguson in here for a few minutes."

"Very well, Your Honor," I say, heading for the door. Now I know that Carswell is not going to put any real pressure on Ferguson to settle; we may as well pack our briefcases and head out.

Back in the courtroom, I tell Ferguson it's his turn and grab a seat. My worst fears realized, within five minutes Ferguson enters the courtroom. He is grinning widely as he walks over to where I am sitting.

"My turn?" I ask, not acknowledging his contentment.

"Not yet," he says, now beaming. "Wise old Judge Carswell thinks that I ought to pay forty thousand. He says that if I can get it, he'll apply some pressure on you to take it. I just have to make a call and get that authority."

"Save your quarter," I say.

"Oh?" Ferguson says, feigning surprise.

"You asshole," I say, only somewhat playfully. We both know that you have that authority already, and we both know that we're not going to take forty thousand." Ferguson silently shrugged, obviously enjoying himself.

"Okay," I say, "call the office and say hello to your secretary, like you guys always do, then tell Carswell you used all your powers of persuasion to get the authority he recommended. I'll decline, and we can get back to our offices."

Ferguson shook his head. "Maybe you should listen to the learned judge's valuation and settle this frivolous case."

"You're a joy, Doug. I think I'll do whatever a jury says, instead; twelve of my client's peers, who have been waiting all of their lives to rectify social abuses."

Ferguson gives me a thoughtful expression, then a raised eyebrow. I sense a gem coming. "You know, Scott, there are a lot of conservative juries out there these days. You may get a cross section of retirees and human resources managers; not exactly your client's peers."

I reflect on this philosophical offering and then nod. "I don't know about that. I'll pick a jury from the folks walking around Costco any-time. There are a lot of people, much like Ms. Darnell, who just want the right to work without being harassed."

He stops smiling. "Let me level with you," Ferguson says. Now I know there's a barge of bullshit coming my way, so I wait silently.

He gives me a look that says he shouldn't be telling me this. "I think I can get you fifty thousand to settle this, if we do it today, before we spend any more money on trial preparation."

"I appreciate your sharing something so intimate, but all your sin-cerity notwithstanding, fifty isn't going to get it done." I give him a friendly smile. "Now I've saved you two quarters, so you can buy me a cup of coffee on the way out."

I see from his face that he is not amused. "Well, at least I tried," he offers, and then turns to go, either feeling or feigning offense at my failure to heed his heartfelt advice.

Carswell brings us back into his chambers, but this time does not offer us a seat. He stares silently for a time, and then looks from me to Ferguson. "This case should settle, and I don't like my calendar clut-tered with cases that should have settled."

I recognize this line from prior visits. Apparently all my cases should settle, whether we can settle them or not.

"I want you to keep working on it," Carswell says, "and I want a call saying that this case has settled by the end of the week."

Good luck with that, I'm thinking.

"I have to tell you," the judge adds in his best Solomon-like voice, "I think that Mr. Ferguson is being reasonable here, and you need to look at your case again, Mr. Winslow. Your client will be awfully disappointed if there's a defense verdict after you told her to leave $40,000 on the table."

Yeah, me too, I think to myself. "I appreciate your input, Your Honor, and I assure the court that whatever we decide to do, we will thoroughly evaluate and consider all offers that are made."

His gazed is fixed on me, eyebrows raised, as he recognizes my bullshit offered in response to his own. "All right, gentlemen," he says, giving up, "Tell the clerk to send in the next case on your way out. And be sure that all of your trial documents are timely filed per the local rules."

"Yes, Your Honor," we both mutter as we exit. We tell the clerk the judge is ready for the next case and walk toward the door of the courtroom.

"Let me know if you get serious about trying to settle this case," Ferguson says, unable to resist a parting shot.

I was going to leave it alone, but this pisses me off. "I will, Doug, and you be sure to call me if you find any money in the area of what the case is worth."

He turns and walks down the hall without answering, followed a half-step behind by the young adjuster, who seems new enough at the game to be trying to assess who is full of shit, and who really has it right.

I see where Linda Darnell is waiting to find out what happened. She smiles nervously as I approach her.

"We're done for now," I say, and I can see the disappointment in her face. "Let's walk out together." As we walk down the almost deserted hallway, I continue. "They told me that they believe they can get fifty thousand to settle the case if they do it now." We had previously agreed to accept 150 thousand, but in the silence, I can tell she is weighing this offer against her desire to be done with it all. I give her a little time to work it through.

"You don't recommend that then?"

"I think the case is worth more, but like I said, I support whatever you would like to do. These are always hard decisions, and it's always possible that things could go badly at trial and there could be a defense verdict. I don't think it should happen that way, but there are no guarantees."

"I understand," she says, reflectively. "Let me think on it."

I nod. "Sure. Give me a call tomorrow and let me know what you're thinking. If you're inclined to settle it, I will try to talk them up a little higher."

"I will. I'll talk to you tomorrow." She turns to go, then stops and looks back. "Thank you for everything, Scott. I never would have been able to stand up to them without you."

"My pleasure," I respond, as she turns to go, and now I'm smiling. That is the best part of the whole damn job.

* * *

On my way out of the courthouse, I stop in the clerk's office and file the Kevin Walters lawsuit. I check the case documents assigned by the court. The end of the perfect day. The judge assigned to this case will be Roy Carswell—my best buddy.

I return to the office, page through and begin returning a stack of messages from clients and opposing attorneys, and then I work on trial preparation for Darnell until I've had enough. It's ten o'clock when I leave the office, for the second time this week, and it's only Wednesday. This sucks.

When I get home, the full weight of the day catches up with me, and I am exhausted. The house is quiet and dark. I make my way upstairs, stopping at the second door to look in on Katy, who is hanging over the edge of the bed, challenging gravity. She clings tightly to Mr. Zanzibear, a stuffed bear she named for "Zanzibar," which is tattooed across his right foot. I scoot Katy back into bed, tuck her under the covers and give her a smooch on the cheek. Without opening her eyes, a grin washes across her angelic face, and she says, "Hi, Daddy. I'm glad you're home now."

My turn to smile. I kiss her forehead and mumble, "Me too, sweetheart," but she is already asleep. It's amazing how kids can do that. If I wake up in the middle of the night, I could be up for an hour, or for the duration of the night. I grin and walk out, slowly pulling the door almost, but not quite, closed, just the way Katy likes it.

A few steps farther down the hall, I open the door marked "Keep Out," and go inside to check on Joey. He is on his back, mouth wide open, snoring loudly. I turn him on his side, and the snoring stops. "Hi, Buddy," I say, looking at the unconscious face. There is no reply. I am not surprised, because Joey sleeps through anything. I could take his bed away and he'd never know it. I give him a kiss, and then I just stand and watch him for a minute. It's amazing how quiet he can be when he's asleep. I turn and walk to the door and leave my little man to his dreams of kings, castles, and pitcher's mounds.

Chapter 4

January 12, 2016

Linda Darnell is still not sure whether she wants to accept the $50,000 settlement, especially with me recommending against it, so we hold out and prepare for trial. Five days before our scheduled trial date, the attorneys for both sides are required to appear for the Trial Readiness Conference. This is the date that the parties announce whether they are ready to proceed or are urging some good cause for a continuance of the trial date. It is also an opportunity for the judge to tell counsel that the matter will be continued because of the court's congested calendar, priority given to some older and dustier case, or just to further harass counsel.

This particular conference, as I will soon learn, is strictly for the purpose of harassing counsel, and Judge Carswell is in rare form. He leans back in his chair and purses his lips, signaling his readiness to impart some judicial wisdom. Doug Ferguson and I occupy the two visitor chairs on the other side of his wide walnut desk and wait for Carswell to complete his contemplation and then break the silence. When he speaks, we have no idea whether it would be about the file on his desk, our case, or the Lakers' latest standings. Carswell leans forward and nods, having come to terms with himself.

"Mr. Winslow and Mr. Ferguson, I don't believe that you have taken my instructions seriously enough." He sits back and waits for us to consider this, as if he has spoken a complete thought.

"Excuse me, Your Honor?" I reply.

"I asked the two of you to do the work it would take to settle this case. I don't know if the problem is someone's ego, or if you're not working hard enough, but I am not satisfied. So here is what we will do about it." He paused, apparently to allow us to contemplate our mutual shortcomings. "Starting now you will both be here for trial, with your respective clients, every day, all day long, until one of two things happen: either we can start trial, or you can settle this case. I suggest you spend each moment productively. Good-bye, gentlemen. I have a jury waiting. Talk to you later in the morning."

I spend the next two days, between 8:30 a.m. and 5:00 p.m., sitting in conference rooms with Doug Ferguson, exchanging occasional offers and periodic barbs, while evenings are spent focusing on all the work I couldn't do during the day. When I get home late at night, Lisa and the kids are asleep. After two full days, the insurance carrier raises its offer to $70,000, and we reduce our settlement demand to $150,000. Neither side is moving any further.

On Friday morning, Judge Carswell calls us into chambers, waves us into chairs, and glowers at us silently. After a time calculated to build the tension, Carswell shakes his head and says, "I gave you gentlemen every opportunity to get this case resolved, and you didn't do it. Is that right?" His tone makes clear his level of disappointment in us as human beings.

"We are not able to settle the case, Your Honor," I offer.

He shrugs. "We have a jury panel on the way up. I want the jury sworn today, opening statements Monday morning." With that he waved us off dismissively and stared at the pretrial documents on his desk. It was our fault he was going to have to try our case, and Carswell was pissed. We spent the afternoon selecting the jury. The process was complete and the jury sworn by 6:30 p.m.

I spent the weekend in the office, trying to catch up with an in-box that consumed two chairs, and attempting to return a handful of messages to attorneys who were not smart enough to be at home with their families for the weekend. When this trial was over, I would have some serious apologizing to do. Lisa was always understanding when I disappeared into trial mode, missing meals and freeway off-ramps while I repeatedly spoke and adjusted my opening statement in empty rooms and cars, but I knew it took a toll on her; and on us.

* * *

January 18, 2016

On Monday morning, I rise to address the newly impaneled jury.

"May it please the court, counsel, ladies and gentlemen of the jury. You know from the jury selection process that this case involves sexual harassment issues. The undisputed evidence will show you that Linda Darnell was an employee of the defendant for seven years, and her performance throughout was excellent, as recognized by the defendant's evaluations of her work, bonuses, merit raises, and countless accolades she received. This case is not about her performance. This case is about the rights of a good employee to be free from intrusion into her personal life, to be free from sexual and demeaning comments and to be free of unwelcome and offensive touching by her boss. It is about the right to be free from statements that your career is conditioned on "putting out." And it is about the company's obligation to promptly investigate and take all steps to make sure sexual harassment is immediately stopped.

"The evidence will show you that Linda Darnell was subjected to ongoing verbal and physical harassment by her supervisor, that the company had the opportunity to stop that conduct but didn't make it stop. While Ms. Darnell attempted to do her job, the harassment continued for almost two years, even though Ms. Darnell complained on three separate occasions. The evidence will show you that no one listened, and, as a result, the conduct continued and worsened.

"You will hear Ms. Darnell's supervisor, Carl Chambers, deny that he inappropriately touched Ms. Darnell, that he ever made sexual remarks to her and that he never conditioned her future or career upon sex. An important part of your job is to weigh the credibility of the testimony you hear, so keep that in mind when you hear the denials by Mr. Chambers. Assess his credibility when you hear the testimony of other employees who will tell you of specific incidents that they witnessed, which are inconsistent with Mr. Chambers's across-the-board denials. These coemployees have the courage to come forward in the face of the fear of how their own careers might be affected, and with nothing at stake for them but the truth. These employees will tell you that they witnessed specific inappropriate touching and sexual statements: the same ones Mr. Chambers will tell you never happened. And some will tell you that they heard Ms. Darnell ask him to stop these behaviors. All Ms. Darnell wanted was the right to do her job at the same professional level she always had, without being groped and without hearing about what he wanted to do to her and how good it would feel. Chambers wouldn't stop, and the company didn't care enough to stop him or even to properly investigate."

The jury is attentive as I describe what the evidence will show: the sexual statements regularly tossed out by Chambers about her body and her sex life and how he could make it so much better, his periodic touching and rubbing of her legs and buttocks, Linda Darnell's complaints to management, and, finally, the toll taken on Linda Darnell coming to work in this environment for two full years.

Doug Ferguson then describes what sounded like a different case: long-suffering supervisor faced with false charges and bravely moving forward to do his job. He urged the jury to consider that two of the coemployee witnesses they would hear no longer work at the company and had axes to grind, which he asserted was the real motivation for such testimony. This one I like, because I knew he can't prove it. I scribble furiously to record his statements in my notes, and I will order the transcript of his opening statement. When he doesn't provide proof of the "axe to grind," I will quote him to the jury in my closing argument, reminding them of what the defense promised to show, and what never was shown. Ferguson tells the jury that Linda Darnell was a willing participant in sexual conversations around the office, and now sought to turn these conversations to her advantage. He assures them that she had no real injury. He then thanks the jury and sits down. I watch their faces as he spoke his concluding words and like what I see: skepticism.

On the ensuing break, the insurance company's offer was raised to eighty-five thousand dollars, which we rejected. When we returned from break, Linda Darnell took the stand and answered questions about Chambers's daily behaviors, her complaints, the company's repeated statements that they would investigate, and their failure to ever get back to her. She was even better than she had been in our pretrial dry runs. Chambers was up next and offered his well-rehearsed denials, which weren't bad either. I then proceed to call four witnesses who had all seen or heard actions and words by Chambers that are inconsistent with his denials. After the fourth witness, the court admonishes the jury not to speak of the case until we return at 9:00 a.m., and recesses for the day.

Ferguson walks over to me and suggests we speak for a few minutes. I know it is good news because he looks like he is about to choke on his words. Fifteen minutes later, we settle the case for $200,000.

The settlement is put on the record before the jury is called in, and Judge Carswell is now in an uncharacteristically good mood. "I want to thank both counsels for the hard work in achieving a resolution of this case. In my opinion, this is a settlement that was fair to both sides." I am amused because this was the same insightful purveyor of justice who thought I should take forty thousand and run, just a couple of weeks ago.

Judge Carswell then has the bailiff return the jury to the box. "Ladies and gentlemen, I have some good news. The parties have now reached a settlement agreement in this matter, and it was your preparedness to serve as jurors that made this possible. You are dismissed, and the court and the parties thank you for your service."

As we walk from the courthouse, Linda Darnell expresses her relief that it is over and thanks me profusely and gives me a hug. She is grateful, happy, and relieved in equal proportions. She wears a big smile, and I am reminded why I like this job so much. There is nothing like a happy client, smiling ear to ear, with a sense that they actually found justice, turned loose in the world to sing the praises of their favorite lawyer. The legal community needs more of those.

When I return to the office for long enough to focus on my depressingly full inbox, my mood changes. At the top is Consolidated Energy's response to my Request to Produce Documents in Kevin Walters's case. All twenty-nine categories of documents requested were objected to as burdensome and oppressive, irrelevant, violative of the attorney-client and attorney work product privileges, and several other objections aimed at keeping us from the Consolidated files. My request for documents pertained to Kevin's duties, background, performance, complaints regarding company activities, and the reasons for his termination. According to Bob Harris, all were irrelevant, and not a single document had been produced. We were about to do this the hard way, and I wasn't at all surprised.

* * *

When I first received the Answer to the Walters lawsuit with Bob Harris's name on it, I knew that the battle would not be pleasant. I have dealt with Harris before, and this classic attempt at a stiff-arm was exactly the reason for my unease. Harris is a senior partner in a law firm of two hundred lawyers and countless staff; his minions are sent scurrying to do his will as he attempts to overpower plaintiff's lawyers with vast sets of document requests, interrogatories and requests for admission, and then set the deposition of most everyone who had known the plaintiff since birth. There was no such thing as too much work to heap on the other side and no such thing as too little cooperation for Harris's scorched earth philosophy. Bob Harris made Doug Ferguson look like Mother Theresa.

I pick up the phone and dial Harris's direct dial number.

"Robert Harris," comes the response.

"Bob, Scott Winslow here."

"What can I do for you, Scott?"

"Well, you can produce the documents I requested, for starters," I say impatiently. "I waited a month for documents and got nothing."

"You'll have to fix the problems with your requests if you want anything produced; you know that," he says, as if trying to be as condescending as possible.

"Perhaps you can explain to me why documents pertaining to the reasons for Mr. Walters's termination are not relevant. I don't think the judge will have much trouble seeing the relevance."

My law partner, Bill Simmons, walks through the open door to my office carrying two beers and hands me one of them. It looks great, so I take a swig while I wait for Harris to respond.

"Your requests were too broad, too many, and too burdensome to deal with. If you want to narrow them—a lot, maybe we can do something for you."

"That's it?" I ask, wearily.

"Yeah, that's it," Harris responds confidently.

"Okay," I say. "I guess we know where we stand. Tomorrow I will send you a letter telling you all the reasons your objections are not well-taken. If we don't make significant progress, I will file my motion to compel responses seeking attorney's fees for being put to the trouble."

"Fine," Harris said in a controlled voice. "Do what you have to do," he retorts, and the line goes dead.

"Good-bye, Bob," I offer to a dial tone. "Always nice catching up."

Bill grins widely at this exchange, and I motion to him to pull up a chair. I tell him about the day at Linda Darnell's trial and the surprise settlement. The beer we share tastes great.

"And for your reward," he says grinning, "enjoy Bob Harris on the Walters case."

"Yep, and to top it off, Carswell as the judge."

Bill starts to laugh, much too amused by all of this. "Well, look at it this way. At least you got one more satisfied client before you were cast into the ninth circle of hell."

"And that is encouraging in some way I can't see?"

Bill shakes his head. "You remember that Harris was my opposing counsel on Johnston v. Markham Hotels?" I nod and wait. Bill continues, "He's a smart guy, but everything is a dick-waving contest. He'll make a big fight out of the smallest discovery disputes—he just never learned to pick his fights so he fights everything. He doesn't seem to care so long as he inflicts a little pain."

"I'm with you," I say. "Works well with the fact that he bills by the hour."

"Amen, to that. The son of a bitch really billed the Johnston case into the ground."

I drain my beer and hold up the bottle. "Thanks. Now I'm good for a couple more hours."

"My pleasure" he says, grinning. "Good nutrition is important."

* * *

March 27, 2016

The rotund bailiff with the nameplate that said Wilcox stood and cried "All rise," as the judge emerges from his chambers wearing his flowing black robe and strolls to the bench. Carswell sits and looks unhappily at the files in front of him, as Jerry the bailiff stares over the heads of the spectators in the courtroom and calls out, "Department 39 of the Superior Court for the State of California, County of Los Angeles, is now in session, the Honorable William B. Carswell presiding." Wilcox, who looks bored during his announcement, sits down as if winded after a hard day's work.

"You may be seated," Carswell says, and then adds, "Case number one on today's docket, Walters vs. Consolidated Energy; Plaintiff's Motion to Compel Further Responses to Request to Produce Documents."

I approach the counsel table, where a sign read "Plaintiff," and remain standing while Robert Harris stands at the defense table. We stare at the judge and await his attention. When he looks up, I say, "Scott Winslow for Mr. Walters, Your Honor."

The judge looks to the defense table. "Robert Harris for Consolidated, Your Honor."

Carswell looks at me and then at Harris, as if he were sizing us up to determine who was going to be the bigger annoyance. "Mr. Winslow," he said, sounding as if he had made that decision. "You may begin."

"Thank you, Your Honor. We have requested that the defendant deliver documents that are not only relevant, but central to the issues in this action, and we have received across the board, and I believe frivolous, objections." Carswell's eyes were locked on me as I continued. "Twenty-nine categories of documents sought, all relevant to Mr. Walters's performance, the reason for his termination, his complaints regarding illegal activities and the mining operations specifically involved in this case. This is not a fishing trip, Your Honor; every item is specifically related to the allegations of this case.

"Every one of these Requests to Produce seeks documents that may tend to prove facts placed in issue by the allegations of the complaint, including the alleged unlawful conduct of Consolidated, Mr. Walters's complaints about safety issues, and the resultant termination or the affirmative defenses raised by defendant in the Answer to the Complaint."

He nods, and then turns his attention to Harris and waits. Harris shakes his head to show his annoyance and then begins: "Your Honor, counsel is seeking volumes of documents here, many of which are not relevant to this action."

Carswell frowns. "I'm looking at the list, Counsel; tell me what's not relevant."

"Everything except the reasons for the termination is irrelevant."

The judge looks my way, and I do not hesitate to jump in.

"We obviously have a different belief about the reason for the termination. Mr. Walters's complaints of illegal conduct by the company are at the heart of this action, but they will obviously not be tagged by the company as the reasons for the termination. Likewise, Mr. Walters's history of positive performance, raises, bonuses, and accolades are relevant to the credibility of the company's purported reason for the termination."

Carswell is nodding again. He looks at Harris. "So when you say only the reasons for the termination are relevant, Mr. Harris, do you mean your reasons or his?" Carswell says, looking at me.

"The reasons," Harris said quickly, emphasizing the "the" and sounding dangerously close to condescending. I like that because I knew Carswell will not.

"As in, 'take our word for it,' right?" the judge asks.

"It's not a subjective thing. If we have documents that address the termination, those would be relevant."

"How about documents that pertain to the reasons the complaint alleges for the termination? Do you dispute he is entitled to discovery on those issues?"

"Yes, Your Honor. This is fantasy land. If it doesn't actually pertain to the reasons for the termination, then he is attempting to go fishing through proprietary documents."

Carswell's brow furrows, and it is clear that he is not impressed.

"And how many of the documents that pertain to any reason for the termination have you produced so far?"

"Until plaintiff properly narrows the requests, we don't know what documents he is entitled to."

The judge looks at me. "Anything else to add, Mr. Winslow?"

"No, Your Honor," I say earnestly, having long ago learned when to stop talking.

"Okay, gentlemen, the court finds that full and complete responses to each of the twenty-nine categories of documents are required within fifteen days of today. Also, defendant's failure to produce any documents is without substantial justification, and defendant is ordered to pay attorneys' fees to plaintiff in the amount of $2,000 for time expended in making this motion."

"Thank you, Your Honor," I say, solemnly.

Harris snatches up his materials and strides over to the court reporter, handing her a business card and making a show of requesting that a transcript of the hearing be prepared so that he can take a writ, which we both know is not something an appellate court will grant except in extreme circumstances.

I do my best to suppress a grin, enjoying how pissed off Harris is and confident that the Court of Appeal will not grant a writ so that this guy can stiff me on discovery he owes. I chalk it up as a triumphant morning and a good way to set the stage for the Walters litigation.

A week later, having heard nothing from Robert Harris, I expect to be served with the writ. Instead, I get a phone call from Harris.

"Scott, I wanted to take that writ, but in the spirit of cooperation, my client is going to make the documents available to you."

Now I am on my guard. When a lawyer like Harris tells you that he is going to do something in the spirit of cooperation, you can be assured that K-Y Jelly will be required at some point during the process. "I see," I offer, without enthusiasm.

Harris takes this as his signal to push onward. "Anytime you want during the next five days, you can view all the documents at the company's Los Angeles warehouse, and," he says, emphasizing the *and* to make sure that I understand the extremes to which he and his client are going to help me out, "we will make copies for you at a nominal charge right there at the warehouse."

"Uh-huh, and what quantity of materials are we talking about?" I ask, my skepticism peaking.

"I'm told there are a couple of hundred boxes of documents," he retorts, and then there is silence.

Even Judge Carswell would make him dig the responsive documents out and deliver them. This "if you can't get away with giving them nothing, drown them in everything" strategy is bullshit, and I am about to tell him so. I open my mouth to speak, but I have second thoughts.

"Where is the warehouse?" I ask, and jot down the address. It occurs to me that while Harris thought he was getting away with something, there was no way that he had taken the time to go through two hundred boxes, so I might just find something helpful. "I and my paralegal will be there for as much time as we need. I assume you will arrange with your client to let us in?"

"Yes," Harris says, "not a problem."

I hang up the phone and buzz Donna. "How did it go?" are her first words.

"I'm not sure. One of us probably got screwed. Make a note to ask me who next week. You and I are going to the Consolidated Distribution Center to search through two hundred or so boxes of documents."

There was a momentary silence, and then she says, "Want to hear my guess as to who got screwed?"

"Never mind," I say, "this may turn into something." But I know that she is probably right. I think I know who got screwed, too.

April 18, 2016

We meet in the parking lot and are escorted into the warehouse at eight in the morning. We are taken down two long corridors and into a massive, windowless room, filled with boxes. It is daunting.

"Are you kidding?" Donna asks, as she scans the seemingly endless rows of storage boxes.

"I'm afraid not. Where shall we start?" I ask, trying to muster some enthusiasm.

"How about Hawaii?" she replies.

I walk to the closest of the boxes and open it up. There is nowhere to sit, so we stand in the aisles and begin to review one box after another. By noon we have been through eighteen boxes. Only four contained anything relevant. When we are asked to leave at 6:00 p.m., we have been through thirty-eight boxes. I copy only fifty documents that may be marginally relevant. I have 162 boxes to go, and I am annoyed. Somewhere this evening, Harris is having a real belly laugh at my expense.

The next morning, I get smarter and call Kevin Walters. He meets us at the warehouse at eight o'clock. It occurs to me that Consolidated might resist letting him in the warehouse, terminated employees being persona non-grata, and in the corporate mind-set, apt to steal, pillage and plunder, so I call Harris, and have him authorize it with his client. There are too many documents, and I need help at getting through them. I also need interpretation of some of the more technical energy documents before I can decide whether they have any relevance. Kevin has the expertise I need, and he doesn't hesitate to jump right in.

During the next two days, we spend thirty hours making our way through 112 boxes, and we find nothing worth reading. It is Friday afternoon at four thirty, and we are blurry-eyed and feeling down. The day's take was a total of eighteen pages marginally worth copying and of dubious value. The real giggles come when I call the office at three o'clock and pick up a message from Bob Harris that my client's personnel documents were not in any of these boxes. They had been left behind and would be mailed next week. Harris is such an asshole. Anyway, an hour and a half later, finding a whole lot of nothing and entirely out of gas, Kevin and Donna are still digging but looking exhausted. As I watch, Kevin pulls the top off another box, notes its number on the yellow pad he carries with him and begins to sort.

"You guys ready to call this a night?" I ask.

Donna nods vigorously. "Yeah, I'm about to go nuts looking at requisitions and invoices that, as far as I can see, have nothing to do with Kevin."

"Don't remind me," I say. My hopes of finding anything of worth were long gone, and I was feeling properly had by Bob Harris. We are searching through voluminous documents that had no more to do with Kevin than the fact that purchasing was under his chain of command: purchasing orders for office supplies, fuel, digging equipment, and everything else a big company can buy. I thought of Harris, enjoying every moment of his revenge for his loss of the motion. He had me looking at every requisition and invoice for shovels, laundry, and paper clips he could line up. "Kevin, you good to get out of here?" I ask.

He is holding a document and nodding, but suddenly stops, and his expression changes to shock. "Scott," he says, his eyes fixed on the page, "I have something."

Chapter 5

As I drive home too fast in some vain hope of making up for lost time, I check my watch every couple of minutes, finding that nine thirty has passed, and ten o'clock is getting closer with each glance. A familiar feeling of guilt overtakes me as I think about having missed another night with Lisa and the kids. I need a different job or, maybe, a little more self-discipline. I recognize that no one ever regretted not having worked more when they got to their deathbed. I know that the kids are growing up too fast, and one day they will want to be with friends, and then they'll want to go on dates, and then they will move out, and they will have families with colds, soccer, school open houses. Then they will have more difficulty finding the time to come home to visit than I have getting home on time now. I really know all of this, so why haven't I fixed it? Good thing the question is rhetorical because I have no damn clue.

As I walk from the garage into the kitchen, the house is quiet and dark. There is faint illumination I recognize as coming from the family room; time to see what kind of a mood Lisa is in. As I walk through the door of the family room, she looks up from the recliner where she sits sewing and gives me that killer smile that melted me the first time I ever saw it. It still takes my breath away.

"Did you have a rough one?" she asks, earnestly awaiting my response. She's not even a little pissed off, which makes me feel even guiltier.

"Yeah, pretty crazy," I say, and then I get to what I need to say. "I'm sorry to be so late again. I really hate missing time with you and the kids."

"I know you do," she says, standing. She gives me a kiss. "You have a whole lot happening these days, and we know it. The kids and I are all right."

"Thank you," I say lamely. "What are you working on?" I ask, indicating her sewing. "I thought with all these late hours that we were earning enough to avoid having to make our own clothes."

"I'm making a costume for Katy," she says. With her serious voice aimed at making sure I pay attention, she adds, "Her play is Wednesday night at six thirty. The last thing she said as I tucked her in was to remind Daddy to be there." I smile like an idiot. It is truly amazing what even secondhand comments from little girls do to their daddies. "It's so cute," Lisa says. "The whole class is going to be fruits and vegetables."

"Really?"

She nods, "They are reading about food supply, nature and ... Well, they're not calling it that, but ecosystems. But you didn't hear all this from me. Katy wants you to be surprised by what they're doing when you come to the play."

"I will be," I say, with the same stupid grin on my face, as I consider what a cute fruit or vegetable Katy will be.

Lisa smiles at me and says, "You want to fool around?"

The phone rings at that moment. "I'll get it," I say, and turn to pick up the phone on the end table.

"Hello?"

"Scott?" a deep male voice says.

"Speaking. Who is this?"

"Jack Logan. I'm sorry to call you at home, but I have a couple of questions about the settlement agreement, and I know you need it signed by the time you go back to court on my case in a couple of days."

"Sure, Jack," I say, "fire away." Jack is a client whose case has recently settled, and we are working out the details of the agreement. Jack did not try to reach me at the office during business hours, and I am not an emergency room doctor, and people don't need to call me at all hours. A mental note to me: stop giving out my home number and my cell phone number to clients. Focusing on Jack's question about the confidentiality provision in the agreement is difficult; it's well after ten, and I really want to go upstairs to give Joey and Katy a goodnight kiss. Fortunately, the question is one I hear on a regular basis, so I can respond on autopilot. Jack thanks me profusely and hangs up.

"Where were we?" I say.

She gives me her best seductress smile. "You were going to kiss the kids and then meet me in the bedroom. I'll be the one who's waiting naked."

I check my watch and say, "Two minutes. Don't start without me." As I walk up the stairs, I glance back at Lisa to see her holding up the costume under construction and smiling broadly.

I lie on my back with my arm around Lisa, and she presses against me; one of our favorite after-lovemaking positions. I love the feel of her body against mine, and there is a wonderful feeling of closeness as I hold her in my arms.

After a time, she asks, "When did you first fall in love with me?"

I reflect for a moment, and then say, "When we went swimming, and you flashed me."

"That's when you first fell in love with my boobs," she says. "When did you first fall in love with me?"

"You're right," I say. "When I first fell in love with you, huh?"

"Yeah."

"I guess that would be the first blow job."

She hits me in the ribs and says, "You really are an asshole, you know that?"

"Yeah, I know." I squeeze her. "I really do remember when I first knew I loved you."

"Yeah?" she asks. "Tell me."

"We had been going out for about four or five months when we took that weekend camping trip to the beach with Brian and Liz. It was somewhere around Ventura," I offer.

"I remember," she says.

"It was Saturday night. I went into the woods to pee, and when I came back I saw your profile as you were looking into the fire talking to Liz and Brian. You were smiling; actually you were glowing, and I realized it wasn't just the fire. Those beautiful, loving eyes and that warm laugh of yours felt like they had been a part of me for as long as I could remember. It suddenly hit me hard; I could spend the rest of my life with this woman."

"Truly?" she gushes.

"Yeah, truly," I reply.

"That's wonderful. I never knew that." She props herself up on her elbow, and the blanket falls down. "You really can be a romantic," she says.

I look in her eyes and nod, and then lower my gaze. "Yep. But you still have great boobs."

Chapter 6

April 21, 2016

Victoria Constantine arched her back and moaned. She opened her legs wider and grabbed the back of his head as his tongue moved firmly against her. As she began to cry out, he repositioned himself, and then he was inside her. They thrust with all of their might, and finally cried out as they come together. He stayed on top of her for a time and held her tightly. She drifted off with him still inside her. When he rolled off, she curled up under his arms, and felt as she thought a cat would at moments of maximum purr. "That was wonderful," she whispered.

"Oh, my God," Michael Constantine said, "I'll get hard again just thinking about it."

"Works for me," she said softly. There would be one hell of a wet spot tonight, but it was more than worth it.

She began to recover normal breathing, and turned the conversation to something that she wanted to talk about but had been dreading. She ran a hand through her hair and sat up in bed. She was almost fifty-three, but had few wrinkles and somehow managed to look five years younger. She took a breath and began. "Michael," she said softly, "Jerry gets out tomorrow." There was silence, but she could feel him tense up. "He needs a place to be for a time while he finds a job and gets back on his feet, and I want to let him stay in the guest house."

The response is immediate. "What?"

"He's my little brother," she said.

Michael considered her, and his blue eyes flashed as he spoke. "Vickie, your brother stole from us last time he stayed here, remember? And that was just the beginning."

"I remember, but he had a disease. He was addicted to drugs."

"No," Michael said, "he was addicted to everything. You don't need ten thousand dollars to get a drug fix. The son of a bitch went to Vegas and lost the ten thousand he stole from us and another five, remember? We had to make that debt good too, just so your little brother would be allowed to keep walking upright."

"Vegas hotels are corporations now," she said. "They don't bury people in the desert anymore."

"Not the ones he found. He didn't gamble at Caesar's. Somehow, he found Lefty's House of We'll Cut Your Throat. He lost all that money, got drunk, and fucked Lefty's girlfriend. You remember the guys who were looking for him? Cauliflower ears and misshapen noses—they looked like thugs from an old Cagney flick. As I recall, you were the one who talked me into paying the whole fifteen thousand to save his sorry ass."

"I know," Vickie said, "but he did three years. He got treatment while he was in prison. He wants to stay clean and pay you back. If we help him get on his feet, he can start making restitution that much sooner."

"Yeah, he's in great shape until the next temptation passes him on a street corner. Then he'll buy it, sell it, fuck it, or smoke it."

"Dammit, he's my brother, Michael," she said, annoyance finding its way into her voice. She waited through a prolonged silence.

"All right," he said, grudgingly, "he can stay in the guest house for one month, and we tell him that from the start. One month to put himself together if he stays out of trouble. No drugs, and he keeps his dick away from the staff around here."

"Thank you," she said, feeling relieved. "Speaking of dicks, how's yours doing? She grabs him under the sheets, and he is instantly aroused. "Looks like we're ready to stand up and move back into action." She stroked him playfully. "All right," she said, "I told you about what was troubling me, now you tell me about what eats at you these days. How's the lawsuit with Kevin?"

Instantly, his erection started to lose traction. "Not a good time to bring up that topic?" she asked.

"No."

"You're worried about it." It was a statement rather than a question.

"We spent a lot of years together, and it's a mess."

"So settle it, and put it behind you."

"The lawyers say we can squeeze him hard and get him to go away for almost nothing. Besides, he betrayed me, and I don't want to give him shit," he said in an angry tone.

"Betrayed you how?" she asked.

"I don't want to talk about this," he said sternly.

"I can tell," she replied, holding his now flaccid penis.

"That's right," he said, "talking about traitors won't get you laid."

She moved under the covers and took him in her mouth. His recovery was immediate.

April 22, 2016

Jerry Anders walked across the familiar prison yard, surrounded by high brick walls topped with razor wire and lookout towers spaced at forty-feet intervals. A short and stocky correctional officer walked beside him. Gray hair pushed out from under his cap, and sweat beaded on his forehead.

As they reached one of the six buildings that formed a rectangle around the yard, the officer paused at a big steel door and waited. There was a metallic clicking followed by a heavy scraping sound as the door inched slowly open. The officer stepped through the door and Jerry followed. Another steel door just like the first stood closed twenty feet in front of them, and they had to wait for the first door to lumber closed before the second would open; one of many holding pens at Renmont State Prison. There was a solid metal on metal sound as the first door closed. Moments later, the sounds began anew, and the second door began to open. The officer gave Jerry a nod, and they walked through the massive door and down a long, narrow hallway, both sides of which are fenced to a height of twenty feet, with razor wire along the top of each.

Less than fifty steps from his release, Jerry was seized by a sudden rush of fear. It was all up to him now, and he was smart enough to know how little faith he should have in himself. He did three stints in rehab that didn't take and then twenty-three months here when he tried to sell some cocaine to the wrong guy. Then came the grand larceny conviction when he stole from his sister and her husband, Michael Constantine, among others, to support his habit. He was a two-time loser, and if he fucked up this time, he would come back for good; or until he was too old to care if he ever came out again.

"I'm going to make it, Willie," Jerry said.

The officer gave him a nod. "Good," he said, without conviction. Jerry understood; being jaded comes with the job. Everyone said they wouldn't be back, but most returned.

"Really, Willie, I'm going to do it."

Willie forced a smile. "I really hope you do."

Another uniformed guard stood in the doorway and checked something on a clipboard. "Anders, right?" Jerry nodded. "I need a signature from you, Anders, and then you're on your way."

Jerry signed a form that the guard presented without any attempt to read it. The guard gave him a small package of belongings and some cash. Without speaking further, Jerry turned and walked toward the door at the end of the hallway, which began to swing open as he approached. He walked out into a sunny day, looked around the crowded parking lot, and saw nothing familiar. It had occurred to him that Vickie might be waiting, but there was no sign of her. How could he blame her, after everything he had done to her and Michael? Their forgiveness would have to be earned, and it would take time. He told himself that this time he would make it work, and one day he would pay them back and earn their trust.

He gave one last look to the expanse of ominous wall and razor wire behind him, and then began walking across the hot pavement toward the prison access road. He decided to walk, getting a fresh look at birds, trees, and all things not captive, for as long as he could before calling a cab; freedom had been a long time coming. As he walked down the narrow access road toward the highway, he looked up at the sky and held his arms high. It was a gorgeous day, and the first of many to come. There was the sound of an engine approaching where the road crested slightly higher ahead. A Mercedes glided over the slight hill toward him, and he saw Vickie's smiling face as she waved vigorously. This was a good day—a really good day.

Chapter 7

I am caught up in the deposition of my client in an age discrimination case. There are two defense attorneys, one representing Starlight Conveyers, the Fortune 500 company where my client had been employed as a middle manager, and the other representing the manager accused of firing her based upon her age. I tell both attorneys that I have to be done at five o'clock because I had a commitment that I couldn't miss. They grumble, as lawyers do whenever the opportunity arises, but ultimately acquiesce after being assured we would reschedule to allow them to complete the deposition. At five fifteen, they are still going strong, so I tell them time is up, and we need to reschedule. One of the defense attorneys states that he has no further questions; the other has just a few more. As attorneys are notorious for having just a few more questions that wind up taking hours or days, I know better, but I let him go a little further. He says, "One more question" about five times, and finishes at five thirty-five.

I say good-bye and run out the door as soon as we are off the record, charging toward my car and cursing under my breath. Dammit, this is Katy's big night. This time of day I will need forty-five minutes to cover the distance, and the program begins in fifteen minutes; I am now in the process of letting my little girl down. Traffic crawls at a snail's pace, but the level of my frustration moves much faster.

At six thirty-five I arrive at the school to find the visitor lot and the surrounding street parking full. I park three blocks away and hustle into the auditorium in time to catch fifteen minutes of the play. Most of the seats are taken and everyone is quiet and absorbed. On stage, a pumpkin speaks to a head of lettuce about the warmth of the sun, gesturing to the painted sky overhead. As I move toward the front of the auditorium, I see Lisa wave and make my way down the row to the seat beside her, excusing myself as I step over feet, hoping that there might be some way Katy doesn't see me arriving so late.

After a few minutes, I see Katy run across the stage in her red, round costume. She does a graceful pirouette, and then twirls with what appears to be a turnip, as a banana slides across the stage on his knees. Flashes go off all around as proud parents of all this produce try to preserve the moment.

"Isn't she adorable," Lisa asks, leaning in my direction.

"That she is," I say. "Nice work with the costume." She squeezes my hand and looks on as the fruits and vegetables formed what looked like a conga train common to wedding receptions and snake across the stage. Peas and onions float around grapes and melons, while apples and broccoli bob and weave, and then reach for the sky and sway in unison. They break off into semicircles and dance around a farmer for the grand finale.

Parents are suckers for this stuff, and the kids scurry off stage to more applause than a Beatles reunion would bring. As the lights go on and the crowd stares at the stage, Lisa says, "The kids are going to come out and see us in costume."

"Great," I say. When nothing happens after a few moments, the parents begin to whistle, yell, and stomp their feet, rock concert style, one of the talents of our generation.

The fruits and vegetables begin pouring onto the stage with the farmer, and they all hold hands and take bows as parents and grandparents go crazy, bringing thunderous applause and loud whistles. The howls continue as the kids move down the steps and into the audience. As I search for Katy, she appears next to me.

"Daddy," she says, "you made it!" Her eyes are wide and fully animated by the excitement.

I am saddened by her shock that I had made it, but then I reminded myself that I almost hadn't. "You were great, sweetie," I say, bending to give her a hug but held at bay by the costume.

"You know what we are?" she asks.

"Yes," I say proudly, "you're a tomato."

"Not what I am," she says, "what we all are together?"

I thought for a moment. "You're a salad," I say.

She put her hands on her tomato hips, the costume making her usual indignant stance impossible. "We're not a salad; we are the harvest," she delivers with some disappointment in her voice. I almost joke that the harvest would be salad next week but thought better of it. "I have to go get my stuff," she says.

"All right," Lisa says, "we'll wait for you right here, and then we'll go get ice cream."

An hour later, Lisa and I sit around a long table with Katy, still in her tomato suit, and three of Katy's friends; two turnips and a pumpkin. The vegetables chatter tirelessly as they spoon hot fudge sundaes into the holes in their costumes that hide their mouths. I grin at Lisa as we watch this great scene, and I feel like I am a million miles from work.

"Where's Joey?" I whisper to Lisa. "I thought he was coming along."

"He was," she says, "until he got a better offer. Marty Pierce wanted him to come over and play some new video game involving nuclear weapons and wagon trains. Then he made some crack about Katy and her fruity friends, so she told him she didn't want him to come anyway because he was a major idiot. After five minutes of that argument, I was happy to have them go to different places."

"Yep," I say, "sibling exchanges get a little grueling sometimes."

She nods. "At least you got past it when you and your brother grew up," she says. "Maybe the same will happen with Joey and Katy."

"Don and I got past it because he moved to Indianapolis. If you only talk three times a year, it's easier not to get pissed at one another. But we still each think the other is an asshole."

"And with good reason," she says and grins, proud of the jab.

"Oh, I see," I say, giving her a poke in the ribs. Suddenly, all the vegetables are silently staring at us, assessing. "Sorry to interrupt the party," I say.

Katy looks at her friends. "My Dad's not really sorry. He's being amusing," she says, solemnly.

Ouch. The fruits and vegetables all seemed to understand this and return to consuming ice cream and having conversations that had been interrupted. There was a sudden gagging sound, and I turned to see the pumpkin throwing up her ice cream and hot fudge on the table.

Chapter 8

The next morning, Kevin Walters and I sit side by side at the table in our conference room, several documents covering the tabletop between us, with one in particular that we are focused on—Kevin's last-minute find at the Consolidated warehouse.

"So," Kevin says thoughtfully, "we have this $50,000 invoice for work performed by J. Andrews Company on the date of the accident. It says unit 319, which internally means Wheeling, so they cleaned that up before they produced it. But they missed a more technical issue—the invoice is for repair and removal of oak substructures, and the oak substructures are in Ruston, not in Wheeling."

"You're sure about that?"

"Definitely. I was familiar with documents at both locations. That's something Michael's people and the lawyers wouldn't know they needed to address when sanitizing documents before the production to us. So I called my connections inside Consolidated."

"Any helpful witnesses for us?" I ask.

"Well, I contacted my three closest friends inside the company who know what was going on here. The lawyers had already met with each of them and instructed them that they are not to talk to me at all, under unspoken threat of personal disaster. Two of the three told me that they were sorry, but there's no way they can help me. They said that they do want us to stay friends even if Constantine doesn't like it. The third guy is Don Parson. He doesn't like what Constantine did to me, and he's going to give some thought to how he might help. I'm still not sure he will, but I can't hold it against him if he walks away. After all, the survival instinct is as basic as it gets. So, I called J. Andrews yesterday."

"Any luck with them?"

Walters shakes his head. "The documents all say the work was done at 319. I talked to two of the people who went out on the job. Both say they did the work at Wheeling, but it's pretty fishy. They call it just an inspection and repair. When I asked them how much the work they did cost, it was clear that they weren't prepared for the question. One said he didn't know, but the other one said $15,000."

"That could help," I say, "and I'll request reports on the work performed, but I expect they will be closely reviewed and cleaned up before we see them."

"Can we go to the mine and look at the substructures and what work was done?" Walters asks?

"Yes. I'll set up an inspection. Let's bring along an expert of our own to assess what they've done in there and with what materials."

"I know the right guy," Walters says, enthusiastically. "Jack Bernard is a structural expert I worked with five or six times. He likes me, and I know he'll help."

"All right." I lean back in my chair. "I hired an investigator, Lee Henry, and he got started a few days ago. He's good at what he does, and I've worked with him for over five years."

"Sounds good," Walters replies. "What's he finding?"

"Closed doors so far," I say. "He approached the employees who were injured. None of them will talk to him about the accident or the company. He also tried talking to the family of the employee who died, but didn't come up with anything. None of them really wanted to talk either. It's almost like answering any question is some giant act of disloyalty to the company."

Kevin nods. "I'm not surprised. They will have been assured that all expenses will be covered—and they will. Plus some additional benefits for the families. Constantine will see that they are taken care of, and they will take care of him in return."

"You think Constantine will be personally involved in this?" I ask.

"I don't know, but Constantine is a master of two things; manufacturing loyalty and not allowing people to look behind his curtain. He can take loyalty to the extreme, making employees grateful that he gave them the opportunity to be injured for the benefit of the rest of the team. He can also be their savior, helping these folks survive a rough time." He shakes his head. "He is resourceful and can be relentless. He also has the assets and the reach to accomplish whatever he wants." He is momentarily quiet, and then he asks, "So what happens now?"

"Next Lee is going to meet with Carl Miller, the Easton County inspector, to see if he can get to the document trail to prove what happened at which mine. So, here is our game plan. You talk to Jack Bernard over the next day or two. If he's willing, I'll talk to him about the expert opinions we need. I'll get hold of Lee and see how his meeting with Carl Miller went."

Walters asks, "Sounds like your investigator is pretty sharp. Is he an ex-cop?"

I smile. "He's actually an ex-ghost. Worked for the CIA for a number of years."

"Why did he leave that gig? I wasn't entirely sure one was allowed to leave the CIA," he says, grinning.

"He liked the agency but not the politics, so he walked after a dozen years and went into business for himself. As you might expect from a guy with that kind of a background, he is pretty resourceful."

"Glad he's on our team," Kevin says.

"Yep. Me too."

He stands and shakes my hand. "Thanks, again."

I find myself smiling. "Whoever gets to information first calls the other, right?

"Right," Kevin says, and then walks out of the conference room.

I look down at the Andrews Company invoice, and the foreboding I had experienced after first meeting with Kevin inexplicably returns. Kevin is a good guy, and I am not predisposed toward any strange paranoia. I need to shake this off.

I am swamped, and the rest of the day flies by. At five o'clock, Donna buzzes me on the intercom. "Scott, Lisa is on line two," she says.

"Okay, thanks." I pick up the phone. "Hi, sweetheart, how are you?"

"I'm going crazy," she says, frustration in her voice. "I gotta get out of here for a while tonight. Joey and Katy have been fighting all afternoon. Is there any way you can come home early and let me go see Lindsay for a while?"

I look at the piles in my inbox, but I can hear the plea in her voice, so I don't hesitate. "You got it, babe. I'll leave within fifteen minutes."

"Oh, bless you," she says. "I owe you for this."

"No you don't," I say. "I've been pretty absorbed lately, and I owe you some sanity preservation."

* * *

When I walk into the house, I see Lisa and Joey standing two feet apart, with Lisa giving him a stern look. "Hi, gang," I say, walking into the room.

"I told you two hours ago I wanted that room cleaned, mister, Lisa says, in her best tough mom voice."

"Well, I would have it done if she hadn't been bugging me the whole time," he retorts, throwing his chin in Katy's direction.

"Hey," Katy chimes in, "it's not my fault. I got my room cleaned, and I saw you watching that cartoon show."

"Enough!" Lisa shouts, with a pained expression. "Can you do dinner?"

"We got it covered," I say. I give her a hug and a kiss. "Have a good time."

She whispers, "Thanks for the rescue," then turned to the kids. "Good night guys." She hugs Katy, then Joey.

"We'll make sure that room gets cleaned too," I add, much to Joey's dismay.

When Lisa leaves the room, I look at the kids. "You guys hungry?" Katy nods. "Yeah," Joey says.

"All right, how about I make something?" They looked at me expectantly. "I know," I say in my most serious tone, "I'll barbecue spaghetti."

Joey shakes his head, which is not an unusual reaction to my jokes. Katy's brow furrows. "You can't do that, Dad. The stringers will fall into the barbecue."

"Oh, yeah," I respond, enlightened. "Well, if that won't work I guess I better take you guys out for dinner." At this there were cheers from the crowd. "First, though, Joey's got to finish that room." His smile begins to fade. "Come on," I say, "do it quickly and we're out of here. Otherwise, we starve."

Twenty minutes later, we walk into Jacey's Coffee Shop and seat ourselves in a corner booth. A waitress appears in a pink dress with a white apron. She holds up a small pad and pencil and says in a practiced manner, "What's it gonna be, kids?"

"Katy, you know what you want?" I ask.

"I want Joey to give my pencil back."

"To eat," I say. "The lady is waiting for your order."

"Okay. I want a baked potato and french fries."

The waitress giggles, but looking at Katy, she saw hurt feelings. "I'm sorry, sweetie," she offers apologetically. "A baked potato and fries sounds yummy. What do you want to drink?"

"Coke, please," she says.

"Coming right up," the waitress says. "How about you, young man? You want a hamburger with a steak on the side?" I give the woman a smile.

"I'll have a hamburger and a slice of pepperoni pizza," Joey says.

"That was my next guess," the woman replies. "How about you, Dad?"

"I'll have a chicken sandwich with salad, blue cheese dressing, diet Coke."

"I'll be right back with your drinks. Don't riot while I'm gone." She smiles and walks away.

"She's pretty crazy," Katy offers thoughtfully.

"Yeah," I say, "I like her, too."

* * *

The next day, I am in court in the morning and back in the office in the afternoon. At a little after three, Donna buzzes. "I know you wanted me to hold your calls for a while, but Lisa is on line two. I figured you better take this one, unless you like sleeping on the couch."

"I will take it," I say, "and you're giving me a lot of insight into the tools you use to keep John in line."

"Damn right. Our couch isn't real comfortable, either."

"Thanks, Donna." I hit the button. "Hi, babe."

"Hi, honey. I just wanted to say thanks again for last night. You're a very sweet husband."

I smile, feeling comfortable that my immediate destiny was not the couch. "I'm glad you and Lindsay had a good time."

"Actually, we didn't. She spent the whole time bitching about how Bob doesn't help her and I spent the whole time thinking about how lucky I am to have you."

"Sounds like time well spent to me," I say.

"Will you be home for dinner? I'll send the kids to my mom's and wear just my apron."

"I'll be there."

"I love you," she says.

"I love you, too. One more thing."

"What?"

"No need for the apron," I add, and she laughs. "Bye."

"Bye. Don't be late."

Donna buzzes again as we hang up. "Lee Henry on line one," she says.

I hit the button. "Lee, you got some news for me on the Walters case?"

"Hey, Scott. Actually, I hope you're doing better with this case than I am. I have news all right, but none of it is good. There's something weird about this one. No one has anything to say. It's like we're trying to get people to take the stand against the Godfather or something. I tried again and could make no progress with the families of the victims who didn't make it or the injured who are well enough to talk. They won't even discuss what happened.

"Then there's our friends at the county. Miller is now on a milk carton—just gone. For all they know, the earth opened up and swallowed him. I talked to five of his coworkers, and the line is always the same. He suddenly retired, and they don't have any idea where he went or how to reach him—and one of them was his buddy for ten years. And get this; there are no documents in any of his files concerning Consolidated Energy mines and no other file they can find, regarding any recent inspections of Consolidated mines by Miller. Recent reports concerning these mines have somehow disappeared." He pauses, and then adds. "So, I did a little covert work, which got me into Miller's personnel file. The only address they have for Miller is a PO Box in Tennessee where his check gets sent. Some place called Covington. Maybe our man Miller is living in this Tennessee town. I'm going to see if I can pay him a visit."

I'm always in awe of how Lee comes up with this stuff, but given his covert connections, which he never discusses, I decide that I am not going to ask how he got there. "You're amazing," I say, and mean it. "Let me know as soon as you make contact with our man."

"Shall do."

"You do great work, Lee. Hang in there."

I lean back in my chair and think about all the evidence I don't have. My gut tells me that Kevin Walters is a straight shooter, and he had his facts right, but I long ago learned that being right isn't worth much if you can't prove it to a jury. One thing I do know is that if Walters is correct about the games being played, then Constantine is a master at hiding the ball, and we are going to have our work cut out for us. Between Consolidated's sleight of hand and Bob Harris's stonewalling, I was going to be up to my ass in good times by the time trial rolled around.

Chapter 9

On Saturday morning, six- and seven-year-olds in blue and white uniforms dot the baseball field, wearing expressions far too serious for such youthful faces. Joey stands on the pitcher's mound, kicking at the dirt as he has undoubtedly seen done on television. I wonder if he knows why he is kicking at the dirt, and if he is going to adjust himself and spit tobacco next.

He gives the signaling catcher a confident nod, and then winds up to pitch. Joey shows the batter his best evil eye as he holds the ball and his glove together, and then rears up on one foot. The recipient of this psychological warfare is a neighbor of ours. He is a nice kid, but this is great theater. Joey throws a fastball, high and outside, that the batter swings at far too late. Strike one. This poor kid is so nervous he can barely hold the bat. Joey struts back to the mound and kicks a couple more ruts beneath it, leading me to believe he'll soon be standing in a hole. He shakes off the catcher once, and then nods and fires one low and inside. Another swing and a miss. Now Joey's really into it. He hurls the next pitch perfectly down the pipe, and the cute neighbor kid takes the strike without swinging. The ump yells strike three, and the youngster shakes off a momentary look that says he might cry and moves toward the dugout to face the wrath of his team. Joey is looking really confident now.

Next to the plate is a much bigger kid. I almost want to ask the kid for some proof that he belonged in this league, but I've seen too many intrusive parents causing trouble at their kids' sporting events, so I let it slide.

Lisa and I stand behind a backstop that separates spectators from wild pitch injuries. "What a ham," Lisa whispers, and we both chuckle. She adds, "I wonder where he gets it." It was not a question.

"Moi?" I ask, using my best incredulous voice.

Joey fires a fastball low and outside. The big kid steps in and connects with a huge swing. The ball takes off, clearing the outfield fence in left field, as the kid jogs the bases victoriously. Joey stands with his hands on his hips, watching his opponent round third and head for home. As he makes his way back to the mound, his swagger is gone, and he looks worried.

Lisa gives me her "my poor baby" look, and I nod in understanding. Even though we know it has to happen, it's tough to watch your kids suffer disappointment. Joey shakes off the effects admirably, striking out the next kid and throwing the final batter out at home. In the fourth inning, we score two runs, and in the seventh, Joey hits a line drive down the third base line to bring in a third. We watch the excitement of the blue and white team as they hold on to win three to two. Everyone on the red team looks like they just lost their best friends. The teams line up facing each other and walk toward one another, slapping hands in the air as they pass and repeatedly reciting "good game." Sportsmanship requires these statements go in both directions, even though only one team thought it was a good game.

In the car on the way home, Joey wears a disappointed expression, which I attribute to the fact that he was tagged for a home run. "You okay, buddy?" I ask.

Joey nods. "Yeah, I'm okay."

"You played a good game, you know?" He is silent. "Are you re-thinking the home run that the big guy hit?"

"No," he says. "I was thinking about Jason Barber."

As he says the name, it comes back to me. Jason Barber is the nice neighborhood kid Joey struck out twice during the game. Now I'm intrigued. "What about him?" I ask.

"Well," he says thoughtfully, "I was just thinking that he's probably kinda disappointed not getting on base. Maybe when we get home I can go hang out with him for a while."

Wow. I am more proud of him than I can say. "That's a really nice idea. I bet he would like to see a friend right about now, just to let him know that friends stay friends even on bad days." It sounded so corny I expected a raised eyebrow and a groan, but it didn't happen.

"I'd probably want that if it happened to me," he says. Wow again. "Besides," he added, "his mom makes milkshakes every time I go over there."

* * *

Michael Constantine sat at one end of the long mahogany dining room table. Vickie sat to his right and Jerry Anders to his left. Jerry looked at Mike nervously every few minutes.

"Jerry, there's something I want to say to you." Anders put down his soup spoon and looked at Constantine with the expression of a kid who knows he is in big trouble. "It's okay with us that you use the guest house for a month, but that's it."

"I know," Anders said, nodding, "Vickie told me that."

Constantine studies him. "I heard you got past the drugs, and I hope that's true. I don't want to worry about anything coming up missing this time."

"I understand," Anders said. "You won't have any problem this time, and I want you to know that I'm going to find a way to pay you back."

Constantine nodded in understanding, but didn't believe a word of it. Leopards don't change their spots, and Constantine doubted Anders would ever be anything but a liability. "Well, I hope you're right, Jerry."

"You'll see," Anders said. "This time I'm going to make it. I'll be looking for a job starting tomorrow, right after I check in with my parole officer."

Constantine decided to run his own little test. "I might be able to get you a job offloading trucks. It'll pay about twelve bucks an hour to start."

"Thanks," Anders said, "but with my bad back I can't do heavy labor."

"You have a bad back?" Constantine asked.

"I thought you said you spent a lot of time pumping iron when you were in jail."

"I did," Anders said. "That's how I got a bad back."

Constantine tried not to roll his eyes. "So what will you do?"

"I don't know, but I'll know it when I see it, kinda like pornography," he added, hoping to lighten the moment with a joke.

"Better not be too much like pornography," Constantine said, "at least not while you're staying here."

"It was a joke, Michael," Vickie says, coming to her brother's rescue. "It was a joke. Jerry told you he's going to find a job."

Constantine held up a hand. "Okay, I hope he does."

Everyone returned to eating and an uncomfortable silence crowded the room. Jerry told himself that he would convince Michael that he was going to stay on the right road; it will just take a little time. It had taken time and bad decisions to lose respect, and it would take work and a few good decisions to get it back. He commended himself on having the right attitude as he finished his chicken stir fry.

Constantine wondered how long it would be until drugs surfaced and belongings started disappearing. One time and he's out of here, Constantine thought to himself, whether Vickie likes it or not.

Chapter 10

Lawyers get home-field advantage when they set a deposition. Sometimes they seek to create an atmosphere of physical intimidation for the other party—anything to gain a psychological advantage.

I follow a red-haired woman in her mid-twenties down a short hall to an opulent conference room that features travertine, marble corner tables, and a huge mahogany conference table in the shape of a *U* that seats twenty-four with large leather-backed chairs. Overhead are three enormous chandeliers that have to be a nightmare for some poor soul to dust. This forty-fourth-floor cavern for the wealthiest of clients is, I guess, where the Michael Constantines of the world expect their lawyers to hang out. I thank the young escort and move to the top of one side of the "U," where a court reporter is setting up. Next to her, the videographer is getting his camera set up. They and their equipment are dwarfed by this cavernous room. I cup my hands around my mouth and warble "hello down there" to emphasize the absurdity of this. The reporter and the videographer laugh as I walk over to them.

"Good morning. I'm Scott Winslow," I say to both of them.

"Hi, Mr. Winslow. I'm Lynn Hernandez," the court reporter replies.

"Mr. Winslow," the videographer said, extending a hand. "Jim Roybal. Good to meet you."

"Please," I say, "call me Scott." I look around the room and then add, "I guess the Convention Center was unavailable this morning." They both laugh.

"Yeah," Frank says, "the room is a little large for this group."

I sit down beside the empty seat one away from Lynn, leaving a vacant seat for the witness between us.

The redhead reappears with Kevin Walters in her wake and says, "Here you are," waving to the three of us in the distant corner of this cavernous room.

"Hi, Kevin," I say, standing to shake his hand. He shakes my hand and then glances around him and shrugs.

"Yeah," I say, rolling my eyes, "very modest and unassuming." Come take the seat of honor next to the court reporter. Hook the microphone to your lapel." I do likewise. The lawyers and the witness wear microphones for the audio portion of the deposition video that is being prepared. At trial, a jury can see the witness on tape while hearing questions and answers to the extent allowed into evidence.

Kevin sits, and we wait fifteen minutes past our scheduled start time. One more of the games Harris likes to play. Harris then walks in and sits, placing his laptop in front of him. He hooks his microphone to his shirt. When all is set, he says, "Good morning," and then adds, "Are we ready?"

"Yes, we're ready." I look around the gigantic room. "Unless you are expecting others?"

"No," Harris says. He looks at the videographer and says, "Let's get started."

The videographer announces the deposition of Kevin Walters, the date, and the location, and Harris and I introduce ourselves for the record. Then he asks the court reporter to administer the oath to the witness, which she does.

Never to disappoint, Bob Harris is every bit the horse's ass I expect. Kevin is poised, calm, and professional, just as he had been during our many hours of preparation, when I played the role of the horse's ass.

Harris leans over the long, polished table and the camera remains focused on Kevin, videotaping his testimony throughout. The first four hours are spent going through Kevin's work history, from his first part-time job in high school and then through his entire history with Consolidated Energy, every position ever held, to whom he reported, how his performance was reviewed. He is asked ad nauseam about all prior jobs held, what he did at each, who he reported to, who reported to him, who he had lunch with, and why he moved from each position. Then Harris takes him through his education at tedious length. He almost goes back as far as Montessori before progressing to high school, college, and grad degrees.

After lunch, he inquires at length about Consolidated, its structure, subsidiaries, the mines it owns, and management personnel who operated them, as well as Kevin's role in each. Then it gets more entertaining.

Harris sits back and tosses out, "Mr. Walters, isn't it accurate that on a number of occasions, Mr. Constantine, had expressed dissatisfaction with your performance?"

"Objection," I say. "Vague and ambiguous as to what's a number of occasions. And expressed dissatisfaction to whom? If we are talking about anyone other than the witness, it lacks foundation and calls for speculation." To Kevin, I say, "You can answer if you understand."

"No," Walters says.

"So you're telling us that Mr. Constantine never told you that he thought there were problems with your performance?"

"That's right," Walters says.

"Why do you think you were fired?"

"I know why I was fired," Walters says.

"How do you know?" Harris asks. "Did someone tell you?"

Walters leaned forward in his chair and looked Harris in the eyes. "Indirectly, yes."

"What does *indirectly* mean?"

"Michael Constantine told me that I was fired because I betrayed him."

"And how did you betray him?"

I raised a hand to stop Kevin from answering until I get my objection on the record. "I object. The question assumes facts not in evidence and is argumentative. He did not say that he betrayed Constantine, he said that Constantine said that."

"All right," Harris said, annoyance in his tone. "Did he say how you had betrayed him?"

Kevin nodded firmly. "From the context of our conversation at the time, yes."

"What was said?"

"He said I had no business going out and talking to Carl Miller, the Easton County inspector. That conditions of our operations were to be discussed in-house only. He asked me if that was clear."

"And you said?"

"I told him that the company failed to correct violations that endangered its employees, and that I was not okay with that."

"What did he say?"

"He said I didn't have to worry about it anymore. That my services were no longer required."

"Did you respond?"

"Not at first. I was stunned that it was over just like that after so many years of being a part of management. When I recovered, I said, 'I didn't expect this from you, Michael. Is it all about profit? Is there no room to do things right?'"

"He was angry. He stared at me and said, 'This meeting is over.' So I left."

"Anyone else there for any part of this meeting?"

"Yeah. Larry Hanson, VP of administration, and a senior personnel guy whose name I can't remember."

"Is he someone you knew before the meeting? Can you describe him?"

My turn to be heard. "Object as compound. Answer one of those questions, Kevin, but don't tell him which one."

"You think you're funny, counsel," Harris said in a raised voice. It was not a question.

"Well, yes." I say. "But I also think your question was bad."

"Yes," Kevin says, and then adds, "to both questions. I had seen him around, although he had only been with the company for about a year. He was about forty, clean shaven, wore wire rimmed glasses, and was balding on top. He was a tall, slender fellow."

"He say anything during the meeting?" Harris asks.

"Not that I recall."

"Were Mr. Constantine and Mr. Hanson still there when you left the room?"

"Yes."

"So they could vouch for your story about what happened in this meeting?"

"They could if they were inclined to tell the truth," Kevin says in an even tone. I love this answer and have to suppress a grin.

"So they'd be lying if they said it happened differently?"

"I object," I say. "You're asking him someone else's state of mind. It calls for speculation. You can answer to the best of your ability," I told Kevin.

"Lying or misremembering," he says, evenly.

Harris pauses and grows a smug look. "Were you a named defendant in a sexual harassment lawsuit against the company?" Harris asks.

Kevin shakes his head in a manner that suggests he was annoyed. "Yes," he responded.

I felt like I had not been told about an important piece of information. "Wait a minute," I say. "Let's take a break."

"In a few minutes," Harris says, "after I finish this line of questioning."

"No," I respond as evenly as I can, "right now."

"Counsel, you're interfering with my deposition," Harris complains.

"No, I'm just taking a break. Come with me, Kevin." We step outside the conference room and walk out to the lobby. "Something you should let me in on? What's with the sex harassment lawsuit?" I ask, after making sure that we were outside the range of hearing of those in the area.

"It shows what they will do to get to me, that's for sure. A director who reported to me was accused of coming on to his secretary. Her name was Jane Evans. There was no allegation against me except that it involved one of my subordinates."

"What happened to the case?"

"It settled."

"Were you accused of doing anything inappropriate by anyone in the company?"

"No, never."

"Did you testify?"

"No."

I nodded. "How long ago was this?"

"Maybe six or seven years," he says.

I nod. "If I'd known the story, I never would have forced a break."

"I'd have told you about it," Kevin says, "but I would never have imagined they would attempt to use something like that against me. It had nothing to do with me."

"Tip of the iceberg, Kevin. They will use anything and everything that will stop you, and we have to be ready for all of it."

When we step back inside, Harris is grinning again. I pretend not to notice. So much damned theater in the process.

"Are we ready to go back on the record?" Harris asks.

"Yes," I say evenly.

"Any part of your testimony you would like to change after meeting with counsel?" I suppress a grin.

"No," Kevin says, "we're fine."

"So then," Harris asks, did you violate policy in connection with the sexual harassment matter we were discussing?

"Not that I'm aware of," Kevin says.

"Did you report the matter to your supervisor?"

"What matter are you speaking of?"

"The sexual harassment claim of Ms. Evans that we have been discussing."

"Sure," Kevin says.

"When?"

"You want the date?"

"Yes, the date," Harris says.

"I don't know. It has been a number of years."

Harris leans forward in his chair, eyes fixed on Kevin. "Weren't you criticized by Mr. Constantine in connection with your handling of the matter?"

"I was not," Kevin says.

"Did you have any disagreements concerning how it should be handled?"

Kevin paused. I had no idea what was coming next. "Yes," Kevin says, evenly.

"Why don't you tell me about that?"

"Do you know what this incident involved, Mr. Harris?"

"Yes, and so do you."

"Objection, counsel. Argumentative and hopelessly ambiguous. Whether what you think you know is what Mr. Walters knows is unknown because you haven't asked. As such, the record is not at all clear that the two of you are on the same page."

"It's my record, counsel," Harris growls, sounding annoyed.

"It is," I respond. "And if you like ambiguity, it will be perfect for you."

Harris gives me daggers. Kevin starts to speak, and I say, "Wait for a question."

"There is a question," Harris retorts.

"All right, then, wait for a question that makes sense."

"Counsel, you are pushing the limits," Harris snarls.

"Thank you. Is there a question you would like to ask?"

Harris gathers himself and says, "What was the disagreement between you and Mr. Constantine concerning how the matter should be handled?"

Kevin pauses to see if there would be any more argument from anyone and proceeds when the silence persisted for longer than five seconds. "There were allegations that a subordinate of mine had been persistent in asking Ms. Evans to have a relationship. She resisted for a while, and then she complained. When I told Mike Constantine of the events and the discipline I laid on my subordinate, he had another view."

"Which was?" Harris asked impatiently.

"That they were both a pain in the ass, and I should dump both of them."

"And what did you say?" Harris asks.

"I said we shouldn't, and we can't fire someone for complaining about improper conduct of a coworker. He just told me to handle it one way or another."

"There was a lawsuit thereafter, right?"

"Yes, there was."

"Did it cost the company money?"

My turn to chime in. "I object. Lacks foundation, calls for speculation, vague and ambiguous, and may violate a confidentiality agreement, but you represent the company, and if you want that on the record, I'll let him respond."

Harris put on a thoughtful expression, but didn't speak further.

Kevin responds, "Most lawsuits do."

"It was made clear to you that Mr. Constantine held you responsible for this lawsuit, wasn't it?"

I watch Kevin's brow furrow. He pauses and then simply says, "No."

Harris sits back in his chair. "Mr. Walters, do you contend that you complained to anyone about unsafe conditions at any of the mines?" Harris asks.

"Yes."

"Which one?" Harris asks.

I chimed in, "Objection. Lacks foundation and assumes facts not in evidence."

"Several over the years," Kevin says. "Most recently, however, it was Ruston."

"And what was the nature of your complaint about Ruston?"

"Assuming there was only one," I say.

"And there wasn't only one," Kevin responds. "They were numerous."

"What complaints did you make?" Harris asks.

"They all related to the fact that the mine was unsafe, and workers were at risk. My complaints were inadequate tunnel maintenance, failing substructures, inadequate safety equipment, and failure to make corrections to bring us into compliance with law."

"How were you out of compliance with law?"

"I wasn't," Walters says. "The company was."

"Okay, fine," Harris says, frustration apparent. "How was the company in violation?"

"Much of it is documented," Kevin says. "The company was cited for twenty-two violations for unsafe conditions. Additionally, I documented shortcomings when they were made known to me."

"Do you have those documents?"

"No, unfortunately, the company has them, though they haven't been produced as requested by my counsel."

"Move to strike that last statement as nonresponsive," Harris says.

Kevin gives me a look, and I say. "He is moving to strike your statement from the record because he didn't like it."

Harris glares at me. "I moved to strike it because it was not responsive to my question, counsel."

"Okay, fine. He moved to strike your statement because he didn't believe it was responsive to his question and because he didn't like it."

Harris gives me another sharp look, and then continues, "To whom did you make your complaints, Mr. Walters?"

"To a number of managers inside the company, including Michael Constantine, and when it was clear it was to be swept under the rug by Michael, I went to Carl Miller, the county inspector."

"And where is Mr. Miller now?" Harris asks.

"Right now? How would he know that?" I interject.

"Counsel, I don't appreciate your obstreperous behavior," Harris says.

"I think he means these days rather than today, I say to Kevin."

"I don't know."

"Does he still work for the county?"

"Apparently not," Kevin responds.

"And you have no way of contacting him?"

"Correct," Kevin says.

"Well, that's pretty convenient, isn't it?" Harris says.

"Don't respond, Kevin," I say. "That is argumentative, and it's not even a question."

"All right," Harris says, "here's a question. The mine you complained about, Ruston, is still operating just fine, right?"

"Object. Vague and ambiguous and argumentative, but you may answer."

"No, it's not *just fine* by any reasonable definition."

"What specific conditions did you complain about?"

"I complained that there were documented violations from the MSHA, the governing federal agency with jurisdiction of mining operations, that had not been corrected, some of which were S&S violations and some of which had also been the subject of repeat violation. I complained that records weren't being kept as MSHA required—problems were being reported on project documents but not the records MSHA reviews." Kevin draws a breath.

"That all of it?" Harris asks.

"No." Harris waited and Kevin said no more. I suppressed a grin at how well Kevin was doing following my instruction that he answer only the question asked and volunteer nothing more.

"What else?" Harris asks.

"I complained that these were knowing cover-ups and that these conditions were dangerous to our miners whose lives were on the line. I also complained that those hiding the ball rather than fixing the problems should be fired rather than encouraged."

"What's an S&S violation, for the record?"

"It means significant and substantial. Per MSHA standards, it is one likely to lead to serious injury or illness."

"Anything else you complained about?"

"Yes." Silence in the room.

"What else did you complain about?" Harris asks, pulling teeth.

"That it was clear that the failure to document and failure to correct violations were starting to become part of the culture, and that managers seemed to be condoning such failures."

"You would expect the records to bear you out concerning the conditions you were reporting, right?" Harris asks.

"I surely would," Kevin says.

Harris was grinning. "But they don't, right?"

Kevin looks at me, not wanting to give what we believed away yet.

I jump in. "I object. Vague and ambiguous, compound, overbroad, calling for improper opinion and legal conclusion. Are you asking him to analyze and conclude on the significance of about twenty thousand documents circulating in this case? If so, I am not going to let him. Do you want him to tell you what he read in the newspapers about what happened—how can he possibly answer that?"

Harris thinks a moment, and then nods. "Okay, I'll strike that question. Tell me what documents you created about the complaints you had."

A much better question, and one that I knew Kevin could run with very well. "I wrote several e-mails about a number of these events. First, to the managers who needed to act on the particular violations that were identified, and, on a number of occasions, to my boss."

"Did you do that to build a claim?"

"No, this was as the events occurred. I was trying to get someone to fix important safety issues. I had no idea that I would ever have a claim of any kind. I had no idea that the company—meaning Mike—would fire me for trying to fix safety problems."

"What documents do you have in your possession to substantiate that these communications occurred?"

"I do not have the e-mails; the company does. They fired me and aren't allowing me access to the system."

Harris smirks in a self-congratulatory way. Such a dick. He leans back in his chair and asks, "Mr. Walters, you knew that you were an at-will employee, right?

"Objection, calls for a legal conclusion, lacks foundation, and calls for speculation," I interject.

"You can answer, Mr. Walters," Harris says.

We had prepped for this one as well, so I just wait while Kevin looks contemplatively at Harris. "I have heard the term, but I don't really know what that means, legally," he says, thoughtfully.

"It means that you can quit anytime you want, and the company can fire you at any time."

"Was that your understanding of your relationship with Consolidated?"

"No," Kevin says and then waits.

Harris shakes his head disapprovingly. "You could have quit at any time and without notice, couldn't you?"

"Well, I suppose that would be possible, but I would never leave the company in a bind."

"But to your understanding, you could, legally, right?"

"Object as calling for a legal conclusion, but you can answer."

"I suppose so, given that slavery was abolished some time back."

"All right," Harris says. "And likewise, the company could have fired you at any time, right?"

"Object as calling for a legal conclusion." I look at Kevin. "You can respond."

"No."

"Why not," Harris says, sounding annoyed once again.

"Because it is my understanding that an employee cannot be terminated for an unlawful reason, such as retaliation for raising safety issues."

"Where did you come by that understanding?"

"I don't recall specifically, but at various times during my career. I've been in the workforce a long time."

Harris wasn't happy. He peruses his notes and then begins asking questions about Kevin's efforts to find reemployment. "So," Harris asks, "did you find another job?"

"No."

Harris nods. "So why can't a guy with your level of experience find a new position if working that hard at it."

"I object. Argumentative, calls for speculation, lacks foundation, and an improper question. But you may answer," I add, smiling inwardly as I knew what was coming.

"Because Consolidated is preventing me from finding reemployment," Kevin says.

"What evidence of that do you have?" Harris sounds angry and indignant.

"There is anger in your voice, counsel. Can you simply ask your questions without a show of disapproval or incredulity?"

"There is nothing wrong with my tone," Harris almost yells. "As for incredulity, a lot of your client's testimony is hard to believe."

I raise a hand. "Save it for the jury. Do you have another question, or are we done here?"

Harris is now pissed. "You know, counsel, your conduct here has been highly inappropriate and obstreperous all day long. I'm about that far," he says, holding up a thumb and index finger, "from halting this deposition and getting an order for sanctions."

I lean back in my chair as Kevin looks on, concerned. I look at him for a moment and then I nod. "If you want to go now, we can still beat traffic. I'll be happy to oppose the motion and convince the court that you had the one and only shot at this deposition that you are entitled to. Just let me know if this is a good time." I waited.

Harris, now completely pissed off, turns to my client shaking his head, and asks his next question. So it went, all day. At 5:00 p.m., Harris says, "Let's quit for the day and arrange a second day later."

"How much longer do you have?" I ask.

"Probably another three hours."

"Do you want to push on and do them tonight?"

Harris sits back and contemplates. "Yes, let's push on," he says, probably figuring he could score more points with a tired witness.

"Let me talk to my client," I say, and Kevin and I step outside and walk down the hall together.

"How are you doing?" I ask.

"A little tired but okay."

"You want to wrap up for the day or push on and get it done? If you are too tired to have your head fully in the game, we should can it, and come back another day," I add.

"I'm okay," Kevin says. "I'd really like to get this all done today." I nod, and we return to the conference room.

"We are good to go on if the court reporter is okay with it."

"The reporter tells us she will be okay if we proceed further."

We reattach our microphones to our lapels, and the videographer announces that we are on tape four of Kevin's deposition.

"Mr. Walters, I am going to ask you about a number of documents. Let's start with what we will mark as Exhibit 1, your employment application with Consolidated."

"Did you prepare this document?"

"I did."

"When?"

"Well, from the date on it, I would say about twenty-eight years ago."

"Is everything on it true and correct?

I chime in with, "Read it all carefully to assure there are no mistakes before answering." In fact, Kevin and I have been through this and all the documents we have, so I know what he will say.

"It's accurate," Kevin says after reading it over again.

Harris then proceeds through forty-four documents, marking each as exhibits and asking questions about the authenticity and context of a number of them. The deposition continues until 8:10 p.m., when Harris finally states that he has no more questions. With Kevin off the hot seat, and having done a great job, I hand Harris a notice of deposition for Michael Constantine in three weeks. "A present for you," I say. "It's the deposition notice for Constantine on the date we agreed." Harris nods, and then says, "Good night," to the room and walks out. When Harris leaves the office, I thank the court reporter and videographer, who are in the process of packing up their equipment, and Kevin and I walk out together.

"Did I do okay?" he asks.

"You did a good job. You came across as direct and honest."

Kevin gives a slight nod. "Thanks," he says, then adds, "The company is either hiding or has destroyed all those memos I did. I probably shouldn't be too surprised at this point but after working somewhere for twenty-seven years, you want to think that ..." He let his words trail off.

"I know," I say, "it can be really disappointing to find that documents are gone without explanation and to listen to what you know is pure bullshit. I can almost guarantee there will be a lot more of the story they try to tell about you that you won't recognize."

Kevin nods. "Thanks for bailing me out in there. I didn't know where to go with a couple of those questions. I also didn't want to talk about that Andrews Company invoice until we can find some backup."

"I am with you all the way."

We hop in the elevator alone, and Kevin says, "You know, Scott, I think I have told you that Constantine can be a pretty ruthless son of a bitch. Worse yet, there's something pathological about the way he does it. When you take his deposition, you will see it. He comes across like he believes every word he utters, even when it's pure bullshit."

"Sounds like a great guy," I said. "I'm looking forward to meeting him. I'm just hoping we can come up with a little more evidence before that happens. Maybe a document or two or maybe a way to get to Carl Miller and convince him to talk to us."

"There's something very weird about Miller being suddenly unavailable," Kevin says. "This guy was around inspecting for years, and then all of a sudden he evaporates without a trace—vaporized into some retirement. Maybe we should start checking the trunks of abandoned cars."

"Maybe," I say, reflecting on the vast resources available to Constantine to change history as reflected in records, to intimidate witnesses, and to accomplish anything else he chooses. "Except that these guys are smart enough to see that the car disappears, too."

"Unfortunately, that seems to be true." As we step out of the elevator on the first floor of the building, Kevin says, "There's one thing I've always wanted to ask you about litigators."

"Yeah, what's that?" I ask.

"Do you really go to war with these guys on a case for two years and then when you are off the record talk to each other like casual friends?"

"We sometimes do that. We're advocates, and argue our positions zealously, but try to stay objective knowing that everyone is doing a job."

"So will you have a beer with Harris when this is over?"

"Nope. Harris is an asshole when we are off the record as well."

Chapter 11

The wake-up alarm gently comes to life, and I hear Dan Fogelberg sing, "Longer than there have been fishes in the ocean." I smile and roll over to find Lisa looking at me. "Good morning, my love," she says. She stands and sheds her nightgown, and then lays down and pulls me to her. "Did you notice that they're playing our song?"

"I did notice that before my senses got taken over by thoughts of what is about to happen," I say, smiling and kissing her softly.

"You get distracted?" she asks continuing her movement beneath the covers.

"Yeah, seems like all the blood left my head, and I can't think."

She smiles. "Shouldn't be a problem," she says. "I know which head you think with anyway."

I pull her to me and kiss her deeply. She puts her hands on my face and caresses. "I love you," she says. "Seems like I just love you more and more. Maybe it's because you're a good dad." She smirks, and then says, "Or maybe it's because you're pretty good at this." She climbs on top of me and places me inside her. She smiles and begins to move, and we are instantly transported to paradise. God, I love this woman.

* * *

Jerry Anders arrived at the County Probation Department twenty minutes late and informed the receptionist he overslept. She told him to take a seat and someone would be with him shortly. Fifteen minutes later, a tall, thin man with a thick mustache and thinning brown hair emerged from the back offices into the reception area.

"Mr. Anders?" he called.

"Yes, I'm here," Jerry said, putting down a magazine.

"Hi. I'm John Linder, your probation officer. Follow me, please."

Jerry followed him down a narrow corridor past groupings of cubicles thick with files, loose paper, and employees on telephones. At the end of the corridor, Linder walked into a conference room Jerry thought to be about the size of a closet, housing a small round table and two chairs. When Jerry walked in, Linder closed the door behind them. Jerry had a sudden claustrophobic sensation. The room was even smaller than the cell he had occupied.

Linder directed Jerry to a chair and sat in the other one. "Mr. Anders," he began, "you and I don't know each other well, but we will. Today was the first and last time you will be late for our meetings. I have a large case load, and I have to report monthly on every one of them. You don't show up on time, I write that down, and you are one step closer to back inside. It won't matter to me because they are going to give me two new cases for every one that goes away. You with me so far?"

"Yes," Jerry said. "Sorry for being late."

"Good. Here are the written rules that govern your probation," Linder said, handing Jerry a two-page document. He looked directly at Jerry and spoke slowly, in a way that suggested he had spoken the words a thousand times. "No drugs, weapons, or associations with known criminals or anybody who I think is shady. You report two times a week for the first month. You find a job, and I make sure you're doing what the employer says you should be. You don't show there, I violate you. You don't show here, I violate you. You comply with all the rules I just gave you, or I violate you and send you back, no second chances. Still with me?"

"Yes," Jerry said softly, feeling suddenly like he was already back inside.

Linder softened his expression. "I'm not that hard to deal with if you toe the line. If you don't," he shrugged, "then at least you know the deal."

Jerry manages to respond with, "I understand."

"Good," Linder said. He threw a five-by-seven card on the table in front of Jerry. "Here are three potential jobs. I suggest you start with number three, Home Town Printers. The owner knows you're coming."

"Okay, thank you," Jerry said, suddenly feeling good about his prospects.

"Needless to say, anything goes missing, and you know who gets looked at first."

Deflated, Jerry says, "I'm not going to take anything." There was a slight edge to his voice.

"Good," Linder says. "Sounds like you mean it. See you here Thursday at 8:00 a.m. Don't be late." He handed Jerry a business card. "Call me if there's anything I need to know, okay?"

"Yes, sir," Jerry said as he got up from his seat. Linder turned his attention to a stack of documents in a folder.

* * *

When Jerry returned to the Constantine guest house that evening, he was ecstatic. He landed a job. He was now a printer and on his way back to fitting in with the crazy ways of free citizens. He called Vickie to share the news, and she invited him to dinner in the main house.

As soon as they sat down to eat, Jerry shared his news with Constantine, who seemed to consider it carefully.

"What are you going to be doing?" he asked.

"I'm going to operate a printing press, processing orders and such."

"You going to stick with it?"

Jerry glanced at Vickie, who looked uncomfortable but remained quiet. "Yes, I plan to make this work."

"Well, I hope you do," Constantine said, unable to keep the skepticism out of his voice. The remainder of dinner passes in discussion of

Vickie's day, sports, and what was needed around the house. As was always the case, Constantine said nothing about business.

After dinner, Vickie walked her brother back to the guest house. "I want to tell you that I think you're doing great, Jerry. Don't worry about Michael; it may take a little while to ..."

Jerry finished the thought. "I know. Look, I fucked up pretty bad. I taught Michael that I couldn't be trusted. It's going to take some time to fix that, but I intend to do it."

Vickie lit up with happiness. She squeezed his arm and said, "I know you're going to make it. Your time has come." She gave him a hug, and they said good night. Jerry couldn't remember the last time he felt such a sense of pride.

After Vickie left, Jerry drank a beer and watched Robert Redford's emergence from prisoner to warden in Brubaker. He thought about his own new emergence into a role he could respect. He felt almost euphoric as he opened a second beer. When he finally fell asleep, he dreamed he was back in prison, and all of his progress in moving into the real world had been a dream. At 2:00 a.m., he awoke startled and crying. He knew this new dream would be hard to hold, but he at least hoped to make it through the night. He went to the kitchen and made hot chocolate, just like Vickie had done for him when they were young, and he was stressed out. He needed something stronger, so while the milk was heating he went to the refrigerator and found the chocolate chip ice cream.

* * *

As Jerry Anders ate ice cream, Lee Henry sat at the desk in his study staring at the computer monitor, searching through data that he had no authority to access in order to find answers to some private questions. His years in covert actions came in very handy, both in terms of the contacts he had and what he could do with any available technology. Lee stroked his closely trimmed wraparound beard and then pushed a hand through his thick, black hair. There had to be a way in—victims and their families weren't talking about what had happened or why it happened, and they had nothing to say about conditions at Ruston. Scott Winslow thought that something critical had been hidden, and Lee was going to make or break his theory.

He moved through the property ownership records of the victims and their families. Then he searched their bank records, looking for assets, debts, and changes in financial circumstance that might tell him something. He found nothing that shed light on the reasons for their silence. They were all working people with more debt than asset. He glanced at the clock on the mantle as the clock hit 3:00 a.m. He rubbed his eyes, not yet ready to give up for the night. Could all of this be about some kind of loyalty without any payment or benefit attached? Why would they do that? Someone would need help with medical bills and discomfort. It seemed plausible that one of them would use the events that Consolidated wanted to keep quiet for leverage to get what he or she needed, but there was no trail. Lee methodically searched financial trails because following the money was what usually worked. It was almost 6:00 a.m. when, in frustration and with no answers, he decided he had to get some sleep. As he walked toward the bedroom, he told himself that there had to be something he was missing. Either that or there was no motivation for this bizarre loyalty in the extreme; maybe nobody was hiding any secrets. Was Scott Winslow wrong? Were the deficiencies at Wheeling, not Ruston, as Consolidated urged? He told himself that was his last rhetorical question that he was going to entertain. His head hurt, and he was going to bed.

Chapter 12

I can't sleep, and I am not sure why. It is one of those times when the combined weight of all the loose thoughts permit no relaxation. At 3:30 a.m., I kiss Lisa good-bye and tell her I am going to the office. She nods through a fog and then becomes conscious enough to glance at the alarm clock next to the bed.

"What?" she asks as the pieces come together. "Are you filling in for the janitorial crew as well?"

"Yeah, I know it's early, but I have a lot going on and most of it won't leave my head."

"Okay," she says, still only half-awake. "Does this change of shift mean you'll make it home for dinner?"

"Yeah, it does. I'll be home by six thirty."

She nods and then drifts off to sleep.

I sit down in the chair next to the bed and watch her sleep. She really does it beautifully. The graceful way she seems to do everything. How did I get this lucky? I stand and walk from the room with Lisa's image on my mind and a smile on my face. I kiss Katy and Joey on the way out, neither stirring.

I am at my desk at 4:45 a.m., coffee in hand, staring at my inbox. Normally it was the stack on the left corner of my desk. Over the last couple of days it has overgrown its boundaries and now threatens to consume the rest of the desk. I check my calendar. After my 9:00 a.m. Case Management Conferences on two cases in two different trial departments, I have appointments with prospective new clients at one and two thirty, which will kill at least an hour each. I shake my head. This was going to be my day to get things done in the office.

As I begin working my way through my to-do list, I am consumed by thoughts of the Walters case. At 8:00 a.m., I call Lee Henry to get an update. A groggy but familiar voice answers, "Yeah?"

"Lee, did I wake you?"

"Yeah, I pulled a late one last night. What time is it?"

"It's about eight."

There was an audible groan. "Even I can't get by on less than two hours sleep. I was working on Walters last night. I searched through all kinds of financial data for all of the victims and their families. No deposits, no loans, nothing unusual at all. I'm beginning to wonder if we're on the right track here, Scott."

I drink some coffee and consider the news. "I'm wondering, too. My gut tells me that there's something here. We just have to find the link."

"I'm working on another idea," Lee says. "After I get some sleep, I'll climb back into it. So far, though, I've got a whole lot of nothing."

"Stay with it, buddy. I'll let you know if I come up with more information or any other angles we can work."

* * *

At 9:00 a.m., Jerry awakened and stared at his clock in horror. He was to start work at eighty thirty. The damned alarm never went off. He leaped out of bed and called work.

"Home Town Printers," a male voice answered.

"Hi. This is Jerry Anders. Can I talk to Mike?"

"One minute." There is a click and a moment of quiet that Jerry uses to search for the right words.

"Mike here."

"Mike, this is Jerry Anders." There was more silence. "I'm so sorry, Mike, my alarm didn't go off. I know this is not a good first day, and it won't be my habit to be—"

"All right, it happens. Just get your ass in here. We have a big lot to run today."

"I'll be right there, and thanks for understanding," Jerry said, feeling as if he had just received the most important pardon of his life. He hurried through a quick shower and made it to work in twenty minutes, his pulse still racing.

As Jerry entered the print shop, Mike directed him to the machine he was to operate. He gestured in the direction of a young man with long black hair and tattoos on both arms. "Rocco will answer any questions you have about working the machine. You'll catch on pretty quick."

"Sure thing," Jerry said. As Mike left the shop for the office, Jerry shook hands with Rocco, who walked over to the printer with him and gave him basic operating instructions. "This is Gladys," he said. "She is a monster, but she can generate large volume in a hurry. Pretty simple to operate." He pointed to a gauge. "Here are the alignment settings and job specs. If there is a jam, the auto shutdown should stop it all so we can fix the problem and get it back on line. If for some reason the auto shutdown doesn't take, here's the emergency switch," he said, pointing to a big red lever on the side of the machine. "I'll be right over there working Dexter, if you have any questions."

"Thanks," Jerry said, "I really appreciate the help getting started."

"No worries, man," Rocco said, as he made his way back to Dexter.

After three hours of running the machine with no serious problem, Jerry stepped into the rear alley behind the building and lit up a cigarette. As he took the first drag, a voice comes from behind him. "Hey, man, I heard you were out now."

Jerry turned to see a thirty-something, muscular guy he recognized. "Hi, Bryce," he said.

"You need work?"

"No. I'm good man," Jerry said evenly.

"I have some avenues opening up you could step into. Pay you a lot more than this shit," Bryce added, gesturing toward the print shop.

"No, man. I'm out of the business. I'm not using or selling."

Bryce shrugged. "Okay, suit yourself man, but you only turn me down one time."

"Sorry," Jerry said, as Bryce walked away. Jerry drew a deep breath. All of this was a lot harder than he had hoped. He needed to stop the reminders of his old life so that he could get on with the new one. He stepped on the cigarette butt and walked back inside to Gladys.

* * *

At just after 6:00 p.m., I arrived home to hugs from Katy and Joey and a kiss from Lisa, who was making chicken burritos, a family favorite.

Lisa tugs on my tie and kisses me again, bringing groans from the kids.

"Do you have to do that right here," Joey asked.

"Yeah," Katy says. "Get a room!"

"What?" Lisa asks, astonished. "Where did you hear that?"

"I heard it on TV," she says confidently. "That's what you say when you see your parents kissing."

I couldn't hide a smirk. Lisa gives me a look, and I shrug.

"Probably better to think of something else to say, sweetheart."

"How come?" she asks.

Joey was watching, seemingly enjoying the exchange.

"A little hard to explain," Lisa says. "It's kind of a grown-up thing."

Joey chimes in with, "That's what you guys always say when you don't want to tell us something."

"Just the same," Lisa says, "that's the answer." She turns to me in hopes of changing the subject. "Can you set out drinks," she asks.

"Sure. Two milks and two glasses of our best house wine."

Joey brings condiments over to the table, and Katy places a stack of napkins beside each plate. "You think we're going to need that many napkins?" I ask.

"Yes, Daddy. You remember, this stuff is really sloppy. It falls out of the burrito jackets and all over," Katy says earnestly.

I nod. "I do remember that; you're right."

We sit down at the table and pass the condiments. Lisa asks Joey to say grace. He makes a face, and then says, "All right. Thank the Lord for the chow."

"Amen," I say. "And very concise." Joey nods, apparently satisfied with his prayer review.

"Hey, Joe," I say, "Did you ever go see that friend of yours from the baseball game? Jason, was that his name?"

"Yeah, Jason Barber. I went over there and told him I was sorry he struck out."

"That's great, buddy. I bet he appreciated that."

"He told me that I sure got dusted when that big guy hit the home run."

I flinch, reflecting on the fact that no good deed goes unpunished. "Sorry he responded that way," I offer, lamely.

"Oh, it's okay," he says. "His mother made an awesome milkshake, and we played video games for a while. It turned out pretty good."

I shake my head. Kids can be brutal to one another, but they sure heal quickly. "What's new with you, Ms. Katy?" I ask.

"Well, Mommy told me what we're getting you for your birthday. Wanna hear?"

"Sure," I say. "Let me in on it, and I won't tell anyone."

"No way, dude; it's a secret. I'll never tell."

"Okay," I say. "I can live with the secret, but I am not 'dude.'"

Joey says. "When you think about it, dude and Dad are words that are pretty close. You can be Daddy Dude."

Katy giggles, making Lisa start to laugh, and I just shake my head. "Well, this dude says that you people are out of control."

Chapter 13

There had to be something that he missed. Lee Henry spent an additional two hours scouring records of each of the victims in hopes of finding something that would explain why they might support Consolidated as it lied about the location of the most recent disaster to distance itself from county violations and the complaints of Kevin Walters. There was no inflow of cash or other assets he could find and no substantial reduction of debt for any of them. In fact, he could find nothing at all. It occurred to him that threats against victims and their families if they did not keep a secret were a possibility, but these were links that wouldn't be found on the Internet. Besides, Consolidated Energy was a Fortune 500 company, not the Gambino crime family.

Lee next focused his attention on Carl Miller, the county representative who was involved in overseeing the Ruston mine. According to Winslow's client he knew about the prior violations, and both he and the violations had suddenly disappeared. He went back to work on his computer, looking at records he was not entitled to access. He combed through county personnel records, finding that Carl Miller's paychecks were being sent to Covington, Tennessee, every two weeks. The checks were being sent payable to Carl Miller, so Miller must have established an account under his real name in order to cash or deposit them.

Lee then began looking for records of people named Carl Miller in the Covington area. His search turned up only three Carl Millers within fifty miles. The first was twenty-three and worked as a carpenter. The second Carl Miller was a forty-year-old nightclub owner. The third was eighty-four and had retired nineteen years ago after a career with the railroad. One more dead end.

Next, Lee decided to search for relatives of his target. Then he found addresses for all of those relatives and came up with an uncle, David Carter, living about thirteen miles from Covington in the city of Munford, Tennessee. Lee grinned widely. "Bingo," he said aloud. He quickly packed a bag and went back to the Internet to find a flight.

At 7:45 a.m. the following day, Lee would be on a plane to Memphis. When he arrived, he would rent a car and drive the remaining thirty-six miles to Covington. He planned to stake out the post office box and see if Miller came by to grab his check. If that failed, he would go on to Munford, Tennessee, home to about sixty-seven hundred people, one of whom was Dave Carter, the uncle of the disappeared Carl Miller. One way or another, he intended to come away with useful information.

* * *

When I return from court, I meet with Kevin Walters and Jack Bernard at 11:00 a.m. in the larger of our firm's two conference rooms. When I walk into the room, both men are absorbed in a stack of documents. Jack appears to be about forty years old and carries a good thirty pounds of excess weight. He has small, deep set eyes that absorb light and miss nothing. The documents covering the conference room table include mine specifications, notes on substructure, and drawings for Consolidated's Wheeler and Ruston mines.

I look at the stacks of data that Kevin and Bernard had been discussing for the past three hours. "Jack?" I ask, reaching a hand in his direction. "I'm Scott Winslow."

Bernard shakes my hand and smiles. "Good to meet you. Kevin says great things about you, Scott."

"Well, the feeling is mutual. Kevin's a good guy." I pause, and then ask, "You guys able to make anything useful out of this overwhelming sea of data that you can translate for a non-engineer?"

They both smile. "Maybe," Bernard says. "We have been trying to formulate a game plan for how to use some of this information. There are several possibilities to explore. Some analysis is aimed at the differing substructures of the mines and some at variances in other materials used in construction or added for reinforcement. We can also get helpful information from an analysis of the post-explosion condition of the mine."

I nod, absorbing the breadth of these courses of action. "So what do you need to conduct your examination?" I ask.

"Some of it we can get from these and other documents," Bernard says. "But we're also going to need to get into the mine and get a look. I will review the post-explosion reports to see if there is any condition or substructure inconsistent with Wheeler and consistent with Ruston, but in all likelihood the reports will have been carefully sanitized, so I will need to see conditions as they are. The sooner the better, before much more work is done in either mine."

"I am going to have to make a motion to get us into Ruston. They are resisting voluntarily giving us access."

"Really?" Bernard says. "Can they keep us out?

"Not if the judge says we're in," I say, stating the obvious. "How long will you need for the inspection?"

"Better get us four or five hours," Bernard says, "so that we have time to inspect substructures and conditions and see how they compare with the records."

"Right. So I am going to prepare a declaration for you to sign about what we need, how long it will take, why we need the access in general terms, etc. I can file your declaration with the motion so we can convince the judge to give us what we want."

"How do they oppose the motion?" Kevin asks.

"They will say it is an unnecessary waste of resources, that there is not enough evidence to suggest that there is a basis for what we are doing and that costs them in time and money."

"And you think you can overcome that argument?" Kevin asks.

"I think so, yes," I say. "I will argue that you complained about substandard conditions there, and the company was motivated to terminate you because of the safety issues you complained about and to prevent them from coming to light." If Kevin complained about unsafe and illegal conditions and was fired to keep him quiet, and we disagree as to the location the complaints pertain to, we should be able to look at both locations to see who is right." Both men nod. "We also have Judge Carswell. He is a disagreeable old curmudgeon at every turn, but he likes openness in discovery. His philosophy is too much is better than not enough, which also works to our advantage."

"Let's do it," Kevin said, and Bernard nods agreement.

"All right," I say. "I will make an ex parte application to get the motion heard on short notice so that we don't have to kill thirty days getting to court." I pause, and then say to Bernard, "You did work for Consolidated over the years, right?"

"I did. That's how I came to know Kevin."

"You know that Consolidated's door is likely to close to you permanently after you attempt to help Kevin in this case?"

He gives me a sideways smirk. "If that happens, so be it. These guys screwed Kevin big time. I think I have my priorities where I want them." He put a hand on Kevin's shoulder, and I can see that Kevin is visibly touched by his colleague's sentiment.

"Well, welcome aboard," I say, glad to have one more committed member on our team. "Give me as many facts as you can over the next couple of days about why we have to see both mines."

Kevin regards me thoughtfully and then says, "Can we use the fact that being able to view the different substructures will help us show that we made some corrections to comply with regulations in Wheeling, and that we should have done the same in Ruston?"

I nod. "That's good. I'll put that in your declaration, Kevin. Give me specifics that you reported concerning conditions at Ruston that were addressed in Wheeling. If Judge Carswell is half as confused as I think he will be, he may throw up his hands and let us in to both."

* * *

Jerry Anders completed his fourth day of work and it was payday. Everything looked good for the first time in a long time. He was learning the job and feeling comfortable with Gladys and a couple of the other machines. He had a paycheck he earned and Vickie told him that he was on the way to convincing Michael that he was going to make things right.

It was time to celebrate. He had earned a night out and decided to check out Sally's Suds, a hole-in-the-wall beer bar he passed on the way home from the print shop each night. He left the shop at 5:25 and by 5:35 he sat at the small, dark bar with a draft beer, savoring the moment. Country music played on a dinged-up jukebox in the corner. The bar was weathered oak with a burgundy edge of intermittently torn and taped vinyl over thick padding. There were two couples in the corner of the bar and two women in their thirties seated together at the other end of the bar. The music changed, and Jerry sang about having friends in low places along with Garth Brooks. One of the two women at the end of the bar looked at him and smiled. She had long brown hair and a sweet smile. She wasn't gorgeous, but she was cute in her way. He smiled back.

Half an hour later, Jerry finished his fourth beer. He felt a little buzz. He suddenly remembered that he was supposed to stay out of bars as part of the terms of his parole. He found himself looking around for his parole officer, John Linder. He didn't see Linder but figured he should make a quick exit. He left a tip on the bar and stood to find the brown-haired woman standing behind him.

"Hello," she said, smiling.

"Hi," Jerry said.

"I wondered if you would ever get around to coming by to say hello to me," she said. She saw the tip on the bar and his readiness to leave. "I guess you weren't going to," she says, as if her feelings are bruised.

"Well, I'm glad you came over here," Jerry said, "but I really have to go."

"You don't have time to buy me one little beer?"

Jerry hesitated. "Yeah, I guess I could do that."

"What's your name, cowboy?"

"Jerry."

"Hi, Jerry. My given name is Margaret, but everybody calls me Mindy." She extended a hand.

"Okay, Mindy, sit down here and tell me about you."

She sat and put her arm on his. "Well, I was raised in Chino. Came up here with my ex-husband when he found work here. Then when we split, he moved back, and I stayed. I'm really a homebody," she said thoughtfully.

"A homebody?" he questioned, looking around.

"Yes," she said defensively, "a homebody. But nobody wants to be home alone every night."

Jerry could definitely relate. "I agree with that, Mindy."

"Tell me about you, Jerry."

He selected his words carefully. "I'm kind of new in town. I got a job working for a printer, and I like it. So I'm going to be staying awhile."

At ten o'clock, they had gone through several more beers and were still talking at the bar. "You said you had to go earlier, but you don't have anyone waiting for you, do you?" Mindy asked.

"No," Jerry says, "unfortunately I don't. I'm in between ladies waiting for me to come home at the moment."

She liked his response and smiled at him. "I like you, Jerry."

"Well, good," he replied. "I like you, too, Mindy."

She touched his hand. "Want to take me home?"

He smiled widely. "Yeah, I do."

"You got a hundred dollars, darlin'?"

He was taken aback. "You mean you're a ..." his words trail off.

"No, I'm not. But I have bills to pay, Jerry," she snapped. "No need to be judgmental. My waitressing job doesn't pay all the bills, and I thought maybe you could help a little." He was quiet, digesting what felt like too much information, so she added, "Okay, I like you Jerry. How about seventy-five? I just need a little financial help. This is not money to sleep with you."

He thought about his check. She would get about a fourth of it, and he couldn't afford to spend it, but he heard himself say, "Yeah, that will be okay." He was so damned lonely. "You got a car?" he asked. "Mine's in the shop."

"Yeah, if you don't mind riding in an old pinto."

"Good. Let's go to my place," he said. Jerry put his arm around her. *What a day*, he thought to himself.

She looked up at him and saw the smile. "You really do have a great smile. Let's go, cowboy."

He kissed her on the forehead. "Great," he said. Jerry was taking good news where he found it, and there was more of it today than he had known in some time. He thought that in the new life he was building, he would like to have a girlfriend. Maybe in this new life he and Mindy could share expenses, and she could sleep with him every night. Suddenly, anything seemed possible.

Chapter 14

It was midafternoon when Lee arrived in Covington, Tennessee. He picked up a rental car and drove the short distance from the airport into town. He cruised past the town's focal point, a beautiful red brick courthouse with steep stone steps leading to huge white pillars. Beyond the courthouse and an adjacent park, he turned left and moved through the downtown area toward the post office. He stopped in one of four parking spaces outside, three of which were unoccupied. He went inside, where he found one service window, unmanned, and two adjoining alcoves, each with mailboxes on three walls.

Lee hunted until he located box 1731, the address designated for delivery of Carl Miller's retirement checks. The box is about knee high and located at the back of one of the alcoves. He looked around, processing surroundings and identifying locations from which to observe anyone accessing the box. Satisfied, he made his way back to the customer window. An elderly man with a gaunt face and a contrasting paunch is now at the window, wearing a nametag saying "Barney."

"Good afternoon," Lee said, warmly.

Barney gave him a nod, and then said, "What can I do for ya?"

"Well, I was just wondering what it costs to rent a small box."

"Seventeen dollars a month," the man said, and then added, "Movin' to town, are ya?"

"Thinking about it," Lee said. "Oh, one more thing. What time is the mail put in the boxes each day?"

"Usually gets in around ten thirty," Barney said.

"Okay, thanks," Lee said, walking from the window. Satisfied, he checked his watch. It was four thirty, and he hadn't eaten all day. He made his way to a diner down the block and sat in the window with coffee and a sandwich, watching some of the town's nine thousand inhabitants beginning to close and lock stores and leave offices to make their way back to their homes.

Some people don't like unfamiliar places and the feeling of being an outsider looking in. Lee relished being a fly on the wall and watching others' lives unfold. His business was all about obtaining information critical to a client. Watching and listening was how he did that. Lee had developed being inconspicuous into an art form, and he had the ability to hide in plain sight. He could talk to people casually without being remembered. He garnered information from strangers in a subtle way that left them unaware that that they had provided information, or even been asked for anything.

After finishing his sandwich and watching the post office close for the day, Lee decided to find a hotel and settle in for the night. In the morning he'd find Miller picking up his paycheck, and they would have an interesting talk. Unless Carl Miller didn't pick up the check personally. With that thought, he punched a number into his cell phone and waited.

"Again?" a male voice offers.

"What kind of a greeting is that for someone you consider among your very best clients and who provides you with challenges to keep your job interesting?"

"Oh, oh, here it comes. What do you want?"

"Funny you should ask," Lee said. "There is one little favor you can do for me. I need info on vehicles registered to a David G. Carter, resident of Munford, Tennessee."

"One little favor, my ass. I suppose this is a rush job, too?"

Lee smiles. "Not a real rush. I need it in about twenty minutes."

"You are a funny guy. Give me an hour."

"You're the greatest."

"I'll call you as soon as I have it."

"Perfect."

At 7:00 p.m., Lee's phone rang. "Yeah," he said.

"Yeah? What kind of a way is that to answer your phone?"

"It's how you know that I'm really me."

"Good point. At least you are aware that your social skills are lacking."

"Right," Lee said, "but fortunately, I have you making great strides toward my personal betterment." He paused and then said, "Did you get it?"

"I did."

"And?"

"So impatient. One vehicle. A 2001 Silverado, white in color." The caller then recited a license number.

"Terrific," Lee said. "Great work as always."

"Not that easy. Don't forget who you owe."

"Never," Lee said. "I'll even make sure I pay your bill."

* * *

At 10:00 a.m., Mindy climbed out of bed and began to put her clothes back on. Jerry glimpsed at her through half-closed eyes and a throbbing headache, noting that she had a great ass even in daylight—it wasn't just a 2:00 a.m., six beer ass. He drifted off again, and next time he awoke she was fully dressed and smoothing her skirt as she looked in the mirror on the dresser.

"Come back to bed," he said. "I need more of you." He had a vague recollection of being inside her briefly before passing out, but he had been too drunk to retain the details he now wanted to savor.

"Sorry, lover boy," she said, pushing a comb through her hair. "I have to go to work now."

"Can I see you again?" he asked.

She looks over at him and reflects momentarily. "I think so," she said. "I think I might really like you if you were sober."

"Maybe tonight ... " he said, letting the words go as he became more conscious. "What time is it?" he asked.

"A little after ten."

"Oh shit, oh shit," he said. "I'm late for work." He looked around and focused on the alarm clock, as if some explanation might be found on the digital readout. "Did you turn the alarm off?"

"Yeah," she said. "After you had me hit the snooze button about three times."

"What the fuck are you trying to do to me?" he screamed. "You're going to get me fired."

"Hold on," she replied. "I tried to wake you up three or four times, and you just shook me off." She paused, now angry. "You can't blame me because you didn't get up." She grabbed her purse and walked for the door, where she stopped and turned back to look at him sitting up in bed. "And I've changed my mind about wanting to see you anymore. Fuck off." She slammed the door behind her as Jerry climbed from bed in a panic. He would have to hurry to finish the big order that needed to be finished by noon today. "Shit, shit, shit," he said to the empty room as he threw on his jeans, shirt, and shoes and ran for the door, the familiar feeling of his heart racing as it did whenever he had screwed up.

* * *

At 9:00 a.m., Lee sat outside the post office in one of the locations that allowed a clear view of the mail alcove containing box 1731. He moved between two locations that allowed visibility from outside the post office, in an attempt to minimize attention he might draw by lingering too long in any one location. He wore magnifiers when any nearby box was approached to assure that he could distinguish access to the subject box from access to the surrounding boxes. At 11:45 a.m. he was still waiting, and no one had accessed the box. He found a bench that allowed him a view of the alcove, although he had to walk to find a better angle whenever someone approached the area of the box.

At 2:30 p.m., Lee watched a white, 2001 Silverado pull into the parking lot. He checked the Tennessee license plate against the one he had been given earlier in the day and saw that he had a match. He slipped a GPS inside the wheel well of the Silverado, then watched as a white-haired man of about seventy got out of the pickup and went directly to box 1731 and opened it up. Lee got into his car and pulled up to the curb. He watched as Miller's uncle, David Carter, returned with the mail and climbed into the Silverado. He stayed a comfortable distance behind the pickup and followed as Carter began the thirteen-mile trip back to Munford, Tennessee.

Lee considered his options. His illicit research through county records told him that the check should have been delivered to the box yesterday or the day before, so Carter should have it now. Would Carter now lead him to Miller? If not, things might begin to move too slowly. He needed to know where Miller was, his research showing no trace of him in either Covington or Munford. There were two things he felt confident about. The first was that Carter knew where Miller was, and the second was that, through one means or another, Carter would get that check to Miller. He had to follow that delivery. He had one more idea. Lee decided to beat Carter back to Munford and bug Carter's phone before Carter arrived. All he needed was ten minutes, so he hit the gas pedal hard and flew past the 2001 Silverado.

Chapter 15

Lee found the house without difficulty. It was a small, one-story structure, with white trim and blue shutters that were probably very attractive twenty-five or thirty years ago, but had long since fallen into a state of disrepair. Every part of the property appeared to be the subject of a little too much deferred maintenance. The exterior paint was faded and chipped. The underlying wood was splintering as it began to rot. The lot was entirely unfenced, and there were no lawns, just patches of dirt punctuated by weeds and wild growth; a patchwork that was left to its own determination without assistance from the resident. The good news was that the nearest neighbor was about a quarter mile away, and the house was shielded from view by trees and brush.

No cars were in the driveway, and the carport was empty. Lee walked the perimeter of the house, glancing through windows as he moved. The first window yielded a view of a small kitchen with a dropped ceiling and tiled countertops. In the second window, on the side toward the rear of the house, Lee saw through a bathroom and into a hallway. Seeing no sign of movement and hearing nothing inside, Lee walked to the back of the house, where he found a cement porch raised from the surrounding dirt by two weathered cement steps. He walked up the steps and then paused to look around. No one was watching. He turned the door handle and gave a slight push. The door creaked open, revealing a short, narrow hall that he followed to a small kitchen.

Before attending to his intended task of planting a bug in the phone, Lee searched for anything that might show Carl Miller's presence as an occupant or a frequent visitor. There were no decorative picture frames, and for that matter, no pictures at all. There were no flowers or plants. Lee opened the refrigerator and found no Tupperware and few groceries. The freezer was stocked with microwaveable meals. There were few furnishings, which included one recliner and a television with a fifty-inch screen. He walked down the hall to the only bedroom and directly to the closet. It contained only men's clothing, mostly jeans, overalls, and pullover shirts.

Lee looked briefly for documents that might be of assistance, but finding none, returned to his primary task. Where was the phone? He walked room to room and found that there was no land line. If Carter was going to call Miller to tell him the check had arrived, it was going to be on a cell phone, and he may already have done so. On the other hand, this check came every two weeks, so maybe there was a regular delivery or pickup routine and no call was needed.

He checked his watch and decided he was cutting it too close and needed to get out. He walked to the rear door and reached for the door handle in time to see the Silverado stop at the base of the steps. He turned and walked to the front of the house. As he quietly pulled the front door closed behind him, he could hear Carter coming in the back way.

Lee walked the two hundred yards to his car at a brisk pace. With about a hundred yards to go, two eight or nine yearold boys dressed in shorts walked toward him. As they approach, the bigger of the boys, who had uncombed black hair and an inquisitive expression, spoke to him. "Hey, mister, who are you?"

He thought about ignoring the boys, but that was not consistent with his desire to be as inconspicuous as possible. "Just a visitor," Lee said, matter-of-factly.

The inquiring boy folded his arms across his chest to make it known that there were answers needed. He would be a lawyer or a detective one day, Lee thought to himself. Right now, he was just an annoying kid.

"You know Mr. Carter?" the kid demanded.

Lee thought for a moment about how to handle this underage neighborhood watch program, and then said, "No, not well. How about you?"

"Yeah, he's our neighbor," the kid replied.

Lee nods. "You like him?"

The kid was taken aback for a moment, and then, being a kid, his compulsion to honesty outweighed any toward discretion, and he said, "Well, sorta, but he's kind of cranky."

Lee acknowledged with a thoughtful nod. "Well, you know, if you kids are a little nicer to him, you'll probably find he's not so cranky." While the kid thought this over, Lee walked on. He glanced over his shoulder to see Carter step onto the front porch and look his way. Lee picked up the pace and disappeared into the trees. Now he would have to watch and wait. He scanned the area for a few places he could park and watch the house without being observed. With no other way to locate Miller, it was going to be a long day.

* * *

I look up from the e-mail I am writing at 6:30 p.m. to see Lisa standing in the doorway. She wears a black evening dress, a string of pearls, and a warm smile. "Hi, sweetheart," she says.

"Wow. You look gorgeous. Please come into my office and take your clothes off; er, I mean, have a seat."

She laughs, and then looking around adds, "Wouldn't be the first time we got naked in your office. Although your conference room table isn't exactly the most comfortable surface to ..." She stops and smiles.

"You're getting me aroused. You do realize that, don't you?"

"I hope so; it takes me a while to get this dressed up. Besides, the kids are staying at my mom's tonight, so I intend to keep you hard all night. May as well start now."

"Don't forget, we have to make it through dinner first."

She grins widely. "We do unless you're real creative. And not the emergency button in the elevator. I don't want to feel rushed."

"Let me grab my briefcase, and we are out of here," I say.

"I saw that you let Donna out of here at a decent hour tonight."

"I had to. It's her anniversary, and she had plans to celebrate." I consider for a moment. "Could be that she and Jim are already naked on some table."

"You'll know for sure tomorrow if she's complaining of a backache."

* * *

The restaurant ambience is perfect. Soft lighting, tables placed in private inlets and servers who stayed only as long as necessary to bring the food.

"I've missed you, lately," I say to Lisa when we are alone awaiting drinks. "We've both been so busy lately, and I know I've been getting home late."

"I've missed you, too," she says softly, taking my hand. "I know you are doing what you can to spend less time at the office, and I get that you're doing what you have to do. Don't worry, the kids and I are okay."

The waiter puts our drinks on the table, takes our order, and moves away.

I lift my glass and she does the same. "To you," I say. "You are truly amazing, you know that?"

"I do, but don't hesitate to remind me whenever it occurs to you.How about to us," she says, and we drink again.

I look into her eyes. "You are also beautiful," I say. "Have I told you that lately?" Lisa gives me her, *You're laying it on a little thick—you already had me at let's get naked* look.

"No, really," I say. "You are gorgeous."

"Thank you," she says, smiling the smile that has turned my heart upside down since the first day I met her. There truly are things in this world that never get old.

I take both of her hands and momentarily get lost in her eyes, something that has happened to me for as long as I can remember.

"What?" she asks, studying my apparently idiotic expression.

"I'm thinking that I am a lot more lucky than deserving."

She smiles widely. "You are certainly in a romantic mood this evening."

"Yeah, I guess so. You do that to me, you know."

"You still trying to get laid?" she whispers.

"Does it show? And I thought I was pretty smooth."

"You are. That's how you got me in the sack the first five thousand times."

"You keeping count?" I ask.

"Not any more. Once I found out I couldn't bill for it, and it wasn't deductible, there seemed to be no point." There were a few moments of silence, and her expression became more somber. "I got a call from Joey's teacher today," she says.

"Is everything okay?" I ask.

"She wants to make sure we were aware of teacher-parent conferences next Tuesday. I was a little concerned about the fact that she was calling to make sure we were coming—sounded like there might be some problem she needed to talk about, so I asked. Apparently not. It seems that our Joey is regarded as pretty sharp. Responds in class, does his work, and participates in class."

"Wow," I say. "What's the bad news?"

"I pushed for more information, and she found a delicate way of saying that he can be pretty direct with other students and teachers. Something like, he knows his mind and can be assertive."

"You mean he's rude or something?"

"No, she said he wasn't rude or out of line. Just that he says what's on his mind."

"I thought all kids did that," I respond.

"Apparently, your son does so more than the average bear."

"He's my son when it comes to this particular attribute?" I ask, feigning indignation.

"Absolutely. All the other good characteristics I mentioned come from my side of the family."

I grin. "Well if she thinks Joey speaks his mind, wait until she spends a semester with Katy."

We laugh at the prospect. "I bet we get more than one phone call once Katy puts her hand on her hip and sets their world straight," I say, and we both visualize.

The waiter drops off chicken curry for her and shrimp scampi for me, and we begin to eat. We are quiet and thoughtful for a while, and then I ask what I've been wondering. "Do you wish we had decided to have more kids?"

She looks at me with wide eyes. "What brings that on?"

"I don't know," I say, "just wanted to see how you felt about it."

She looks like she's not entirely buying my motivation. She reflects a moment and then says, "I did for a while, but now I think our family is just perfect. I wouldn't change anything." I nod. She studies me, waiting, and then asks, "And you?"

"I think our family is just as was meant to be," I respond.

She gives me a flirtatious grin. "We should continue to practice, though, in case we change our minds."

"Definitely," I say, and then ask, "Do we have to wait an hour after we eat or can we get right to it?"

"Wait an hour?" she asks, furrowing her brow. "Only if we're going to do it while swimming laps. Otherwise, I think we're good to go."

"What time do we pick up the kids?" I ask.

"I told mom we had to pick them up by 8:00 a.m. for school, although she looked disappointed."

"Well let's hurry up and finish dinner. We've only got eleven hours, and I want to allow at least an hour for sleep."

"You're feeling pretty ambitious there, sailor."

"Damn straight."

Lisa's expression turns more serious. "Thanks for taking some time tomorrow morning to come speak to Katy's class."

"Yeah, sure," I say, fighting back sensations of guilt about all of the events that I seem to have missed lately. "It should be a gas. Although, they may be a little young to decide their career direction this semester. College and postgrad work are a little ways off yet, so maybe they can think about it until they graduate elementary school."

She grins. "You may be surprised. From what Katy tells me, you've got your work cut out for you if you're going to sway the career direction of her class."

"Yeah?"

She nods. "Let's see, one guy wants to be a painter, although not in the conventional sense. He doesn't want to paint portraits or houses. He wants to paint billboards and T-shirts. One of the girls wants to sell makeup, another wants to be a telephone operator, and a third an Olympic gymnast. One guy wants to be a veteran so he can help animals, and one guy wants to drive a cab in Minneapolis."

I furrow a brow. "Why Minneapolis?"

"No clue. Katy thinks maybe he likes snowball fights."

A busboy who looks fifteen stops by and collects plates. On his heels is the waiter, who asks if we need anything else and prepares to leave the bill. I hand him a credit card, and he quickly disappears from view.

I regard Lisa a moment and then ask, "Have you considered what you're going to tell Joey's class about a career in real estate when it's your turn?"

"Still working out the fine points," she replies, "although Joey has given me a few instructions." I make a *this oughta be good* face, and she continues. "I should avoid too much detail about the paperwork cuz no one likes that stuff. I should tell them they can make lots of money if they sell a bunch of houses and, there was one more thing." She reflects and then adds, "Oh yeah, this is a good one—Don't say anything embarrassing."

We both laugh, and then she says, "You mean you didn't get any instructions from Katy?"

"Just one," I say, considering the words. "She said I should talk more like regular people."

With this, Lisa begins to laugh hysterically and then to nod.

"You think that's pretty good, do you?"

When she can get control of herself enough to speak, which takes some time, she says, "She's got you pegged."

"Come on, now," I say, a little defensively. "I talk like everyone else."

She shakes her head. "Other lawyers maybe, but not regular people." She looks at me and then adds. "I'm used to your style, sweetheart, because we've been together a long while, but you could be a little more ... " She searches for the right word, although I'm not sure whether she wants to be diplomatic or just accurate. Then she adds, "folksy," apparently satisfied with her word selection. "Don't worry," she says, "I find it endearing in a crazy way. It's only your children who need an interpreter."

"Ouch," I say, but looking into her face I see no judgment; she is simply delivering a message. "I'll try to keep it in tune with my audience."

"Good. Now, let's go home and share some intimate sensations," she says taking my hand and standing to leave.

"You know, you've got a pretty interesting way with words."

"That's just the beginning, big boy."

Enough said, I see my credit card has returned, grab it, and we are on to better things.

Chapter 16

May 12, 2016

At 8:45 a.m., I greet Ms. Parsons at the door to Katy's classroom. Ms. Parsons, who Katy regards as old and wise, had to be about twenty-five years old, with short blonde hair and eyes that danced around a small nose and dimples. She is one of those teachers who oozed excitement about the children she taught and spoke of as her own.

"Hi, Ms. Parsons," I say, extending a hand.

"Hello, Mr. Winslow. So glad you could make it."

"Please, call me Scott," I say.

She regards me as if assessing whether this is appropriate, and then says, "Okay, and you can call me Betsy."

I nod, reflecting on the fact that Betsy Parsons seems an older name than the face that presents.

"I was named after my grandmother," she adds, as if having read my mind. Then she says, "I know the kids will enjoy hearing from you. I also know you're busy, so we won't keep you too long. As soon as we go inside, I'll have Katy introduce you."

"Katy will introduce me?" I ask.

"Yes," she says, regarding me carefully. "Unless you would prefer not."

"No, no, that's great," I say.

Ms. Parsons and I walk into the rear door of the classroom, where she gestures to a seat at the back of the room. I regard the desk chair combination a moment, and then squeeze my six-foot, two-inch frame into it, wondering if I will ever be able to extricate myself. The students are all looking at me and probably wondering the same thing. A couple of them appear to be suppressing laughter.

Ms. Parsons takes her place at the front of the room. "Class," she says calling the group to attention with raised arms. When they look at her she announces, "We have the pleasure of having Katy Winslow's dad here to speak about his career today. Katy," she adds, looking down toward Katy's seat in the second row, "would you like to introduce your dad?"

From where I sit, I have a profile view of Katy, who momentarily looks as if she is considering the question but is undecided. She then stands and moves to the front of the room. She looks at me without expression and then at her classmates. "Boys and girls," she announces, "my dad is here to talk to you about being a liar."

"A liar?" one of the kids says. There is some scattered laughter, and she looks both concerned and indignant. "You know," she adds to clarify, "A tourney. He goes to court and gets judges to listen to him."

Ms. Parsons stands up and says, "That's right, Mr. Winslow is here to talk to you about being a lawyer. Thank you, Katy."

Katy nods, seemingly satisfied that all has been clarified, though probably not sure why there should have been any confusion in the first place.

I squeeze from my containment and make my way to the front of the room. "Hi, boys and girls. I'm Scott Winslow. Being Katy's dad is the job I like best, but I am an attorney for a living. Let me tell you a little about what I do." As I begin to speak, I see Ms. Parsons easily sit down in one of the minidesks from which I could barely escape.

"I am an employment lawyer, so I represent people who are fired for unlawful reasons or are treated unfairly in connection with their jobs. Like people who were discriminated against because they have a disability, or because of race or age, and people who aren't paid what they are owed. I prepare the cases for trial, and then I go to court and argue the cases to judges and juries, so that they can reach a verdict." I let that settle in and then add, "It's a pretty interesting business because you learn a lot about all kinds of other jobs and businesses. I guess I think it's most fulfilling ..." I briefly consider my word choice, "most rewarding and fun, when I get to help someone who really needs help and who hasn't been treated fairly."

I look around the classroom and see that all the eyes are fixed on me. "Anyone have questions?"

There's a moment of quiet, and then a couple of hands go up. I point to a young man in the middle of the room with short dark hair and a worried expression. "You are s'posed to argue in your job?" he asks with great concern. "Cuz my mom always tells me not to argue."

I see Ms. Parsons grinning, but as I look around, I quickly see that all others regard the question seriously. "That's a good point," I say, "but it's really a different kind of arguing. It means explaining the facts of your case rather than being rude." I make a mental note to tell this to Bob Harris, who seems to have missed this distinction.

Three more hands go up, and I select a girl near the front. She stands to speak, locks her hands in front of her, and then asks, "My daddy is a sturgeon, and he says they get sued all the time and don't want to. Do you sue my daddy?"

I want to smile at this because, if I have to be a "liar," I'm glad that her dad will be introduced as a "sturgeon" when he comes to speak. "No I don't. I don't work on medical malpractice cases." I look at Katy, who is scrutinizing me carefully. "Malpractice cases happen when someone believes a doctor made a mistake and hurt someone, but those aren't the kind of cases I do."

The girls sits, seemingly satisfied that I am not suing her father. I call on a young man at the back of the room. "How much money do you get?" he asks.

Ms. Parsons stands up and says, "Blake, and all of you, that is a privacy question like we talked about. You can ask about the job but not how much money someone makes."

Blake looks concerned. "I want to make a lot of money," he says. "How do I know if I want this job if we can't know how much he gets?"

Ms. Parsons looks at me, and I give her a nod. "Great question," I say, already convinced that Blake probably will make a lot of money. "You can make a good income as an attorney. The most important thing to remember when you choose your career is to do what you really like. A career lasts thirty or forty years, so you want to be doing something you care about."

Blake is still considering, and then says, "I like to play video games and ride my skateboard. Are those jobs?"

"Maybe. I know that there are people who make a living creating new video games or improving old ones. I'm not sure about professional skateboarding."

Another hand goes up, this time attached to a young lady who has dainty features and a ponytail. When I call on her and she stands, she is shorter than most of her classmates.

"What's your name," I ask.

"Emily."

"Okay, Emily. What is your question?"

"What do the people get if they win the court case?"

"Another good question," I say. "Ms. Parsons you have a very smart class." I glance at Katy, and she actually rolls her eyes at this comment. "As part of our case we have to prove the amount of damages suffered because of what happened. Like lost wages or benefits of employment and sometimes emotional distress." I look around the class and see questioning and confused expressions. "Money. We get an award of money to pay back the losses the judge or jury thinks we suffered after they consider all of the facts." This seems to settle a little better on the crowd.

Ms. Parsons stands. "All right, class, one more question, and then we need to let Mr. Winslow get back to work."

There are four more hands, so I select one I recognize as having been up for a little while. It belongs to a young man with ears that are too large for the remainder of his head, red hair, and a large number of freckles.

"Your name, young man?" I ask.

"Justin Franklin Mason," he says.

"Okay, Justin, go ahead."

"What happens when you lose your case?" he asks.

"Well, then my client doesn't get any money, and he or she has to pay for court costs of the other side."

"Do you get money if your client loses?" he asks, as if worried about my welfare.

"Usually not," I say, "because I often make a deal where I get a part of what they receive."

"That's not good," he says earnestly. "Why do you do that?"

Ms. Parsons moves as if to jump in, but I give her a smile and address Justin's question. "The reason I do it is because many people can't afford to hire an attorney any other way. So it is how I am able to help them with their case.

"I have an uncle who only gets paid if he sells stuff," Justin adds. "Sounds like that."

"I guess it is like that. If what we do doesn't work, your uncle and I don't get paid."

"I think I want a job that pays all the time," he says. "Maybe a paperboy."

I smile, and Ms. Parson jumps up. "Okay, class, let's thank Mr. Winslow for being with us to tell us about his career and answer our questions today."

There is applause around the room, but the kids look worried. I don't think I made any converts to the legal profession. They seem too worried about contingency arrangements and not getting paid. "Thank you, girls and boys, and it was good to meet you all. Bye," I say as I and Ms. Parsons walk toward the door.

"Lips sealed," she says to them as she approaches the door, and the murmur around the room goes quiet.

We step into the hallway and she says, "Thanks so much for coming in to talk to the kids, Mr. Winslow. I know they will reflect on what you told them."

"My pleasure," I say. "It's fascinating how they call it as they see it."

"It is that," she says, grinning. "Good to meet you" she says, and we shake hands. "Katy is an amazing child."

"She's doing well?" I ask.

"She is doing very well. Works hard and cares a lot about what she does."

"That's great to hear," I say lamely, but feeling good.

"And say hello to Lisa for me, will you? She is really wonderful."

"Yes, she is. I will tell her." I turn to go, finding myself smiling as I reflect on the kids and their direct questions. I'm not at all sure it's always such a good thing that our directness and honesty gives way to subtlety and discretion as we get older. You know just where you stand when talking to one of these kids—no hidden agendas. As I race toward the office and appointments that are scheduled, I wonder how Lisa will do explaining the real estate brokerage business to Joey's class.

* * *

It's a cool day, but Jerry Anders was sweating as he walked into the print shop after running all the way. He walked over to the time clock, where he could see that his machine was idle across the large room. He quickly punched his card and raced over to start up Gladys. He has some work to do to make up for lost time if he is going to get this job out on time. He looked over at Rocco, who was working his machine and didn't look up at him.

Jerry fired up Gladys and began to stack the first cycle for printing. He set the ink tray, started the feeder, and checked the quality of the job as Gladys spit out the finished product. He gave a nod of approval and told himself that he would catch up and get the job done pretty near schedule if he punched it and passed on breaks. His thoughts turned to Maggie, and more specifically, how he had shifted the blame to her for his failure to get up for work on time. He reminded himself that he could be such an asshole sometimes. He liked her and wanted to call her and make it up to her. Tonight, right after work, that's just what he would do. He would make everything right.

At one o'clock, Rocco disappeared for lunch and left Jerry working. Jerry checked his count and found that he was not making up much time. He was still about three hours behind on the job. He could work through lunch to get one of those hours back, and maybe stay a little later tonight after clocking out. With any luck, he told himself, he would be within an hour of schedule by tomorrow at the same time and have the job completed on Wednesday, pretty close to schedule.

Jerry worked through lunch and was able to make up some ground. At three o'clock, he felt like he was well on his way back. He did a spot check on the quality and, to his horror, found that there was a faded section in the middle of each page that Gladys was producing. Oh, my God, he thought to himself, there is an inking problem of some kind. He checked the finished product to find that the problem existed on all of the documents produced in the past twenty minutes. All that time would now have to be made up. There was no way. As he stared at the deficiencies in the finished product, Mike walked over to him.

"Problem?" he asked.

Jerry could only nod. He showed Mike what Gladys was most recently turning out.

Mike studied it for a few minutes. "We need to rework the ink tray," he said calmly. "How many units look like this?"

Jerry felt himself shaking as he spoke. "About twelve hundred," he said, feeling ashamed.

Mike waited until Jerry looked at him, and then said. "When you don't get in until almost eleven o'clock, you're already two hours behind. That doesn't leave much room for contingencies like machine breakdowns, you agree?"

Jerry was suddenly short of oxygen. He took a moment to find words, but was finally able to say, "Yes, Mike. I agree. It is my fault, and I made a mistake. I can ..."

Mike interrupted him, making a halting gesture with his hand. "Jerry, I really want to help you, but I have a business to run. If you don't show up we're both fucked, you understand that."

"I'm so sorry, Mike. I really am ..."

"Jerry, you're not hearing me. I don't need apologies, I need reliability. If you don't show up on time, we are screwed. No amount of apologizing will fix the problem when we can't deliver to the customer on time. We on the same page here?"

"Yes," Jerry said, "we're definitely on the same page."

"Okay, well let's get it fixed up. I'll help you get restarted and we'll get it moving."

"Am I okay, Mike?" Jerry asked. He could feel his heart pounding so hard he thought Mike might hear it.

"I'm not sure," Mike said. "You know I have to give status reports to Mr. Reynolds each night and the final call will be his. Let's do what we can to get back on track."

"Okay," Jerry said, nervously. "I can work through lunch to make up time."

"I can't let you do that, Jerry. Mr. Reynolds doesn't want any Labor Board issues, so he says everybody takes lunches and breaks. Go take your lunch now, and I'll get Gladys right while you're gone."

"But Mike, if I just work through ..."

"We can't do it. You have to hear me when I tell you something, Jerry. No schemes that will get both of us into some shit. Now, go take your lunch," Mike said, raising his voice for the first time.

Jerry turned and walked out of the building. He walked down the street without direction, his whole body shaking and not able to get enough air. He sat down on a three-foot-wall surrounding an auto repair place, reliving the conversation again and again. Each time it seemed worse. He went from scared to terrified, and then found himself becoming more and more angry. Mike didn't have to treat him like that. He made a mistake, that's all. And he was willing to pay for it—working through lunch or staying late, but Mike wasn't going to let him do it. Did he want to cause Jerry to fail? He had thought Mike wanted to help him, but now he harbored grave doubts. Mike was undermining his ability to fix the problem.

When Jerry stood and continued walking, he was not sure how long he had been sitting there, but he was angry with Mike, who had the power to make this all okay and was going to use his power to make Jerry look bad to Mr. Reynolds instead.

Jerry walked on, no longer recognizing his surroundings. He turned left at a busy corner, figuring he would make his way back to work. His stomach in turmoil, there was no way he could eat anything. He walked for about five blocks and then made another left. He passed a massive metal warehouse that appeared to be a block long and entirely abandoned. There were padlocks on the front door of this lonely monstrosity. He continued walking until he saw a flashing neon sign that said, "Sally's Suds." He had no idea how he found his way to Sally's, but it was familiar and looked like a friend where none could be found. He needed just one beer, and then he could return to work with renewed strength and get caught up on the job. He and Mike would get back on the right track and everything would be okay.

He walked into Sally's to find it empty, with the exception of a guy with a beard behind the bar. "What'll it be, buddy?" the man said.

"I'll have whatever you got on tap," Jerry said, selecting a seat at the bar.

"Coming up," the bartender said. He topped off the beer and placed it on the bar in front of Jerry. The chilled glass of beer had a head on it that wanted to run down the side of the glass and it looked wonderful. "Want me to run a tab?"

"No, no." Jerry said, "I'm only having one beer."

"Okay, buddy, whatever you say."

"What do you mean by that?" Jerry asked, upset by the suggestion that he wasn't going to have just one beer.

"Nothing personal," the bartender offered. "You get to decide that."

Jerry nursed the beer for a time, and then took a strong pull. It was perfect. The cool sensation of the beer going down immediately relaxed him, and he felt stronger. He took another big gulp, and his fears began to fade. Everything would be okay. He kept the beer in the glass as long as he could, avoiding confrontation with the issue presented by an empty glass. By the time the glass was empty, Jerry felt good. He was relaxed and feeling just the slightest buzz. He was no longer stressed out, shaking, angry, or out of control.

"Want another?" the bartender asked.

"Maybe just one more," Jerry said, feeling good and forgetting about his anger. The second beer was better than the first. It was cold, quenching, and in some undefined way, reassuring. He felt a little stronger with each swallow of the beer. When it was gone, he stared at the empty glass. He decided that just one more beer would be perfect. Then he would go back to work, and the rest of the afternoon would be a breeze.

When the final beer was gone, he put a ten dollar bill on the counter and stood up. He walked out into the sunlight, squinting as he emerged from the dark, windowless bar. He started walking past the massive warehouse next door and suddenly remembered that Sally's was a good distance from the print shop. It would take him another fifteen minutes to make his way back. Checking his watch, he wondered how long he had been gone. It couldn't be. He shook his wrist, as if it may somehow unwind the time. "Oh, shit," he said aloud, stopping in his tracks. He was instantly back from his euphoric escape when he realized he had been gone for an hour and a half, and he was going to return with beer on his breath.

"How fucking stupid are you?" His anger at himself gave way to a sudden feeling of panic. He couldn't afford to lose this job. This was his only chance to make good.

Jerry found it hard to breathe and he sat down on the curb. If he went back late and reeking of beer, he was done. He told himself to relax, and to take a deep breath. As he did, his panic suggested the answer.

He was having some kind of attack. He would call in sick and describe his symptoms and then go to a doctor so he could produce a note.

Jerry ran back into Sally's. "Hey, buddy, can I use your phone for a local call?"

The bartender considered this and furrowed his brow. "Please," Jerry said, "it's just a local call, and it's really important."

The man shrugged. "Okay, Mack, no skin off my nose so long as it's local." He passed the phone across the bar to Jerry.

Jerry dialed the phone and then spoke nervously. "Mike, I am not feeling well. I am going to go sleep, but I will be there early in the morning."

Chapter 17

May 6, 2016

Lee began his day at 5:00 a.m., with coffee at the almost empty diner. After finishing his second cup at a small, wobbly table near the rear of the restaurant, he took a third cup and a jelly donut for the road and drove in the direction of David Carter's place to wait for something to happen. The morning was damp and chilly. He wore a faded gray sweatshirt without markings, black pants, and black slip-ons, the art of blending in and remaining unnoticed never far from his thoughts. He was all about blending into crowds and being entirely unmemorable. He was confident from years of practice that 95 percent of the people who saw him would have no recollection that he was ever there, and the remaining 5 percent would be unable to provide any meaningful description.

Lee dictated an update into a handheld recorder and then called and left early-morning voice mail updates for a couple of clients, including Scott Winslow. When he arrived at Carter's, he parked the car in one of the previously selected spots, allowing him a clear view of the residence from about fifty feet to its left side. He quickly noted that the Silverado was the only vehicle present outside the residence. The lights in the house were already on, so he concluded that Carter was up and moving around.

Lee dialed a number and waited while it rang several times.

"Yes," was the cryptic response.

"I need another favor."

"Of course you do. I've noted that there is no end to the favors you need."

"True, but no need to get testy. Those monthly checks do keep coming, right?"

"What do you want?"

"Cell phone calls for a David Carter, incoming and outgoing, between noon yesterday and noon today." He recited Carter's address.

"Not a problem."

"When can I have them?"

"I'll call you back around noon."

"Perfect, thanks."

"Now you know why we're worth the money."

"I never doubted it," Lee said.

Lee surveyed the residence. The bedroom and kitchen lights were on, but he saw no movement. He settled in with his now cold coffee and jelly donut. He decided that if nothing happened by midafternoon, he would have to make something happen. He would confront Carter, and they would discuss the whereabouts of Mr. Miller. This was not his preferred course, because he had no real leverage to make Carter talk. It would also sound alarms and give Miller the opportunity to go further under cover, if, as all indications showed, he didn't care to be found.

* * *

Jerry arrived at 7:35 a.m. feeling that he had dodged a bullet yesterday and wanting to make up for his shortfall. He planned to start early and work hard to get the job out quickly. He would make himself an asset to Mike and Mr. Reynolds.

As Jerry walked across the shop to where Gladys awaited, he saw Mike's office door open. Mike stepped out with a somber, almost sad expression.

"Jerry, I need to see you in the office, please."

Jerry felt his chest grow tight. He followed silently, feeling himself sweat as he walked through the door. Mr. Reynolds and a woman in her mid-thirties were already seated in the office.

Mike looked at Jerry and said, "This is Mr. Reynolds, our owner, and this is Allie Morgan from personnel."

Jerry could not find words but extended a hand that each shook briefly. Mike gestured to the only remaining chair in the office, and then perched on the edge of his desk, folding his arms.

"Jerry, this is a hard conversation to have. I want you to know I really like you." Mike stopped and took a breath, as Jerry sensed what was coming and felt panic rising within him. "I think you will find a niche; I just don't think it is here with us." Mike was quiet for another moment, and then softly added, "We are going to have to let you go, Jerry." He wore a pained expression.

Jerry wanted to yell, 'No, you can't do this. This can't happen.' He was shaking and could almost hear his heart beat as he groped for words.

"Oh no, Mike. I want to work for you. I'll work really hard. I'm getting to know Gladys now, and I think we can really get the orders out at top speed. It just takes a little time—"

Mike shook his head. "It's not your work, Jerry. We know it takes time to learn. We just have to be able to trust each other."

Jerry was lost. "What? Is it about me being out yesterday? I couldn't help it; I got sick, Mike. I called in, remember?"

There was a heavy silence in the air and a knowing look was exchanged among the others in the room. Jerry felt like an outsider; the only one in the room who didn't know an important secret.

Mike wore a sad expression as he spoke his final words of the meeting. "Jerry, your call came from a bar." The statement fell across the room like an immense, dark shadow. Jerry felt his throat constrict, and he could find no more words.

Mike put a hand on Jerry's shoulder. "I'm sorry, but trust issues are critical." He handed Jerry an envelope. "Here's your final check and a week's severance pay. We wish you the best, Jerry." Jerry couldn't find any words, not even to say how sorry he was for his terrible mistake. "I'll walk you out now, Jerry."

On the way home, he thought about how he had let Mike down, how he had ruined his shot at making a new life, and how Michael Constantine, if not his sister, Vickie, would find this last failure impossible to forgive. Perhaps worst of all, they wouldn't be surprised that he had failed again. He found himself outside of Sally's Suds. He would have one beer and make a plan. Then he could face Vickie and Michael.

* * *

I check in with the Carswell's court clerk at 8:20 a.m. and find that my motion to compel Consolidated to give me access to both of its mines for expert analysis on the Kevin Walters case is number four on a courtroom calendar of twenty-two motions. This was a stroke of luck. If I was called fourth, I might be out of Carswell's court within the hour, rather than spending the entire morning watching him rant and rave indiscriminately, whenever some unseen force moved him to do so. Some judges give tentative rulings on motions, so that you can see the court's thinking before you argue. Carswell does not.

At precisely 8:29 a.m., the bailiff stands and says, "All rise and come to order. Department 39 of the Superior Court is now in session, the Honorable Roy Carswell presiding."

A robed Judge Carswell emerges from his chambers through a door to the left of the bench. He sits down and looks out at the crowd of attorneys waiting for their cases to be called while they wish they were somewhere—anywhere—else.

"This is the law and motion calendar," he announces. The court first calls number twenty-one, Dyer v. Community Hospital. The fact that we were number four on the calendar was of less benefit than hoped. Why would I expect Carswell do anything predictable?

A female attorney in a gray suit strode to counsel table. "Jennifer Simon for the defendant, Your Honor."

"Where is Mr. McKenzie?" Carswell asks, already sounding annoyed.

"I don't know, Your Honor. I haven't seen him."

Carswell regards his watch. "We have any call-ins?" he asks his clerk.

"No, Your Honor."

Carswell shakes his head. "Counsel needs to respect the court's time and the time of opposing counsel. Ms. Simon, I will call the case again in five minutes. If we have not heard from plaintiff's counsel, I will rule on your motion."

"Thank you, Your Honor."

Before Jennifer Simon could move from counsel table, Carswell moved on. "Case number four, Walters v. Consolidated Energy." Just that quickly, we are ready to proceed.

Harris and I make our way to the counsel tables.

"Good morning, Your Honor. Scott Winslow for the plaintiff, Mr. Walters," I state.

"Robert Harris for Defendants Consolidated Energy and Michael Constantine, Your Honor."

"Let me hear first from counsel for defendants. You think that plaintiff should not be allowed any access to inspect conditions at either of the mines?"

"Yes, Your Honor."

"Why? This is discovery, isn't it?"

"Well, Your Honor, it is our position that the actual condition of the mines has nothing to do with this lawsuit. The issues in this action are whether the plaintiff had a reasonable belief that there was unlawful conduct on the part of the defendants and whether he was fired for voicing that reasonable belief. Of course, in reality the answer is a resounding no on both counts; nonetheless, the actual condition of the mine makes no difference. The conditions don't alter whether or not there was a reasonable belief on the plaintiff's part or whether he was fired for voicing it."

"Hmm," Carswell grunts. "Mr. Winslow, you have anything to say?"

"Yes, Your Honor. First of all, the defense argument has a couple of logistical flaws. The affirmative defenses alleged in the Defendants'

Answers to the Complaint include the position that there was no unlawful condition in the mines—

"Yes," Harris interrupts, "but that doesn't mean the actual conditions
are relevant. Just—

"Your Honor, I believe that I had the floor," I say.

"I believe you did, too. Continue. Seriatim, Mr. Harris; you'll get
another opportunity, but now isn't it."

This heaping of Carswellisms on Harris made my morning. "As I
was saying, Your Honor," I want to add before I was so rudely interrupted, but thought better of it, so I continue, "defendants contend that
there was no unsafe or unlawful condition in the mines. They also take
the position that Mr. Walters did not have any reasonable belief that
any such unlawful or unsafe conditions existed. If the defendants are
now prepared to stipulate that the unsafe and unlawful conditions that
Mr. Walters complained about actually existed, we will waive the right
to inspect. Otherwise, the inspections are necessary to determine that
the conditions he complained about existed. If these conditions existed
and can reasonably be seen as dangerous to those familiar with mines
and their safety, then we have established reasonable belief, and the
defense goes away. The inspections will allow us to identify conditions
consistent with Mr. Walters's complaints leading up to his termination
and refute the defense position that no dangerous conditions existed.
Defendants want to argue that there is no basis for a belief in unsafe
or unlawful conditions and then deny us access to evidence that we
believe will establish that such dangerous conditions existed."

Carswell nods. "Now is your opportunity to respond, Mr. Harris."

"I think counsel's argument misses the point on the law here. As I
was saying, it makes no difference if there were unlawful conditions;
the question is simply whether my client reasonably believed there
were dangerous conditions at the time of the making of the complaint.
Looking at the mine adds nothing to this."

Carswell furrows his brow as he does in contemplation of forthcoming thought or perhaps ridicule. "Are you planning to argue that

Mr. Walters's belief in unlawful conditions was not reasonable or that the conditions he references did not exist?"

I glance at Harris and could see he was not comfortable with this direction. "Well, Your Honor, perhaps, but that doesn't make any differ—"

"I think it does," Carswell says, interrupting and ending the dispute. "Next issue," he says. "I want the plaintiff to tell me why he needs access to both mines—Wheeling and Ruston."

"Didn't your client complain about Ruston conditions?"

"Yes, Your Honor."

"No specific conditions at Wheeling are in issue in the case, right?"

"Yes, Your Honor, Ruston conditions are in issue, but we believe that conditions in both will provide critical evidence for two reasons. The first is that the defendants had acted to address deficiencies under Mr. Walters's direction in Wheeling, but they failed to correct violations in Ruston. Our expert will be able to attest to what was done with respect to certain conditions in Wheeling. Some of those conditions also existed in Ruston. Defendants will not be able to deny that those specific conditions needed addressing, as they had admitted it and addressed them in Wheeling. Mr. Walters pointed out these and other serious corrective actions needed in Ruston but was fired for insisting on safety measures to address these issues because it would have cost money to shut the mine to make the corrections. All of this is supported by the declarations of Mr. Walters, and our mining expert, John J. Bernard, of Mining Enterprise International. So the examination of both mines is essential and can be completed expeditiously to allow us to properly prepare for trial."

"I've read those declarations," Carswell says, nodding.

"May I be heard, Your Honor?" Harris asks.

"You can, Mr. Harris. This is your time."

"This is wholly unwarranted and nothing but a waste of corporate assets. We are now talking about the operation of a mine not even in issue in this case based upon some wild speculation about similar conditions. This is way over the top, Your Honor, and my client should not be required to interrupt business to allow inspections of a mine not involved in this lawsuit. Plaintiff's own allegations are that he was fired for complaining about conditions at Ruston, not at Wheeling. This is like losing your car keys in Los Angeles and wanting to look for them in San Francisco."

"Hmm," Carswell mumbles, and then he leans forward in his chair and looks at me. "You said you had two reasons, Mr. Winslow. What is the other one?"

Here goes, I think to myself as I take a breath. "The other, Your Honor, is that we believe that conditions referenced by defendants as occurring in Wheeling, were in Ruston. They are conflating the two, and we can establish this with the help of our expert." Carswell is listening intently and quietly, so I continue. "Ordinarily, county records regarding inspections and citations would help, as would the testimony of the county inspector assigned to oversee these mines and their inspections for the past fifteen years, but he is suddenly gone, and no one knows where he is. I have a declaration from the county addressing that issue. At the same time, the records are unexplainably intertwined—matters pertaining to Ruston appear in the Wheeling records and vice versa. Mr. Walters's declaration addresses that issue based upon his personal knowledge of conditions in both places." Carswell is nodding and definitely intrigued.

"Now we are in the land of conspiracy theories and entering into the *Twilight Zone*," Harris says, disgustedly. "This is ridiculous, Your Honor."

"Hang on, Mr. Harris." Carswell says. "Do you dispute what counsel says about the records and the missing inspector?"

Harris shakes his head. "Records that are known to exist have been produced. I understand the inspector retired and moved. No big mystery there; people get older and retire. Again, Your Honor, this is a waste of time and money in the extreme. We shouldn't even have to be here today to oppose nonsensical motions like these."

"I do not agree with you, Mr. Harris. The court's order will be that plaintiff and his representatives will have the right to inspect conditions at both mines. The inspections shall be limited to six hours each and will be scheduled by the parties. Counsel, you need the court to order a specific date, or can you work that out between you?"

"I believe we can reach agreement on that issue, Your Honor, although I request that the order specify that the inspections are to occur within fifteen days."

"Fifteen days is too short, Your Honor; we need a reasonable period of time to set this up," Harris says.

"The inspections will both occur within thirty days of today," Carswell responds.

"Good-bye, counsel. Next case is number fourteen, Maxwell v. Lamont," Carswell says without wasting a word or taking a breath.

* * *

At five minutes past noon, Lee's phone rang. After four hours of watching the house and seeing nothing, Lee was growing impatient and stiff.

"About time," he said, dispensing with any greeting. "What have you got?"

"Carter got one call from his wife and one from his mother. That's it."

Lee reflected for a moment, and then asked. "Where's mom?"

"Orlando, Florida."

"All right, thanks," Lee muttered unhappily, hanging up the phone.

Lee decided he had to approach David Carter because he was out of other ideas. As he lifted the handle to open the car door, he saw Carter step from the house and walk down the front steps. He didn't walk toward his car, but directly to the old wooden mailbox in front of the house. He opened the box and pushed mail inside. Then Carter looked around him as if to see if anyone was watching. For a moment, he seemed to stare in Lee's direction. Then he turned away and walked back to the house. When he disappeared inside and closed the door, Lee moved quickly to the box and pulled out three letters. One was an unopened letter to Evan McMahon, with the handwritten words "wrong address" added. The second envelope was to the gas company and looked like a payment. The third envelope was addressed to Eric Darden in Magnolia, Mississippi. Lee cautiously opened the envelope. Inside was the current month's retirement check payable to Carl Miller. "Bingo," Lee said aloud, as he raced quickly toward his rental car and wondered how far it was to Magnolia, Mississippi. Whoever Eric Darden was, he was going to bring Lee that much closer to Scott Winslow's missing witness.

As Lee climbed into the car, he punched the redial button on his cell phone. It rang once, and then the familiar voice answered.

"What now?"

"Time to earn your money again. I need all you can find on Eric Darden in Magnolia, Mississippi."

"Is that it?"

"Yeah. And I need it in the next couple of hours."

"Of course you do," the voice said without surprise. "We'll get back to you."

The phone went dead as Lee smiled to himself and turned on the radio. He joined Bob Seger in a chorus of "Old Time Rock and Roll." This was going to be a good day.

Chapter 18

June 3, 2016

The Ruston and Wheeling mine inspections were scheduled for one week apart. The first inspection occurs at Ruston. Kevin Walters and I meet with Jack Bernard outside the gates twenty minutes before the scheduled inspection.

Bernard says, "I brought two engineers with me to observe and operate equipment. We will confer to determine the best testing and sampling areas. We are going to sample physical materials in the shaft, and we will take samples of the air in various locations in the shaft." He stops long enough to draw some air and see if we were going to jump in. We didn't, so he continues, "We can also compare what we find with what was on the invoice you guys found. Shall we get started?"

Nods all around, and we walk toward the mine. Harris stands with two other men a few feet from the mine access area.

"You can start anytime. Your clock is running." Harris says. "We will be here to monitor."

"That's fine," I say, and with that, Harris and the others with him move away without speaking further.

"Nice guy," Bernard says, grinning.

"Yep. A real sweetheart," I say, shaking my head.

Bernard and his team say a few words to a supervisor and the process begins. Small quantities of materials are removed from the primary vertical shaft and shaft junctions. Measurements are taken—both physical measurements of the shaft and surrounding areas and air volume and content measurements. One of the engineers takes photos at the locations they visit. Kevin periodically interacts with Bernard and the team.

Harris and a more junior attorney from his firm stand by and watch everything. Harris speaks while the junior attorney takes notes. They watch our team carefully, lest we should plant bad air or do something else untoward. I suspect that the other man standing with Harris is a company engineer supplied to provide him insight as to what he is watching. They huddle frequently, and then look in our direction, the junior attorney notating throughout.

On several occasions, Bernard interacts briefly with Consolidated Energy employees on site, which causes Harris visible angst. He appears ready to complain about this on a couple of occasions, but the conversation stops before he approaches me to discuss his concerns. We have been on site for almost five hours when Bernard nods, indicating that he and his team had completed their work.

I signal completion to Harris, who looks visibly relieved. As we walk out to our cars, Bernard says good-bye to two engineers and turns to speak to Kevin and me. "I will have the tests for both facilities completed within a week after next week's Wheeling inspection."

"Okay, great," I say. "Any initial impressions?"

He looks thoughtful. "Was there any discussion about when they would stop operating prior to this inspection?"

"No, although I assumed that they would operate until very close to the time of the inspection because they complain about the substantial costs of any period when they are not operating," I reply.

"Yeah," Bernard says, "but that's not what happened here." He observes what must have been a puzzled expression on my face and continues, "This mine has been shut down for at least a couple of days before this inspection."

"What?" I reply, shocked.

"Yeah. You can tell nonoperation several ways, like air content and movement."

"Why would they do that?" I ask.

He smiles. "One reason is to assure we don't get any usable information that would establish issues with air content. If they just let the shaft sit and breathe the air for a couple of days, it gets much cleaner than it would be if operating."

I respond, "So, do I need to go to court to try to get an order requiring that they keep working the mine until a designated number of hours before the inspection?"

He shakes his head. "No. And it wouldn't do you much good. They can find a number of ways around the order. They operate on a very limited basis, they stop certain types of work, leave certain areas alone—there are endless possibilities."

"So what do we do?" I ask.

"Nothing. Let them think that they are getting away with something." He smiles widely. "They're not."

We shake hands, and Bernard turns and walks to his car, leaving Kevin and me alone. "What do you think?" I ask.

"I told you he's good. I worked with him for a lot of years. He says just what he thinks, and he knows stuff. I think he can also help us prove our theory." He pauses and then adds, "And whatever he says, he's probably right."

* * *

Lee arrived in Magnolia, Mississippi, at 6:00 p.m. He found a roadside hotel that featured nothing in particular—no Internet, no cable, no gym, and nothing in the room but a standard double, one end table with an oversized lamp, and a thirteen-inch television suspended where the wall meets the ceiling in such a manner that a neck ache was guaranteed after a few moments of watching. The view was a potholed parking lot and an adjacent old building that housed a delicatessen. The room was twenty-four dollars, including tax.

As he opened his bag on the bed, Lee's cell phone rang. He recognized the number. "About time," he said. "What have you got for me?"

"Eric Darden is an appraiser at a three-person firm called Property Values. Been there about six months. He lives at 174 Hinden Court. No property ownership in the county.

"Before that, what do you have on this guy?" Lee asked, playing a hunch.

"That's the interesting part. Before that nothing. DL issued for the first time six months ago. I'm checking other states and sources, but it looks like this guy was born six months ago."

"Nice," Lee said grinning. There was no doubt in his mind that Darden was Miller. "Thank you. Nice work. Let me know if you find anything else on Darden or any connection to a prior life."

"Shall do."

"I owe you for this."

"Yep. What's new?" the voice said as Lee disconnected.

Lee thought about his approach to Darden as he walked from the room. Somewhere in this town there had to be a place to find a beer and a burger. Both sounded great.

The town was a throwback to an earlier time. Old clapboard houses were set back from tree-lined streets. The weathered homes made Lee feel as if he had suddenly been transported back to the early 1960s. The houses were modest, the lawns manicured, and the streets empty.

As Lee approached the downtown area on Main Street, a row of shops came into view, all one story, many with windowed offices upstairs. Every fourth or fifth shop was for rent, most bearing the same agent's sign. Neon flashed shop and restaurant names as Lee followed Main Street, which meandered to the 1890s courthouse on the edge of town. He drove past Rigby's Beef Barn, suddenly putting his hunger on hold. He had the overwhelming urge to get a look at Darden's place and, maybe, at Eric Darden.

Lee traveled farther on Main Street and then out of town for seven or eight miles, as he watched the scene turn rural. The pavement ended, and the road narrowed to a single lane serving both directions. At first, houses were on each side of the road. They became more and more sporadic until they were few and far between. As the surroundings became more rural, a five-foot ditch appeared on each side of the narrow, dirt road, so if a car came the other way, someone would have to back up for some distance. This was not a big concern, as there was no other car to be seen. Lee bounced onward to the next dirt road intersection. He grinned at a battered street sign identifying this cross street as Bel Air Drive. Lee made a left turn to find that the roadway narrowed even further, and now the potholes were frequent and jolting. After bouncing for a half mile, and passing only a few houses, Lee came to Hinden Court, his destination. He made a right turn and saw two small houses about two hundred yards away on the right side of the road and nothing on the left. He identified the house numbers with field glasses, realizing that there was no way to get much closer without being seen. This would be the ideal place if you were trying to escape. About as remote as possible and anyone approaching can be quickly spotted. Surrounded by dirt fields and with no other cover, he could probably already be seen by anyone in these houses. Worse, there was no shoulder and no place to park without driving into the ditch. Lee locked the car where it was and began walking toward the house. He pulled his cell phone from his pocket and started dialing. He then saw that there was no service, which made perfect sense as he looked around him. No cell towers and not much of anything else.

Chapter 19

The day of Michael Constantine's deposition is sunny, breezy, and beautiful. I am in the office at 6:00 a.m. looking through hundreds of pages of documents and organizing my cross-examination for the tenth time.

At 8:00 a.m., Donna walks through my open door smiling. "Beautiful day to talk to an emperor," she says. "Be sure and get under his skin for me, too."

"Yeah? You're after this guy, huh?"

"Damned straight. Not only do I think he screwed Kevin over, I'm still harboring animosity about the days spent searching through a sea of documents in a warehouse."

"That strategy was more Harris than Constantine. Besides, we did find something for the expert to examine, right?"

"That's true, and I'll enjoy the moment we get to spring it on these guys. You know, this is one of those cases where I really don't like the other side. I think Mrs. Walters has it right—kick them in the balls." She smiles. "What can I do to help?"

"I need three copies of each of that remaining pile of exhibits. That should be all of them."

"I'm on it," she says, grabbing the stack and walking from the office.

The deposition is taking place in my firm's conference room—I get home-field advantage this time. The cherry wood conference table seats twelve and fills most of the room, with cupboards and a marble counter at one end of the room and a long, cherry wood lateral file at the other. Windows run the length of the conference room, making the videographer work hard to obtain correct lighting conditions for the camera. The conference room is comfortably roomy, but unlike Harris's conference room, it could not host the UN General Assembly in the off hours.

I sit in my chosen spot for taking depositions, looking at my notes and reviewing exhibits. I look up to see Donna escort Kevin into the conference room and stand to shake his hand. "Hi, Kevin. Take the seat next to me." As he settles in, Harris and a tall man I know to be Constantine appear at the door.

Harris says, "Hello," to no one in particular and sits down. What a dick. "Mr. Constantine?" I say, standing and extending a hand. He nods. "Scott Winslow," I say.

"Yes, Mr. Winslow. I know who you are." This is not a happy camper.

"Great," I say. "Shall we get started?"

"What is your estimate for this deposition, Scott?" Harris asks, as if it were already too long for his liking."

"Well," I reply, "what day is it now?"

Again, Harris fails to appreciate my humor. He says, "Mr. Constantine has an appointment this afternoon at three o'clock that he must attend."

"You never mentioned that when we were selecting agreed dates for depositions, or we would not have agreed to do this deposition today."

There was quiet, and then Harris says, "Mr. Constantine is a busy man, and things come up." I love it when some arrogant son of a bitch thinks his time is more important than everyone else's. I am sure my expression shows my displeasure.

"Well, if he must leave, then we will go until 2:30 and continue on another day. You should plan on two full days of deposition."

"We will see if that is justified," Harris says.

"Any way you want it, Bob. You can produce Mr. Constantine to finish his deposition, or we can ask the judge to order you to do so. Either way, this depo is not going to be over by midafternoon today.We are ready," I say. The videographer announces the case name, the deposition of Michael Constantine, and the location. The court reporter gives Constantine the oath, and we are set.

"Ever had your deposition taken before, Mr. Constantine?"

"Yes."

"How many times?"

"I'm not sure. Maybe six or eight."

"How many of those depositions were on behalf of Consolidated?"

"All of them."

"When was the last?"

"About two years ago."

"In connection with what kind of a matter?"

"A contract dispute with an equipment provider."

"What was the case name?"

"I don't recall."

"Are you able to identity each of the cases in which you have testified on behalf of Consolidated?"

"Not now."

"By looking at documents available to you, are you able to do so?"

"Yes."

"Were you a defendant in any of these actions?"

"No."

"You understand that you are testifying under oath, Mr. Constantine?"

"Yes."

"Do you understand that the oath that you have been given is the same one that you would take in any court and subjects you to the same penalties of perjury?"

"I do."

"Please answer verbally rather than with a nod or shake of your head, because the reporter is making a written record, and we want your testimony to be clear, agreed?"

"Yes."

"If you don't know or don't recall the answer to a question, it is acceptable to say so. Understood?"

"Yes."

"No one wants you to guess as to information you don't know. On the other hand, if you have a best estimate as to a date or time, or a general recollection as distinguished from a guess, I am entitled to that information."

"Fine."

"Any questions about this proceeding you would like to ask me or stop and ask your counsel before we go further?"

"No."

"Since Mr. Walters's termination, have you discussed the conditions at the Ruston mine with any employee?"

"I object. Overbroad, seeking information not calculated to the discovery of admissible evidence, but you can answer," Harris says.

"No. It was not an issue," Constantine replies.

"How about at Wheeling? Did you discuss conditions there with anyone since Mr. Walters's termination?"

"Object. Overbroad, seeking information not calculated to the discovery of admissible evidence," Harris states.

Constantine looks at Harris, who nods. "Yes, there were corrections needed there."

"Who made the corrections?"

"I don't recall. A contractor."

"What conditions existed that needed correcting?"

Harris chimes in with, "Lacks foundation, calls for speculation, improper opinion."

"I don't know the specifics, just that there were some items that needed addressing, so we addressed them."

I hear annoyance creeping into his response, which I like. When witnesses are pissed off, especially the arrogant ones, their testimony comes quickly and is not well considered. "Do you know any of the corrections that were made?"

"I might have at one point. I don't recall at this time."

"Who was in charge of making the corrections internally?"

"Object, vague and ambiguous," Harris says, finding his rhythm.

"Do you understand the question, sir?" I ask.

"Yes."

"Well, I don't," Harris says. "It's your deposition, so if you want to ask ambiguous questions, that's up to you."

I smile. "Thanks, Bob, but two out of three of us understood that one."

"Who was in charge of making the corrections internally?" I ask.

Constantine thinks a moment and then says, "One of the operations managers. I can't specifically say which one."

"But you have documents from which you can obtain that information?"

"Yes."

"What documents would you look at?" I ask.

"Well, letters and forms addressing the conditions will be signed or initialed by one of these managers. That will tell me who had been assigned."

"Who have you personally instructed to keep you informed of any conditions that may pose a threat of injury?"

"I don't recall."

"Is there anything written that states that you are to be kept informed of conditions that may threaten serious injury?"

Constantine is now suppressing anger that his eyes give away. He clearly wants to be done with this, which is one of the reasons I am not done. He responds, "Not that I am aware of, no."

"So there may be matters of great significance to the safety of your employees that you have never instructed managers that you need to be kept informed about, right?"

Harris chimes in. "Object, counsel. Asked and answered and argumentative. Don't answer the question."

Now they are both pissed off, so I know we are on the right track. "Is that right, Mr. Constantine? That there may be matters that threaten injury or death that you never asked to be informed about?"

"Objection," Harris says, louder. Asked and answered and argumentative. Don't an—"

But he is interrupted by Constantine. "No, that's not right."

"Really?" I say. "How is that inaccurate?"

"Don't answer. Argumentative, asked and answered." Harris says, now sounding pissed off.

I lean back in my chair. "You need to rethink that one, Bob. Mr. Constantine just told me that it is not accurate that there are conditions that threaten injury or death that he did not ask to be informed about. I think that I am entitled to know why that is so."

"We are taking a break," Harris says.

"Let's answer my pending question and then take a break," I respond.

"No, we are taking a break now. Mr. Constantine, let's talk." Harris walks out of the room and Constantine follows. I look at Kevin, who grins and says, "Wow, you really got under his skin."

"Which one?" I ask.

"Both of them, but Mike is really angry. He's not used to having to answer to others."

We take a short break and then return. We wait another fifteen minutes for Harris and Constantine to return. I tell Sheila, the court reporter, to make sure she identifies the length of all the breaks, because I may want to use that information if they attempt to avoid returning for a second day.

Constantine and Harris take their seats. "Are we ready to resume?" Harris grunts in the affirmative.

"Do you have the pending question in mind, Mr. Constantine?" I ask. "Yes."

"And your answer?"

"I do expect to learn if there are conditions that threaten health and safety, although I can't say how I communicated to people that they had to keep me informed."

"But do you know that you did communicate that to your managers?" I ask.

"I don't know. We've had our procedures in place a long time."

I watch his expression and ask, "Do you know what S&S violations are?"

He does not react, answering with a simple "Yes."

"What are they?"

"Violations that present an immediate safety issue."

"Does it also mean that they present an immediate risk of serious injury or illness?"

"Lacks foundation, calls for speculation," Harris says.

"Yes, that is my understanding," Constantine admits.

"In the twelve months before Mr. Walters's termination, were there S&S violations of record for Ruston or Wheeling?"

"Yes."

"Which mine?"

"Wheeling."

"Were there also S&S violations at Ruston?"

"Not that I am aware of."

"Didn't Mr. Walters complain to you about dangerous conditions or violations at Ruston?"

"I really don't recall that," Constantine says. I note that Kevin is looking directly at him, but Constantine does not look his way.

"It didn't happen, or you don't remember?" I ask.

"I said I don't recall," the anger starting to emerge.

"Did Mr. Walters ever complain about dangerous conditions at either mine?"

"I don't recall that."

"Did Mr. Walters complain about dangerous conditions at any Consolidated mine?"

"I don't think so."

"But you aren't sure?"

"Object as argumentative. Don't answer further," Harris says leaning toward me.

I glance at notes to make him aware I have documents to address what comes next, and then I ask, "Well, sir, didn't Mr. Walters complain about inadequate tunnel maintenance?"

"I don't recall."

"Did he complain about failing substructures?"

"I don't recall," Constantine says again.

"Did he complain about inadequate safety equipment?"

"I don't recall."

"Did he complain about ventilation issues at any of the mines?"

"I don't recall that."

"How often did you see Mr. Walters in the normal course of business?"

"It varied," Constantine says.

"Between what and what?" I ask.

"Between daily and a couple of times a week depending on travel schedules."

"And did the two of you speak on the phone as well?"

"Yes," he says.

"Mr. Constantine, did Mr. Walters raise concerns about the need to make any mine comply with legal requirements?"

"I don't recall; I already told you that."

"Did either Ruston or Wheeling have violations for unsafe conditions last year?"

"I believe there were some," he acknowledges calmly.

"How did you learn that?"

"I can't recall specifically. It would have been in the course of normal reporting of information."

"How often did you get such reporting on mine conditions?"

"I don't know."

"Did either Ruston or Wheeling have twenty-two violations for unsafe conditions last year?"

"I don't recall the specific number."

"How about an approximation?" I ask.

There is momentary quiet while he thinks, and then Constantine says, "I don't have one."

"You recall which of the two mines had the greater number of violations?" I ask.

"No."

"How many S&S violations?"

"I don't know."

"To what conditions did the violations pertain?" I press.

"I don't know," now suppressing annoyance.

"Did they include tunnel maintenance inadequacies?"

"I don't know," he says.

"Did they include citations for equipment failures?"

"I don't know."

"Did they include citations for ventilation issues?" I ask.

"I don't know," he says again.

"Let's take a break," Harris said, taking off his microphone and standing. He waves at Constantine, urging him to follow.

"Sure, this is a good time," I offer.

Harris and Constantine go outside and disappear for about twenty-five minutes. My guess is that Constantine is probably pissed off and venting. We are all in our positions at the conference table when they return and take their seats.

"Ready?" I ask.

Harris nods, and the videographer announces the deposition, tape number, and time.

I next take Constantine through all the positions held by Kevin Walters and the duties. I then have him acknowledge each of the positive evaluations that Kevin received, his bonuses, and his promotions based on excellent performance reflected in his evaluations. Constantine has no choice but to concede each of these facts.

Then I address Kevin's termination. "Mr. Constantine, why was Mr. Walters fired?"

"I was not happy with his performance," he says, ready for this one.

"For how long a period were you dissatisfied with his performance?"

"I'd say the last year."

"Didn't you compliment him on the job he was doing about two months before his termination?"

"No."

"Did you compliment him on the job he was doing in front of others within the last two months of his employment?"

"I don't recall that."

"Well, you wouldn't have done it, right? You already told me that you did not compliment him in those last two months, so you couldn't have done so in front of others—is that right?"

"Object. Vague and ambiguous and argumentative."

"I guess that's right, yes," Constantine answers.

"Did Consolidated give executive bonuses in the last year of Mr. Walters's employment?"

"Yes."

"And the executive bonuses were based on what?"

"They were based on how well the company was doing."

"Anything else?" I ask, suppressing a smile.

"Not that I can think of."

"Well, were they performance based?"

"No."

"So every executive at the same level got the same amount?"

"No."

"What accounts for some getting more than others?"

"Their rank and role within the company."

"Now, there were two others of Mr. Walters's rank, right?"

He visibly squirms in his seat. He knows where this goes. "Mr. Walters got appreciably more of a bonus than both, didn't he?"

Harris is on it. "Objection, the rights to privacy of third parties not a part of this lawsuit are involved here. You are instructed not to answer."

I look at Harris. "For clarification, what privacy rights are you asserting?"

"The rights of the other two employees involved. Their rights are entitled to protection even though they aren't part of this proceeding," he says somewhat indignantly.

I pull two documents from my file. "Okay, well, here are the signed consents to release of this information from Mr. Clayton and Mr. Peters, the two employees we are talking about." There is silence and shock from the other side of the table as I return to my questioning. "How much did Mr. Clayton get?"

"I object, this is not relevant, invasive of privacy, and inappropriate," Harris says.

Constantine looks at Harris. "Do I answer?"

"We are taking a break," Harris says and stands again.

"Bob, we just took a lengthy break at your request. Let's not do it again."

"We're breaking now," he says.

They return fifteen minutes later, and we go back on the record.

"Do you recall the question that was pending when your attorney took the last break? It was how much of a bonus did Mr. Clayton get?"

"I don't recall."

"Less than Mr. Walters?"

"Yes."

"And you told Mr. Clayton that he was getting the amount he got because he was doing an excellent job, right?"

"I think so, yes."

"Do you remember how much of a bonus Mr. Peters received?

"No."

"Did you tell him his bonus was based upon his excellent performance?"

"I think so, yes."

"And did he receive a smaller bonus than Mr. Walters?"

Momentary silence, then, "Yes."

I take a deep breath. "Mr. Walters also got an award about three months before his termination?"

He is quiet for a prolonged period. "Yes."

"From whom?"

"An energy association of which Consolidated is a member."

"What was the award for?" I ask, suppressing a grin.

Constantine says, "It was for going above and beyond for the industry."

"Were you there?" I ask.

"I was," he says. I can see he knows what comes next.

"Did you say a few words about Mr. Walters at that event?"

"Yes."

"What did you say, sir?"

"That we appreciated his efforts," Constantine responds.

"Did you say anything else?" I ask, expectantly.

"Not that I recall."

"Did you say that Kevin did a wonderful job for the organization?"

"Maybe. I don't recall."

"Did you say that Kevin was a dedicated executive who always did great work?"

"I don't recall that."

"Did you say that Consolidated was lucky to have him?"

"I might have said that."

Harris looks at his watch. "It is two forty-five, and Mr. Constantine has to get to his meeting, so we need to end the deposition."

"For today, you mean."

He hesitates and then says, "Yes, for today."

For the record, I state, "We've agreed that because the witness has another engagement this afternoon we will stop for today and reconvene on another date within the next thirty days."

"How about thirty days if we can make it work, otherwise within six weeks," Harris responds.

"Too long. I'll compromise with you. The parties will make diligent efforts to have day two within thirty days, but, at the latest, the deposition will occur within five weeks from today."

"Okay, agreed." Harris picks up his briefcase, and he and Constantine walk from the room.

Kevin looks at me and shakes his head. "That was something," he says. "Glad I was here to see it." He pauses and adds, "And I'm glad you're on my team."

"Thanks, Kevin. I'm glad I'm on your team, too."

I spend a few minutes debriefing with Kevin, going over the day's testimony while the videographer and court reporter gather their belongings. I then say good-bye to everyone and walk back to my office. It is about 3:10 p.m. as I look down on the parking lot to see Harris and Constantine still standing and talking. Constantine's 3:00 p.m. meeting must have a start time that is a little more fluid than was conveyed to me by Harris. Constantine was probably used to making people wait, and most meetings that he was involved in were not going to start without him. He looks unhappy. It has been a good day.

Chapter 20

Michael Constantine arrived home at 7:30 p.m. the day of his deposition. He was exhausted. The deposition had been grueling, and the board meeting about the case almost as bad. He walked into the kitchen and mixed a drink.

Victoria appeared at the kitchen door as he stared into his glass. She walked into the kitchen and looked at him tentatively. "How did the deposition go?" she asked, not really expecting him to be forthcoming.

He shook his head. "It was even worse than I thought it would be. I spent all day trying to answer as best I could without getting painted into a corner. I also had to work not to be pissed off at Kevin's lawyer, who is an aggressive son of a bitch. He keeps a straight face while turning the knife." He took a drink from the glass. "And this was day one of at least two. Then I went to the board meeting, and the case was the most controversial item on the agenda."

"You thinking about trying to get it settled? How about bringing Kevin back?"

"Yeah, I told my lawyer to get a mediation set up so we can get this thing resolved." He pauses a moment. "I think there may be too much spilled blood for Walters to return to Consolidated, but I am considering trying to make that happen. He was a key player for a long time."

She smiled and said, "You two were always a great team." She let that settle and then added, "And you were friends."

He nodded. "Yes, we were. Maybe I saw disloyalty in him when I should have seen that he had the character to stand up to me."

"I'm glad you are keeping an open mind," she said.

Jerry sat alone in the living room, nervously awaiting dinner, when he would have to explain to Michael that he lost his job. He could hear, and listened carefully to, the conversation taking place in the kitchen. Michael's bad day would not make this conversation any easier.

Vickie put her arms around Michael and kissed him. "I'm really sorry you had a rough day," she said.

He smiled at her. "Thanks for that. It helps."

"You give this company everything. The board needs to support whatever decision you make about resolving the case."

He shook his head. "A number of them are supportive of whatever I want to do. Some are angry at Kevin for this lawsuit. And I had a go-around with three of the board members who think this lawsuit is my fault. There was also a good deal of discussion about the potential for bad press coming from the case. They want it contained, so the majority want it settled with a confidentiality agreement."

She nods. "Makes sense to me." She draws a breath. "I know that this is probably not a good day for this, but Jerry is here for dinner."

"Tonight?"

"Yeah, I'm really sorry, but something happened that he needs to tell us about." She whispered, "He lost the job."

"The perfect day," he said.

"He's been thinking hard about how he is going to tell you about this. He is very nervous."

"How many times do we deal with his crazy shit, Vickie? This was his last chance, remember?"

"I remember, Michael. He hasn't done well, but he's still my brother."

"I know that, but it's time to cut the cord. We gave good words to the print company and the probation officer to help him land this gig, and these guys wanted to help make it work." He studied the sadness in Vickie's eyes. "All right, we'll listen, but I think it's time for him to make his own way."

They walked into the living room and found Jerry sitting on a couch in the closest of the three conversation areas spread across the expansive room. They sat in armchairs across from the couch, a large coffee table filling the space between them and Jerry.

Michael looked at Jerry and said nothing.

"I lost my job," Jerry said, resisting tears. Admitting to Michael Constantine that he failed again was devastating. He had promised he was going to make Michael proud, and he meant it. But somehow, the job and the new start were gone.

"What happened?" Constantine asked.

"I really tried to make it work. I learned the job, and I could do it."

Victoria looked at her brother, and then in the direction of her husband to gauge his response. Constantine looked at Jerry, silently awaited more of an explanation.

"I stopped at a bar at lunch and lost track of time. They wouldn't give me another chance."

"This was your other chance, Jerry."

"I know. I know that. I learned the job, and I was doing okay. I just let time get away from me."

"Jerry, come on. You were drinking, right? That's how time got away from you. Own it."

Jerry looked at the floor. He rubbed his hands together and closed his eyes. "I want you guys to know that I can do this. I can make things work."

Michael looked at Vickie with a "this guy just doesn't get it" expression.

Vickie said, "Jerry, you know we want to believe that. And we have helped you because we believe it. You know that, right?"

"I do. I know that, and I am so sorry I let you both down." Tears were flowing as he spoke.

"Have dinner with us, Jerry. Then go home and start looking for jobs," Michael said.

"I will. I will look hard, but you know how hard it is for someone with a criminal record."

"We know," Vickie said. "It means you have to work that much harder. You are the one who has to make this work."

Jerry looked at Michael. "I know what you did for me, Michael, and I won't forget it. I will find a way to pay you back, I promise."

"You don't owe me anything, Jerry. You owe yourself the opportunity to make a go of it in the world. Focus on that," Michael said.

"I will find a way to make you proud of me, Michael. I will find a way to help you in return."

Michael found this puzzling. All he could think of to say was, "Pick yourself up and find a way to support yourself, and I will be proud of you."

Jerry nodded, tearfully. Vickie looked at Michael and mouthed a "thank you."

After a quiet dinner, Jerry thanked Michael and Vickie and again swore that he would make them proud. He bought a six pack of beer and went home. He started his secondhand computer and made a couple of notes on a pad beside him. The name he had heard was Kevin. Kevin what? Walters—that was it. Kevin Walters and Consolidated. He began searching the web for information about the lawsuit between Walters and Consolidated that had caused Michael so much distress. He will find a way to help Michael be done with the case. After the way Michael had helped him, he had to find a way to make Michael proud.

* * *

Lee knocked on Darden's door at 3:00 p.m. It had been twenty-four hours since he first arrived at Hidden Court, and he had used the time productively. He knocked twice more before the door opened slightly and a man with short dark hair, a close cropped beard, and wire-rimmed glasses said, "Yes?" through the crack in the door.

"Mr. Darden?"

"Yes."

"Good afternoon, Mr. Darden. My name is Lyle Redmond, and I'm vice president of the Tennessee Association of Professional Engineers."

Lee wasn't making up the organization. He found them on the Internet, gave himself a nice title and had business cards printed, one of which he now handed to Darden. It always amazed Lee that people accepted a business card as some sort of real identification when for twelve bucks you could be anyone you wanted. Lee could see that Darden now breathed easier after that introduction. He was understandably concerned about strangers.

"I understand that you are an engineer?"

"Yes, although now retired."

"How about joining our organization? Not only do we support other engineers, we do association funding for research and development and scholarships through the foundation, and we keep you abreast of all that is happening in your discipline. We also do monthly luncheons to discuss new ideas, and we provide mentoring to new members. What do you think? Can I count on you to be a part of our organization?"

Darden was quiet for a moment, so Lee said, "Dues are only $125 a year, and you get the monthly magazine and great comradery. We have a general coming from the Pentagon to discuss air force programs this month, and lunch is included. It's really worthwhile, and we can always use new ideas."

"Well, why don't you leave me your card and material, and I will think it over," Darden said.

"Sure, happy to do that." He presented a packet that contained the business card he had printed and a brochure he picked up at the Chamber of Commerce. "Anything I can say to get you to sign up with me today?

"The career was crazy time-consuming, so I'm taking things a little easy for a while, but I'll think it over."

"Fair enough," Lee said and turned to walk toward the front door. At the door he turned and said, "Where did you work the longest?"

Not surprisingly, Darden had an answer ready. "I spent almost twenty years with a small firm in Juneau, Alaska.

Lee almost laughed. Darden may as well have said the South Pole. He was being careful to make it hard to check on him.

"Oh, okay," Lee said. "Please call me as soon as you decide."

"Yeah. Thanks again for stopping by."

Lee walked back into the living room and sat down on the couch. "We really need to talk, you know."

Darden stood frozen in place, trying to gather himself. "We just did."

"No, we really didn't. So far we've only talked about what got me through your front door. Now let's talk business."

* * *

At 9:00 a.m., Jack Bernard arrives. I sit expectantly in the conference room with Kevin Walters and Donna while Jack grabs coffee from the table and sits back in his chair.

He grins.

"What, already? What did you find?"

"It's not what I found; it's what Kevin recognizes." He takes a sip of coffee and made us wait. "The roof supports and stabilizers that Kevin knew were purchased and used in Wheeling are in Wheeling. Our tests and the manufacturer confirms it."

Kevin smiles.

Donna stops taking notes. "Does that mean what I think it does?"

"Yeah," Bernard says. "The records show that those supports and stabilizers are in Ruston. It lends a lot of support to your argument that the mine records have been conflated."

"Yes," Kevin says, thumping the table. "I knew it, damn it."

"That's all you, Kevin," I say, in genuine admiration of his powers of observation. "After staring at a warehouse full of documents for two days, to come up with that is amazing. I can't help but think that if I or Donna had been the one to find that invoice, it would have meant nothing to us, and we'd have blown right by it."

Kevin's expression changes. "So this means that someone really did switch the records for Wheeling and Ruston, doesn't it?"

I nod. "Some switched, and some just missing. Net effect to eliminate what points to Ruston. Ballsy as hell."

"Whoever did it wanted to show Wheeling records as Ruston to eliminate the impact of the uncorrected S&S violations in Ruston. Those violations would put the company in a public shitstorm after this latest accident," Kevin adds.

"Who could have done this?" Bernard asks. "This is a big time gamble for someone."

"I think we have a pretty good idea who did it," I add. "And we are in the process of locating him so that we can have a discussion about the right thing to do."

"Anything else?" Kevin asks.

"I can't draw any conclusions from the equipment. Nothing looks out of whack, but they have had plenty of time to make changes since the accident, so who knows. From the records, we know that there are three times as many reports of excessive methane in one mine than the other. The records now show that was a bigger problem in Wheeling."

"I know that's not true, and I can identify other witnesses who can testify to it too," Kevin says.

"One other item," I add. "The production records for the mines show that the smaller mine was generating the greatest output."

"Nice," Kevin says. "Use that for day two of Mike Constantine's deposition. He will tell you that the larger mine would be substantially more productive."

"Good thought. I'm looking forward to day two of his deposition already." I looked up at Kevin. "Do you think Constantine engineered this reversal of records?"

Kevin pushes his glasses toward the bridge of his nose and then says, "There is no way he was engaged in carrying this out. It would have been undertaken at lower levels of management, and there would always be distance to protect him and give him plausible deniability. But I think he knows what happened." He paused and shook his head. "But proving that he was involved is something else entirely."

* * *

Lee stared silently at Darden. He could feel the man starting to sweat.

"So what is your business? Are you with Tennessee Professional Engineers?"

Lee sat back and looked directly into Darden's eyes. "No, I'm not."

"Then you need to leave, sir. You are not welcome in my house."

"No," Lee said evenly, "not just yet."

"What do you want from me?" Darden asked.

"Well, first you can tell me how much you were paid."

"What? Paid for what?" He was talking faster. "You are out of your mind, and I am going to call the police."

"In a minute, maybe we will both call the police. But for right now, tell me what you were paid."

"I don't know what you are talking about."

"Is that a fact, sir?"

"Yes. Yes it is."

"You know," Lee said calmly, "I just cannot abide someone who lies to me."

"Lies to you? I don't even know you."

"Yeah, so you said." Lee leaned forward in his chair. "Sit down here, Mr. Darden," he said, pointing to the couch.

"I am just fine, and you are not staying that long."

"Sit down now," Lee said quietly, and the man sat.

"You are trespassing—breaking the law."

Lee nodded. "You know, Mr. Darden, I was raised in a small Pennsylvania town, almost right in the middle of the state. A little town that had only one real employer. The coal mine." Darden stared at him, but said nothing. "You know, three generations before me worked in the coal mine for their entire careers. My grandpa died of emphysema before he got to retire. My dad made it to retirement, but he could hardly pull in enough air to keep breathing once he retired. And he died two years later."

"Why are you telling me all this?"

"Hang on, sir, just hang on a minute." Lee shook his head. My uncle died in an explosion in that mine. You know how the methane gas collects into pockets and then some little spark can set it off." He watched as Darden began to sweat. "And you know how those little coal towns are. There were little clouds of gas and unbreathable air that just hung there—hovering above everyone as they attempted to go about their business. Except that they don't just hang there, do they? Instead they poison the air, and, gradually, everyone who is stuck there breathing." Darden was now turning white. "You know how it is; even in grammar school, the kids have respiratory problems and lung issues. And you know, all most of them can look forward to is thirty or thirty-five years in those mines, if they don't die first. You with me?"

Darden clenched at the arms of his chair and tried to sound unaffected as he spoke. "I don't know why you are telling me all this, sir, but you need to go."

"Yeah, so you said. You know Mr. Darden—how long have you been Mr. Darden, anyway." Silence. "I have it at about six months. Seems like before that, your new character just didn't exist. Oh, and I did a little more research, and it turns out the Social Security number you use belonged to a guy name Ted Mannis, who died about twenty years back. So someone did a really half-assed job with your new identity, don't you think? You might want to ask for your money back, as I'm sure it wasn't cheap."

"What do you want with me?" he asked, almost in a whisper.

"Well, Mr. Darden—no, I mean Mr. Miller, I need you to come back home and testify about the exchange of records you carried out. You know, you really hurt some people with that."

"Miller? I don't know what you are talking about."

"I have your fingerprints and your DNA," Lee lied. "So you want to tell me that one more time? Or would you prefer to call the police now, and we'll both explain our stories. I really think mine is more believable, don't you?"

"Who are you?" Miller asked again.

"I'm the guy who is going to help you confront your demons and tell the truth. You want to share what you were paid yet?" Silence. "Well, you can tell me or you can tell the local police and then the FBI. You understand that you could do some real time for this, right? Altering county records and getting paid for doing so may be profitable, but it is also several felonies. It really doesn't matter to me, but I can be much more forgiving if I get some assistance."

"Meaning what?"

"How much, Mr. Miller? How much were you paid?" No response. "Who paid you, Mr. Miller?

Miller was visibly squirming. "I don't know the guy."

"Whose money, Mr. Miller?"

"I don't know. I can only assume it was Consolidated Energy's."

"Mr. Miller, you are going to come back and testify in a deposition about which records pertain to which mine, and how they got switched. You can also testify about how you were bribed, threatened, and paid off to swap the records of the two mines."

"I can't do that," Miller said. "No way."

"Why not?"

"Because as soon as I testify to all of that, I am under arrest and off to jail."

"Well, I see your concern. But here's a couple of things that might change your mind. First, if we don't reach this agreement, you are going to get arrested now, so you really don't come out ahead, wouldn't you agree? Second, if you come testify, my client and I won't mind if you walk right out of your deposition once you have testified and disappear all over again. You with me?"

"You think I'm going to be given a chance to do that?"

"Maybe, and sometimes there can be distractions that occur and give a person the opportunity to walk quietly away."

"Oh my God," Miller said.

"At least you have a chance of not going to jail that way. If you don't help, it's a sure thing."

"If I agree to this, you go away, and tell me when I have to show up?"

"You are dreaming. You already disappeared once, and you won't get another chance. If you agree, you and I are leaving here together tomorrow. Then, you and I will be joined at the hip, every day of both of our lives, until you testify. You won't even take a piss without me looking over your shoulder to make sure that your dick is the only thing you're hanging on to and that there are no hidden escape plans in your underwear."

"I don't know. I just don't know."

Lee nodded and pulled out his cell phone. "I understand. Let's explain all of this to the local cops and the FBI and see what they suggest." He began to dial.

"Wait," Miller said. "Just wait a minute."

Chapter 21

For two full days, Jerry stayed in the Constantine guest quarters, watching television and trying to reconcile the hope he had for a better life and the unpleasant reality that surrounded him. He replayed everything that had happened to him over and over on a continuous loop—the voices of those that gave him a new chance and the mistakes that took it all away. The tools he found to construct a new life were gone. No job, no respect, and no tomorrow.

Jerry paced for hours, seven steps across the living room and then five across the kitchen, over and over again. His anger burned and his feeling of hopelessness was overwhelming. He stared out the window at nothing in particular, and it was then that his thoughts returned to what he heard before dinner with Vickie and Michael. He had to find a way to help Michael Constantine with the lawsuit that was causing him such distress, and then Michael would only see that he was a friend and someone worthwhile. He could rescue Michael and redeem himself all at the same time. As the hours passed, he became more hopeful and found himself becoming excited about the prospects of this new plan.

Jerry continued to search through every article about Kevin Walters and Consolidated Energy that he could find. He found Scott Winslow's statement to the media in response to inquiries when the case was filed. "This is a whistle-blower case. Kevin Walters was a career-long and exceptional employee who was fired for raising safety issues concerning mining operations. Consolidated knew that Mr. Walters was right about conditions that threatened employee safety; they just didn't want to spend the money to halt operations and fix the problem. Apparently, they thought it cheaper to get rid of the source of the complaints."

Jerry next found a statement by attorney Robert Harris on behalf of Consolidated. "This lawsuit has no merit. Safety issues were attended to as they arose. This is simply sour grapes by an at-will employee who was fired because the company was dissatisfied with his performance."

He then read a brief article about the court allowing Walters access to the mines for inspections, and the most recent, stating that the Consolidated CEO was to testify in deposition. He found pictures of Constantine and Walters at various events together over a number of years. Michael had been good to Walters, and Walters had betrayed Michael with a lawsuit. Something had to be done. Then Jerry found clips of Scott Winslow talking about different employment cases over the years. He studied every picture and every quote he could find until he felt like he knew both Walters and Winslow. He found himself getting angry at both of them. What they were doing to Michael just wasn't right, and he had to do something about it.

It occurred to Jerry that if he was going to get rid of this lawsuit, he had two possible targets. He had to convince either Walters or Winslow that the case had to be dismissed. He began to think about how he would go about it and which of the two would be the better target. Jerry decided that he needed more information about both of them to make that decision. He felt the adrenalin rush—he was excited to have an important project that could make Michael Constantine realize what an asset he could be. This was a project that could help him put past mistakes behind him and make everything right again. He looked up the address on the Internet, and then he got into his car and drove to Scott Winslow's office. He parked across the street where the front door of the building was plainly visible and waited.

* * *

"All right, in the car you guys."

"McDonald's!" Katy yells.

"Yep," Joe echoes.

"Are you sure that McDonald's is where we have to go, you guys?" I ask, almost pleading for a reprieve.

"Yes, Daddy," Katy said without hesitation. "You promised us that we could choose."

"I did. I remember," I say regretfully. "Sure there is nowhere you prefer? Maybe Chinese food or subs?"

"Stop it, Joey."

"What happened?" I ask.

"He is in my space. And he is giving me that look," Katy says in a frustrated voice.

"Uh-uh," Joey replies.

"What look?" I was foolish enough to ask.

"You know, that look he gets when he is about to make trouble. It's his trouble face."

"Stop it, guys." I almost say that I am going to turn this car around but, fortunately, came to my senses. "Who started this argument?"

"She did," Joey says.

"No way, Dad. He did. He hit me back first."

"He hit you back first? Does that mean you hit him and then ... never mind, I have a headache," I say. "Just stop and be good to each other. We're family."

"Yep," Joey said thoughtfully. "I want a chocolate milkshake, Dad."

"He shouldn't get it," Katy says. "He's being a jerk."

"Katy, stop. We don't call each other names like that."

"Well, okay, but he is."

"I didn't do anything to her, Dad. She's just being a butthead."

"What? Are you kidding?"

"No, she really is a butthead."

"Joey, I mean we don't talk like that to each other either. You know that. No more." They must both detect my level of frustration, as the car is suddenly quiet.

I glance in the rearview mirror as I change lanes and see an old Toyota. It's a distinctive car because its hood was an unpainted gray, while the rest of the car was green. I remember seeing the same car yesterday afternoon. I watch it follow as I make a left turn, and again a few blocks later as I make a right. I make another right, changing my direction to see if the car follows. It does. Now I make a left, and it follows. I can't see the figure behind the wheel, but the car stays back, keeping the same distance as it follows. I make another right, and it follows. I slow, and it slows. I pull over and watch as it slowly drives past me. I memorize the license plate number, and then I watch the car gradually move into traffic and out of view.

"Why are we stopped? This isn't McDonald's," Joey says.

"Yeah, I know. I just wanted to check something. You guys still hungry?"

"Yep," Joey says, "and I need that milkshake."

"I am going to starve, Daddy," Katy adds.

"Well I better hurry then—before you pass out." As I move away from the curb, I survey the road for the discolored Toyota until I am satisfied that it is no longer around. The incident makes me feel inexplicably ill at ease as I move toward McDonald's to overcome the starvation that surrounds me.

Chapter 22

"So what can you tell me about this case, Mr. Winslow?"

"What do you want to know?"

"Are you going to win it?" Pat McCormick asks me. I can almost hear the quiet that follows and know from experience that he is ready to take down a quote.

"You know how to stir up a quote, don't you," I ask, and we both chuckle. "Let me put it this way. Kevin Walters was a long-term employee who helped build the organization. He has an excellent track record, and the guy knows his stuff. He also cares about workers and the communities that Consolidated operates in." I actually pause at this point, reflecting on the fact that I ended that last sentence with a preposition, and then I continue, "And he was fired right after complaining about unlawful conduct that posed serious danger to Consolidated workers. We believe that people who hear this evidence will see that there was no other good reason for terminating this great employee. So, yes, I think so. Does that help?"

"Yeah, it does. So will this case settle?"

"I don't know. But what you should know is that we will be happy to take this case to trial, and let a jury decide what is right."

"Do you have some kind of smoking gun?"

"Is that just a shot in the dark?" No response, so I just couldn't resist running with it. "If I tell you about our secret evidence, then it won't be a secret anymore." When I looked up, I saw Donna standing at my open door grinning.

"Anything else you can tell me?" McCormick asks.

"I'll keep the *Times* posted. Feel free to check back with me as you get word of new developments in the case—and I'm confident you will."

"Okay. Bye, Mr. Winslow."

"Good-bye Mr. McCormick."

"You were messing with him," Donna says with a smirk.

"A little bit. I want them in a speculating mode as they publish. Tends to shake things up."

Donna put two messages on my desk, and the phone rang again. She picks it up and says, "Simmons and Winslow. How can I help you?"

There was a pause, and then she says, "Hang on one moment, Mr. Harris. I'll see if he is available."

She raises eyebrows and says, "Want to talk to your favorite defense counsel?"

"Makes my day." I punch a button on the phone. "Hi, Bob."

"Hello, Scott. How's it going?"

Already weird. Harris doesn't give a shit how things are going with me. "Fine. You?"

"Oh, you know, busy, but good." I say nothing in response. "A couple of things," he says. "First, can you give me an additional week to respond to your outstanding interrogatories and request to produce documents. We're close, but the client still needs to review the final responses."

"No problem, just confirm by letter or e-mail, and we will calendar the new due date."

"Okay, great." I am already convinced this was not the reason for the call. He would have an associate attorney or a paralegal get a week's extension to respond to discovery.

"What's the other item?" I ask.

"We wanted to see if you want to mediate the case. Seems like the right time to set something up, particularly given that the judge will ask us about whether we have mediated when we go back to court at the end of the month. Why don't you suggest a couple of possible mediators?" Way too nice for Bob Harris.

"Maybe," I say. "But I need some reason to believe that it will be productive before agreeing."

"Meaning what?" Irritation in his voice. The Harris I know is on his way back.

"Meaning that I think mediation is a good idea if the parties are in the same universe with their case valuation, but if not, we should acknowledge it up front and not waste the time."

"Well, I need to know your demand before we can make an initial offer," Harris says.

"Okay, we'll work on that and get back to you."

"Why don't we at least pick a mediator and get the process started? Who do you think we should use as a mediator in this case?"

"Maybe Jake Billings or Margaret Flynn."

"Okay, I'll recommend Billings. Should we set it up?"

"After I hear your initial settlement offer."

"Come on," Harris says. "Your initial demand will be too high, and our initial offer will be too low, but closer to reality, and then we will work from there."

"I'll get back to you with our demand so that we can hear your offer."

"Fine." Click.

"Bye, Bob, lovely speaking with you," I say to the dial tone.

* * *

Jerry followed Scott Winslow to work, to court, and to another law office in a single day. Then he followed Winslow and his kids until it appeared that Winslow was on to him and making random turns to see if he would follow. At that point, Jerry knew he was at risk and thought he had better stop tailing Winslow. He made a left and went away from Winslow as quickly as possible. Winslow was alert and checking his rearview. Jerry had to be careful. If it took a little longer, that would be okay. He decided to buy some beer and try again tomorrow.

The next day he followed Winslow from home to his office. Jerry watched Scott Winslow park and go inside, and then he parked outside and watched the building until about 10:00 a.m., when Kevin Walters pulled into the parking lot. "Perfect," he thought to himself. At noon, Walters came out and led Jerry to his house.

Jerry waited in his car for hours, just watching the front door of the house. He told himself he had to do this right. He had to wait for just the right opportunity. If things went badly, he wouldn't get another shot. Walters was at home most of the day, periodically venturing out and then back again. Jerry followed him to what was signed as some kind of any energy association meeting that went on for a couple of hours. He then followed Walters to a restaurant where his wife joined him for a late lunch. Then Walters and his wife drove home in separate cars. Three hours later, they had not emerged from the residence. It was after 6:00 p.m., and Jerry decided this would not be the day. He was back in front of the Walters house at 5:30 a.m., his car parked in front of brush that separated the large homes, where he had a view of the front door, but neither Walters nor the neighbors had a clear view of him.

At 9:30 a.m., Walters went back to Scott Winslow's office and was there for a couple of hours. Pretty damn boring, Jerry thought to himself as he waited. When Walters came out, he drove home. Jerry found another discreet place that gave him a view of the residence. He felt frustrated and anxious. He had to make something happen.

At 1:30 p.m., Kevin and Julia Walters came out of their house together. They got into a Volvo talking and oblivious to his presence. Jerry followed them at a careful distance for several miles, where they entered the mall parking lot. He parked a few rows away from them and watched as they entered a main mall entrance. Jerry followed on foot.

This was it. Right here in plain sight he would do this. Jerry walked through the mall until he saw Walters and Julia standing in the Starbucks Coffee line. He positioned himself about thirty feet away and waited until they got their coffees and sat at a small table in the mall area. He pulled a burner phone from his pocket and dialed the number. Jerry stood against the wall, leaving Walters no direct line of vision to his position. People moved between Jerry and Starbucks in every direction.

As he watched, Walters looked at his phone and put it to his ear.

"Hello." Jerry considered his next words as Walters repeated the greeting. "Hello."

"Hello, Kevin Walters."

"Yes."

"It's time for you to dismiss your lawsuit."

"What? Who is this?"

"I'm the guy who is going to make sure you do the right thing. You have three days to get your lawsuit dismissed. Do you understand?"

"Who is this?" Kevin looked at his phone. The readout just said unknown caller.

"Three days, Mr. Walters. That is all." He paused and then added, "Enjoy your coffee," before hanging up.

He watched as Walters ran from Starbucks, looking around in all directions, searching desperately to identify the caller. Jerry smiled as he walked along slowly, staring into store windows and not looking in the direction of Walters. The adrenalin coursed through him, and he knew that he was on his way to redemption and to earning Michael Constantine's respect. Maybe he would find a place to celebrate this great day.

* * *

Lisa Winslow stood behind a lectern and addressed the local association of Realtors at the monthly meeting. "We all want our deals to work. If we don't get the deal to the finish line, we don't get paid, right?" Nodding all around. "But not at any cost. Look, we have a legal and an ethical obligation to our clients to disclose what we are aware of. And we have a legal obligation to the other side to disclose what might make a difference to them in whether they go through with the transaction. I'm a believer that if we do it right, a deal may or may not work, but the folks we take good care of will come back to us and will recommend us. And on the practical side, anyone who has ever been named in a lawsuit because of some condition on a property knows that it is stressful regardless of whether there is merit to the claim." She stopped and took a drink of water as heads nodded around the room.

"In conclusion, let me say that my rule is easy to remember. If I know something about a property, I disclose it. If it concerns you at all, disclose it. When in doubt, disclose it. Nobody ever got sued for disclosing too much information about a property." There were smiles around the room. "You will still close most of your deals, and the ones that don't go forward may have caused you heartburn for some time if they did. Thanks, everyone. I have to run off to my next presentation today, at my son's school." There was enthusiastic applause as Lisa walked from the lectern.

An hour later, Lisa walked into Joey's class and was introduced by Ms. Hammond. She was not only Joey's teacher, but a former client who had purchased her house through Lisa. Audrey Hammond addressed her class. "Boys and girls, we have a real treat today. Joey's mom, Lisa Winslow, is here to talk to us about her career in real estate. She is not only a successful real estate broker, she is a friend who helped me find my house. Let's welcome her," Audrey Hammond said to the class and began clapping. The class followed suit.

"Good morning, everyone. I'm happy to talk to you this morning about what I do because I really like it. You guys all have a home you go to every day, right?" Nodding all around. "Ever wonder how that ended up being your house?" Some head-shaking, some vacant stares. "Well, if your folks bought a house, they probably used someone like me to help them find it. Part of my job is to figure out what people are looking for in a house, such as the number of bedrooms and bathrooms, how much space they need, what they need in a kitchen, and where they would like to be so that they can get to work. After we have that figured out, I find houses that come as close as possible to what they want, and then I show them those houses. We try to find the one they like the most and that they can afford." She glanced at Joey, who didn't look embarrassed yet.

"If you think about how your house is different from some of the houses where your friends live, you can see that there are a lot of choices when a family is buying a house. You want your house to be comfortable and a good place to raise your family. So part of my job is to help people find a house that they can afford and that works really well for their family. Another part is helping them make the deal once they find that house. Does anyone have questions?"

A girl in the front row raised her hand. "Yes. What is your name?" Lisa asked.

"My name is Sophia Sanchez."

"And what is your question?"

"Houses cost a lot, right? So where do people get money to buy them?"

"A very good question, Sophia. You are right, houses are expensive, so most people get loans from banks that they pay back every month for about thirty years."

"Thirty years?" a boy in the back said, incredulously.

"Put your hand up first, Phillip," Ms. Hammond said. Phillip's hand flew up.

"Sure, Phillip, go ahead," Lisa said, with a smile.

"So you have to pay this money your whole life—until you're almost dead?"

"Well, hopefully, you are not almost dead by then," Lisa replied, "but a big loan is really the only way most people can buy a house."

"The young man in the middle. What is your name?"

"Ethan Thomas."

"Okay, Ethan, go ahead with your question."

"How do you get money?"

"Well, I get a very small percent of the price of the house when it sells."

"That could be a lot," someone added.

Another hand went up. The young lady looked perplexed.

"Yes, ma'am," Lisa said. "Your name?"

"I'm Megan Littlefield. So you get paid from the money the guy selling the house gets, right?"

"Yes, Megan, that's right."

"So you help someone find a house and that person doesn't pay you anything. Instead, the person who sold his or her house pays you?"

Kid is brilliant, Lisa thought. "Yes, that's right. Seems a little weird to you?"

Megan nodded.

A young man at the back of the room raised his hand, and Lisa pointed to him. "Your name?"

"Jackson Oliver."

"Go ahead."

"What if there is something wrong with your house when you buy it. My mom and dad bought a house, and the heater did not work."

"Another great question. So there are now insurance policies available in case there is a problem with the house. Also, sellers and real estate representatives like me are required to tell buyers what we know about the house that might affect whether someone wants to buy it. If I know that there are problems with the air conditioner or heater or some system in the house, I have to write that down for the buyer."

Another hand shot up. "Your name?"

"Lucas Crandall."

"Go ahead, Lucas."

"Well, my mom and dad sold our old house, and we moved this year, and they had to tell people that grandpa died upstairs." The class went silent.

"That's right, we are required to write that down, too."

"Why?" someone asked. "Is it in case they know your grandpa?"

They are so cute, Lisa thought, trying hard not to smile. "No, it is because some people don't want to buy a house where someone recently died."

Lucas said, "Why not?"

"I'm really not sure, Lucas, but for some people that is important." Ms. Hammond stepped back in front of the class. "All right, class, let's thank Mrs. Winslow for sharing her time and talent here today." Rousing applause from the class.

"Thank you all; it has been great having the chance to speak with you." Lisa just couldn't help it. In a moment of weakness, she looked at Joey and winked. He rolled his eyes and then furrowed his brow as she turned to walk from the room. *Damn*, she thought. She had avoided embarrassing him until the very last minute. Well, at least she hadn't blown him a kiss.

Chapter 23

June 15, 2016

"Lisa is on line three," Donna told me through the intercom.

"Okay, thanks." I punch a button. "Hi, babe. How did you do?"

"Well, I think I almost pulled it off."

"Almost?"

"Yeah, you know those kids are really sharp."

"Tell me about it. They sure have penetrating questions."

"And they say exactly what they think."

I laugh. "So tell me about the shortfall—what's the *almost*?"

"Well, I did my pitch, and they listened carefully. Then I answered their amazing questions. All was good. Then I got ready to go, and, in a moment of weakness, I looked at Joey and winked."

"Ow. I bet he loved that."

"He rolled his eyes at me, and I know he'll have something to say about it tonight."

"Well, congratulations. Mostly well done."

Donna came through the door and handed me a note.

"Lisa, I have to go. Looks like I have an emergency. I'll call you back later."

"Okay, call me sooner and tell me what the emergency is."

"You got it. Bye."

I pushed the button for line one and said, "Lee, what's happening."

"I got him."

"Miller, you have Miller?"

"Yep, and I am going to bring him back."

"How did you get him to agree to that?" I ask.

"Agree might be a little strong. I told him he comes with me and takes his chances on testifying, or I turn his ass over to the cops and the FBI now. You may want to set up his deposition because I don't know that I can contain this guy until trial happens."

"Lee, I'm worried that he has to admit on cross-examination that he was threatened with criminal prosecution if he didn't testify."

"I understand, but we either leverage this son of a bitch, or he doesn't show."

"All right, we'll figure that one out. You think he will come back?"

"Not if we give him five minutes to find an exit. He's living under an assumed name with a dead guy's Social. He's a major flight risk and will blend into a small community in another state if we give him a chance."

"So how do you get him here?"

"I persuaded him that he and I should drive back together."

"Persuaded? As in convinced him with compelling and reasoned arguments?"

"Yeah, something like that. I convinced him that it was better to ride up front with me than in the trunk." He pauses a moment and then adds, "Mr. Miller and I are going to have some discussions about who approached him and how it all happened. It should keep us entertained all the way home."

Donna came in with another note. "Kevin Walters has an emergency. Line one."

"Okay, Lee. Good work, but try not to do bad things to him before you get him here. Another emergency."

"See you soon," followed by the click.

I pushed line two. "Kevin, what's up?"

"I got a threatening phone call while I was at the mall. I was in Starbucks' and the caller said I should enjoy my coffee after telling me I had three days to dismiss my lawsuit."

"What?"

"Yeah, three days."

"Or what?"

"He didn't say."

"Call the cops, Kevin. I'm on my way over."

"You think so? I didn't know how seriously to take it. The case is getting media attention, so this could just be some crank."

I said, "It could be, but don't chance it. Take it seriously. Get the cops on the way, and I'll be at your place in twenty minutes." I hung up and looked up at Donna, who was staring at me with wide eyes.

"Kevin was just threatened. Somebody called him and said that he has three days to dismiss his lawsuit. I'm going over there."

She nods and says, "Call me if I can do anything from here."

On the way to the Walterses' house, I call Lisa and tell her what had happened.

"Oh my God. What do you think they should do?"

"I think we let the cops handle it. They are equipped to deal with this kind of thing."

"I suppose. Pretty damned scary though," she adds.

"Yeah," I respond. "We really have no idea who this person is or what he might do. Hopefully, nothing. I have to run. I'm pulling up to their house now."

"Okay, call me later." She pauses. "And tell them we're both with them."

* * *

A uniformed officer with a name tag that says "Braddock" sits in one of two armchairs in the Walterses' living room and scribbles in a small notebook as Kevin describes what happened at the mall. Julia Walters sits in the other armchair while Kevin talks. There are brief introductions, and then I take a seat on the couch looking across the coffee table at Braddock.

"So you never saw anyone that you thought might be the caller?" Braddock asks.

"Right. I looked around the mall but couldn't identify anyone," Kevin responds.

"Is there anyone that you believe would want to threaten you?"

"No, not in terms of a specific person, but given this was a threat requiring me to dismiss my lawsuit against my former employer, it seems reasonable to think it may be someone connected to the company. Not sure who else would care about getting my lawsuit dismissed."

"Right," Braddock says, and then he is silent for a few moments as he considers the matter. "Can I take your cell phone?"

"You want to take it with you?"

"Yeah. I want our techies to look it over and see if there is any evidence to be gathered from the caller info. I can get it back to you tomorrow. We'll also chase phone records, but it won't get us far if the call was made from a burner."

"Okay, sure," Kevin says.

"What's next, officer?" Julia Walters asks with concern. "I'm worried about the fact that there is only about two and a half days before this person carries out some unknown threat."

"Yes, Ma'am," Braddock responds. "Given the tight time frame here, a detective will be getting back to you today, after my report is turned in. You have voice mail set up on your cell?"

"Yes," Kevin says.

"And on your home phone?"

"Yes."

"All right. We have your cell and will monitor anything incoming. Write down your voice mail retrieval numbers for me." Kevin complied and handed Braddock the note. "Okay, now don't answer your home phone if it rings. At least not until you hear from us. Anyone who needs to talk to you can leave you a message."

Kevin nods. "Sure."

"What about Julia's cell," I ask. "Same procedure?"

"Right," Braddock says. "And if there is any further contact of any kind, call us right away."

"Thanks for your help, officer," Kevin says, extending a hand. They shake and then Julia and I each shake his hand.

"If the phone is in your possession when a call comes in, can you get info about a private caller?" I ask.

"I'm not a techie, but I know that the answer is *sometimes*."

I nod, and we watch Braddock walk out the front door. "You guys okay?" I ask Julia and Kevin.

Julia nods. Kevin says, "Sure, Scott." He thinks for a moment and adds, "I don't know who is doing this, but it really pisses me off. I will not dismiss this lawsuit, and these guys can go pound sand."

I looked at Julia, who shrugs. "Yep. We're both okay. And these guys should know that this kind of shit will never work with Kevin."

"Call me if anything else happens, okay?"

"Yeah," Kevin says. "Thanks for coming, Scott."

As I walk out of the house, I find myself looking up and down the street—looking for some clue and seeing nothing out of place. I hear the phone ring behind me, and I run back inside, I join Kevin and Julia in staring at the phone readout. It said private caller. The temptation to pick it up is almost overwhelming, but we resist and wait for a voice mail. Instead the caller hung up and we had no idea whether it was him or just a solicitation. Even more unsettling.

* * *

Lee began the drive with Carl Miller as his reluctant passenger. "So tell me who approached you."

"About what?" Miller asked.

"Don't fuck with me," Lee said. "About switching the Wheeling and Ruston records for Consolidated and making some records disappear."

Miller was quiet.

"What now?" Lee asked.

"I'm not sure I want to do this," Miller replied.

"What?" Lee snarled. "We've been through this shit."

"I don't think you know what you are asking here," Miller said, defensively.

"Okay," Lee replied calmly. He said nothing further. Lee drove for about ten minutes into the downtown area and pulled up in front of the Police Department.

"What are you doing?" Miller asked, sounding panicked.

Lee turned off the car. "I am not wasting my time with you. We had an agreement. Now you tell me you're not sure you are going to cooperate. Okay, your choice. So let's just go talk to the cops, and they can contact the FBI for us. We'll all meet right here, and you can explain everything to their satisfaction." He opened the car door and got out. He leaned in and said, "Let's go."

"You are blackmailing me," Miller said, without moving.

Lee looked back into the car and stared at him. "And your point is?"

"There could be people very unhappy with me coming forward."

"Yep. Could be. You ready to walk in or do you need help?" Lee said evenly.

"All right, all right. I'll do it. I'll tell you."

"Good," Lee said, getting back into the car. "But just so that we understand each other, this is going to be the last time this happens. You stop talking again, and I will drag your ass to the closest FBI office. I am not going to fuck around with you."

"I understand," Miller said, resignation in his voice.

"So who approached you?" Lee asked as he started the car.

"A guy who called himself Mr. Valentine."

Lee furrowed his brow. "Who was this Mr. Valentine?"

"I don't know."

"Where did he approach you?"

"I was having lunch at a restaurant called Boca, sitting outdoors on the patio. This guy walked up to my table, pulled out a chair and sat down. I was puzzled, and I said, "Can I help you?""

The guy looked at me and said, "No, but you can help you."

"What did he look like?" Lee asked.

"He had a closely trimmed beard and a moustache and dark eyes. He was tall and thin."

"Then what?" Lee asks.

"Then I listened, and he told me that he needed some records fixed. He said that the records for the Ruston and Wheeler mines needed to be switched. Ruston needed to become Wheeler and Wheeler needed to become Ruston, and whatever documents are inconsistent with that realignment needed to disappear." Lee nodded and waited for him to continue. "I told him I have no idea who you are and that we had nothing to talk about. The guy just stared at me. And then he said it's going to be easy. You know how to deal with the physical files, and we can help with the clearances needed for the electronic files."

"What did you say?" Lee asked, as he listened to tone and delivery and tried to assess whether Miller was telling the truth.

"I asked him, 'Who is we?' He said that information was beyond what I needed to know. At that point I said we had nothing more to talk about, and I stood up to leave."

"What did he do?"

"He stood and walked with me. He told me that I better listen to the rest of what he had to say before walking away. At that point I was pissed, and I said, 'Or what?' "

"That's what you get to find out. You need to know what might happen before it actually happens to you."

Lee was now convinced that Miller was telling him the truth. "How did you react?"

"We just stared at each other for a couple of moments. I noticed at that point that he was wearing a wig. But that told me I didn't know his real hair color, and I wasn't sure if the beard was real. It occurred to me that the intent might be to assure that I couldn't describe this guy accurately." Miller shook his head as he reflected on the conversation. "Anyway, I let him walk next to me for a couple of blocks. He tells me that he can arrange for me to have a great retirement. Full retirement, full benefits, and a cash bonus of $50,000 to walk away with."

"Sounded tempting, I bet," Lee responded.

"No, it didn't. I am a career guy and care about protecting public safety. So I told this guy I had nothing more to say to him."

"He said, 'I guess that's your choice, but there is one more thing you should know. If we don't reach an agreement, you are going to be fired and never get to that pension.' I watched him in stunned silence, and he told me that they had the goods on me. That there were going to be questions raised about whether violations existed that were not reported by me. Then he said that the next thing they would do is present evidence that I was paid not to record violations that I was made aware of, and several people who uncovered these events would be prepared to testify about them.

"I was angry and ready to strike back by then. I said that none of that was true. He shrugged and told me that there would be very credible witnesses who said otherwise. I told him that he would be implicating his own client if he did that. The son of a bitch just grinned at me and said that his client would be nowhere near the incidents that had been discovered. I told him again that this was all bullshit. The guy said that I should watch the six o'clock news for the first hint. He said he would meet me back at the restaurant tomorrow at the same time, and he turned and walked away."

"Then what?" Lee asked.

"Then I watched the news and heard a headline about a possible investigation into bribery of county employees."

"I get it," Lee said. "So did you meet with him again?"

"Yeah. The next day. This time his beard was longer and both his hair and beard were a different color. He asked me if I saw the news, and I said that I did. At that point he handed me a briefcase. He said that the instructions were in there along with the fifty thousand. He told me that I had twenty-four hours to make the changes, and if I do it, the investigation story ends, and they set up my retirement. He asked me if I had any questions and then walked away, telling me that we would have one more lunch the next day."

"So you did it?"

"I did it. I stayed awake all night turning it over in my mind and concluded I had no way out. I did it, and I met with the guy, who looked different again—no facial hair and a double chin that wasn't there yesterday. It was only the voice that convinced me it was the same guy. He asked me if I watched the news, and I told him I did. Then he asked me how I want the rest of the story to go. I tell him that this story isn't true and whoever was doing this was manipulating facts. The guy shrugged and said that the story was going to be believed. He said I could take my chances, but the odds weren't good. By then, I was really scared. So I went along with the deal. I agreed to do what they wanted over the next couple of days. Somehow, Valentine knew when I had done it without me showing him any proof, so this guy was somehow plugged in. He then called me and said that I had done the right thing, and within two days I got a statement confirming my date of retirement and retirement benefits."

"And then you changed your name and moved a long way away."

"Right. After what I did, I didn't want to be findable by anyone connected to my old life. So I blended into a small town with a new name to live my life out peacefully, which I might have done if you hadn't tracked me down."

Lee nodded and then said, "If all goes well, you still might get to be that guy."

* * *

At three thirty, Kevin Walters opened his front door to see Officer Braddock with a man in blue slacks and a bluer jacket. The man was built like an NFL receiver, but approaching NFL retirement age. He was tall and wiry but clearly muscular.

"Mr. Walters?" the blue man said.

"Yes."

"I'm Detective John Landon. You remember Officer Braddock?" he adds, referencing the uniformed officer.

"Yes, sure. Come in gentlemen." They walked into the living room. "This is my wife, Julia," Walters tells them. "Julia, Detective Landon and Officer Braddock."

"Hello Ms. Walters." They shake hands.

"Anything learned from the analysis of the phone?" Julia asked.

"No. The lab got nothing from the phone." He paused and then asked, "Any calls on your home phone?"

"One, Julia replied. The readout said private caller, and there was no voice mail message." She drew a breath and then added, "I' can't help but be a little nervous about all this, Detective. Kevin is not dismissing his lawsuit, and we have no clue what happens after the three days are up."

"I understand," Landon said, "but we don't have much to work with here unless there is another call. We set up your cell phone so that we get to listen to and record any calls." He returns the phone to her. "With your permission, we will do the same with your home phone. The techs will be here shortly. The problem is no one has seen this guy; we don't know that he has a prior record, and we know nothing about him. So we don't have enough information for much of a search."

"Yeah, that's fine," Kevin says.

"Anything else you can tell me about the voice? Any other facts you remember?"

Kevin shakes his head. "No, I told you all I know."

Landon nods. "Okay, we'll be prepared to listen, and we will also roll a patrol car by here every couple of hours around the clock. Please call us if you see or hear anything else."

"Sure," Kevin says.

They shake hands again and open the door to leave.

* * *

From across the street in a neighbor's front yard, Jerry watched as the cops walked outside and down the driveway to the unmarked car at the curb. Walters had fucking gone to the cops. Jerry was angry, but he knew what it meant. Any incoming calls and visitors to the Walterses' would be monitored. Technology would be used to identify anyone who contacted them, and if he got close, here would be a search for any kind of hair or fiber of DNA evidence. He wasn't going to walk into a hornet's nest, so he told himself that he had to be done with the Walterses.

Jerry walked back to his car frustrated and angry with himself for failing to account for the obvious. He had made no plan in the event that Walters called the police. He had naively assumed that they would fear the threat and comply, dismissing the lawsuit, without going to the cops. Jerry slapped the hood of his car in anger. The thought then occurred to him that he had simply lost one battle—not the war. No one knew who he was, and he was still free to act. He would make a new plan.

Chapter 24

When I get back to the office, it is almost five o'clock. Donna hands me a stack of messages and says, "Well?"

"No clue," I say shaking my head. "Some guy calls Kevin on a blocked cell and tells him that he has three days to dismiss his lawsuit. The police took the phone yesterday but came up with nothing. No one has any idea who this is, where the call emanated from, or how to determine any of it. The Walterses' phones are being bugged, and marked cars are going to patrol the house, but that's all the news."

"Wow, crazy."

"Yeah. Anything critical?"

"Yeah, Lee just called for a second time. Says that he has Miller, and Miller told him how he was approached."

I dial Lee. "Did you get the update?" he asks.

"Well, I heard he talked to you."

"Right. Here's the scoop. Miller is contacted by some guy who calls himself Mr. Valentine. Valentine tells him that if he switches records between Ruston and Wheeling and purges anything inconsistent with that reversal, he gets a great retirement package plus fifty grand in cash. When Miller resists, they blackmail him—I can give you more on that later. So he meets with this Valentine guy in public places three times, and each time the guy changes his appearance. Ultimately, they use a news release to convince Miller that they will get him fired or worse if he doesn't cooperate. So he takes the deal, changes his ID to a dead guy's and moves to a small town where he wants to remain a hologram."

"Amazing story," I say, marveling at all this. "I set his deposition for next Friday at my office. The other side knows that we put his deposition on calendar, but they have no idea that he will actually show up."

"So I will find him a hotel when we get back and have him lie low," Lee replies.

"Yeah, that's good. I want to ask you how you got all this out of him, but I know better."

Lee laughs. "We are working on our relationship and have a long ride and lots of time to share. You know, I think he's actually a decent guy. My take is that someone at Consolidated—whoever this Valentine is—really worked this poor bastard over. I think he'll come across okay."

"Is he nervous about getting busted when he comes back to testify?"

"Yep. I told him that we need his testimony, and if he can deliver and then disappear, we won't be spending time or money looking for him."

"Okay, thanks, Lee. Great work."

As I hang up, Donna's voice on the intercom says, "Bob Harris on line two."

"I was just wondering how this day could be even more fun." She laughs as I hit the line two button.

"Afternoon, Bob."

"Hi, Scott. I was wondering if you got a settlement demand from your client yet."

"No, I haven't had an opportunity to do that."

"Okay, well look. You were worried about whether we were going to low ball you if we went to mediation, right?"

"Yes, that's right."

"My client is operating in good faith here and would like to get this case settled. They have authorized me to give you an opening offer of $100,000 to show you that we are serious."

I think that sounds like a good faith opening offer, so I say, "Okay, Bob. We are on board."

"So I have two dates from your proposed mediator, Jake Billings, three and four weeks out. I just e-mailed both to you, and you tell me if you can make one of them work," Harris says.

I glance at the e-mail he referred to and then look at my calendar. "I will confirm with my client before committing, but I think the second date works."

"Perfect. I will have Billings's office block the date for us."

"Okay, Bob. I will get back to you to confirm in the next day or two."

"Also, let me have your initial settlement demand so I can share it with my client."

"Shall do."

We hang up, and I sit back in my chair, genuinely confused. Consolidated wants to work on settling this case while someone is threatening Kevin if we don't just dismiss it and walk away? If you want to settle the case, why go over the line in an attempt to blackmail someone? Is it possible that the caller was not with Consolidated? But who else would need to have this case dismissed? I can't think of anyone else who would want to make sure that a lawsuit against Consolidated didn't go forward. Could the threat be intended to make sure we settled? Seems unlikely. Crossing the line to blackmail in order to assist in getting a good settlement is not the kind of practice that a major corporation can afford to engage in. And then there is Harris. A complete asshole, to be sure, but seemingly representing a client who wants to get this case resolved by settlement. And I can tell that Harris is carrying out his client's intent to get this case set for mediation, or he wouldn't have called me back again before I even gave him a settlement demand. They offer six figures without even knowing how high the demand will be in order to get us to go to mediation. So if Consolidated wants to work toward settlement, then who wants to exhort a dismissal of the case without payment? I play it over and over in mind, and I get nowhere. It just doesn't make sense.

At 6:00 p.m., my partner appeared at my doorway with a grin on his face. Bill says, "I just met with a woman who has a sexual harassment case against the county."

"Good case?"

"Yes, but more relevant, she worked with Carl Miller in the inspection division. A name I know you're familiar with."

"No shit. What does she say about him?"

"That he was the only decent human being in the bunch." Four others in the division spend half their time asking her about her sex life, and the other half telling her how they could make it better for her. Frequent comments on her boobs and her ass. Pretty serious stuff."

"She report it?"

"Yeah. After your man Miller retires, someone pins her in the corner and kisses her, and she takes it to personnel. They tell her they will review it and get back to her. Two months later, she's still waiting for the call back."

"And Miller is not one of the assholes doing this stuff?"

"Right. According to her, he was always a gentleman. Thought you might want to know that."

"I do. That is fascinating. My witness can be impeached by the fact that he manipulated public records, ran away with cash, and took the identity of a dead guy. But at least he's not a sexual harasser. He has to be everyone's hero, right?"

Bill shrugs. "No one's perfect." But I guess I should get his deposition about the harassment in the work environment before the cops lock him up for excessive creativity with public records."

"Wish I could say you're making me feel better," I add.

"See you tomorrow, buddy. I am out of here." He waved and headed for the door.

As Bill approached his car, he glimpsed a figure sitting in a car across the street, staring directly at him. Bill stopped for a moment and then starting walking toward the figure. At that point, the old car with the discolored hood took off in a hurry.

* * *

They were passing through Oklahoma just a couple of hundred miles from the New Mexico border when Lee got back to a topic that he had already probed at length. "Let's talk more about Valentine," he told Miller, who did not respond. "You told me that you met with this guy three times, right?

"Right."

"And each time he looked entirely different than he did the time before?"

"Yes, correct."

"Do you have any idea how we can identify this guy?"

"Well, we don't have any clue which one of these three people he is—maybe he doesn't really look like any of them. That's why the picture doesn't help."

"What? What picture?" Lee said, incredulously.

"I paid the waiter fifty bucks to take a picture of me and this guy together on the third day, but then he showed up with the double chin that he never had before, so it all seemed useless," Miller replied.

"Where's the picture? Do you have it?"

"Yeah, it's on my phone." He pulled out his phone and searched for the picture as Lee hit the brakes and stopped on the side of the road.

"Are you fucking kidding me? You have a picture of the guy?"

Miller handed Lee the phone. "Here it is, but who knows if this even looks like the real guy."

Lee wrote a text using Miller's phone. "Scott, this is Lee from Miller's phone. Attached is a picture of Mr. Valentine in one of his disguises. I'll hook up with some facial recognition software and see if we can ID this son of a bitch. This is their third get-together. When Miller saw him on the two prior visits, he had a beard and no double chin." Lee attached the picture and sent the text.

"You think that might do some good?" Miller asked.

"Are you for real? Why did it take you so long to getting around to telling me you had a picture of this guy?" Lee said, sounding annoyed.

"I just didn't think it would help. The guy may not look anything like this."

"That's possible," Lee said, deliberately calming himself. "On the other hand, it may be enough to identify him."

"I guess I should have considered that," Miller said.

Lee wanted to smack him, but said nothing. What a dipshit.

* * *

June 16, 2016

At 6:30 a.m., Lisa and I sit at the kitchen table drinking coffee and waiting for the kids to emerge for breakfast. The morning we see through the window is a beautiful blue and cloudless.

"Anything more on the Kevin Walters threatening call?" Lisa asks.

"Nothing. The police are set to record on any phone the calls come in on, but there are no more calls. Maybe it was just a prank of some kind."

She gave me her skeptical look. "Do you think so?" she asks.

"I don't know what to think. Yesterday I get a call from Consolidated's lawyer making a settlement offer and seeking to mediate the case to see if we can get it resolved. I find that hard to square with Consolidated demanding a dismissal without payment as a threat of some kind. And if Consolidated isn't threatening Kevin, then who else has a horse in this race? It's just baffling."

"I see your point. It is very weird." She goes quiet a moment and then adds, "Don't forget, tonight is my regional board meeting, so I need to hand off the kids at 5:30 p.m."

"Got it. I'll meet you here at five thirty and take the kids to dinner. They've been wanting to get Chinese. Katy actually wanted to know if we can buy a whole box of fortune cookies so she can find the fortunes she likes best."

Lisa laughs. "Sounds right. Good luck with that—she may want you to organize the fortunes alphabetically."

I kiss Lisa good-bye and take off for what started as a reasonably uneventful day.

* * *

With cops circling all around the Walters residence, Jerry decided to focus on Scott Winslow. If Winslow was convinced to dismiss the case, he could get Walters to go along with it. It was about three thirty when Jerry started toward Scott Winslow's house. Having followed Winslow home a couple of times, he knew exactly where he was going.

Jerry arrived at the Winslow house at about 4:00 p.m. and parked two houses down and across the street. He was still contemplating how he would approach Winslow, but he had concluded that Winslow had to be scared—he had to have a strong motivation to dismiss the case. He pulled a towel up from the floor on the passenger side and placed it on the seat beside him. He unfolded the towel to reveal the small handgun that he had purchased. He had never used a gun, and it made him nervous, but he felt it was the best way to make his point. It looked like the safety was on, so he put the gun back on the towel beside him. He picked up a can of beer and took a deep pull. Nothing to do but wait.

* * *

It was 5:25 p.m. when Lisa pulled into the driveway. "Okay, guys, let's drop your books and grab coats for tonight. Everyone get their homework done?"

"Yes," Katy said.

"Joey, how about you?"

"Mostly. I have to look over my spelling words one more time for tomorrow's quiz, but it's a no-brainer."

"It's a no-brainer, huh?"

"Yeah. I been looking at these words for the past two days, and they're not that hard."

"Dad will be home in about five minutes to take you to dinner. I have to run when he gets home." She looked at Katy. "Where is your other shoe?"

"I had it a while ago."

"Where were you just now?"

"In the bathroom." When the bathroom was found devoid of shoes, Lisa located the missing item on the coffee table.

"Can we turn on the TV for just a little while?" Joey asked.

"No time. We're down to just a few minutes. Grab your coats."

"Can't we just see a little of *The Big Bang Theory*?"

"No time. Besides, you guys have seen every episode of that show."

"But it's good, Mom," Katy said pleadingly.

"No, can't do it."

"Where is Dad taking us to dinner?" Joey asked.

"I heard something about Chinese. What do you think?"

"Yeah, awesome," Joey said.

"I want a whole box of fortune cookies," Katy said. "So I can pick the best one."

"That's not how fortunes work, nerd. You don't get to read a bunch and pick one," Joey responded.

"Why not?"

"You guys stop, okay? Come on, let's go."

Lisa led the way to the front door. "Dad will be here in just a minute, so let's head outside."

"She stepped outside, and both kids grudgingly followed. "All right, guys, hop in the car. Katy, buckle yourself in your car seat."

"I thought we were going with Dad."

"You are, but we'll just trade cars so we don't have to shift your car seat."

"I almost don't need it anymore," Katy said, confidently.

"Yep, you almost don't. Maybe just a couple more months."

I pull into the driveway next to her Lexus and see Lisa wave to me and smile. The kids are waiting in her car, although Joey is absorbed in something he is holding. Katy waves to me, and I wave back. I walk over to where Lisa waits and kiss her to booing and hissing from within the car. "Gross." "Yuk."

We laugh and then turn to see a man standing in the driveway with a gun. He is staring at us silently.

"Instinctively, I put my hands up, palms facing him. Please, point the gun down."

He is unsteady and shakes violently as he continues to point the gun. He has deep-set, dark eyes, stringy blond hair, and slightly sunken cheeks. He looks almost undernourished, and his expression is intense. I do not recognize him, but I know instinctively that this has to be the guy who threatened Kevin Walters. "We are not moving," I say. "Please be careful with that, and we will give you whatever you need."

The guy stares for a time and then says, "You need to dismiss your lawsuit."

"Okay. What lawsuit?"

"Walters."

"Okay, why?"

He raises the gun higher. "You don't get to ask why. You just have to do it."

"Okay, okay. Like I said, you've got the gun, and I will do whatever you want. You want the case dismissed, it happens."

"Tomorrow. You do it tomorrow."

"Okay, tomorrow."

"If you don't, I will find you." He pauses and then adds, "And your family."

"I understand." The guy is shaking so much that I thought the gun might go off accidentally. "Please put the gun down now."

He seems momentarily satisfied. He lowers the gun slightly, and I am able to breathe. He backs up and then slowly turns to leave, but there is a sudden squeal of brakes, and a car stops in front of the house. Bernie climbs from the car and yells, "What's going on here?"

In an instant, the gun goes off, and Bernie ducks behind his car. The man panics and scrambles into Lisa's car. I hear her scream, "Oh, my God, no."

I hear Katy crying as the man finds the keys in the ignition and starts the car. He flies backward out of the driveway, smacking the tail end of Bernie's car as he roars out onto the street. I run down to Bernie's car and climb behind the wheel. He jumps in beside me, and we take off, following the Lexus, which is moving quickly through residential streets. Bernie pulls out his cell phone and calls 911, giving the details of where we are and which way we are heading. He provides the license plate number of the Lexus, and then describes what had happened. He tells them that two children are in the back of the stolen car. His voice breaks as he speaks excitedly.

My whole body is shaking as I focus on the Lexus, trying desperately to keep it in sight. The traffic is getting worse as we reach commercial areas. The Lexus is running red lights as cars honk and brakes scream. I follow through all of it, hoping that we aren't broadsided as we run through intersections at high speeds. We race westbound, the Lexus about five cars ahead of us and changing lanes wildly. Traffic is entering the road we occupy from all intersections, and getting through is getting harder. I am slowly gaining on the Lexus, which is sprinting around traffic, sometimes in the lanes of oncoming traffic. I follow.

The Lexus makes a sharp left and then another. I barely make the second turn, passing another car and moving into oncoming traffic as I do. My body is shaking, my heart is pounding, and I have feelings of fear as I desperately try to keep up. I lose sight of the Lexus for a few moments and then see it again as it surges around another vehicle. The Lexus sprints straight ahead and then makes a sudden right, tires squealing through the turn. I follow, the car fishtailing as I make the turn and then try to correct. The Lexus roars through a red light, narrowly missing being broadsided by a fast-braking garbage truck, which is coming to a stop in front of me. I bear left to go behind the truck, but several other cars are coming right at me, and I cannot find a path. There is nowhere to go. I am trapped, honking and yelling; watching helplessly as the Lexus moves ahead, and slowly out of my view. I work my way past oncoming traffic and then back into my own lane, following the path the Lexus had taken, but the Lexus is no longer in view. My stomach is knotted, and I can feel a rising sense of terror as I think of my kids alone with a crazy person. Bernie and I race ahead, looking left and right at every intersection, speeding recklessly and running red lights. After a couple of miles the reality hits—we have lost them. The Lexus is nowhere to be found. Bernie is on the phone with 911, telling them where we lost the Lexus, where we are now and the route we have covered. We go on as fast as possible, covering ten additional miles, searching for clues in every direction, as the weight begins to settle on us. We stop by the side of the road, having no idea what direction they went, and I begin to weep. My world is in that car, and I have no idea what to do next.

Chapter 25

I sit on the couch next to Lisa, and we clutch hands. Her eyes are red from crying and are filled with pain. Our living room is now a satellite operation for police agencies, and cops are all around us. Detective Landon sits across the coffee table, while the tech team hooks up recording and monitoring equipment. Detective Landon provides recollections about the initial threat to Kevin and Julia Walters to supplement the report that he prepared and that they are reviewing. Two FBI agents, Becky Sandoval and Greg Edmonds, review the notes they have taken.

"How tall?" Sandoval asks me.

"About five feet ten inches, I say."

"And no other distinguishing features you can think of? No facial hair, moles, scars, anything distinctive?"

"Just those dark eyes. Almost sunken in." I pause. "A couple of days' growth on the beard, uncombed blond hair. And skinny. They guy was pretty thin."

Edmonds is now on the phone relaying the description. He adds, "Along with the APB on the car, get a list of all hotels, restaurants, and convenience stores within a twenty-mile radius. Contact them all and have them look out for the Lexus and a guy who meets this description traveling with two kids. Put out the Amber Alert with the car description and license plate." There is a brief silence and then he says, "One more thing, get the description of this guy to managers at

Consolidated, and let's see if anyone knows who he is. That's it for
now." He hangs up and turns to us. "I know how hard this is," he says,
"but we are going to need your help. This guy has an agenda. That
agenda is not kidnapping kids, and as far as we know, this guy has no
motive to hurt children; they just happened to be in the car he used
to get away." He pauses. "But they are now new leverage to get what
he wants. And we know what that is. He wants you to dismiss this
lawsuit. So we think that he will likely call you today or tomorrow to
talk specifics."

"And if he doesn't?" I ask. I see the look on his face and wish I could
retrieve the question. The impact on Lisa is immediate, so I don't wait
for an answer. "Okay, but you need to know that we will give him
whatever he wants. You understand that, right?"

Sandoval says, "We get it. We want to make this come out right, so
you need to do a couple of things for us. We don't care what you have
to promise to give him. We have to keep this guy in play. Ask to speak
to the kids, to make sure that they are okay. Then, keep the guy on
the line as long as you can. And if there is going to be a drop-off or
a meeting, we want it to be in a public place, so we can be there to
watch it all without being seen. That okay?"

"Yes," I say, in a painfully weak voice. "We can do all that."

"When should we—when would you normally expect a call to occur?" I ask.

"Depends. In a kidnapping for ransom case, we usually expect a call
within twenty-four hours, but this is not that case. Our guy didn't go
after the kids; he simply took the vehicle they occupied. He may be
shaken up and looking for a way out of all this. We will give him any
opportunity to return the kids and think he can walk away."

"What else can we do?" Lisa asks.

"Our people will be looking at employee photos of present and former Consolidated Energy employees tonight and trying identify this
guy. We will chase every lead that comes from calls in response to the
Amber Alert and the word we put out to all of law enforcement. And

we will also get in touch with all of your contacts to see if anyone might know something. We will have teams following every lead."

"Okay," Lisa says, "but I mean what else can *we* do? I mean Scott and me."

"Keep each other company and try to stay calm to be ready for that call. And we have a sketch artist on the way. You can help him develop a sketch of the guy, okay?" Lisa nods. "Then we'll get that sketch over to Consolidated employees as well to see if it results in any identification. It makes sense that this guy will have something to do with Consolidated. Why else demand dismissal of a lawsuit against them?"

"I feel like I should be out there," I interject, "beating the bushes and looking for them. Not just sitting here, uselessly worrying. I feel like I am wasting time."

Sandoval nods. "I understand, but we need you here, looking normal and nonthreatening. For all we know, he could be watching the house to see if the police are here. That's why, in twenty minutes, every visible trace of police presence will be gone, and you two will look to be home alone. We will set up a perimeter to see anyone who is watching the house, but that person will have no idea we've been here." She pauses and then adds, "I know it's hard to sit here when your kids are out there, but it's what will work best. We have every law enforcement officer in the state as well as federal officers on the lookout."

"I understand," I say reluctantly. Then I stand and walk to the window and examine the street out front.

"One more thing," Sandoval says, looking at me. "Sorry, but I need you to stay away from windows."

"In case this guy shoots us?" I ask, incredulously.

She shrugs. "We don't know who we are dealing with here or what to expect, but this guy could be somewhat irrational. We also don't want him to see you and be scared away. If he is watching the house, we want him to think no one sees him. We will have the whole area under a microscope, but he can't see any trace of what we're doing."

I nod and walk over to Lisa. I have never seen such fear and worry on her face. I take her in my arms and whisper, "This guy is not after the kids. Everything will be okay." She nods agreeably, but neither of us is convinced.

Twenty-five minutes later, Sandoval says, "Everything is in place, and we are exiting. The phones will record every call, and we will be listening to every call from a few blocks away, okay? We nod, saying nothing. "One more thing. This phone on the end table," she points, "is connected directly to us. You pick it up, and we answer."

"Thank you," Lisa says.

Sandoval gives her a sad smile and then a quick hug. "We are with you."

With her phone on speaker, Sandoval talks to an unseen observer. "We are ready. Are we clear?"

"Affirmative," is the audible reply from a male voice. She nods to her team, and they all walk quietly through the back door of the house, leaving hidden technology as the only trace of their visit.

* * *

Jerry was shaking so hard he could barely hold onto the wheel. He looked in his rear view mirror every few seconds. Had he successfully ditched Scott Winslow? To make sure, he spent ten minutes making a random series of rights and lefts. He didn't seem to be following anymore. He tried to calm himself as he considered what he had inadvertently done. He turned into a residential neighborhood and pulled the Lexus over to the curb. He had crossed a line. He had kidnapped the lawyer's two children. *Jesus help me*, he thought to himself. *What do I do now?*

The kids were crying in the backseat. Jerry looked at the tearful faces in the mirror. The little girl was openly sobbing, and the boy was pushing tears away and looking at him like he was expecting to be hurt. Jerry's heart began racing as he looked at them. He suddenly felt trapped; like the air around him was getting thicker, and breathing was difficult. Could he just take them home? Drop them off and run? The cops might be there waiting for him. When they caught him, he would go back to jail. This time, forever.

"Mister," the boy said through tears, "you can just let us out and take the car. We can call and get a ride home."

Jerry looked at him. "I didn't mean to take you kids," he said, "but they will say I kidnapped you and send me back to jail if I go back."

"We won't tell anyone, Mister," the boy said. "We don't want you to get in trouble; we just want to go home."

Jerry considered him in the mirror. "If you are good, you will get home. Just not yet. I have to do something first."

Jerry told himself that he couldn't go back to his place with kids that don't belong to him. If they figure out who he is, they will be all over the guest house. And they will figure it out; it was just a question of time. Winslow and his wife had seen him. And before too long, Michael and Vickie would learn that he had let them down again. He had no choice. He had to leave town. But how? He had a stolen car and not much money.

Maybe he could let these kids out of the car close to town or near the police station. He quickly decided that there were too many problems with that plan. He was still here and not going to get what he needed without these kids. They were the leverage he needed to find an exit and to keep him out of prison—he just couldn't go back there. It was then that Jerry remembered the abandoned warehouse next to Sally's Suds. They could spend the night there, and in the morning, he could make a deal and give the kids back.

"Please," Katy cried. "I really want to go home now."

"You'll get to go home. Just not yet." Jerry drove in the direction of Sally's Suds, wanting to get there as quickly as possible, before the license plate on the Lexus was spotted.

After ten minutes of avoiding major streets for fear that the road-blocks would be set up or the license plate would be spotted, Jerry reached the abandoned warehouse. The block-long building made of aluminum was just as he remembered. Jerry pulled a lug wrench from the rear of the car and used it to pry open the padlock on the front door of the building.

"Okay, you kids. Let's go." Neither Katy not Joey moved. "Now. Get moving," Jerry yelled. They released their belts and climbed from the car, following Jerry inside the warehouse. Inside was a cement floor. There were no rooms, just vast open space with a small mezzanine about twenty feet up and accessed by a rope ladder on the far side of the building. There were several piles of rusted metal objects that were broken and scattered. Stacks of rusted metal fixtures protruded from seemingly random locations throughout the building.

Katy and Joey stood against the wall and watched as Jerry started to drag some of the heavier metal beams and fixtures toward the door. He made about five trips with heavy metal objects until he was satisfied that the access door was completely blocked, and there was no way the kids could get out.

He turned and looked at the fearful faces of the kids. "We are staying here tonight," Jerry said. "Tomorrow, we will see about getting you home."

"Why are we here?" Joey asked.

"Because it's safe here," Jerry said. "You guys sleep. I will be right here."

Joey looked around. "There's nowhere to sleep," he said.

"Do your best. We just have the floor."

Katy and Joey sat down together in the closest corner of the warehouse, leaning against the aluminum wall and keeping their eyes on the man. It was uncomfortable, but occasionally they drifted off to a few minutes of sleep, then they awoke to find themselves in this strange, cold, and empty place. Katy began to cry again. Joey put his arm around her and tried to resist crying so that he could make Katy feel better. The strange man at the door just looked at them. It occurred to Joey that he looked scared, too.

* * *

We wait impatiently for something, anything, to happen. I pace, drink coffee, and stare at the wall. I am still suppressing the urge to go out looking, but I know that I can't. Lisa lies on the couch, then walks aimlessly around the house, and in and out of the kids' rooms, crying anew with each look at their belongings.

"What are we going to do if we don't hear from him?" she asks, terror in her eyes.

I shake my head. "We can't let ourselves think about that," I say lamely. Then I take her hand and say, "I don't know."

June 17, 2016

At 3:00 a.m., I can't take it anymore. I pick up the directly connected phone and say, "Are you there?"

"Yes, sir. Is something happening at the residence?"

"No, we just can't cope with nothing happening. Do you have any new information? Anything on the identification of this guy? Has anyone spotted the car?"

"Not yet, sir. Nothing yet. Agents are still questioning employees of Consolidated." I shake my head in Lisa's direction to let her know that they had nothing more.

"Okay, thank you."

"Yes, sir." There was a pause and then the voice adds, "We will contact you as soon as we have more information."

"Yes, okay."

I put down the phone, as Lisa walks over to me. "What are we going to do?" she asks again, in desperation.

"We are going to get our kids back," I say with false confidence, but she can always see right through me. She nods and walks toward the stairs. "What are you going to do?" I ask.

"I'm going to clean the kids' closets," she says. I nod, but say nothing more. She always needs a way to expend energy when she is nervous.

I stand beside the living room window looking out at the street. I move from one side to the other, hoping for some sign that someone was out there watching us. I need to find the skinny guy with the sunken eyes, but there is no movement and no sign of anyone.

It is 8:30 a.m. when the phone rings. I race to the phone and pick it up on the second ring. "Hello?"

"Scott?" The voice is Donna's.

"Hi, Donna," I say, letting my guard down.

"He just called here," she says. "He said that you have thirty minutes to be here when he calls back. He also said that it needs to be just you and that he is watching to make sure. Anyone else around, and he does not call back. That was the message exactly."

"I need a strong tail wind and no traffic to make it in thirty minutes, but I'm on my way," I say, slamming down the phone.

I turn to Lisa. "He called the office and is calling back in thirty minutes. He says anyone comes with me, there will be no call back."

Lisa cupped her hands over her mouth and then said, "What do we do?"

"I don't know. I guess we comply."

"What about the FBI?"

"I'll start for the office. Give me a five minute head start and then pick up the direct contact phone and let them know what's going on. That way if he's watching me leave, he sees that I am alone."

"Okay," she replied, nodding. She kissed me and said, "Go fast. I'll tell them that he has to know it's you alone, so they have to stay out of sight."

I run into the garage and open the door. As I pull out of the driveway I search all around me for anyone watching, but I see nothing. I race toward the office as fast as traffic will allow.

* * *

Jerry decided to make good use of his time while he waited thirty minutes before calling Winslow's office again. He saw a small used car lot not yet open for business. He walked to the back of the small office and saw a few more cars in the rear yard that were not yet priced for sale. He picked a five-year-old Buick because it was the least visible from the street. He bent down behind it and quickly removed the license plate, replacing it with the plate he had taken from the Lexus. He went back to the Lexus and quickly put the newly obtained plate on it. If the police ran the plate, they would see that it did not go with a Lexus, but at least he no longer had a plate that would be the subject of a stolen car and Amber Alert APB.

Jerry stayed away from the car and walked two blocks, checking his watch. He dialed the number. It rang three times, and then a female voice said "Law offices of Simmons and Winslow. How may I help you?"

"It's me," Jerry said without inflection. "Is he there?"

"Not yet. He's a few minutes out."

"Five minutes," Jerry said, and hung up. He checked his watch and paced. He thought about the two kids he left back in the warehouse. They were scared, but soon he would be able to give them back and disappear.

* * *

As the light of morning came, Joey and Katy had seen their captor climb the mountain of metal debris and squeeze out the front door. Then they heard the padlock snap closed behind him. They waited a few minutes and then pushed on the door several times, but there was no give. They hit the door, screaming for help again and again, trying to make as much noise as possible, but there was no reply. The warehouse had grown cold during the night, and they were both chilled to the bone.

"Let's see if there is another door or a hole in the wall," Joey said, and they began a walk around the interior of the warehouse. Every place that looked as if it might be weak or faded in color, they struck at and pushed as hard as they could. The siding did not give. Joey saw scraps of wood in one corner and picked up a stick about two feet long. He began striking at the building as they walked around, thinking that even if there was no give, maybe someone might hear the noise. They walked the entire building and did not find a spot that would open, crack, or break. As they reached the original starting point, they were out of ideas.

Katy started to cry. "I'm scared," she said.

"Yeah, me too," Joey said, still looking around the building for anything that might help.

"Do you think that he will be back?" Katy asked.

"I don't know. Probably," Joey said, not thinking that that was good news. As he spoke, Joey focused on the mezzanine in the corner of the building and the rope ladder that could take him up there. "Maybe we can get out up there," he said. Katy looked worried but said nothing. "I'll climb up there and take a look," he said, beginning his walk toward the ladder. Katy sat down on the cement floor and leaned against the side of the warehouse, wrapping her arms around herself in an attempt to get warm. She watched her brother make his way to the rope ladder and look up twenty feet toward the mezzanine floor. He grabbed the unanchored rope ladder and began to climb.

* * *

I run into the office as the phone is ringing. Donna visibly tenses as she picks it up. "Simmons and Winslow. How may I help you?" Her countenance relaxes. "Good morning, Ms. Ramirez. Not right now, but I will have him give you a call as soon as he is available."

I recognize the client name. As soon as Donna hangs up, the phone rings again. "Simmons and Winslow. How may I help you?" She looks at me and nods. Into the phone she says, "Yes, he's here; hang on one moment."

I take the phone, and then I take a deep breath. "This is Scott Winslow."

"Mr. Winslow, your kids are okay. I need something from you, and then they will come home."

"Let me talk to them," I respond.

"You can't right now," was the cryptic response.

"Why not?"

"They are not here with me now."

"Damnit, where are they?" I said, raising my voice.

"They are okay, and if you cooperate, they come home."

I know I have to stay in control, so I make myself take a breath. "What do you want?"

"I want the dismissal of the lawsuit, stamped by the court, and I want $20,000."

"Money? This is about money?"

"No, it's not." The man was momentarily quiet and then said, "I just need money to leave now. You'll get your kids back, but I need to be able to go away."

"I will get both, but I need a few hours. When and where do we meet?"

"I will call you at your office at noon. Then I will tell you what to do." Then the man hung up. I tell Donna to prepare a Request for Dismissal of the Walters case with prejudice. I have to call Kevin Walters and Bob Harris about that, but I first start making calls to arrange for the money in a hurry. Two minutes later, FBI agents Sandoval and Edmonds walk into my office.

* * *

The rope ladder swung and twisted unpredictably as Joey climbed. With each new step to a higher rung, he had to pause while the ladder's violent movement settled. He was halfway up the ladder, and his hands were tired and his body tense from gripping so hard.

"Joey, I'm scared," Katy said, looking up at his moving form. "Come back down."

"I have to see if there is a way out up here. Maybe we can get out of here before that guy comes back." He took another step, and the ladder began swaying and twisting again. "I'm really getting tired," he told her.

Five minutes later, with arms and legs hurting, Joey put a knee up and hoisted himself onto the mezzanine. He stood up and looked down at Katy without speaking. She looked up with big eyes and waited for her brother to do what came next. After he recovered his normal breathing, he walked away from the edge and out of her view. Katy could hear the mezzanine creak and groan as Joey walked around. Then she heard him pound on one area of the wall after another.

A few minutes later, he came back to the edge where Katy waited. "I need that stick," he said.

She gave him a puzzled look as she picked up the wood. "How do I get it up there?"

"Stand on the first step and point it up. I will reach down and get it," Joey said, looking around to make sure that man wasn't coming back yet.

Katy held onto the ladder with one hand and the piece of wood with the other. She stepped up onto the first rung of the rope ladder and began to swing and twist, almost letting go of the ladder. "I'm scared, Joey."

"I know. Here, just reach up and lean the wood against the ladder." She did, although it was hard for her to hold the wood upright, even using the ladder as support. "Good, Katy. Hold it there, and I think I can reach it." Joey stepped onto the first rung of the ladder and found the top moving in different directions than the bottom. They both held on tightly as the rope ladder whipped and turned. As it began to stabilize, Joey reached down toward the wood. "Push up just a little bit more," he told Katy, and he reached for the wood. Katy pushed with all her strength, and Joey reached down even farther. With one final reach, Joey lost his grip on the ladder. He fell and narrowly missed Katy. His head struck the cement floor of the warehouse with a horrible popping sound, and he did not move. Katy came down off the ladder and ran to his side, yelling, "Joey, Joey, are you okay?" She shook him and called out, "Please wake up, Joey." He didn't open his eyes. He didn't move.

* * *

At noon, Donna announces, "It's him on line one." I answer as Sandoval and Edmonds looked on. "This is Scott Winslow."

"Do you have both things?" the voice asks.

"Yes."

"Good. Here's what you do next. Go to 2316 Western Avenue. There is a bank of three phones in front of the grocery store. The call will come in at 12:50 on one of the phones not in use. Understand?"

"I understand. What about my kids?"

"You will deliver the two items to me, and I will provide the location of your children. They are safe. Same rules apply. You come alone, or you do not hear from me."

"Okay," I reply as calmly as I can. "I'm on my way now." I hang up, and Sandoval nods. We will give you a wide perimeter so that he has no idea you are not alone."

"You have to be sure," I say, imploringly. "You can't scare him off. He disappears and ..." I let the words trail off.

"We get it," Sandoval says. "Trust me, he will have no clue that we are in the area at all. Now go."

I rush to my car, where I already have the Request for Dismissal with Prejudice and a gym bag containing $20,000 in cash. Ten thousand of the money came from our savings, and occupies the top half of the gym bag. The other ten thousand in the gym bag comes from the FBI, and it has been marked and identified, bill by bill.

After a brief conversation about what was occurring and the threat to my children, Bob Harris quickly obtains consent from Consolidated to set aside the dismissal and reinstate the action after the dismissal was delivered to the kidnapper. Today Bob Harris is not an asshole.

I race down the freeway so that I can make the designated location by 12:45 p.m. I see red lights go on behind me. This can't be happening. I say a brief prayer, seeking any kind of help. Then I punch a button and hear, "Sandoval."

"I am being pulled over," I say into the phone line. "If I get stopped, I won't make it in time."

"What agency?" she asks.

I check my rearview to be sure. "Highway Patrol," I say.

"Here's what you do. Put on your signal and begin to slow down, but take about thirty seconds to pull over. We'll take care of the rest.

I'll stay on the line with you. Do you have your signal on to signify that you are going to pull over?"

"Yes."

"Are you slowing?

"Yes."

"Current speed?"

"Forty-five miles per hour and slowing."

"Perfect. Just a little longer. Keep slowing."

"Okay, I'm down to thirty-five and pulling over."

"Just a few seconds move," Sandoval says. I can hear Edmonds talking in the background. "Okay," she says, "you should be getting a signal shortly."

I look in the rearview, and the lights go off. The Highway Patrol car begins to fall back. I pick up speed, and he stays behind me, moving slowly, no longer following. "Looks like I'm clear," I say. "He backed off."

"Do what you need to in order to get there on time. You won't be stopped again," Sandoval says.

"Thank you," I say, and I accelerate to over eighty miles per hour. I check the clock on the control panel. It is twelve thirty-two. I think I can make it. I race around other freeway traffic, drawing one finger salutes from two different drivers. I race down the off-ramp for Western Avenue and swing a right turn against the red light at thirty miles per hour. Ahead traffic is completely stopped. I don't have the time to wait, so I drive the shoulder between parked cars, and then force my way back into traffic. There is a red light two hundred yards ahead, and traffic is getting through at only a few cars per green. I launch into the opposing traffic lanes and roll down the road at forty miles per hour. As I get to the light it turns green, and I force myself back in with traffic that will make it across the intersection. I strike the front bumper of a green Ford and keep going, weaving in and out of cars on the other side of the light. Three miles to go, and it is 12:44 p.m. I know that I am not going to make it, and I am starting to panic. I am swerving left and right through traffic relentlessly. Twice more

I venture into oncoming traffic lanes to pass someone. I double-park in front of the grocery store at 2316 Western and leap from the car. People are blasting their horns as I tie up traffic and run, leaving my car double-parked.

It is 12:50 p.m. as I stand in front of the market and stare at the three public phones that sit on a metal rack against the red brick wall. No one is using any of the phones, and none of the phones are ringing.

My heart is racing a mile a minute. I am still waiting at 12:53 and there has been no call. I look all around me but I see no signs of anyone watching. I don't see him, and I don't see any police. Carrying the gym bag, I pace nervously in front of the phones, partly to be ready and partly to keep other potential users at bay. *Please, phone, ring*, I think to myself, not wanting to consider the implications of me arriving too late to receive the call.

A young woman in a tight black skirt approaches, and I place myself between her and the phone bank. She looks momentarily puzzled and then says, "I need to use the phone."

Before I can speak, the phone in the middle of the three rings. I pick it up. "Yes?"

"Winslow?"

"Yes."

"Okay, listen carefully. Walk through the market and out the back door. You will be in an alley. Walk directly across the alley from the rear of the store, and you will see a wooden fence. Throw the container with the items in it over that fence. Got it."

"I have it. What about the location? Where are the children?"

"After you have thrown the container, turn to your right and walk down the alley. You will see a series of closed garage doors. You will find an envelope containing the address on the lower right of the seventh garage door on your left. Got it?"

"Yes."

"You will find the children waiting at the address in the envelope provided both items are in the container. If not, they will be moved before anyone can get there, understand?"

"Yes, I have it." The line went dead, and I move into the grocery store and toward the rear door as fast as I can. I can see the rear door, and it has a closed screen.

Someone yells, "Can I help you?"

"No," I say and keep rushing toward the rear door.

* * *

Katy sat against the metal wall and held her brother tightly. "Please be okay, Joey. We have to get out of here, and I don't know how to do it." He was not responding. "Are you sleeping?" She pushed tears away and said, "Help me Joey. I don't know what to do."

Katy heard the distant sound of cars going past, but no one heard her continual cries for help. She kissed Joey on the forehead and again said, "Please be okay, Joey."

* * *

Jerry saw the bag come over the fence. He heard the footsteps on the other side running toward the envelope pasted on the garage a hundred yards away. He picked up the package and moved from the backyard of the condemned house to the front yard. He walked quickly across the street and into a mobile home park. He walked through eight streets of mobile homes and then threw the bag over a brick wall and followed. As he leaped over the wall, Jerry heard footsteps closing behind him. He grabbed the bag, climbed into the waiting Lexus and drove away quickly, telling himself that his next task was to get rid of the car.

* * *

I see the envelope taped to a closed garage and run toward it. I pull it loose and open the envelope, glancing at the only thing on the enclosed note—an address and the word "warehouse." I pull out my cell phone and hit the direct dial number.

"Sandoval here."

"I have the address," I say breathlessly, and read it off to her. "It's a warehouse."

"We're on it. I'll call you back as soon as the closest police officer gets there."

"Thank you, agent Sandoval," I say again, as those are the only words I can find. I say a prayer that Joey and Katy are where the note says they are. My worst fear is that the warehouse will be empty when the police arrive. What do we do then? I can think of no answer, so I just keep praying.

* * *

I get back to my double-parked car, which has not yet been towed away. Motorists are still grumbling with their horns as I climb in and start the drive back. Five minutes later my phone rings, and I recognize agent Sandoval's number.

"Scott Winslow," I say with anticipation.

"Scott, we have the children." I take a breath in relief, and then I hear the rest of the news. "Katy is fine, although a little shaken. Joey is unconscious and being taken to Cedars Sinai Hospital by ambulance. We are bringing Katy to the hospital and will meet you there."

"What's wrong?"

"Katy says that Joey climbed up a ladder in the warehouse to look for a way out and fell from the top rung. Lisa is going to meet you at the hospital."

* * *

I run into the emergency department and am directed to the neurology department. In the corridor I see Lisa with her arms around Katy; I throw mine around both of them. "Katy, are you okay? Did you get hurt in any way?"

"I am okay, but Joey got hurt."

"We know sweetheart, and the doctors are going to take good care of him."

She nods. "I was nervous." She tears up. "I was asking him to talk to me, but he couldn't."

"The scary part is all over now," I say, even as my thoughts return to new fears about Joey's condition.

We keep asking, and Katy repeatedly assures us that she is okay and that she didn't get hurt at all, and that the man didn't do anything bad to her. A hospital nurse informs us that they looked her over and found no signs of physical injury or assault. Katy appears to be physically okay, though the emotional impact of being a kidnap victim and her brother's injuries remain to be determined.

Katy sits quietly between Lisa and me in a row of chairs in the neurology waiting room at Cedars Sinai. It is now 4:30 p.m., and we have been waiting for some information since about 2:00 p.m., when we were told that tests were going to be undertaken to determine the nature and extent of Joey's injuries. We sit on pins and needles, hugging Katy and waiting anxiously for an update. There are ten other people in the room, all of whom share the same pained look of worry about someone close to them. It is a community of shared anxiety and fear among strangers.

Just after 5:00 p.m., the neurologist heading the team working with Joey emerges and calls out, "Winslow family?"

"Yes," I say. "Right here."

He wore the blue physician's uniform, inclusive of the shoe covers on his feet. He walked slowly toward us and extended a hand. "I am Dr. Mitchell, a neurologist and neurosurgeon."

"Scott Winslow, my wife Lisa, and our daughter Katy." I say. Then we just waited.

"Joey remains unconscious. He has swelling of the brain tissues that we are studying closely. We will do a couple more tests, and then I should be able to give you more information and a recommended course of action."

"Is he going to be okay?" Lisa asks.

The doctor goes momentarily quiet and then says, "In many cases, we can reduce swelling and the patient improves dramatically. I don't know if this is one of those cases, but I can tell you that Joey has experienced significant trauma." He took a moment and then added, "If you can give us a couple more hours, we will give you more specific information. My team will be here until we have completed the tests and are ready to make recommendations to you, however long that takes."

"Thank you, doctor," we both mumble and then sit down without the feeling of relief we had wanted so desperately.

It is 8:30 p.m. when we see the doctor again. His face says the news is not good. We stand, but he waves us seated and then brings a chair over to join us. By now Katy, who wants to stay at our side rather than going home to rest with Bernie and Kathy, is exhausted and asleep.

"Tell us," I say. "Tell us everything."

He nods. "As I mentioned, there is swelling in and around the brain from the traumatic impact of the fall. That swelling is substantial, and it is life-threatening at this point." Lisa lets out a cry and covers her mouth. The doctor just nods understanding. "So what we feel strongly is the right course at this point is a medically induced coma."

I feel like I have been hit in the gut, and the doctor's face says he sees it. "What does that mean?" I ask. "And what is the effect?"

Seeing our expressions, Dr. Mitchell says, "It is scary; I understand. What a medically induced coma really is …" He pauses to find the right words and then says, "Think anesthesia. We use it to put everyone under for all kinds of surgery. Well, this is the same thing except it is a greater dosage. It is monitored and kept up for a longer period of time. When there is brain swelling, there are certain areas of the brain that don't get adequate blood flow. So the medically induced coma allows the affected areas to require less energy so that they get some protection while the swelling decreases." He glances at each of us and then adds, "The critical difference between a coma and a medically induced coma is that we can slowly bring the patient out of it when medical conditions warrant it."

"How long?" I ask. "How long will this continue?"

"We don't know," he replies. "We can only monitor the results and act based upon what happens."

"So it can go on forever?"

"No. It is often for a matter of days, but it can be a number of weeks. I've never known of an instance that went beyond five or six months. If it is going to provide relief at all, it will be within that time."

"And what if there is no change?" Lisa asks.

The look on his face says it all.

"Oh, my God," Lisa says.

"But we are at the beginning of this, and it does help in many cases."

"What are the risks of the procedure?" I ask.

"Well, we are slowing down the systems. Blood flow slows and blood pressure goes down. So when you slow systems down, the unexpected can happen, but we are monitoring all the time, so if something happens, we can respond with other appropriate treatment. I should add that right now Joey is breathing on his own, but it can become necessary to use a ventilator if he struggles at some point after the coma is induced."

Lisa and I are quiet for a time, absorbing the shock of the injuries and the proposed treatment. "Can we visit him and talk to him?" Lisa asks.

"Anytime and all the time. I believe in the positive effects of loved ones nearby the patient. Talk to him as you normally would. Tell him about your day and what's going on in the neighborhood—new toys and new television shows. At some level, I believe that people who are comatose hear and respond to their families." He rubs his chin and adds, "For the next two or three days, Joey will be in the critical care unit. Once we administer the drugs and assure that he is stable, he can be transferred to a patient room. Then we watch and see how the swelling is doing day by day."

I give a nod and shake his hand as all of this continues to settle on me. We say good-bye to Dr. Mitchell, who gives us a card with a number where he and the other two neurologists on his team can be reached. As he walks away, I put my arms around Lisa, and we cry together, as softly as we can so that we don't wake our other sleeping angel.

Chapter 26

The next day the police gave the artist's drawing of the suspect to the press for distribution, so that the public would help identify the suspect. The national media picked up the story, and it was in print, on cable, and a topic of conversation on social media. Articles about the kidnapped children of an employment attorney by a man who wanted a whistle-blower lawsuit dismissed dominated the news cycle. There are passionate pleas to the public to provide tips to the FBI about who the skinny, gaunt man with the sunken eyes might be. Television and newspapers reported the kidnapper's demands for dismissal of the lawsuit and for money. They showed pictures of Joey and Katy, and reported that they are at the hospital, and news of their condition will be shared when known. The media even posited possible directions of travel by the kidnapper, which were largely speculation.

We are in the hospital with Joey the day after his admission at about 6:00 p.m. when agent Sandoval walks into the room. She asks if she can speak to Lisa and me outside in the hall for a moment. We step outside, and she opens the artist rendition of the kidnapper. "We have an ID on the guy," she says.

"Who is it?" I ask.

"Jerry Anders." We stare at her blankly, as the name means nothing to us. "He is Michael Constantine's wife's brother. Constantine called the office and identified him a short time ago. Constantine says the guy is troubled. Apparently, just recently out of prison and trying to make up for his past theft from the Constantines by helping dispose of the lawsuit against Consolidated."

I stare at the deep-set eyes in the picture. The guy didn't look evil. He looked a little nerdy and a little lost. "Any leads on the whereabouts of this guy?" I ask.

"Yeah, too many to chase down yet, but nothing that we know is really credible. But we'll get him."

I just nod, feeling weary.

"Thanks for coming to tell us, agent Sandoval," Lisa says.

Sandoval nods and then says, "On a personal level, I'm praying for your son's recovery."

"Thank you," Lisa says, and we shake hands and step back into Joey's room as she walks away.

* * *

Jerry left his car and all his other possessions behind. He couldn't chance stopping at the guest house. He hid the Lexus in one of the long-term lots that were provided for airport parking. Then he left town on foot, hitchhiking toward San Bernardino. He called someone he met in prison and, for a thousand dollars, ordered new ID. Within seventy-two hours, he would be Frank Adams, from Boise, Idaho.

After taking three rides and seven hours to get to San Bernardino, he found a used car dealer and paid cash for an old Toyota with too many miles on it. Then he stopped at a discount store and bought a couple of pairs of jeans, five shirts, and packages of socks and underwear. He also bought a small suitcase to keep it in. Then he connected with Route 15 and drove toward Las Vegas. He was keeping it together until his name and his picture hit the news services. Then he knew he couldn't check into a hotel without fearing that he would be recognized.

Jerry had to change his appearance, and do it quickly. He stopped at a pharmacy as he hit the outskirts of Las Vegas and bought black hair dye and scissors. He also bought makeup and three different-sized application brushes. Jerry next drove to the Flamingo Hotel and walked into the casino area. He located the closest bathroom and went inside. There were a couple of people in the stalls, but no one was near the mirrors. He cut his hair short and then quickly followed the instructions in applying the black hair dye. He carefully used the makeup to create a mole high on his left cheekbone. People came and went, but no one paid much attention. He then applied small amounts of makeup to his eyes and eyebrows to eliminate the sunken-eye look that the media was describing. When he was done, he thought he looked a little weird, but he didn't look like Jerry Anders. All he needed was his new ID. For now, he would find a small strip motel that would take cash and ask no questions.

* * *

At the end of the first week, Dr. Mitchell approaches us in Joey's room, peeling his surgical mask to allow him to communicate freely. He sits down beside us and asks, "Are you guys hanging in there?"

"No." I say. "We are struggling."

He nods. "So far, there is no change in Joey's condition." He stops and seeks his words cautiously. "The brain swelling has not yet changed. But I don't want you to be disheartened. Joey's bodily systems are working well, and no changes are warranted. He is holding his own with all of this. And remember what I told you before, significant progress can take weeks, and in some cases even months."

We nod and thank him, looking and feeling disheartened by this news. Our son must remain in a coma for an indefinite period. No progress. None of this registers as good news.

* * *

There are now constant calls from the press requesting comments and interviews. Our days are long visits to the hospital, sitting next to Joey, and talking to him about anything and everything. He sleeps through it all, and I stop sleeping almost entirely. I stay awake all night, listening to the ticking of the grandfather clock and obsessing over what had happened and how I might have prevented it. I spend the quiet hours worrying about whether Joey will recover and the psychological damage done to both kids.

The articles and news stories keep coming—pictures of Joey accompanied by reporting that he was now in a medically induced coma. There are profiles of Lisa and me and our careers. There are stories about Joey and Katy and how their teachers and classmates love them and are praying for Joey. There are vigils at school and a local park, with pictures of Joey all around. And there are stories about Jerry Anders, his criminal history, his failed rehabilitations, and his twisted obsession with finding a way to help Michael Constantine end Kevin's whistle-blower suit.

The media discusses the Walters case. They shine a light on mining accidents and industry practices. They address Kevin's claims of corporate failure to remedy dangerous conditions and the abrupt termination of his long-term career with Consolidated Energy. The media even addresses whether the conditions that Kevin complained about were actually in the Wheeling or Ruston mines. Some suggest that Kevin was confused in what he was urging, as the conditions and the accident did not coexist in the same mine. Some suggest that there are things that they just didn't know being hidden behind a corporate veil.

For the first three of weeks after the kids are recovered, the media appears daily outside of our home, watching where we go and what we do, and they constantly seek any statement. On a couple of occasions, we did make statements thanking everyone for the concern, good wishes, and prayers we received for Joey's recovery. After the first three weeks, the media outside the house slowly begin to dissipate. They return in force with each new story about Joey or the case, sometimes trying to get us on camera.

They run earlier interviews with Kevin, Constantine, and me. They isolate specific words we said along the way and seek to determine whether what we said was actually what we meant. And there is an outpouring of sympathy for our family that is remarkable and touching.

News shows and social media gather public comment about all of it. Some people blame Constantine, suggesting that he had to be behind the attempts of Jerry Anders to blackmail first Kevin, and then me, into dismissing the case. Some callers think that I am responsible by bringing the lawsuit for Kevin in the first place, arguing that we should have turned the other cheek instead of seeking legal recourse. Others respond that the courts exist so that people have a right to have their claims heard and determined, and it is not about retribution but fairness and accountability.

We receive hundreds of letters in the mail. Most are sent in sympathy and express good wishes for Joey's recovery. Some of the letters support us in the fight with Consolidated Energy. A few letters tell us that Anders was right, and the lawsuit should be dismissed or state that the Lord does not approve of litigation. A couple of the stranger ones are threatening in tone.

After ten days of Joey's coma, we fall into a pattern. I go to court or the office in the morning for a few hours and arrive at the hospital around midday. Lisa arrives at the hospital at 7:00 a.m. and stays until 2:00 p.m., and then she tries to catch up on her work for a few hours. We have dinner with Katy around 6:00 p.m., and then Lisa and I go back to the hospital, leaving Katy with Bernie and Kathy, until about 11:00 p.m. Then we come home and try to sleep, which I cannot do. I get no more than two hours a night. When I do fall asleep, I often have nightmares about missing and injured children, my own and others.

Most nights, I stare at the wall, playing the blame game, unable to forgive myself for what happened. In the middle of the night, I look at our family photos. Joey and I hiking through a narrow canyon, all of us sitting around a campfire, and Joey and Katy on their bicycles. Can any of this ever happen again? Will I ever have another conversation with Joey? Will he have the opportunity to live this precious life? Will he come out of this, grow up and go to college, and raise a family of his own? Or will he never experience most of what we cherish in this life? There is no answer to any of these questions, but I keep playing the tape.

When I am at the office, my focus is still the same. I can't stop the tape, and I can't find any rest. When at home, I make coffee and walk around the house. I try to read a book. I look at files that I brought home from work. And I play the tape again. This night has played out like all the others since the event. The sun will be coming up soon, and maybe Joey will awaken today.

Two cups of coffee later, it is 4:30 a.m., and I see that Lisa is awake. She sits up in bed and calls me over. She takes my hand and says, "You didn't do this, Scott. A demented man kidnapped our children." She looks away and then back at me. "Whether you can forgive yourself is something you will have to come to terms with, but if you think you need forgiveness from me, you have it." She puts her arms around me and says, "Now you have to figure out how to sleep so that you can make it through this."

"I know. I am really struggling with letting me off the hook."

"I think you should talk to a counselor. We need you in good shape so that you can help us make it through this."

"Maybe you're right," I say. She gives me a kiss. "And thanks for all the ways you love me."

She smiles. "Ditto, Daddy dude." And that almost makes me cry.

I show up for work at 5:30 a.m. I can't sleep anyway, so I may as well get as much as possible done so that I can get back to the hospital. I am also going to meet with Kevin Walters this morning at eight o'clock, and I sense that this meeting will be emotionally difficult for both of us.

I'm sitting at my desk reviewing documents when I look up and see Donna standing in my doorway. "Come in," I say, waving her to a chair. She sits and I grope for words. "I want to say thank you for keeping everything going while I've been consumed and for ..." I pause, searching for the right word. "For being there for me."

She nods and forces a smile. "You going to be okay?" she asks.

I open my mouth, but I can't make any words come out, leaving no doubt that I am not okay. I know that if I speak, I will come apart midsentence. She seems to know it too, because she doesn't make me answer. She touches my hand and says, "I'm praying Joey will be okay."

I want to say something to her, but I still can't speak, so I swallow hard and nod.

She gives me a warm smile. "Kevin Walters is here. Are you ready for him now?"

I nod slowly. "Okay," I say, doing my best to pull myself together.

"I'll put him in the large conference room," she says, and disappears down the hall. I force myself to stand and walk down the hall to the conference room. I walk through the door, and Kevin stands and reaches out a hand. His eyes are deeply pained as he looks into mine. The reflection of my sorrow is painful to see in his eyes. I shake his hand while I search for words, but I can't find any. Nothing will come out of my mouth at all.

Walters says, "Scott, we can end all this. This has cost you far more than I could ever have imagined, and I never would have … " his words trailed off. He takes a breath and continues, "We can end the case right now. Take the hundred thousand they are offering, or just dump the case, and we'll walk away."

I finally manage to say "Thank you, Kevin. You are a friend." I shake my head. "No," I say, in a suddenly strong voice, "we can't." I lean forward and lace my hands. "This fight has to be for something. You had the guts to stand up and say Consolidated is endangering its workers, and we can't let it end without accomplishing something that helps to protect employees in the future. Accountability will help to do that. Even a significant verdict of settlement will shine light on the issue, but these guys can write a $100,000 check without blinking and bury all of this."

He reflects for a moment and says, "You really want to fight further, Scott? I would understand if you were done with this."

"They ruined a great career because of legitimate safety complaints. I know I have been pretty distracted lately, but I still want to hold them accountable."

He nods. "Okay, I'm with you."

"I mentioned to you that we need to give them a demand for the mediation. I want to start at five million if that is okay with you."

He nods and then adds, "Okay, but I want you to know that this is not about money, and I could just walk away. To tell you the truth, I blame me and my case for what has happened to your family and ..." his words trail off as emotion takes him. He works to hold back tears.

"You didn't do this, Kevin. A madman did this." As I say this, I hear Lisa's words as she attempted to console me the same way. I search for the right words and then add, "For me, it would be a tragedy if what this guy did is successful in ending the litigation. It is one thing to go to trial and lose. It is another to have someone take away your right to pursue a legitimate grievance by blackmail and personal attack. I believe in what we do, and I can't let that happen."

Kevin smiles weakly and says. "It is a pleasure to know you, Scott. You are a good man, my friend."

* * *

It is 6:00 p.m. as I climb the stairs. At the top of the stairs, I find a single door. I push the adjacent buzzer, and there is an electronic tone. A green light goes on, and I walk into what looks like a living room. It is all so stereotypical shrink. I sit on the couch and wait, rubbing my eyes and wondering if I should leave. I just don't want to be here. I'm a guy who grew up with boundaries, and it is hard for me to talk to a stranger, even a licensed stranger, about personal matters. Besides, what can this guy do? He can't wake up Joey. He can't bring the kids back to the innocence of lives before they were kidnapped and held for ransom. He will want me to talk, and I have nothing to say—there is nothing I can say. I remind myself that I promised Lisa I would do this to save me from the blackness that has been eating me up.

The inner sanctum door opens, and a balding man, looking over wire-rimmed glasses, looks at me and smiles. "Mr. Winslow?" he says, as if I might be one of many other patients scheduled for this hour.

"Yes," I say, standing and extending a hand. He shakes it and then gestures me into the interior living room, decorated with a ship motif, whales, and lighthouses, some of which are pictured and some are trinkets assuming spots on bookcases. There are two chairs and one couch. He directs me to the couch with an extended hand, and I sit and wait.

He sits, and there is a moment of silence. He must get this often. Another minute goes by, and he finally says, "How can I help you, Mr. Winslow … Can I call you Scott?"

"Sure," I say. "And I don't think you can help me."

"How do we know until we try?" Dr. Jackson asks with a smile that is intended to break down barriers. "You can call me Pat," he returns. "I've seen a good deal of the media about you and Lisa and the kids, of course, but that just tells me what happened. So you tell me how you're doing."

"Not great," I say. "I have two precious children who were kidnapped and held by a madman. One of them is now in a coma, and I am not sure he will ever be back." My heart is beating loud, and I can feel the blood pulsing through my veins. I look down at the floor and add, "And this is my fault. So you tell me how you think I'm doing."

He nods. "I can tell you're hurting badly." He folds his hands in front of his mouth thoughtfully. "I'm not going to bullshit you, Scott. I have no magic way to make this better, and you know that." He leans back and looks straight at me. "But this is a place where you can say anything you want. Where you can talk, vent, scream—anything at all with no judgment. And maybe we can help you make it through this."

"I want that son of a bitch," I say, shocking myself with the first acknowledgment that I am deeply angry with Anders. "If I found him, I would consider killing him myself." I smile at Pat. "Do you have to turn that statement over to the police as a threat of imminent bodily harm?"

"I don't know. Do you intend to find and kill him?"

"I don't know either. I can't get past step one anyway. I have no idea where the son of a bitch is."

He raises an eyebrow. "Have you thought about how you would do it?"

"Actually, I have considered countless ways, but the one I like best is walking him to the edge of a cliff and pushing him off—after telling him what's coming."

"You want him to know it because you want him to be scared?"

"Damn it, yes. I want him to be scared, just like my children were scared. I want him to know what he's done."

"I get it," he says, nodding. "I can let you in on a little secret, though."

"What?" I ask.

"It probably wouldn't help. I've known people who took their retribution and killed or tortured someone who hurt their family. It didn't bring the catharsis they thought it would. It just brought more pain."

I think about that, glancing at the room around me. It was a well-lit living room where friends would hang and drink beer while watching the game, and I decide that this was no accident. Glancing at the pictures, I ask, "Were you a sea captain in another life?"

"No, I just love the ocean and escape to it when I can. Weekends here and there, vacations. That kind of thing."

I nod, no longer paying attention. "So you've worked with others who went through this? Their children injured or lost, I mean."

"Yes."

"And they make it through?"

"Mostly," he says. I think that this guy is pretty credible—the answers aren't over the top or hard to believe. He is working on his credibility and rapport building, and it must be working because I am listening.

"Sometimes not?" I ask.

"You and I both know that this is not an easy situation. Lots of people suffer some kind of situational anxiety—relationships and careers gone bust, kids on drugs or in jail. And family members dying—shot, stabbed, cancer. It's devastating."

"Holy shit," I say, "now I'm cheered up."

He grins. "I won't bullshit you, Scott. I see some bad stuff. Sometimes people get up and run. Their pain isn't gone; it's just lived with."

"And others?" I ask, rhetorically.

"Others don't do so well." He shrugs. "I don't know if the strength is innate or environmental, but I know that most people can make it through more that they know. And I regard them as heroes for being able to go on. And I will always be there for them."

I hear a slight break in the last words. "Jesus, you've been there yourself."

He is quiet.

"Wow," I say.

"First piece of advice, Scott. Keep talking to Lisa about all this. Doesn't matter what you say, just talk. When you're silent for protracted periods, you start thinking maybe she can't forgive you or that you can't talk anymore, and when you stop connecting, you just remind each other of the worst. Say anything. Words are comforts—both the heart-felt ones and the innocuous day-to-day conversations. Talking to one another keeps you connected despite the elephant in the room."

We talk about both of the kids and their personalities. We talk about Joey's absence and its effect on Katy, and then on Lisa. We talk about Joey and what a great kid he is.

He says, "And now you see him unconscious every day at the hospital."

"Yes."

"You go through emotions throughout your visits?"

"Yeah."

"Can you tell me what you experience?"

"Everything," I say. "I remember the things we've done. Playing catch, walking in the woods, doing homework. And every time I think of something we've done, I play the tape that says we may never get to do it again. I think that he may never wake up and that he may miss the rest of his life, and that is the worst. All the great things that lie ahead: graduations, marriage, family, career. I think that he may never get to know any of it, and my heart crashes in an instant. I stand there, and tears come as I look at him."

"You are doing a good job, Scott, as a parent and in coping. I think that after you leave today, you will be glad you came. I want to encourage you to come back. Just the opportunity to off-load can assist you, my friend." He checks his watch and then says, "Our time is up for today."

I chuckle, and he smiles. "I thought they only said that in the movies," I say.

He grins and says, "Turns out that some of what's in the movies actually happens." His expression turns solemn. "I know that you probably have doubts about all this, Scott, but I hope you'll come back."

I nod. "Okay, thanks," I say, noncommittally, but I'm thinking that I might. As hours go, this one has been less painful than many I'm living.

I leave the office and walk, thinking, and for the first time noticing surroundings. I walk from the business district into a nearby residential neighborhood as dusk settles around me. There are children playing and people watering their front yards. There are dogs on leashes and kids and cats on porches. There are signs of normality. There are wafting smells from barbecues and splashes and screams from backyard pools. For some, it seems that life goes on as usual. Then I think about Lisa and telling her about my experience with Patrick. I'm not sure the visit will help me get any more sleep, but there is something positive in being able to share the pain with a good listener.

* * *

In the morning, I return a call from Lee Henry.

"Yes."

"Lee, it's Scott."

"Oh my God, my friend, I'm so sorry."

"Thank you, Lee." I take a deep breath, fighting off rising emotion, before I can go on. "Have you been able to keep our friend captive and under wraps?"

"Yeah, he's at the Sheraton. He started making noise about leaving all this behind when I served him with the subpoena you guys gave me for his deposition next Friday."

"Do you think he will stay?"

"Yes. He'll stay."

"You sound confident."

"I can be persuasive."

"Don't tell me anymore. Does he still have all of his parts?"

"Yep. He is still in one annoying piece."

"Have you talked to him about the documents we are working on?"

"No, I'm keeping that in my back pocket."

"Okay, I think that's a good decision." I thought momentarily and then said, "I hear you have a photo of this Mr. Valentine character in one of his incarnations."

"I do, and I have a couple of law enforcement friends working on it with facial recognition software. As of yesterday, there was no match in their data banks."

"Can you get them to run the picture against Consolidated Energy employees in the region?

"Yeah, if you are okay picking up the additional tab."

"Let's do it. I really want to know who that guy is," I say.

"You bet, and I'll keep pushing."

"Lee was quiet a moment and then says, "Scott, I am really so sorry …"

I interrupt. "Thanks, Lee. It's hard for me to talk about, and I'm trying really hard to hold myself together."

"I understand. Take care and don't worry about our friend; he'll be there next Friday."

When we hang up, I return a call from Bob Harris.

"Scott, Jesus, man, I'm really sorry."

"Thanks." I take a deep breath. "I know you are waiting for our settlement demand in advance of the mediation. Our settlement demand is $5 million." I don't wait for a response. I add, "This guy is Constantine's brother-in-law." I'm not sure why I say it. Maybe I just need to hear the reaction.

"Yes, he is." He pauses and says, "Mike Constantine wants me to assure you that he had no knowledge of Anders pursuing you or Mr. Walters to drop the case. He says that he will come to your office to tell you that in person if you would like, so that you can look him in the eye while he says it."

"Thanks for that."

After an awkward, quiet moment, Harris says, "Okay. I will pass on your settlement demand." There was a moment of quiet. "I have a little girl, and I'm really so sorry, Scott."

'Thank you, Bob. May your baby always stay safe."

He clears this throat. "Thanks, Scott." A brief pause and then, "One more thing, I assume the deposition of Miller that you set for next Friday is off given that no one can find him."

"No, it's on. He has been subpoenaed, and I expect him to appear."

There is a protracted silence, which I interpret as surprise, and then Harris replies, "Okay, see you then."

Chapter 27

June 20, 2016

On Monday evening as we are finishing dinner and are preparing to run back to the hospital, there is a knock at the door. I open it to see an attractive woman who appears to be in her late forties. She wears elegant clothing and a distressed expression.

"Are you Scott Winslow?"

"Yes," I say and wait.

"I am so sorry to bother you, Mr. Winslow, but I have to talk to you."

"All right, would you like to step inside?" I ask.

She hesitates and then says, "Okay, thank you. I hope that I am not disturbing you."

"No, it's okay," I say, still waiting to find out who she is and what this is about.

I wave toward the couch, and she sits. Lisa and I sit down on the love seat across the coffee table from her. This woman looks like she might burst into tears any moment. She takes a deep breath and says, "My name is Victoria Constantine. I don't know if you know who I am—"

I am instantly angry, and I interrupt her. "I know who you are, and if your husband sent you to talk about the case at all, it is not going to happen."

"No, definitely not. Michael did not send me, and I don't want to talk about the case at all."

"Okay," I say, "so what do you want?"

"Mr. and Mrs. Winslow, Jerry Anders is my brother. He is deeply troubled. I just want to tell you personally how sorry I am for what he did. I know that in some twisted way he thought he was helping us." She shakes her head and adds, "He has done many bad things in the past, and I have tried to help him to find his way. This time I can't forgive him." She draws a deep breath and pushes back a tear. "I am here to let you know how sorry I am and to tell you that if there is anything I can do for your family, I will do it." She looks tired and vulnerable. And genuine.

Lisa says, "Thank you, Ms. Constantine. I can't think of anything that you can do, but we appreciate the thought and your concern."

I say, "Thank you, Ms. Constantine. The support is appreciated. Sorry I assumed the worst."

"There is something I would like to do, for me, but it may be too early for you. Don't answer today, but please consider allowing me to pay for the medical expenses you incur in taking care of your son. I mean now and all those needed in the future."

"We can find a way to pay what we have to," Ms. Constantine," I say.

"I understand that. It would be a favor to me to let me help. I know that nothing can ever make up for the horrible actions of my brother, but I can try to help those that he hurt. That's what I want most."

Lisa smiles at her. "We will give that serious thought, Ms. Constantine. Thank you."

We walk her to the door, and she turns and hugs Lisa, and then me. "Thank you both so much for seeing me. And please, let me do something to help you."

As she walks to her car, Lisa says, "I understand. She has her own kind of pain."

In response, I can only nod.

* * *

June 24, 2016

On Friday morning at 10:15 a.m., I am sitting in my conference room with a stack of documents and my notes for the deposition of Carl Miller. Bob Harris, the court reporter, and the videographer all sit at the ready. Kevin Walters sits next to me, and an in-house attorney from Consolidated has come along to witness the testimony and sits next to Harris. We make small talk while we wait for Miller, who is now fifteen minutes late. I am a little worried, but Lee said he would get Miller here, so I haven't given up hope. Bob Harris's mood seems elevated by the thought that Miller might not show.

At 10:20 a.m., Miller walks in and apologizes for being late, saying he was caught in traffic. We all shake hands, and then I have him attach his microphone to his lapel. The videographer announces that we are all present for the deposition of Carl Miller in connection with the matter of Kevin Walters v. Consolidated Energy and Michael Constantine. He states the case number, our starting time, and where we are. We introduce ourselves and our clients who are present for the record. The court reporter then has Miller raise his right hand and has him agree that all of his testimony will be true and correct, so help him God. At that point, I begin to question Miller.

"Please state your full name for the record, sir."

"Carl Edward Miller."

"Are you employed, Mr. Miller?"

"I am now retired from the county."

"Are you here today pursuant to a subpoena from my office?"

"I am."

"I'm sure that you have things you would rather be doing, so we will move it along as fast as we can, but we need your testimony about certain occurrences while you worked for the county. Understand?"

"You are testifying under oath today, just as if you were in a court of law, and the oath that you have been administered subjects you to the same penalties of perjury. Understand?"

"Yes, sir."

"Please wait to hear the entire question before you respond. I will then allow you to complete your answer before I move to the next question. Agreed?

"Yes."

"If you do not know the answer to a question, it is perfectly acceptable to say you don't know, or you don't recall. No one wants you to guess at information you do not have."

"Okay."

"On the other hand, if you have a best estimate about a date or time of some occurrence, or a general recollection of some event, I am entitled to that information. Do you understand that distinction?"

"Yes, I do."

"If objections are made, because we do not have a judge to rule on them, they will be addressed later. Once the objection is made for the record, you answer the question that is pending. Understood?"

"I understand."

Over the next hour, I take him through his dates of employment with the county, all of the positions he has held and the duties of each position. We talk at length about his duties, responsibilities, and authority in the final position, which he held during the ten years preceding Kevin Walters's termination from Consolidated.

Then I ask, "So, it was part of your duties to monitor the violations that were discovered at both the Wheeling and the Ruston mines operated by Consolidated Energy?"

"Yes."

"Was it part of your duty to secure compliance with the legal requirements to operate these mines?

Harris says, "I object, lacks foundation, vague and ambiguous."

"You understand my question, Mr. Miller?"

"Yes."

"Was it also part of your job to follow up with mine operators such as Consolidated to assure correction of deficiencies found in their operations?"

"Same objection."

"Yes."

"At some point, were you asked to alter official records?"

"Yes."

"In what manner?"

"I was asked to switch the Ruston and Wheeler records and get rid of anything inconsistent with that switch."

I glance at Harris, who looks visibly distressed. "Did you do it?"

"Ultimately, yes."

"You say you ultimately did so. Did you resist at first?"

"Yes."

"Were there promises or threats to get you to make this switch?"

"There were both. It started with promises of an early retirement and additional cash."

"Did you refuse that?"

"At first I did."

"What changed your mind?"

"Next came the threats." I took him through the specifics, and he told me about the six o'clock news reporting a bribery investigation of county employees. He said that he had never taken money before in connection with any violation, but that they had people ready to testify that they told him of violations he did not report and paid him not to report these incidents. He felt he could not disprove those statements, so he should take retirement.

"Did more than one person make the promises and threats you described?"

"No."

"Who made these promises and threats?"

"A man who called himself Mr. Valentine."

"How many times did you see him?"

"Three times on three consecutive days."

I have him describe the specifics of each meeting, and he details them just as he had for Lee Henry.

"Do you have an understanding of why he wanted you to switch the Ruston and Wheeler records?"

"He didn't tell me, but I certainly had a good idea of the reason."

"What was your understanding in that regard?"

Harris interjects, "I object. This lacks foundation and calls for speculation. This witness does not have sufficient information to answer that question. You are asking him to speculate."

"We only need a basis for the objection, Bob. The full-blown argument can be delivered when we talk to the judge."

"What was your understanding, sir?"

"Well, there had been a recent explosion, and someone was trying to obscure the connection between that explosion and the conditions resulting in violations that had not been corrected leading to the explosion."

"What did Mr. Valentine look like?"

"He looked different every visit." He describes the closely trimmed beard and bad wig that characterized his appearance at the time of the first visit, the wilder beard of the second, and the clean-shaven double chin on the third.

By about two o'clock, he had fully testified to his switching of the records, all of the events that led him to that point, and the multiple descriptions of the blackmailer. He also verified correct records for Wheeler and for Ruston when shown each as exhibits.

After we take a break, it is Harris's opportunity to question Miller.

"Good afternoon, Mr. Miller. My name is Bob Harris, and I represent the defendants in the case Mr. Walters brought against them."

"Yes, sir."

"Did you ever determine who the person who called himself Mr. Valentine really was?"

"No, sir. I never did."

"So you cannot establish that he was an employee of Consolidated, correct?"

"Correct."

"Or that he was in any way related to or hired by Consolidated, correct?"

"Correct."

"You just have no idea who this guy is, right?"

"Right."

"When you retired, where did you move?"

"Magnolia, Mississippi."

"Why?"

"Nice place, and I wanted a change of lifestyle."

"Did you also want to be far away from the place where you had altered official county records?"

"Yes, sir."

"Did you know that it was against the law to alter public records?"

My turn to jump in. "Mr. Miller, you do not have counsel here, but if I represented you I would tell you that you have a Fifth Amendment right against self-incrimination, which you can assert to answer a question that would be admitting a potential crime."

Harris glares at me. "That is not your job, counsel. You don't represent him."

"I know. Didn't I just say that?"

"You have no business instructing him not to answer any question."

"I never instructed him not to answer. We can read back the record if you like. I simply informed him of rights that we all possess. He can choose whether to exercise those rights."

Miller replied, "My answer is that as a rule, yes, but here I was being blackmailed. I certainly knew that was against the law, but it didn't help me any."

At that moment, my partner appears at the conference room door. "Scott, I need to talk to you about another matter. It will only take a couple of minutes."

"Sure," I say. "Excuse me, everyone. We'll take just a couple of minutes before we resume."

I walk down the hall, and Bill waves me into his office. "What's happening?"

"We have a couple of cops sitting in the waiting room. They are waiting for the depo to be over, and I think that they are going to arrest Miller."

I nod. "Did you call Lee?"

"Yeah, he's on his way over now."

"Did you tell him to come in the back entrance so he isn't seen by these guys?"

He nods. "How much longer?"

"I think we are pretty close. I am guessing that Harris has another half hour, which means we'll be done a little before four."

"I'll have Lee wait for you in your office."

"That works, thanks."

Bill smiles and shakes his head. "This is pretty crazy. I hope it works."

"Yeah. You and me both."

I return to the conference room, and we get under way again. Harris asks Miller about the specifics of record entries and what certain abbreviations mean.

"Have you had conversations about this matter with anyone, at any time since speaking to the man you described as Mr. Valentine?" Harris asks.

Miller nods. "Yes. I talked to an investigator about the matter."

"Do you know who this investigator was representing?"

"I believe that he works with Mr. Winslow."

"What did he look like?"

"A tall man. Short dark hair with a little gray and a wraparound beard. Really penetrating eyes. Maybe a little over six feet."

"And what conversation did you have with this man?"

"We discussed the same things I testified to today. He asked me about who approached me and what was said. I told him the same thing I have told all of you today. Then he asked me to describe the guy, and I gave him the same description of the disguises that we just talked about."

"And where were you served with this subpoena?," Harris asks.

"In Magnolia, Mississippi."

"Were you aware a California subpoena is not effective to compel you to come here from Mississippi? Did the investigator tell you that?"

At this point, I am anticipating Miller saying that Lee didn't really give him any choice. Instead, he just says, "No, he didn't tell me that."

"So you came all the way here based on a subpoena that was not effective?"

I think this is offered in an attempt to get Miller pissed at us so he will stop cooperating. I respond with, I Object. You are arguing with the witness. He doesn't know whether the subpoena was effective to compel his presence or not."

"You can answer," Harris says.

"I don't know. If you say so," Miller says.

"I may be done," Harris says. "Let me just review my notes for a couple of minutes to confirm."

I step out of the room and go to my office, where Lee waits.

"Hi, Lee."

"Scott." He shakes my hand.

"Okay, I think we will be ready in a minute or so. Are you set?"

"Ready."

I return to the conference room, where Harris confirms that he is done. I state that I have no further questions, and we put a stipulation about how the transcript is to be delivered on the record for the court reporter. The videographer does his sign-off at 4:05 p.m., and I give a subtle wave to Miller, and he follows me. We walk to my office, where Lee waits.

I say, "You know Lee."

"Yeah," Miller says.

"So one thing we thought was possible has happened," I say. "We have two cops sitting in the lobby, and I think they plan to arrest you."

Miller looks terrified. He looks at Lee and then back to me in desperation. "So that's it?"

"No," Lee says. He opens a folder and then says, "Here is an Oregon driver's license. You are now Jason Wilcox, and you live in Eugene, Oregon. The address is your new apartment. I have never been there, so I hope it's nice. You owe me $1,800 for first month's rent and security deposit. You can send me the cash. Here is a credit card as a secondary ID. We are going to get you out the back door with all this."

"Really?"

"Yeah, but it never happened. You got that?" Lee says.

"Yes, I have it."

Lee says, "Okay, now these guys know where you were living in Mississippi but not your full name. Cash out of your bank, and get out of your house there right away. They will connect the dots if you stay there, just like I did. Also, no deposits from you in your old life to you in your new one. A bank deposit from Darden in Mississippi to Wilcox in Oregon will connect the dots in a hurry. Got it?"

"Yes."

"All right, let's go," and Lee hustles Miller down the hall and out the back door.

Three minutes later I walk into the lobby where two officers wait. I look at them, taking in their presence for the first time. "Good afternoon, gentlemen. Can I help you with something?" I offer, extending a hand.

"We are looking for Carl Miller, and understand that he's here today."

"He was," I say. "I think he just left a few minutes ago."

"How? How did he leave?"

"I think he went out the back door to the parking lot."

"Which way is the back door?" the taller of the two cops asks.

"Come with me, I'll take you."

"Okay," he says. "'Take the front and go around,' he says to the other officer, who nods and takes off.

I walk him to the rear door, and we go outside. "Any idea what kind of car he came in?"

"No."

He looks around the lot; no cars moving. He sees the other officer come around the side of the building shaking his head. "Okay, thanks," he says to me, and the officers walk to a midpoint to confer. I go back inside and watch the two officers from my office window. After a few minutes, I see them walk toward their marked car and drive off. I guess that somewhere in the midst of all that, Harris left the office. I walk down the hall and into Bill's office, where he is seated behind his desk. He looks up and asks, "What kind of crazy shit are you getting me into?"

I grin. "Interesting day, don't you think?"

"Are they going to be able to track that guy?"

"Probably sooner or later. After all, Lee did it." I add, "But we made it a little harder than it was by eliminating a few connections between his old and new lives."

"Or maybe by making us the connections they will be looking for," he says.

"Something like that, yeah."

Chapter 28

July 20, 2016

It has now been five weeks from Joey's injury, and he has not awakened. It is 8:00 p.m. on a Wednesday, and we are awaiting Dr. Mitchell's arrival to provide a medical update based upon the latest testing. Lisa is holding Joey's hand, and I am pacing by the window. Soft music plays in the background, but the room is otherwise quiet.

Dr. Mitchell walks in wearing his usual garb, peels the blue surgical cap from his head and says, "Sorry to keep you waiting a few minutes."

I force a smile and say, "We have nowhere else to go."

Lisa and I look at him and wait. He pauses before he begins, which is seldom a good sign. "The swelling around the brain has not been reduced. The challenges we now face are that Joey's blood pressure is getting too low, even with the medication we are feeding him, and his respiration is weak."

"You mean his breathing?" Lisa asks.

"Yes, his breathing." He furrows his brow. "So we have to make a choice. Either we start reducing the anesthesia, or we put him on a respirator."

"Life support?" I say, almost involuntarily.

"That term has a pejorative connotation because it is associated with the end of life, but respirators are often interim steps in treatment. It doesn't automatically mean that there is no return."

"If we reduce the anesthesia?" Lisa asks.

He nods. "Then his respiration and blood pressure will strengthen, but we diminish the chances of reducing the brain swelling."

Lisa starts to cry at the thought of her boy on a respirator. I am scared. This now sounds like it won't get better. It feels like we may lose our boy.

"What are you recommending?" I ask, nervously.

"I recommend that we use the respirator and make it easier for Joey to breathe while he fights the swelling."

I look at the deep sadness on Lisa's face, and my heart breaks. She says, "I guess we have no real choice."

We go home that night knowing that when we see Joey again, he will be hooked up to more tubes and machines. It is hard to find any reason for optimism.

* * *

The next morning, I am in the office putting out sparks before they become fires. I am obsessed with Joey's condition, and I haven't slept. I want the focus of work, hopeful that thinking about something else for a few minutes will serve as some kind of temporary escape from the world I now inhabit. I work at a frenetic pace looking for that diversion from the reality that overcomes my mind in waves. I generate discovery on three cases, oversee responses to discovery on two others, and prepare for an upcoming deposition. In other words, a normal day in the office. It is almost 11:00 a.m. when Donna buzzes and says, "Scott, I have Jared McGuire on line one."

"Really. Did he say what it is about?"

"I asked. He said it's personal."

Last thing I knew, I didn't have anything personal going on with the assistant district attorney. "Okay, I got it. Thanks."

I hit a button on the phone. "Jared, our paths haven't crossed in a long time. How are you?"

"I'm okay. Before we start, let me say I am so sorry about what happened to your son."

"Thanks, I appreciate your concern."

"Scott, we need to talk. Can I stop by this morning? How would noon work for you?"

"That's fine. See you then."

When I hang up, Donna stands at my open door. "Strange call. What did he want?"

"He stayed mysterious about it. Says he needs to talk to me. It sounds like a warning call of some kind, so I'm running through our client list in my head, considering whether any of them might be about to be picked up and charged with something. No criminal controversy comes to mind, but you never know."

"Yeah, I remember the Briton case," she says.

"Exactly." Briton was a wrongful termination case, in the midst of which the employer swore out a criminal complaint contending that Mr. Briton had stolen important documents from the company. Ultimately, the case was dismissed for lack of evidence. "It is likely some surprise like that. Although, nobody gave us a heads-up on that one."

"I didn't know that you and McGuire were close."

"We aren't. We see each other at Bar Association meetings and greet each other as we pass in the courthouse hallways. That's the extent of it."

"Hmm. Maybe it is not a heads-up then," she says.

"Right, maybe he's coming to raise money for DA softball, or to arrest me for being a public pain in the ass."

"I'd bet on the latter," she says, grinning.

Turns out, she was more accurate than we knew.

At noon, I greet Jared McGuire. We grab coffee, and I lead the way to our smaller conference room. Jared is about fifty and built like an offensive tackle. Even with a body that size, his head looks large. He has big perceptive eyes that don't look away, and lots of wavy white hair.

Jared sits back in his chair and puts his fingertips together at the base of his chin. "So let me get to why I'm here," he says, evenly. "There has been a complaint that you aided a suspect in evading the police."

"What?" I say, incredulously.

"Yeah. It seems that you had Carl Miller in this very room and helped him exit before police waiting in your lobby could get to him."

I smile. "You're not serious?"

"I am."

"Jared, you would have to agree with me that the essential elements of such an accusation would include showing knowledge on my part that Miller was wanted by the police and that, knowing that, I actually knowingly assisted him in making a getaway. Am I right?"

"Essentially, yeah."

"Well, neither of those things are true."

"I had no idea that the police were looking for Miller before the deposition of Miller. After we completed the deposition, he said he was parked out back, so he used the employee door to get directly to the parking lot. There were two officers sitting in the lobby, but he had already gone before I spoke to them." I shake my head. "It's not like Miller is a friend of mine. He was here because we managed to get him served with a subpoena, and he didn't have a choice."

McGuire is quiet, and then nods reluctantly. "I'm hearing what I thought I would hear," he says. "Doesn't sound like there is anything to this complaint."

"I'm surprised to hear from you about this rather than a detective."

"I know. Two reasons for that. First, with me handling it, I can go more directly to a finding that no action should be taken on the complaint. Second, I heard that Miller admitted to changing official records, and I wanted you to tell me if that is true."

"Yeah," I said, "that is true."

He nods. "Did he say why?"

"He said that he was blackmailed into doing it."

"Really. By whom?"

"A guy who called himself Mr. Valentine."

McGuire furrows his brow. "Let me know when your transcript is done, will you? I want to order a copy."

"Sure thing."

"Sorry for the interruption." He raises the hand holding the cup, "And thanks for the coffee." We shake hands, and I walk him from the office. Carl Miller was lucky to be a new man in a new city, and I would really be in some shit if it was known that I helped set it up and wasn't sharing where he could be found. I knew all this, but I thought that Miller had been fucked over quite enough and could use a little help. I'd have to wait and see whether that empathy would come back to bite me on the ass.

I put a call in to Lee that went directly to voice mail. "You've reached me because you know who I am and how to reach me. Now tell me who you are and how to get even."

"Hi, Lee. This is Scott Winslow. I just had a visit from Assistant DA McGuire regarding our mutual friend, and I wanted to give you a heads-up in case he decides to call you at some point."

Twenty minutes later, Donna said, "Lee Henry, line three."

I punch the button and say, "Hi, Lee. I just had a visit from Jared McGuire, and I wanted to give you a heads-up in case he calls you at some point."

"Wow," Lee says. "Those sneaky little bastards."

"The DA?"

"Yep. At the same time you were meeting with McGuire, I got a visit from Detective Art Scully. He wanted to talk about Carl Miller, too. Seems that our friends at the DA's office wanted to assure that you and I did not have the opportunity to confer before the inquiry was complete."

"Wow is right," I say. "What did you tell them?"

"The truth. I told them that I tracked Miller to Mississippi, and he was living under an assumed as one Eric Dardon. I told them that I paid him a visit and that I was persuasive in convincing him to return to California based on your deposition subpoena."

"How did the detective react?"

"Scully frowned when I talked about being convincing to Miller. He probably thinks that I beat the shit out of the guy, or threatened to, but he doesn't have any information to suggest I did anything inappropriate, so I just gave him my nice guy smile."

"You'll have to show me that one sometime. Sounds unfamiliar."

"Very funny. Anyway, I shared the Mississippi address, told him what I could share about how I got to him. I had to leave a couple of steps out because I accessed certain info I shouldn't be able to get. I told him that they should try him at that same address. I just left out the part about him now being a different guy in a different state. Hopefully, Miller was careful about not leaving tracks to his new life because these guys are going to look."

"What did McGuire say to you?" Lee asks.

"He suggested that I might have helped him to get away while we had those cops in the lobby. I told him that I wasn't aware of any warrants on him, and I certainly had no reason to make him stay around after his testimony."

"I'm glad we were on the same page." Lee adds, again, "Those tricky little bastards."

I laugh. "Let me know if you hear anything else, and I'll do the same. Hopefully, there is just no sign of Mr. Dardon in Mississippi anymore. The neighbors can say he just up and moved out in the middle of the night."

"Amen and farewell to Mr. Dardon—poof."

"See you, Lee. Take care."

"You, too."

* * *

August 3, 2016

The day of the mediation in the Walters v. Consolidated Energy case, Kevin Walters and I arrive at Jake Billings's mediation office early. The office consists of a lobby area and reception desk, Jake's personal office, a kitchen, and five large conference rooms. Jake Billings was a thirty-year employment attorney who no longer represents clients. He mediates employment cases of every conceivable sort, every day, regularly filling his conference rooms with multiple parties and insurance carriers. Jake's assistant, Sara, greets us with a smile. "Good morning, Mr. Winslow," she says enthusiastically, extending a hand that I shook. "And Mr. Walters, nice to meet you, sir." Kevin also shakes her hand. "Jake has you in Conference Room 3; if you'll follow me, please." We followed her down the hall to a room that contained a conference room table large enough for ten people. "Coffee, tea, soda, and food are in the kitchen down the hall to your left. Mr. Winslow, I know that you know your way around from previous visits."

"I do. Thank you, Sara."

"Internet access info is on the credenza. If you need anything else, please let me know. I'll tell Jake that you're here, and he'll be in shortly."

"Great, thanks," I say, unpacking my computer.

When Sara leaves the room, Kevin says, "I want to thank you for everything, Scott. However this comes out, you have been great to work with, and both Julia and I think very highly of you."

"Likewise, Kevin. It is a pleasure to work with you." I pause and add, "And to get to know you. You and Julia are remarkable people." Looking into his eyes, I could see that there was something else he wanted to say. I'm guessing it was something about the family tragedy that had taken us, but he was struggling for the right words. He was relieved of the struggle when Jake Billings gave a knock at the door and then walked into the room. Billings is just over six feet tall, slim, and occupies that area somewhere between a receding hairline and the early stages of balding. He wears a nice suit and glasses, and has a thoughtful expression on his face.

A week ago, I submitted a twenty-five page brief to Jake's office, complete with exhibits that included our expert analysis and a summary of the deposition testimony of Carl Miller. I knew from my prior experience with Jake that he would have read all of it by the time I arrived. Today he will know the strengths and weaknesses of both sides and be ready to use them against one party or another in his efforts to shape a settlement of the case. Jake will look for anything that might settle a case, whether it involved money damages, returning the plaintiff to a position at the same or a different company, and sometimes a mea culpa from an individual responsible for a dubious employment decision.

Jake extends his hand to Kevin first. "Mr. Walters, good to meet you. You have obviously had a remarkable history with Consolidated and accomplished a great deal to make them a better company."

Kevin shakes his hand and says, "It's really good to hear that, thanks."

"Doesn't just come from me. Michael Constantine acknowledges that you are very talented and brought a great deal to the table." Kevin looks a little shocked. Jake sees the expression and adds, "It's really true. They know you are good."

"I'm just a little shocked," Kevin says. "I heard that frequently while I worked there, but since this lawsuit, they've been working hard to paint me differently."

"Nature of the beast," Jake says, "but it doesn't alter reality."

Jake next reaches out a hand to me, and as we shake, says, "Good to see you again, Scott. Very interesting case here."

"It is," I agree.

"I hope all goes well with your son's recovery," he says soberly.

"Thanks, Jake."

We all sit down around the conference table, with Jake's position closest to the door so that he can easily move between rooms. "Can I call you Kevin?" Jake asks.

"Yes, sure."

"Kevin, knowing Scott, you and he have talked about this proceeding, but I do want to hit a couple of the highlights. First, I have no power to compel anyone to do anything. I will work with both sides to reach an agreement while you all still control your own destiny. That is, before the case is turned over to a judge and twelve people selected for their lack of information about your case and your whole industry. Next, I am having everyone sign an agreement acknowledging the law in California that everything that is said here today is confidential and stays that way. People are not able to speak freely if they believe that what they say working to get a case settled can come back to bite them later on, so we have laws that make everything that is said at a mediation confidential and unusable at trial. It means that whatever you say today, no one can put you on the witness stand at trial and say, 'But at the mediation, didn't you say the opposite?' And I cannot be subpoenaed to testify at trial regarding who said what at the mediation."

"I understand," Kevin says.

"One caveat," Jake adds. "Although what we say today is confidential, if a party learns something today, there is nothing that stops them seeking evidence to prove it by other than what was said at the mediation."

"Got it," Kevin acknowledges.

Jake continues. "Today you will hear me make arguments that I get from the other room. Doesn't mean I agree with them; it means those are the positions that the other side is taking. Whether we agree with those positions or not, it's important for you to know what they are saying and what their positions will be if you go to trial."

"I agree," Kevin says.

Jake nods, having completed the informational part of his introduction. He then looks at me and says, "I read all of your material."

"I knew you would," I say, grinning.

"You have a demand of $5 million, and they have a darned good opening offer of $100,000. Correct?"

"Those are the numbers, yes."

He chuckled. "Not conceding that 100K is a good opening?"

"It would be in some cases. Not so much here."

He laughs more openly. "Yep, that's the Scott Winslow I remember."

He looks at Kevin and says, "Kevin, are there any questions that you have about this process before we get down to it?"

"No, not at this point."

Jake looks at me. "I see how you got to your demand, given Kevin's salary and bonus structure, but I hope you are coming with an open mind toward achieving a viable number." This is mediator speak for,

"I hope you will reduce that demand a lot in order for me to get this deal done."

So I give him my equally vague response. "We are certainly here to make good faith efforts to get the case resolved, but we believe that our assessment of value is pretty reasonable."

I deliver this with sincerity, but I would challenge him to find any real message in that answer.

"All right, I'm going to have an initial meeting with the other side. I will be back. You know where to find coffee and food, right?"

"Yes, thanks, Jake."

When Jake walks out, Kevin said, "I'm not sure what you told him about whether we would negotiate or not."

"That's because you were listening carefully, and I didn't really say much. Just keeping our cards close to our vest until we get going."

"I'm following your lead on this, Scott. Like we talked about, I won't react to any offers as they happen, but I want you to know that I will do what you suggest. Julia is on board also."

"Thanks, Kevin. I want you guys to know that I want to do what is right for you. We went through a horror show with Jerry Anders, but I can't let that crazy man succeed in affecting your case. You can never let the terrorists win."

Kevin could only nod.

After almost an hour, Jake Billings returns and sits down.

"So they want me to begin by telling you that your demand is unreasonable. So there you go." He looks at his notes and then says, "Let's get right to key issues. How are you going to establish the connection between Kevin's complaints and the termination?"

"Kevin complained about the failure to correct deficiencies that were serious and ongoing. We will have testimony concerning what the deficiencies would have cost to correct, and it was appreciable. The accident that occurred relates to those deficiencies, and there will be little doubt that the existing conditions are what can cause exactly what happened. They give rise to the likelihood that pockets of methane build up. And we all know what happens when a tunnel full of methane gas meets with a spark in one of a hundred different ways." I pause to breathe. "We also have Carl Miller's testimony that he switched the records, so that we can establish the conditions existed and had been the subject of violations, but remained uncorrected in the mine where the explosion took place. Add to that the fact that Kevin has an incredible performance history, a bonus reflective of his successful performance prior to his termination, personal acknowledgment by Constantine in a group setting that Kevin was outstanding, and several co-executives who will testify about Kevin's competence and support the fact that he had complained about these dangerous conditions."

Billings nods. "Let's talk about the Mr. Valentine character that was mentioned in your brief. How do you establish that he was an agent of the defendants and not some kind of a loose cannon? They say that you can't, and they will make motions to exclude any reference to him at trial. I know it is a sensitive area, but you did have one of those who wanted the case dismissed, right? I mean, can you connect him to the defendants?"

"Not yet, but it doesn't matter." I let that settle a moment. "Now that we have established that the mine where the injuries occurred is the mine where the danger had been presented because of prior documented violations that went uncorrected, I don't have to care who Mr. Valentine might be."

"Why?"

"Well, with Miller's testimony, I can establish that the mine with the uncorrected citations is the same mine where the explosion happened. I don't need to establish how Valentine compelled him to make the switch in order to establish that he made the switch."

"I don't disagree, but if you can associate Valentine's blackmail acts with instructions from the guys in the other room, the punitive damage exposure gets stronger."

"I agree, and we are working on identifying Valentine. But even if we never do, I think that establishing Kevin was fired because he raised serious safety issues and that those same safety issues led to a disaster that could have been prevented had they done what was right for their employees will provide significant opportunity for punitive damages."

"Kevin, how are you doing these days?" Jake asks.

"I'm okay. Thanks in large part to Scott. I mean, when I came to see him I was crestfallen. My whole career was spent with these guys, and I gave everything I had. It has certainly changed my life, but Scott is helping me see what these guys did and that helps me move forward with life."

"What is a good resolution of this case for you, Kevin?"

I jump into this one. "Kevin, don't talk numbers. You and I do that together. If you have other thoughts about what might aid in resolution of the matter, feel free to share them."

Billings asks, "What about returning to work? I know you and Constantine go back a long ways. Is that something you would consider?"

"I don't think so." He shakes his head thoughtfully, and then says, "I used to love the company, and Michael showed his true colors with what he did to me. I don't know that I can ever trust them again."

Jake looks at me. "So do you have a counter for me?"

"It's their turn."

"What?"

"Look, they offered to settle for $100,000. We countered at $5 million. Doesn't that make it their turn?"

"There's a pretty crazy crowd in there. If I can't take something back to them, we may hit a wall early."

"Who is in that room there, and which of them is calling the shots?" I ask.

Billings says, "Bob Harris, Michael Constantine, an in-house lawyer named Jeffers, a risk manager, a carrier with coverage above their retention, and an adjuster. They have the board on alert in case a deal is made."

"So who is calling the shots?"

"Harris is doing most of the talking, but Constantine is the guy to convince."

"Who happens to be the same guy who is personally implicated in all this," I say.

"Correct."

"You can tell them we will take 4.75, but they need to make a significant six-figure move before we go any further."

He shakes his head. "I'm not sure they're ready for that, but I'll give them the message and make the case for why that makes sense."

He departs for the other conference room, and I walk back to see Kevin and to check e-mail. It is ninety minutes before Jake emerges from the defense room. He sits down and says, "They are at $275,000. They continue to tell me that you can't prove who Valentine is, so you can prove that they had any role in Miller's activities."

"I don't think that matters," I reply. "Like I said, once it is shown that Miller changed the records, they have serious uncorrected violations in the same mine where the explosion occurred. This not only makes our case, but they are also probably thinking will come to be a public relations nightmare for Consolidated. We are happy to play out the hand if that's how they want it to go."

We spend additional time talking through the facts. Jake periodically asks Kevin a question, and it is clear he is impressed with the responses and will reinforce to the other side what a good witness Kevin will be if we wind up at trial. Jake considers in silence, and then says, "You are too far apart. I am concerned that if we continue at this rate, we'll hit a wall shortly. Will you guys go to one million if they go to five hundred thousand?"

We ask for time to consider and Kevin and I discuss it for twenty minutes. We then refuse their proposed range, but tell Jake we will go to three million if they go to one million. He disappears for almost two hours, which is not a good sign.

Jake walks into the room and sits down with us at 2:45 p.m. "They will go to six hundred thousand if you go to one million. That's the most I could get them to move."

"Thanks for your hard work, Jake. Looks like they are not ready to settle the case for what we believe it's worth. Please tell them we appreciate the effort, but we are moving forward with the case." I stand and put my jacket on, and Kevin follows my lead.

"I understand, but don't go yet. Let me tell them this is it. That you're leaving unless they do something significant enough to make you stay."

I nod. "Okay, a few more minutes can't hurt."

Jake nodded and left the room. It was 4:10 p.m. when we saw him again.

"They are offering $600,000 and the opportunity for Kevin to return to work at the same salary he was making when he left. They will give you a two-year contract with right to terminate for cause or with six months' severance if the termination is without cause."

Kevin and I discussed it for a half hour, and then relayed to Jake that Kevin would not return to work for them for the reasons previously discussed. We countered the $600,000 offer with $2.5 million. It was then 5:20 p.m. We next saw Jake at 7:10 p.m., and he was looking pretty beat up.

"You look a little the worse for wear," I joke.

Jake grinned. "It is an intense environment in there."

"Is Michael angry?" Kevin asks.

"No, he's the voice of sanity in that room. And I really believe that he wants you to come back." Kevin listens quietly but does not respond.

"Is there another offer?" I ask.

"There is: $650,000, last, best, and final, with confidentiality regarding the settlement terms. And the offer also remains open for you to return to work."

Kevin shakes his head. "I hear what you are saying, but I'm not sure that I can ever trust Michael again."

Kevin and I speak privately again, and then I walk over to Jake's office. All staff are now gone, so it is just he and I in the area. "We are going to decline the offer," I say.

Jake takes on a pained look. "Are you sure? I mean, I really think that they are getting reasonable." He pauses. "Scott, my gut is that Constantine is sincere about wanting your guy to come back to work.

I've seen a lot of empty offers, and I don't think this is one of them. They really believe Walters has a great deal to offer Consolidated."

"Better late than never," I say.

"All right," Jake says, "but I'm going to keep working this. This case should get settled."

"I appreciate that, even knowing that you think all cases should get settled."

* * *

I arrive home at 9:20 p.m. I kiss Lisa, and then I say, "What did I miss today?"

"I can't get used to seeing all of the life support equipment all around him. It's all so massive and mechanical," she says, and I can see the sadness in her eyes. "Joey moved a couple more times, and my heart fluttered. Even though they keep saying that is to be expected and that he is still asleep, it gets your hopes up." She pushes a tear away and adds, "I know he can't wake up until they bring him out of the coma, but with every movement, there is some excitement. I guess my head knows he can't wake up alone, but my heart is looking for any sign."

After we talk about Joey and then Katy, I update her on the mediation. We drink a glass of wine together as we talk, and I remember my visit to the psychologist and what Pat had told me, about the importance of talking and sharing—saying everything and nothing. I know he is right, because I find a glimmer of hope in our conversation.

Just after midnight, Lisa says that she is going to try to get some sleep. I kiss her good night and then walk into Katy's room and kiss my little girl on the forehead. She wiggles but does not awaken. I sit beside her and say a silent prayer that she will always be protected. Then I walk into Joey's room and sit on his empty bed. I look around at his model airplanes and his posters on the wall. Musicians and athletes surround me. His old stuffed bear, Monte Burke, sits there looking worn and lonely. I grin at the fact that Joey selected both first and last names for his bear and neither were names we had ever heard.

There is so much of Joey here that there is a comfort in seeing every-thing he loves. I smile widely as I look at the things that are important to my little boy. And at the same time, I am fighting a dark shadow in the form of a fear that he may never return to all of this. My boy may never be back to this room. It's a gut punch. We may never see the things that would become important to him in the future. That tape is playing again, and I'm finding it hard to get my breath.

It is never far from my mind that I failed to protect him. That he is in ultimate jeopardy because I didn't take care of him—the sacred job of a parent. This will be another long night as I am lost in the feelings of imminent and ultimate loss that sweeps over me in waves.

Chapter 29

August 3, 2016

I arrive at the office at 6:00 a.m., planning to leave by 11:00 a.m. to spend extra time with Joey. I am walking to my desk with coffee when the phone rings.

I pick it up and say, "Simmons and Winslow."

"Hi, Scott. It's Lee."

"Morning, Lee."

"I started looking around last night but wanted to get your blessing before I go much further."

"Looking around for what?" I ask, now curious.

"I want to find Anders."

"You think you can?"

"I don't know. It's like finding a single needle in ten haystacks because I have no clue where to look or even who he is now."

"So where do you start?"

"I know one of the guys who creates needles, so I thought I would start with him."

"Go for it. Just so I have an idea, can you ballpark how much it will cost me to chase down your ideas?"

"Yes, it will cost you nothing in my time—out of pocket expenses only. This is something that I want to do."

I am suddenly silenced. When the words come to me, I say, "Thank you, Lee."

"I will keep you posted on anything I can find out. In the interim, know that I am with you and Lisa."

I feel humbled and grateful—the way you always feel when a friend stands by you during the worst of times. "You're a good friend."

"So are you, Scott. Take care."

* * *

I sit in Pat Jackson's nautical living room, and he hands me a glass of water. He sits down and says, "I'm glad you came back."

I nod. "I found you gave me good advice last time. I talk to Lisa about everything and nothing, and she shares the same way. Some days that alone has kept us going."

"Good work, Scott," he says, nodding. "Don't allow walls to be created by emotional distance."

I smile weakly. "You know, that statement was very shrink-like."

"We all have our manner of speaking, I guess. There are times that you sound pretty lawyer-like, too."

"No doubt. Lisa tells me I could work on being a little more folksy."

He laughs. "Exactly. But you probably can't stay in that gear, right?"

"Right."

He dons a more serious expression. "So what do good days and bad days look like right now?"

I sit back in my chair. "Let me do bad days first, because those are more frequent and familiar. They are the days that I spend obsessing back and forth between fear that I may never get my son back again and guilt about having put him in that position. There are some days when I never think about anything else."

"Let's talk about the guilt," Pat says. "Let's attack this at an intellectual level, which is where you live most of the time. If you can accept what I am about to share at an intellectual level, it may sink in emotionally along the way."

"Okay, I'll try."

"What you are doing is holding yourself accountable simply because something bad happened."

"Well ...," I start. Pat holds up a hand.

"Wait a second," he says. "We all live in a world where bad things happen and where children are particularly vulnerable. Someone can run over your children while they cross in a crosswalk or do a hundred other things that inadvertently cause injury. That's before we get to those who are intentionally engaging in acts that endanger our kids." He watches my expression closely. "We have to accept the fact that those things happen, and they happen to good people. Would you blame the parent of a child who was attacked while walking home from school like he or she did a hundred times before?"

"No, probably not, unless there were other facts that made it clear that that parent wasn't looking out for the kid."

"Scott, you and your family were attacked by a guy with a gun in your own driveway. You were not an accomplice."

"I do know that, but I keep thinking of things that I might have done differently. Maybe put myself between the kids and Anders."

He shrugs. "You can do that all day long. Won't get you anywhere good." He leans forward and says, "As far as I can tell, you and Lisa have been nothing but great parents. Your kids know it too. Give yourself a break." He lets it settle on me and adds, "On the other hand, situational distress and anxiety is a perfectly appropriate and healthy response here. You are still on hold—waiting for Joey to return and not knowing whether it is possible. It's anxiety-provoking, and all you can do is wait and pray. I really get it, and I just want you to know that there is nothing inappropriate in your responses. And if you keep talking to each other, you and Lisa can make it through whatever happens."

I let out a breath and feel my heart pounding hard. "There are just some days when I feel panicked about the possibility that Joey won't come home. I sit up at night and stare at the wall, and I play our memories on an endless loop. Once in a while I drift off thinking about Joey, and it's almost like he's back. Then I suddenly wake and realize where he is all over again. It's like getting the bad news all over again."

Pat nods. "I understand." He reflects and then says, "Have you tried sleeping when you are with Joey?"

"At the hospital?" I ask, and then realize what an idiotic question that was.

"Yes. Pull your chair close to him and sleep next to him in the afternoon or evening. That may make sleep possible, knowing you're right there with him."

"I will try that," I say. "This may sound crazy, but somehow I have always felt like I should be awake and watching him in case he needs something."

"It doesn't sound crazy," he says, and smiles. "How are you doing with all the press coverage?"

I shrug. "I wouldn't mind a day without phone calls or the press on my lawn, but they have a job to do. It has become a fact of life, just like waiting for Joey to be well enough to awaken. We've also been the recipient of prayers and kind words from thousands of people," I say. "There are a lot of good folks out there."

"Yes, there are." He pauses and then asks, "You still think about Anders?"

"Every day. I remember what you said about vengeance not bringing relief, but I might like to test that premise."

"How is Lisa doing?"

"She is amazing. Brave. It seems like we spend all of our time waiting. On hold waiting for Joey to come back."

"Is she talking to anyone about all of this?"

"Yeah. She has a really good support group. Her three best friends from college are an amazing support for her. She also just went to talk to a psychologist—Alexandra Sawyer."

"I know Alexandra. She is a good choice."

The room goes silent for a moment, and then Pat says, "Whatever happens, Scott, come back to see me again. This may or may not get easier, but you should keep up with the good and open work you're doing."

My stomach sinks as I realize that is code for "Joey might die." I nod and then say, "Commitment is hard at this point. I think I will come back, as much as I know anything for sure about what I will do in the future."

* * *

Jerry swept the floor leading into the restroom, stopping to check his watch. Only a half hour left in the shift. The deep voice of a short man who came out of the restroom said, "You work here, right?"

He wanted to say, "No, I just like sweeping floors in public places." Instead, he said, "Yes, sir, how can I help you?"

"Which way is the buffet?"

"Walk straight ahead until you see the bar and then turn left. You can't miss it."

"Thanks," the man said, but did not divert his glance. The man looked at him a little too long.

He returned to sweeping as the man walked away. He had let his now black hair grow long and flip slightly at the back. He had a birthmark on his face that Jerry Anders never had, and he has learned the periodic makeup touch-ups that keep it looking real. He found this maintenance job in a small off-strip casino called Maggie's, where overtime is needed frequently, and low lighting aids anonymity. He has an apartment within walking distance and a solitary life. Pictures of Jerry Anders have periodically appeared on Las Vegas television, so he kept to himself and did not allow anyone a close look in good lighting. He managed to resist the gambling addiction that previously brought him down, and when he is not working, he visited one of two small, dark beer bars where he obsessed over what brought him to this point and what he might do next.

When the news confirmed that Michael Constantine set aside the dismissal of the Walters case, he felt betrayed. It was like he gave his all to help Constantine for nothing. He still has more than half of the money he got from Scott Winslow, which he considered his escape fund. Every day he thought about where he might go and what he might do next, but made no plans. It was hard to give up the inconspicuous life that he had found and take a chance on something new because the risk that comes with change overwhelmed him. For right now, he, Frank Adams from Boise, Idaho, would stay right here.

* * *

We are now less than three months from trial of the Walters case. The trial will involve at least twenty-three witnesses and consume three to four weeks of court time. The press started calling about the trial, and I tell them that we are looking forward to telling our story to the jury and that we are confident that they will do what is right. I have to be careful how much I say when I get these calls, because the more specific information that makes the news, the harder it will be to find a jury with no knowledge of the facts of the case. Because no one wants a jury that comes with inside information that might affect the outcome of the case, jurors are chosen for their ignorance of the facts of the case and their lack of knowledge of the industry itself. Someone who has worked in the industry for a number of years comes with a predisposition that neither side can forecast, so that person will never be allowed to stay on the jury. The process is actually about deselecting jurors, so that at the end of the day you have smart and caring people who have no information about the industry they came to examine; in that way, both sides can be reasonably assured that the information jurors will use to make their decision comes only from the facts of the case and the law that the court provides before deliberations begin.

I am already working countless hours in preparation for trial, working on our trial brief, witness list, exhibit list, and jury instructions for trial. I identify testimony from every deposition that I intend to play for the jury by page and line as the court rules require. The judge will consider objections made by the other side to each side's selected testimony and will rule on all objections before any of it gets shown to a jury.

I know Harris will work hard to try to exclude as much of Carl Miller's testimony as possible because the effects of it can be devastating to his client. I have already prepared a brief arguing the admissibility of that testimony, and why all of it must come in to evidence. We have exceptions to the hearsay rule at the ready, and the deposition testimony of Miller is admissible because he is unavailable to testify at trial. No one can find Miller or his alias, Eric Dardon. Detective Art Scully called to tell me that they have an arrest warrant for Miller, reminding me that if I talk to him, I have a legal obligation to notify the police, or I am aiding and abetting. I tell him that I understand, and I accurately tell him that I have had no contact with Miller since his deposition. Lee tells me that he has had similar calls on three occasions. It seems that Carl Miller, a.k.a. Eric Dardon, just disappeared from his Mississippi home right after his deposition. All I can say to Scully is, "Imagine that."

I am already working on my opening statement to the jury, and, with Donna's help, I am also working on a PowerPoint that I will use to provide visual aids in connection with that opening statement. I am also preparing the timeline that I will use in connection with my closing statement and all of the testimony and documents that tell the story of serious safety violations in the mine and what happened to Kevin Walters when he sought to point out those violations and have them corrected.

Donna and I are talking about the PowerPoint when a call comes in from Harris.

"Yes, Mr. Harris, I'll see if he's available."

I push the button and say, "Good afternoon, Bob."

"Scott, how are you?"

Harris is the worst at small talk because it is pretty clear that he really doesn't give a shit how I am. "I'm well, Bob, and you?"

"Good. Listen, I just wanted to see if we can pick a date next week to meet to start going over proposed jury instructions."

"Great. How about Wednesday afternoon?"

"Let me just check the calendar," he says. "Sorry, can't do that one. How about Thursday or Friday morning?"

I check my own calendar. "Thursday morning will work. Why don't you come here for that meeting, and I'll come to your office for the next one."

"Fine, shall we say 9:00 a.m.?"

"Sounds good. I'll see you at our pretrial conference with Judge Carswell on Monday morning."

"Yeah, see you then. Oh, one more thing; my client has authorized me to go to $700,000 to settle the case. Naturally, with full release and confidentiality provisions."

"I will talk to my client and get back to you."

There is no response, just a click as Harris disconnects.

I relay the offer to Kevin. Later in the day, I call Harris.

"Bob Harris."

"Hi, Bob. Scott Winslow. I spoke with my client regarding the offer you relayed this morning."

"And?"

"And we will counter at 3.5 million."

"Are you kidding?"

"No, I'm really not."

"Well, then, it doesn't look like this case can settle."

"Well, please relay our counter to your client, and I will see you Monday morning." Then I hear the expected click.

* * *

On Monday morning, we arrive in court before 9:00 a.m. as scheduled. The clerk directs us into chambers to meet with Judge Carswell just before 11:00 a.m.

"All right, what have we got here?"

I remind him of the nature of the case.

"Have you talked about settlement?"

"We have, Your Honor; we've also been to mediation but have not been able to reach agreement," I say.

"We've been working at it, Your Honor; it's just that plaintiff wants more than the case is worth," Harris adds, attempting to throw us under the bus because the case has not resolved.

"Mr. Winslow?" Judge Carswell says, raising his eyebrows in my direction. Apparently he needs me to confirm or deny that I am the cause of the congestion on his calendar.

"No, Your Honor, but that illustrates a problem of perspective. When a defendant doesn't want to pay what a case is reasonably worth, they often try to characterize the problem as Mr. Harris just did." I look at Harris, who is scowling before I continue, "We will have expert testimony that establishes the economic losses alone exceed the demand that has been made, so to suggest that we are not operating in good faith here …

"Okay," Carswell says, "but I want you to keep talking. This is not the end of settlement discussions. And if either of you think it is worthwhile, I'm going to order you back to mediation. Who did you mediate with the first time?"

"Jake Billings, Your Honor."

"Hmm. He gets good results. I think you should go see him again."

"Your Honor," I say, "we have had numerous settlement conversations since the mediation, and we are just not on the same page with respect to the reasonable value of the case, so I don't think another day of mediation would be helpful."

"What do you think, Mr. Harris?"

"Well, I would talk to my client about that; they might agree to another day of mediation."

Carswell looks at both of us. "I'm not ordering it, but I am strongly urging you to mediate again. If I think you are not doing all possible to get this case settled, then I will have you here every day between the day you answer ready for trial and the day I actually get the case started, and with my calendar, that could easily be two to three weeks. Get my message, counsel?"

"Yes, Your Honor," comes from both camps.

"Don't forget to get everything timely filed per local rules, and I will see you on the date of trial to go over pretrial motions and evidentiary issues before I get a jury panel sent up. Have a nice day, gentlemen," and he looks to the documents on his desk, making clear that he is done talking to us.

"Thank you, Your Honor," we say as we leave chambers. Time spent with Judge Carswell is always so much fun.

* * *

Lee Henry was on his latest assignment, following a middle manager suspected of embezzlement at a safe distance. Just watching someone for days to see if they go anywhere suspicious, like to a stash of money, seems like a long shot, but one never knows. Besides, that's what the client wants. He drove slowly along Pacific Coast Highway, maintaining a quarter mile distance between himself and the target, just in case the guy is paying attention. And embezzlers do have a tendency to be on the lookout. Lee's phone rings, as he followed his target's right turn into Pepperdine University.

When he saw the number, he knew that he wanted to take this call. He punched a button. "What have you got?"

"We got a hit on your Mr. Valentine."

"What?" His eyes grew wide.

"Yeah. We just got a match on facial recognition."

"How? FBI database?"

"No. Near as we can tell, this guy has no criminal record."

"So how did you get to him?"

"We got access to a data bank for lobbyists and affiliated entities. Our man pops out as associated with the PPC."

"No shit. What's his name?"

"Edward Jamison."

"Where is he assigned?"

"He is on staff with the PPC Washington, DC, office, but that doesn't mean anything because all of their US-assigned people are out of the Washington office."

"Got an address for me?"

"Somehow we knew you would ask. He is living in Las Vegas. I just texted his file picture and his address to you."

"You are amazing. Great work."

"Yep. We know. Just keep the checks coming. They are very motivating."

"You got it." As Lee hung up the phone, he digested what he had just learned. "Wow," he said to the empty car, "unfucking believable." He checked his watch. It was 12:30 p.m. If he could get done with this assignment in the next couple of hours, he could be in Vegas tonight. He was already looking forward to meeting Mr. Jamison.

* * *

When I get my next call from Bob Harris, I debate whether to take it. I was in the midst of juggling about a dozen projects. More to the point, after spending the morning in court with Harris, I had enough of him for one day. But I am curious, so after consideration, I say to Donna, "Okay, I'll take it."

"Hi, Bob."

"Hello, Scott. How's it going?"

This is getting predictable. Small talk, point of conversation, then click. "I'm good. What's up?"

"I spoke with my client, and they are willing to go back to mediation as Judge Carswell suggested."

"Is there a good reason to do that? I just don't want to kill another day if there isn't any reason to expect things to go differently."

"Up to you, Scott. Carswell asked that we do it, so we're ready. When we go back, we can just tell him you weren't interested."

"Cute, Bob. But I really am asking if there is a reason to expect a different position from your clients."

"Here's what I can tell you," Harris says in his most condescending voice, so I could be assured that there was real wisdom coming my way, "my client is ready to engage in good faith negotiations to see if we can make further progress."

"Hmmm. Pretty nonspecific."

"One more thing I can tell you is that Mike Constantine is serious about your guy coming back to work. As a matter of fact, he wants him to return."

"I'll pass that on. I'll also get back to you concerning whether we want to go back to mediation at this point. It may be hard to get another date with Jake's office within the next three weeks."

"I've got one. Two weeks from Thursday. Another attorney in my office had the date for a case and needs to postpone, so we can pick it up, but we need to say so by morning."

I check my calendar and see that if I shift a couple of appointments I can make the date work. "All right, I'll get back to you as soon as possible."

"Great." Click.

I put down the phone wondering whether it was worthwhile to go through another day of mediation. I would kick it around with Kevin and see what he thought. As I turned my attention back to trial preparation, the intercom came to life. "I have Lee Henry on one."

"Okay, got it."

I hit the button. "Lee?"

"None other. I have some pretty amazing news."

"You sound excited. What is it?"

"We identified Mr. Valentine."

"No shit?" I say, at my most eloquent.

"No shit. He works for PPC out of DC and lives in Vegas. I'm at the airport on my way to pay him a visit and have a heart to heart."

"What in the world is PPC?"

"It stands for Protective Partners Corporation. It is a behind the scenes facilitator that works for lobbyist groups. Things that they need done but don't want to get directly involved in doing. The kind of things that the public never hears about."

"I've never heard of these guys. Is this a small outfit?"

"That's the point; they don't want to be known. And no, they aren't small. They have a presence everywhere. Think of the way that Blackwater assists the military, except more opaque."

"Are you kidding? So what are you walking into here? Is it safe?"

"Not sure, but I'll be careful."

"Call me as soon as you have something. You have my cell, and I don't care what time of day or night."

"I'll do it."

"And, Lee, if it gets dangerous, walk away."

"I will. Talk to you soon."

"Bye, Lee." I put the phone down thinking that I'm not sure Lee will walk away from danger. I stare at nothing in particular while the wheels turn.

The intercom buzzes. "What is it?" Donna asks.

"Lee has an ID on the guy who called himself Mr. Valentine. He's headed to Vegas to visit the guy."

"That's amazing! You have to call me tonight if you learn more, okay?"

"Okay, you got it."

* * *

Lee stared at the picture that had been texted to him and realized why the facial recognition software worked. The last Valentine that Miller saw, the one with the double chin, was Edward Jamison. On that third visit, he had appeared without a disguise. Something Lee was sure Jamison would soon regret.

As Lee climbed behind the wheel of the rental car at McCarran Airport in Las Vegas, he punched the address for Edward Jamison into the Waze app on his phone and started out of the airport. The program told him that the trip would take twenty-five minutes. It took twenty-three. Lee drove by the house, a new single-story modern on a half-acre. He circled the block and then made his way to the closest commercial area. He found a Starbucks and parked outside. He dialed Jamison.

"Hello."

"Mr. Jamison?"

"Yes, who's calling?"

"Well, Mr. Valentine, you can just call me Father Christmas. You need to meet with me so that we can discuss something critical to your future."

There is silence, and then the man says, "You don't want to try to squeeze me, whoever you are. Because I can find out who you are."

"Just like I found out who you are, right? Now you need to meet me in twenty minutes at Dante's Bar and Grill right in your own neighborhood."

"Look, I don't think you know who you are messing with here."

"Oh, but I do. Should I start using names? Meet me in twenty minutes, and make sure you are alone. Anyone else in the shadows, and you will have a big problem, Mr. Valentine."

"Look you son of a ..."

Lee hung up. He was under the guy's skin, and Lee was certain that he would show up. He scouted the restaurant until he found a place at the side of the building from which he could remain out of view and see anyone approach the front door. He waited patiently for twenty minutes, at which point he saw a Mercedes stop a block away. The occupant got out of the car and approached the restaurant on foot and from across the street. Jamison first walked past the restaurant on the other side of the street, scouring the faces of passersby for anyone looking for someone. After passing the restaurant, he crossed the street and walked back. When he reached the restaurant, he did a quick visual search of the occupants. He would be looking for a lone male who was waiting for his arrival. After standing at the window for about two minutes, Jamison walked inside and was greeted by the staff. He was taken to a table near the back of the room and sat so that he could watch the front door.

Lee gave it another five minutes, until the man became restless, frequently checking his watch and occasionally sipping his beer. Jamison reached into his wallet to pull out tip money, and at that moment, Lee sat down across the table from the man.

Jamison gave him an angry look. "You a cop?" he asked.

"Something like that," Lee said.

"What do you want?"

"I thought maybe a light beer. Something not too hoppy." Judging by his expression, the man had no sense of humor.

"Listen you son of a bitch, you've got about thirty seconds to tell me what you want, or I am gone."

"You don't want to leave. This is important to you." Lee put on his practiced casual expression to offset the intensity of the other man. "Mr. Jamison, you threatened and then blackmailed a county official. One Carl Miller. You remember him, sir?"

"I have no idea what you're talking about."

"Really? He got your picture, and we identified you, among other ways, by facial recognition software." Lee let that sink in a moment, and then added, "For future reference, it is probably not a good practice to show up on any occasion without your disguise in place. Maybe you were in a hurry, but bad call on your part."

His eyes narrowed, and the man's face showed utter contempt. "You don't know what you're walking into. I can make a call, and you will have serious problems; accidents happen to people all the time, you know."

"So now you are threatening me, too?"

Jamison stared at him. "You think that you are some kind of tough guy?"

"No, I'm a really curious guy."

The man pulled out his cell phone. "I've had enough."

"You don't want to do that. If you're going to call your boss, tell him what's really going on. That you got caught on the assignment with Miller and that you're about to do a long stretch in jail. Let me share how this works. I have Miller identifying you as the blackmailer."

"Bullshit. He's never going to do it."

"Unpleasant surprise for you, he's already done it." The man shook his head. "You having trouble believing? Let me give you a little more detail. Your firm helped establish Mr. Miller as one Eric Dardon, with a brand new life in Mississippi. Pulled some strings to get him his pension and, oh yeah, gave him an extra fifty grand in cash. You with me so far?"

Jamison sat in stunned silence, and then said, "Go on."

"You knew who and where he was because you created the new life for him. But the next news flash is that he's not there anymore. You will find that he suddenly disappeared from his Mississippi home in the middle of the night, and there is no more trace of Eric Dardon. What that will tell you is that I have Miller, and you don't. Still with me?"

Jamison adopted a snarl and said, "You are in over your head, mister."

"Yeah, and it occurred to me that you might consider violence where I was concerned, so I took some steps. First, everything I told you, others already know. Those same people already know I'm here tonight. And, one more thing," Lee pulled out his phone showing a picture of Jamison in the restaurant taken immediately before Lee sat down. "This date-and location-stamped photo has been transmitted to those same folks, so all of my professional friends are in the loop." Jamison said nothing, so Lee continued, "Look, I'm doing you a favor. I could have taken this to your supervisor, but then you'd be fucked. Instead, I came to you to give you first opportunity to work with me and avoid getting your ass in a sling. Up to you, though; I really don't care who I talk to about this stuff. Could be you, could be your boss, could be the FBI. You get to choose."

The man sat back in his chair and stared at Lee. Neither said anything for several minutes. Then Jamison said softly, "So what do you want?"

"I thought you'd never ask," Lee said, smiling. "First, my primary interest is not in coming after you, and if you cooperate, I never will." He let that settle and then said, "I need to know who within Consolidated Energy hired you for the job."

"What makes you think it was someone within Consolidated Energy?"

Lee's expression grew stern. "Now you're just wasting my fucking time." Jamison hadn't seen that level of intensity from him and looked startled. "First, Consolidated owns and operates both mines and needed to switch the records to avoid liability for never having corrected serious violations that led to the explosion. We both know that only Consolidated needed that to happen. Aside from that compelling logic, we also have proof that the decision to switch the records came from inside Consolidated." Lee shrugged. "So, you want to cooperate or you want me to take my concerns elsewhere."

"Look," Jamison said, sounding suddenly concerned, "I didn't take the assignment. It came to me from my boss." Lee gave him a skeptical look. "It's true, man. I was given the assignment, but it didn't come directly to me from Consolidated. That's not the way it works."

Lee smiled. He now had the admission that the assignment came from within Consolidated. "Even if you don't know, you can find out."

"I don't know, man. You don't know the code we have."

"I'm sure your organizational code is staggeringly beautiful, but I don't give a flying fuck," Lee said, staring at the man. "You think you will be keeping with your code when you go to jail for bribery and blackmail, your boss is implicated, and PPC gets known as the company that engages in criminal conduct. It gets a shitload worse if you and I don't get on the same team here." Lee paused and then said, "I want you to understand what kind of shit you're in. You could spend twelve to fifteen years in prison, maybe sharing a cell with your boss so you have lots of time to discuss what went wrong. Maybe you can both write letters to your board of directors to explain how you are going to pay the company back for several million in fines. Or, I can get you a free pass." Jamison just looked at him, all the fire gone from his expression. Lee said, "You have until noon tomorrow to get the identity of the Consolidated Energy representative who hired PPC for the job. If you give me good information, I disappear, and you never hear from me again—and no one knows how you fucked this up." Lee folded his hands in front of him. "On the other hand, if I don't have this information by noon tomorrow, it will be your turn to hit the six o'clock news tomorrow night—remember, just like you did for Mr. Miller. I imagine that would create a few shock waves within PPC, don't you think?"

Jamison was now wet across the brow. He took a few moments and then said, "How do I find you tomorrow morning?"

"You don't. I will call you on another of my burner phones, and you can update me. Pleasure meeting you, Edward." Lee stood and then added, "I never did get that beer," before walking out of the restaurant. He looked back and saw that Jamison was still sitting at the table.

As Lee walked to his car, he took a deep breath and couldn't help but glance behind him. Squeezing people who operate entirely in the dark was uncomfortably dangerous, and he knew he was walking a razor's edge.

Chapter 30

The next morning, Kevin Walters comes into my office to assist in preparing responses to interrogatories posed by Consolidated and to discuss whether we return to a second day of mediation.

"This is your wheelhouse, Scott. If you think we should go back to mediation, I am on board. The part I struggle with is the confidentiality requirement that they want. I understand that employers want that in every case, but part of what I wanted to do in pursuing this case is hold Consolidated accountable for not correcting violations that endanger people. If I sign a confidentiality agreement, they are free of the spotlight. No one learns that they endangered people for money, and maybe it all happens again."

"Yeah, they definitely want that confidentiality provision. But I also keep hearing that these guys want you to go back to work. Harris tells me that you can almost name the post you want."

"And what comes to mind?" Kevin asks.

"I'm not sure, but it occurred to me that if you really could name the position, you could be the corporate safety czar. The guy who gets to make the safety calls."

Kevin looks thoughtful. "Maybe, until he doesn't like a decision I make and fires me again."

"I know what you mean. I thought about that, too. There's definitely some holes in the dike that need plugging. What if you didn't report to Constantine, but straight to the board of directors?"

"Flashed through my head, too," Kevin says. "Two problems with that. The first is that Michael insists that everyone report to or below him, and only he reports to the board."

"And if we got past that problem?"

"Michael controls that board. They buy what he says. I can't remember the last time the board turned him down on anything. He got my termination approved by the board."

"Okay, good point. Maybe the idea just doesn't work."

"That's what my gut tells me," Kevin replies.

"Well, we should trust your gut. I understand about not being able to trust these guys anymore. That said, do we go to a second mediation?"

"I don't know. I'll do it if you think we should, but I'm just not sure where it goes from here."

"I'm not either. Let's just tell them that we see no point. The time is better spent preparing for trial."

"Carl Miller won't be at trial, right?"

"Right. We'll have a declaration from Lee Henry saying that we tried to serve him at his Eric Dardon/Tennessee address, but couldn't find him. If we show he is unavailable, we can then use his deposition testimony."

Kevin looks at me thoughtfully. "Do you know where he is?"

"Maybe, but if I do, he is outside of the jurisdiction and not subject to subpoena. And even if we did get him back here, he'd be arrested as soon as he was spotted."

Kevin nods. "He got screwed over by Consolidated too, so getting him arrested is not part of my agenda. Let's use his deposition testimony, and let him live wherever he is as whoever he is."

* * *

It is noon, and there has been no word from Lee. The phone rings, and I stare at it, as I have the last ten times it rang, always expecting Lee's call.

"Bob Harris," Donna says through the intercom.

"Okay, thanks."

I hit the button. "Hi, Bob."

"Hi, Scott. My client wanted me to give you another call. I have a message directly from Mike Constantine."

"Okay, fire away."

"Mike Constantine is pushing to have this second day of mediation. He wants to try to settle the case, and he wants an opportunity to have a conversation directly with Kevin. He says he has important information."

"Direct—as in alone with Kevin?"

"I told him that you might be concerned about that in case the intent was to set something up for us in your absence. Mike gets that, and he says he's okay if you and I are present as well; he just wants the opportunity to speak with Kevin." I am silent for a time while I consider this. "Scott, it's important. I can tell you that Mr. Walters will want to hear this."

"I will let Kevin know."

"Can you tell me that you will recommend going forward to him?"

"I will take your word for the sincerity of your client, and I will recommend it."

"Thanks. I'll let Mr. Constantine know."

As soon as I hang up, Donna buzzes again. "Lee is on line three."

Thank goodness, I think as I hit the button. "Lee, are you okay?"

"I'm in one piece, and I have what we were after."

"Thank God," I say, with a great sense of relief. "Hi, Lee. What's the update?"

"We scored. The client who hired PPC was a director at Consolidated named Corbin Wilson. I checked him out. He was then in charge of insurance and risk for Consolidated companies."

"And now?"

"He's still there, and he has since been promoted to vice president of administration for the Southwest Region."

I am taken aback and stop to absorb this incredible information, and then said, "Great information, Lee. I am amazed you got Jamison to cooperate."

"Well, I wouldn't exactly say cooperate. His screw-up was going to put a spotlight on PPC's covert activities, and they couldn't let that happen. So they gave me the information with the understanding that we never say it came from them. Jamison's last words to me were that if anyone learns this came from PPC, he will personally track me down."

"How can he find you?"

"You know, Scott, I'm pretty good at tracking people, but these guys really have some resources behind them. Between last night and our call this morning, the guy figured out who I am. He used my name in the call when he threatened to come find me. So, needless to say, it's important that you guys don't let on that this came from PPC or Jamison. I don't want to have to change my name and move in with Carl Miller."

"Understood. The source will never be revealed."

"Thanks. My future well-being appreciates it."

* * *

Jerry sat at a small table in a purposefully dark gentlemen's club at three in the afternoon. He nursed his third beer and considered how he would spend the rest of his day off. A topless woman in her early twenties asked him if he wanted something else. He simply shook his head. Off to his right, in the back of the big room with forty tables, there was a naked woman on a small stage, dancing to a disco song he never liked.

Jerry had been following the story about Joey Winslow's injury in the news and was hoping the kid would be okay. He knew it wasn't his fault. He wasn't even there. The kid had done something stupid and gotten hurt. Just the same, he was hoping for Joey's recovery. He was also lonely. His life was a series of small rooms; his small apartment, this bar, and an out-of-the-way coffee shop that got little business since the relocation of major streets in the area. He avoided other public places as much as possible, keeping his head down. When the ads seeking the public's assistance in identifying him hit the networks, he had seen a few prolonged glances his way, but he kept moving and made it through without any real incident.

Jerry stepped outside and dialed his burner phone. It rang twice, and then a familiar voice said, "Hello."

"Hi," he said. "It's me."

"Oh, my God, Jerry," Vickie Constantine said. "Are you okay?"

"I'm all right. I know it has been a long time. I wanted to tell you I'm okay and hear your voice, sis."

"Jerry, where are you?"

"Better you don't know."

"You have to come back."

"Why?"

"You have to turn yourself in," Vickie urged. "That little boy is barely hanging on. You need to accept responsibility for what you did."

"Vickie, I didn't do it. He fell."

There was a moment of silence, and then she said, "Jerry, you kidnapped that child and left him in a dangerous place. You are responsible for what happened."

"I can't go back to jail for thirty years, Vickie. Don't you know I was trying to do something good? It just didn't work out."

"You did something bad, Jerry. You have to acknowledge it, or I am done with you."

"I have to go, Vickie. Don't tell Michael I called." He hung up, feeling miserable. "Shit," he said aloud. He didn't like feeling like this. He decided he had to do something to make himself feel better. He would take some of the money he still had stashed and try his luck at the tables. He had resisted long enough. If he just took a couple of thousand, he could turn it into some real money and then improve the quality of his life. Maybe he could get a nice new apartment. He told himself that this could turn into something really good.

Chapter 31

Lee started with one of his own contacts—a guy who made needles disappear into haystacks. Art Chase was the talented former counterfeiter who had created the new ID papers to turn Carl Miller from Eric Dardon to Jason Wilcox of Eugene, Oregon.

Lee walked through the back exterior door of an apartment building and entered the open door on the left. He closed the door behind him. Inside, a man sat behind a desk reading a newspaper. The room contained only a desk with one visitor's chair. There was no other furniture, and there were no pictures on the walls.

Lee sat down in the visitor's chair, and a husky man of about fifty with a big grin looked around the newspaper at him. "Hi, Art," Lee said with a smile.

"Hey, brother," Art said, grinning. "What's new?"

"On the hunt, my friend."

"Fire away."

"Here's what I have so far," Lee said, handing the man two sheets of paper. "The first page is the list of inmates in the same cell block as Anders before his release. The second page contains the names of those released from the prison between six months before Anders's release and three months after his release. Seems to me that this is a likely universe of people who have the contacts to get the new identity put together." As Art stared at the pages, Lee asked, "Who on this list does what you do, and who else on the list knows people who do what you do?" Lee reflected a moment and added, "I am not interested in bringing anyone to the attention of any authorities. This is just for my client."

Art said, "First of all, I need to know who you are looking for. I need to make sure that I don't have a conflict of interest."

Lee nodded. "Fair enough. I'm looking for Jerry Anders, the dirtbag who kidnapped the Winslow kids."

"Yeah, I remember the story. Anders was pretty clumsy, but they made him disappear pretty well. Anyway, not my guy, so no conflict." Art returned his attention to the pages in front of him. There was silence in the small room for about three minutes, and then Art set the sheets on the desk and circled three names in black. "I know that these two guys know how to make IDs," he said. He circled four more names in red. "These guys for sure know how to find someone who can do what I do." He underlined three other names and stopped. "I know it's not these guys."

"How?" Lee asked.

"Because they would have come to me," he replied.

"Any thoughts about which one of these guys I should start with?" Art nodded and put boxes around two of the names. Lee nodded and handed him two $100 bills. "Okay, thanks. I appreciate it."

"No problem, man. I hope you can find the guy." He paused and added, "And keep sending me people who need help, man. I'm there for you."

* * *

I sit beside Joey with my hand on his. The room has come to look a lot like his bedroom at home. There are trophies he won playing baseball that occupy a shelf; there is a football sitting on a stand that says "Green Bay Packers," his favorite team despite the fact that he has never been to Wisconsin; there is a chemistry set; and there are four or five video games at the ready. They gather dust patiently awaiting the return of their owner.

I close my eyes and lean against his bed. I fall asleep, but then wake up abruptly as I lean too far forward. It's like dozing on an airplane and being periodically awakened by unexpected turbulence. Between the motions, I manage to sleep for about an hour and a half. Then I wake up to see Katy standing beside Joey. There is a tear in her eye, and she tells him, "Joey, you have to come back now. I miss you too much." She looks at him silently, as if waiting for a reply. When there is no response, she adds, "Please, Joey, I won't call you a butthead any more, I promise." She waits for the longest time, not noticing that I am awake. I find myself trying hard to hold back the tears as I watch.

I check my watch to find that it's now 6:30 p.m. I look up, and Lisa walks into the room. She kisses Joey on the forehead and then gives Katy a hug. "Hi, sweetheart, how are you today?"

"I miss Joey. He needs to wake up."

"I agree, Katy." She looks at me. "You doing okay?"

"Yeah, I guess so. I spent the afternoon revising a brief on the Walters case, and then napped with Joey," I reply. "How was your afternoon?"

"Okay," she says. "These days I feel like I go through the motions at work so I can get back here. Just do what I can to keep things afloat, you know?"

"Yeah, I get it." I take her hand and hold it tightly as we watch Joey sleep, not speaking our shared fears out loud. Fears that time is running out because this induced coma won't protect him forever, fears that he never wakes up, and fears that this is the way we see our son for the last time. We are caught between wanting something to happen if it means getting our son back, but not if it means an end to the hope that we cling to so desperately.

Our weekly updates with Dr. Mitchell are approached with a foreboding that comes with experience and his downcast expression at every meeting. At the last meeting, he told us that there was no change. He emphasized that we are now at six months and that he has never known a successful return from a medically induced coma that went beyond seven months, so we are battling the clock. As much as I don't want to face it, I sense that he is preparing us for the ultimate bad news. It is coming closer, and he dreads the day when he has to tell us what we are not prepared to accept. For now, we hold tight to our last grains of hope while the sand runs through the hourglass ever faster. We are not devoid of hope, but we feel all too helpless.

* * *

"This is it, 1927 East Coleman," agent Becky Sandoval said, pointing to a small gray house with chain-link fence that leaned at about thirty degrees and a dirt front yard.

Greg Edmonds stopped across the street, and they both climbed from the unmarked car and walked quickly to the house. Sandoval gestured to Edmonds with an extended hand. He nodded and then made his way to the rear of the residence.

Sandoval gave him time to get positioned and then stood to the side of the door as she pounded, to stay out of the line of fire. "Open up, Desmond. FBI." There was no response so she repeated the announcement and pounded even harder.

"Just a minute," was heard from inside. A moment later a man with long, greasy hair, and no shirt opened the door. He was thin, about forty years old, and flashed angry eyes. Sandoval pushed in, walked through the living room and kitchen that led to the back door, and let her partner into the house. She walked to the small table in the kitchen, pulled out a chair, and said, "Sit down," to the man.

He stared at her a moment and then said, "What the fuck do you want?"

She looked at him and then tapped the chair. "Sit down."

He moved slowly to the chair, never taking his eyes from her. He sat down and continued to stare at her.

"So you did time with this guy?" she said, flipping a picture of Jerry Anders from her pocket. He looked at the picture and said nothing. She waited, and then said, "You having trouble hearing me, Mr. Desmond?"

"I hear you."

"And?"

"And what?"

"And you did time with this guy, correct?"

"I am not telling you shit. Now get out of my house, lady. I haven't done anything."

She shook her head. "Mr. Desmond, I'm afraid our relationship is getting off to a rocky start. So let me clarify a couple of things. First, I am not 'lady,' I am agent Sandoval with the FBI. Second, I am conducting an investigation into a kidnapping, and you don't want to be anything but cooperative and honest, or I will run your ass in for obstructing my fucking investigation," she said, getting slower and louder as she concluded. "You have any questions now?" There was silence. "You, Mr. Desmond, are on parole, you remember? So I can violate your ass for any of the alarming suspicions that I have about you." She held his eyes for a few moments and then said, "Now, do you have my question in mind?"

"Yes," he said through an angry expression, "I did time with Anders."

"Much better," she said, smiling at him. "And you got out of the system about two months before he did, right?"

"You already know this shit."

"Mr. Desmond, your level of cooperation is slipping again. You and I need to discuss these things because we need to be on the same page about what happened, so that I can then ask about other things that we both know are true. You with me?"

"Yeah."

"Good. So back to the question. You got out about two months before Anders?"

"Yeah."

"And until that time, you and he had spent about a year on the same block, correct?"

"Yeah, we were both there."

"I think you're getting the rhythm of this. See how easy it can be? And you, Mr. Desmond, are an artist when it comes to creating personal paperwork, right?"

"I used to do that, yeah."

"Used to?"

"Yeah."

"Until when?" she asked.

"Until I got caught and went to prison."

"And not since then?"

"No."

"You sure about that?"

"Yeah, I'm sure."

She shook her head, "Well, you see Mr. Desmond, we have a witness who says otherwise. He tells us you connected him to a very nice driver's license and credit card, looking just like the real thing. Just so you know, we can now arrest you for the new fraudulent activity, obstructing this investigation, and for violating your probation by associating with a known felon. You've hit the fucking big winner trifecta." He said nothing, but was beginning to sweat. "You have this wrong, Mr. Desmond. Now is not the time for silence. That will be when we bust your ass and Mirandize you. Now is your chance to talk, and maybe we walk out of here without you. Got it?"

"I didn't do any work for Anders. Nothing. And he didn't come to me."

"Have you seen him since you got out?"

"No."

"Talk to him at all?"

"No, just like I already told that other investigator."

"What other investigator?"

"Come on, he was here just yesterday asking this same kind of shit. Like I told him, I haven't been in touch with Anders since I got out."

"What was this investigator's name?"

"I don't remember."

"Where would Anders go if he didn't come to you? Give me some names."

He leaned back in his chair considering what he would do.

"It would be a shame to get this close to retaining your freedom and then blow it, don't you think?

"Lester Hall and Byron Cerda are possibles."

"Who else?"

"Rim Noll and Burt Snider."

"Anybody else you know?" He was quiet, so she added, "I find another who knows you, and I come back and charge you with everything I can think of plus one, and you will spend twenty-five years making new friends. You follow?"

"The only other I know is Martin Chavez, but I heard he was sick and out of the business."

"I need contact information for all these guys. I won't mention your name when we talk."

"Hall checks in at the Blue Bison once or twice a week. Cerda is all over the street, but I don't have contact."

"Noll?"

Good friend of Brent Ramos, the guy who runs that strip joint near the airport, The Fur Trap."

"You tell all this to the other investigator? The guy you saw yesterday?"

"Yeah," he responded.

"Give me a description of the investigator you saw yesterday, and we are out of here."

Desmond nodded and began to describe Lee Henry.

* * *

Lee knocked on the door and waited. An obese man with a straggly goatee covering a broad jaw, and dull, black eyes, opened the door and stared at him. The man wore a sleeveless T-shirt, revealing extensive inking on both arms. He said nothing.

"Lester Hall?"

"Who's asking?" the man asked.

"I'm an investigator, and I'm looking for Jerry Anders. You know him?"

"You got a warrant?"

"Do I need one?"

"What do you think?"

"Well, I think that neither one of us wants that. I need to find a guy who kidnapped two kids. You've seen the news on this guy, right?" Lee waited but got no response, so he added, "It's easier for me if you and I cooperate. I need to know who supplied paper for this guy. Can you help me?"

There was quiet. After a moment, Hall said, "What's in it for me?"

"How about gratitude and a hundred bucks?"

"How about you keep the gratitude, and two hundred bucks."

Lee nodded. "If you've got information that helps, you've got a deal."

"It's yes or no, man."

"Okay," Lee said. "It's yes." He handed the man two $100 bills.

"I don't know who papered this guy, but I can tell you that I didn't do it, and I know one other scribe who didn't do it."

"Who's the other guy, and how do you know he didn't paper this guy?"

"The guy is Rim Noll, and I know because we talk two or three times a week. We go back a long way, man, and we've talked about not wanting to help this asshole."

Lee nodded. "Okay. Anything else you can tell me?"

"That's what I've got, man. That's it."

Lee offered the man a hand. He stared at it like it might be dangerous, but after a moment he nodded and shook it.

"Call me if you hear anything," Lee said. "There's more money if you can get me to this guy." He handed Hall a card that contained only a name and a phone number.

"Okay, man. You got it."

Lee walked to his car and drove away. He decided that he would find Martin Chavez and then Byron Cerda next. He would see the supposedly ill Chavez first and then drive to the bar Cerda was known to frequent. As he accelerated onto the freeway, his phone rang. He pushed the button on the steering wheel and said, "Go ahead."

"Mr. Henry, this is agent Greg Edmonds."

"Yes, I know who you are."

"Good. We need to meet."

"We do? To what end?"

"We will tell you when we meet," Edmonds said. "Meet us at Matthew's House of Coffee on Ventura Boulevard in twenty minutes."

Lee reflected momentarily and then said, "See you there." He hung up and took the next off-ramp. It would take him fifteen minutes to reach the meeting place, and they somehow already knew he could make it in twenty. Lee pulled into a gas station and walked around his car, looking underneath at various points until he found what he was looking for. The device was about two inches in diameter and had been secreted in a magnetic box above the passenger side rear wheel well. He looked at the device and smiled. He employed several similar devices and had a couple in his tool bag presently. He took the device over to a pickup truck that was fueling. The owner had evidently gone inside the adjacent minimart. He placed the device in the same place on the pickup and then stopped. He had second thoughts and grabbed the device, placed it in his pocket, and walked back to his car.

Lee got into his car and continued toward Matthew's. He arrived at Mathew's with three minutes to spare. Because of the device, they would know he was arriving. Lee looked around the parking lot and saw three cars that might be FBI wheels. He pushed a button and then heard the phone ring. It rang twice and then a voice said, "You need us again?"

"Yep. You guys are the bright spot in my day. Can you run three plates for me, quickly? I have three minutes max."

"Fire away."

Lee recited the makes and models and the plates of each of the three, then said, "I'm looking for a cop plate or government ownership."

The response was, "Just hang on."

Less than two minutes later, the voice said, "The Ford is the car you want."

"Thanks. Gotta go." Lee hung up and got out of the car. He walked over to the Ford and placed the device in its magnetic container above the rear wheel well on the passenger side. That done, he walked into the coffee shop. There were half a dozen high tables that seated three in the center of the room and booths against glass walls around the perimeter. Only one of the high tables was occupied. It was inhabited by three early-twenties guys. Three of the booths were occupied. One by a couple in their sixties who were laughing and thoroughly entertained. Another by two women in office attire. The third was occupied by a man and a woman with no coffee or drinks in front of them. The woman had dark hair and watchful eyes. The man was short-haired and wore a tie, no jacket. They were cops—textbook cops. He walked over and sat down in the booth, across from agent Sandoval and agent Edmonds.

"Good afternoon," he said. "What can I do for you?"

Sandoval sat back in her seat and said, "Mr. Henry, do you represent yourself to the public as an investigator?"

"A private investigator, yes. As I assume you already know, I am licensed as one. Now, why am I here?"

Sandoval regarded him and then said, "You're here because we need to talk to you."

Lee lifted his palms and said, "Please, go ahead."

"We are conducting an investigation. We have spoken to two witnesses in the last two days, and from both of them, we learned that you have been there first."

Lee nodded. "Okay."

"We are conducting an official investigation. We don't need you getting in the way. And, Mr. Henry, we take interference with an official investigation very seriously."

Lee furrowed his brow. "I want to make sure that I have this right. You think I am interfering with an investigation that you are conducting that I knew nothing about. And I'm doing that by talking to the people that I need to talk to in order to represent my client and that I have no knowledge that you are approaching."

"Well, Mr. Henry, you may not have known of our investigation before, but now you do."

"I guess that I do," Lee said. "It does occur to me, however, that we are or should be on the same team here. Aren't we both working to find Jerry Anders? Why can't we work together and share information?"

"Parallel investigations do not work. I am telling you that your investigation may well impede ours, and we won't let that happen. If you have any information from your discussions, we expect you to turn it over." Lee was silent. "You have any information that you want to share with us?"

"Not that I can think of," Lee replied.

Edmonds leaned forward in his chair. "You understand that you can be charged for withholding information in connection with an official investigation?"

"Now you are threatening me based upon not providing information I don't have?"

Sandoval said, "We just want you to know that we're serious and that we expect you to provide information relevant to our investigation. If you don't, we will come after you. Now, what do you know?"

"Can't think of anything I can share at this point. If something comes to me, I'll give you a call." Lee stood up and started away. He stopped and turned back and said, "One more thing. You dragged me to a coffee house to threaten me and didn't even buy me a cup of coffee. I would have expected a little more courtesy for my tax dollars." Lee turned and walked out.

"Interesting guy," Sandoval said. "Come on, let's go."

When they climbed into the car and pulled away, Sandoval said, "Check the GPS in the vehicle, and let's see where he's going next."

Edmonds played with the device with a puzzled look on his face.

"What?" Sandoval asked.

"It doesn't seem to be working right." He fiddled with it for a few moments and then said, "Shit."

"What?" Sandoval asked again. "What have you got?"

Edmonds shook his head. "The GPS is exactly where we are. We are following us." He chuckled. "The son of a bitch not only found the bug, he planted it on us."

Sandoval smiled. "Not bad."

Chapter 32

Kevin and I arrive at Jake Billings's office fifteen minutes before the scheduled start time for day two of the mediation. Within two minutes, we are installed in conference room three with coffee in hand. Jake joins us with warm greetings. "Welcome back, Mr. Walters." He extends a hand, and Kevin shakes it. "Morning, Scott," he says, and we also shake hands. Jake sits down and rubs a hand through his thinning hair. "You may have heard that they want to start us off a little differently today. Mr. Constantine wants to talk with Mr. Walters. No problem if lawyers are also present."

I nod. "We're okay with that plan," I say. "But there are a couple of other things you should know." I sit back in my chair as Jake silently waits for me to continue. "You remember our discussions of the man who calls himself Mr. Valentine?"

"I remember," Jake says.

"We now know who he is."

Jake's eyes widen. "How did you get to that?" he asks.

"A good investigator," I say, and then add, "And that's just half of it. We also determined who at Consolidated hired Valentine to blackmail and bribe Carl Miller to switch county records. That information means significant punitive liability for Consolidated."

"Who is the guy calling himself Valentine?" he asks.

"Valentine is a guy who works for a company known to do covert projects, often for certain lobbyist groups."

"Covert?"

"Right. Think Blackwater with no footprint."

Billings shook his head. "This gets crazier all the time. We should get this case settled before people start finding bodies in the trunks of cars."

"One more thing, Jake. With all of these puzzle pieces now available to us, Consolidated Energy's liability and our settlement demand are both higher than they used to be."

"Okay, but before you tell me any new demand, let's hold this meeting so that Mike Constantine can talk to Kevin. I don't know what he is going to say, but Bob Harris told me only that it is critical that Constantine gets a chance to talk to Kevin."

I look a Kevin, and he nods. "Let's do it," I say. "Where do we go?"

"Let's do it right here," Jake says. "Give me a few minutes, and I will bring Constantine and Harris back."

In a few minutes, Jake enters the room followed by Constantine and then Harris. Jake says, "Mr. Walters and Mr. Winslow, you know Mr. Constantine and Mr. Harris. Vague greeting nods followed by brief handshakes, and then Jake and Harris sit down. Jake says, "Mr. Constantine, you have the floor."

Constantine stands at the head of a table, a man who is used to being in charge and controlling a room. He has the studious look of an accountant and the polish and poise of an army colonel. "Kevin, I have some things to tell you. First, I made a mistake. I somehow convinced myself that your demands to make costly fixes to mine conditions were disloyal—some kind of a betrayal of our relationship. It has taken me time to realize that you were making suggestions that you thought were in the best interests of the company." He lets this settle on the room while Harris stands for the likely purpose of warning his client about giving up information that may come back to bite him. Constantine looks over at him and says, "No need, Bob. I'm going to level with Kevin. I owe it to him. He and I go back, well, forever." Harris returns to his seat, and Constantine continues, "I want you to come back to work, Kevin. You have good vision, great management skills, and you belong at Consolidated."

Kevin responds with, "Is this just a way to end this case or to buy confidentiality?"

Constantine smiles and says, "I always liked how direct you are. Too many people are scared to talk to me that way." He shakes his head. "The answer to both questions is no."

"I can give it some thought," Kevin says, not sounding convinced.

"I am going to tell you something that will let you see that I am sincere. When we were at the first day of the mediation, I heard talk of this Mr. Valentine, who blackmailed Carl Miller into changing records. I had no idea who Valentine is, but I started thinking that someone inside the company might be responsible for hiring this guy. I mean, I couldn't think of anyone outside the company that would have a reason to want these mine records switched. So, I started an internal investigation and quietly probed who might have been involved. My investigative team came up with a name, so I had a one-on-one meeting with the employee. By the end of that meeting, he confessed that he hired this guy to protect the company. I fired him at that moment, and he will face criminal charges." He drew a deep breath. "I will tell you in confidence that the individual who did was then director level, in charge of the risk department, and had since been promoted to vice president."

"Let's cut to the chase. Who are we talking about?" Kevin asks pointedly.

"Corbin Wilson," Constantine says without hesitation. There was stunned silence in the room as we drank in the fact that Constantine just told us the secret we planned to spring on him.

Harris stands and gropes for words. "Michael, don't say any more."

"It's okay, Bob. He didn't give away anything we didn't already have," I reply. More stunned silence, and then I add, "We told Jake we had that information when we arrived. You should know that we have identified both Mr. Valentine and Corbin Wilson. So we have closed the loop for purposes of our punitive damage claim."

Constantine says, "So, Kevin, does that mean that what I confided this morning means nothing to you?"

"No," Kevin says, "it doesn't mean that at all."

I smile and add, "To the contrary, Mr. Constantine, it shows us that you are being forthright. I have no doubt about your sincerity, but the damage was done before we got here today. I think that Kevin and I need to talk at this point." There are nods around the room, and Jake escorts Constantine and Harris back to their conference room and closes the door as he leaves.

"That was something," I say to Kevin.

"It was impressive, and he's obviously working to get me back, but I still have trust issues. Even if I had a contract, Mike could figure out how to break it or pay it off. I don't want to be vulnerable to that son of a bitch after what he did to me the first time."

"I get it," I say. "I had an idea as Constantine was talking. Maybe a little variation on what we are discussing is in order."

"Tell me what you've got."

An hour later, we reconvene as a group.

"Thanks for giving us time to work through this," I say. "We have a proposal. Let me start by saying that with all the information that we have gathered, I believe the case has a settlement value in the area of $7 million." There are shaking heads on the defense side. "Think about it," I say evenly. A Consolidated Energy executive hired a clandestine group to blackmail the county's representative into changing records. We can identify both the person who did the blackmailing and the person at Consolidated who hired the organization he works for. How do you think a jury receives that information about the way Consolidated put its self-interest ahead of public safety?"

There is quiet for a few moments, and then I continue. "This case is about fixing a problem. So, we are proposing that you form a subsidiary whose purpose is to inspect mine conditions and recommend and undertake specific remedies for dangerous conditions, whether or not they have been identified as violations. We would also reach out to the families who were the victims of the explosion with financial support, which serves the employees well and has great PR value." Around the room, faces were inscrutable. "Kevin would be the president of the new company at a salary that is three-quarters of his former salary and a five-year contract terminable for limited causes. There would be a five-person board of directors for the company. Kevin would be on the board, and he initially designates one other member. Mr. Constantine is also on the board, and he also designates one other member. Those four board members then select a fifth member from within the industry." I look around at closed expressions. "Consolidated funds the company with $3 million initially and agrees to put in another $2 million over the next five years. There would be a payment of $500,000 to Kevin to cover some of his losses to date, and there would be an additional payment of $350,000 to my firm for attorneys' fees to date."

Harris looks unhappy. Constantine is deep in thought.

"On these terms, we will also agree to a confidentiality agreement concerning the allegations of the case and terms of settlement."

Harris looks like he is going to speak, but stifles the comment. Constantine says, "Now let us talk for a while."

* * *

Lee Henry dialed the number and waited for the ring.

"Becky Sandoval," the now familiar voice answered.

"Good afternoon, agent Sandoval."

A moment's hesitation and then, "How did you get this number? This is my personal cell phone."

"Didn't you give it to me?"

"I did not."

Lee grinned widely. "Well, you have mine, so it seems fair, right?"

"What do you want?"

"Agent Sandoval, I meant what I said about believing that you and I are on the same team. We both want to help get to Anders, right?"

"And?"

"And I just wanted to update you on some work I had done so we don't duplicate efforts. I met with Martin Chavez, and he really is very ill. Stage four cancer and not mobile, so certainly not working in the past couple of months. Anders did not get his new ID from him, so you can scratch him off your list."

"Cute, Mr. Henry. As was planting our bug on my car."

"What? Were you bugging me? I didn't even know you had a warrant. That would require a warrant, wouldn't it?"

"Good-bye, Mr. Henry."

"Have a nice day, agent Sandoval."

* * *

After two more hours, we all gather in the same room once again.

Constantine speaks first. Shaking his head, he says, "We can't create a subsidiary that decides corporate matters. We are a public-traded company that answers to its stockholders, and all has to come through our board. So we are not going to create a new company as we do not think that is the right way to go." My turn to look inscrutable, and I was doing my best. Turning directly to Kevin, Michael Constantine continues, "Kevin, I think you know how serious I am. I revealed the director who hired, what's his name, Mr. Valentine? I didn't have to share that information today. I did that so there would be no doubt in your mind about my sincerity. I do want you back. I am prepared to offer you a senior vice president in charge of safety at your old wage and a five-year contract allowing termination for good cause only. I will agree to the other terms. We will give you $500,000 to settle the case and pay attorneys' fees of $350,000." He paused and says, "I want you to return, Kevin, and I am putting it in your hands."

Harris interjects, "If we do not reach agreement, we will lay it all out for the jury. We will tell them what Corbin Wilson did, that he did so without authorization, and that Mr. Constantine initiated an investigation as soon as he learned about Mr. Valentine. We will explain to them that Mr. Constantine discovered the identity of the perpetrator, fired him immediately, and turned his action over to the district attorneys' office for prosecution. We will then explain to the jury that Mr. Constantine revealed what had happened to you." He hands me a letter. "I e-mailed a letter to you this morning explaining it all, so there can be no doubt about the sequencing and your awareness. That said, we do not want to go down that legal path; we want to arrive at a settlement if we can."

"I understand your position," I say, "but if the best case you have is, 'We did it, but we admit it,' you may not get all the empathy from the jury that you are hoping for, because you didn't keep safety as a priority, and you fired Mr. Walters for raising critical issues." I stop there, but the truth is, the strategy makes sense.

Kevin looks at Constantine and says, "Michael, let me be blunt with you, the way I could when we worked together all those years."

The room grows quiet as Michael Constantine waits for more. Kevin leans forward in his chair and laces his fingers together. He takes a breath and says, "I am disappointed, and I am hurt. You took a significant part of my life away, and you torpedoed all of the trust that we built over the years. Then I was treated like a pariah—like I had embezzled or intentionally injured the company in some way.

"You said that you won't agree to incorporate a subsidiary. How about if I incorporate, and we will have the relationship you just described by way of a five-year contract with my company. I will work three-quarters of the fifty hours I would work if I was employed by the company, and you pay me three-quarters of the amount we discussed."

"What does that get you?" Constantine asks.

"The ability to serve Consolidated well and build my own company." He leans forward in his chair, still looking directly at Constantine. "Maybe I wind up having consultancy agreements with others in the industry down the road. You and I both know that there are a number of companies that need help with their safety records."

"I'm not sure we're interested in financing a new business. We want you to come back to us." He shrugged. "I'll talk to the board," Constantine says. "Give me a half hour." At that point, everyone except Kevin and I walk out of the room.

Jake sticks his head back in the room and says, "Maybe we have something here. Stay tuned."

As Jake disappears, I say, "I really hope this idea works. It would be great if you could form a company that put safety first and had one big client to get it off the ground."

"Exactly. I want to do more than work for Consolidated. I want to monitor and improve safety for as much of the industry as I can."

Kevin and I spend the next hour talking about the company he wanted to form. He has ideas about the standards it would employ, the testing and reporting it would do, and even some of the people he would hire for key roles. We even kick around potential names for the company, such as Safety Compliance Corporation or Protective Energy Services. As I listen, I am taken by Kevin's knowledge of intricacies and his enthusiasm for this project. I have never heard him so animated.

"Kevin," I say, "I am impressed by these ideas, and I think that this is your calling."

"You know," Kevin says, smiling widely, "I think you might be right. I would really like to do this." While we wait for Jake to return with Constantine and Harris, Kevin makes notes about a possible company, and ideas came to him in flashes. He talks about inspectors, organizational structure, and connections to MSHA and counties with oversight responsibilities. Then he talks about how all of this could coerce mining companies to comply with regulations, address violations, and protect workers, and he does all of it with palpable enthusiasm, despite the fact that it has been a long day, and we are exhausted.

Ninety minutes later, Jake steps into the room alone. After sitting down and searching for the right words, which is not a good sign, he says, "Consolidated does not want to fund a new organization. They are shutting down the idea entirely. That said they are making a final offer of $900,000 to settle the matter outright."

"Is this it? Nowhere else to go from here?" I ask.

"Yeah, I think they mean it. They say it's a take it or leave it deal."

We shake hands with Jake and let him know that we would not take the deal. We thank him for his hard work, and, at 9:00 p.m., we leave the mediation without an agreement.

Chapter 33

As Lee drove up to the small house, he saw an obese man sitting on the porch smoking a cigarette. He drove past the house and to the end of the block, where he made a Y-turn and parked the car. He watched as the man held a cell phone to his ear and spoke animatedly.

Burt Snider then ran into the house as Lee watched from a distance. In a few minutes, Snider emerged with a suitcase and walked toward the classic Corvette in the driveway. This guy was in a big hurry to go somewhere, and Lee was sure it had something to do with the call that just happened—he was either chased away or warned off something.

Lee got out of the car and walked toward the man. Snider saw him and moved faster toward the car.

"Hold it," Lee says loudly. "We need to talk."

"You got a warrant?"

"If I need one, I'll have someone get it while we talk. In the meantime, you aren't going anywhere."

Snider stopped and looked at the car, now just a few feet away. He looked back at Lee, standing by the curb staring back at him. "You don't want to do that," Lee said. "You won't make it." Snider continued to stand and stare. Lee said, "How far do you think you'll get? I call this in, and there's cops all over you in two minutes." No movement. "All I want is a little information. I am not after you. Got it?"

Snider nodded but said nothing.

"Let's go inside and talk. You cooperate, and I am gone in ten minutes. You don't, and this ends badly for you."

Snider turned and walked toward the house. Lee followed. The inside was dark. Darkness composed of windows were blacked out and ancient, wood dark. Snider turned 180 degrees and looked at Lee. "What do you want?"

"I've seen a lot of your work. I know that you are pretty good." The man said nothing. "I'm looking for one of the dirtbags you helped."

Suddenly, a fist flew at Lee's face. He sidestepped the punch, feeling it graze his chin, and hit Snider hard in the gut, causing Snider to double over, and then smacked him in the face with an uppercut. Snider fell to the floor.

"Okay, fucknut, you've made your choice. Let's go."

"Wait," Snider said, climbing to his feet. "What do you want?"

"When I got here I just wanted a little cooperation. Now I might want to put your ass back in jail."

"You don't understand, man," Snider said, still trying to recover normal breathing. "The people I work with are like sources are to reporters. I give up someone I worked with, my business is gone man; no one's gonna come back to me."

"I understand," Lee said. "Reporters go to jail for their sources. I assume you're willing to do that as well?" Snider said nothing. "I don't care. I'm going to find this guy with or without your help. So if you want to go to jail while I look for him, I'm okay with that. But if you do help me, he'll never know how I got to him, and you stay a free man."

"Can't help you, man."

They stood face to face, and Lee looked into the man's eyes so he could see the reaction as he spoke. "I know you papered Jerry Anders." There it was. The momentary flash of acknowledgment in his eyes. This was his guy.

"I don't know who you are talking about."

"You know exactly who I'm talking about." He paused, watching carefully, but now the man's face was impassive. "You don't owe this dirtbag loyalty, man. You want to go to jail for an asshole that kidnapped kids?"

"I don't know who you mean, man."

"You know that there is a little boy barely alive because of this fucking scumbag. You want to be an accomplice to this prick?"

"I don't know this guy, man. Now get out and leave me alone."

"The FBI is on the way," Lee said, in one last attempt to break through.

He shook his head. "They were here this morning. I told them the same thing I told you. I have no clue who you're talking about. I've seen a little on TV about him, but I don't know him, man."

Lee stared at the man for almost a full minute, and then said, "You are going down. And when you do, I want you to remember when you could have avoided it all. When I came here I wanted Anders, not you. Now I'm coming after both of you."

Lee slammed the door as he walked from the house. As he walked past the Corvette, he glanced back at the house to make sure he wasn't being watched, and then he slipped a GPS up in the right rear tire well. He looked back at the house and waited. No reaction, so he walked to his car. He sat in the car and watched the house for fifteen minutes, but Snider did not come out. Lee started the car, and as he pulled away, dialed his phone.

Sandoval said, "This is my personal cell. I don't want you calling this number."

"Sorry, I must have forgotten that you are sensitive about that. How fast can you meet me at the same coffee shop?" Lee asked.

There was a moment of silence while she considered her response, and then Sandoval said, "I can be there in an hour."

"Okay, see you then," Lee said.

* * *

We get the message that Dr. Mitchell wanted a special meeting at noon today, rather than waiting for our normal end of the week meeting, and we are scared. I put my arms around Lisa and hold her tight, but neither of us can find words. We spend the next two hours with Joey and then walk to Dr. Mitchell's office. Upon arrival, we are directed into an adjoining conference room, where Dr. Mitchell and another man wait. They both stand and shake hands with us.

Dr. Mitchell then says, "You remember Dr. Santos? He is the neurologist who has helped us with Joey's situation in the past."

"Do we have progress?" I ask, unable to wait any longer.

"Unfortunately there is no appreciable change in Joey's condition despite everything we tried."

"So what do we do now," Lisa asks, squeezing my hand as she speaks.

"We think it's time to take Joey off life support," Dr. Mitchell says.

For a moment, we take this as good news. "So he no longer needs assistance?" I ask, feeling hopeful.

"I wish that was the case," Dr. Mitchell says. "But the truth is very different." He pauses a beat, confronting the fact that there is no good way to say what he is about to say. "In truth, there is no longer hope. We just don't think this is going to get better. We have used the medically induced coma in every way possible, and there hasn't been any significant recovery. It has been as long as it can be, and we are at that point when it is time to face the news that Joey will not recover. Dr. Santos and our entire team have been consulting with me on this, and we are all of the same opinion. We just wish we could give you some better news, but you need to know the truth."

The room is silent.

After a couple of minutes of digesting this, Lisa says, "What happens when you disengage the life support machines?"

"Joey will pass pretty quickly." His eyes are sad as he says this. "I'm so very sorry."

I momentarily put my head in my hands. Then I look up at Lisa, who looks lost. I take both of her hands in mine. I look back at Dr. Mitchell and say, "So what do you want us to do?"

"You'll have to sign the documents allowing us to remove Joey from life support."

"And what if we don't."

"Then at this point, nothing will happen." He furrows his brow as he searches for the right words, and then says, "We have tried everything we can for as long as we can. At this point, it is not good for you to continue this, and there is no expectation Joey can recover."

"I assume you and the others on the team are in full agreement, Dr. Santos?"

He nods and then says, "I'm so sorry."

"We're not ready to give up," Lisa says.

I nod. "No, we're not."

Dr. Mitchell takes a moment and then says, "I understand how hard this is. If we thought that there was any other way . . ." he let his words trail off and then added. "Now it's really just a matter of acceptance."

Dr. Santos nods in accord, and we sit there feeling lost and desperate as we begin to recognize that what we have so long feared is becoming a reality. "I encourage you to talk further before you reach any conclusion. You know we have tried everything, and there is just nowhere to go from here," Santos says. "Take some time and discuss it."

We nod and leave the room with our hearts broken but not ready to face this.

* * *

The three of them sat at the same table but this time with coffee in front of them.

"What did you want to tell us, Mr. Henry?" Sandoval said.

"I wanted to share information. You interested?"

Sandoval frowned. "Not our job to share information with you."

"Have I mentioned that we are on the same side here? Anders kidnapped two children and hurt one of them badly. Isn't that what matters to all of us?"

"Do you have information?" Edmonds asked.

"Look, I'm trying really hard to work with you. You want to share or not?"

There was only background music for a few moments, and then Sandoval said, "Okay, what do you want to share?"

"Did you get anything from the pictures of Anders you put on television across the country?"

Sandoval shook her head. "Nothing that helps. We got a thousand or so calls with sightings from Anchorage to the Philippines. None of them turned out to be Anders, but we have to spend the time to check out every one of them."

"I understand," Lee said. After a moment of reflection, he said, "You guys interviewed Burt Snider this morning. What are your thoughts about him?"

"I don't hear this as you sharing with us," Edmonds said.

"I talked to him, too. I want to know what you think."

Sandoval nodded to Edmonds and then said, "I think he's the guy. I think he set Anders up with a new identity."

"I'm sure of it," Lee said.

"How?"

"I saw it in his eyes." He waited a moment and added, "Did you get anywhere?"

"No. He denies even knowing Anders."

"Can you search his place? Maybe there's evidence of his business on site."

"Not enough probable cause to get a warrant."

"Hmm. That didn't stop you bugging my car, as I recall."

Sandoval shook her head. "Look, I see this the way you do. I think he's the guy, but I can't toss his house without a warrant, or the bust gets tossed."

"So you need someone else to get you enough to establish PC, right?"

"Well. We need PC. We are not telling you to act to get it for us."

"Now that we all agree who has the information on Anders's new identity, maybe someone can provide you with PC that you can take to a judge."

"Wait. What are you going to do?" Edmonds asked.

"Nice talking to you," Lee said, standing and picking up his to-go cup of coffee.

"You know that you're not authorized to do anything on our behalf, right? And you are not authorized to interfere in our investigation in any way," Sandoval instructed.

"Understood. I'll be in touch."

* * *

"Hello, Mr. Winslow. Have you had a chance to talk further with Mrs. Winslow?"

"Yes, and we are not ready to act yet." *Act*—a euphemism for ending the life of my child. I feel my heart race as I speak. "We can't give up on Joey. We just can't."

There is an awkward silence. After a time, Dr. Mitchell says, "I'm afraid that the time for hope has come and gone, and now we have to deal with reality."

"No, Dr. Mitchell. We are not ready to take any action."

"I understand your wishes, but think about the fact that this is not best for you or Joey. It is time to think about letting him transition."

"We will continue to talk about it and pray about it, Dr. Mitchell, but as of now, we want Joey to remain on life support."

"Yes, sir. I understand," the doctor says softly. "We will talk again soon."

"Thank you, Doctor."

* * *

Jerry put a $200 bet out and waited. He drew a five and an eight. The dealer had a queen showing. He took a hit and drew a queen of his own. That left only $100 of the $2,000 he started betting with two hours ago. He drew an eleven and pulled another hundred from his pocket to go down for double. The dealer had a six showing. He drew an eight, putting him at nineteen. The dealer flipped his down card and revealed a four. His next card was a king and Jerry was beaten again. He stood up and walked away from the table. This was his third outing in three days. He lost $3,000 the first time, $1,000 the second, and another $2,100 here. He realized that he had to stop before his rainy day money was all gone. He was falling into old habits, and he knew that his addictive personality would do him in if he let it. He had to stay away from the tables.

Jerry looked at his watch. He had to be at work in two hours, so that would be a distraction for a while. Then what? Maybe he needed to move away from Vegas and get far away from places that permitted gambling. Maybe he should go to Missouri. A guy he did time with was from Missouri and said it was great. Another new start might be the answer. As he walked down the street, he suddenly found himself thinking about Joey Winslow and hoping the kid would be all right.

Jerry felt the weight of being alone. In his former life he had spent a lot of time alone, sometimes going for days without speaking to another human being, but he could always reach out to Vickie or one of the guys he met in prison if he needed to talk. Now there was no one. It also weighed on him that he might never see his sister again, and Vickie was the one who had always been there for him. She stood by him when they were kids and when he got into trouble as an adult. He cared what she said, and he wanted to please her, but he just couldn't deal with a third conviction and twenty-five more years in prison.

* * *

We sit at the breakfast table. Lisa and I have coffee, and Katy has a bowl of Honey Nut Cheerios and orange juice. With her big blue eyes open wide and moving from Lisa to me and back again, she casually asks, "Is Joey going to die?"

Even after all this time the question is heart-wrenching and soul-crushing. I look at Lisa, and she stares my way in pained desperation. I already know that the pause has been too long as I say, "We don't know, honey. We can't be sure."

She nods as she processes this information. "Are you guys going to die?"

"Someday," Lisa says. "When you are grown up and have a family of your own. But we want to be around to meet your kids and their kids too."

Katy had a look that suggested that she was now worried about that, too. If her big brother could suddenly die, maybe her mom and dad could too. "Joey and I talked about being grown up and still spending time together. Maybe going to the pool or a movie. Joey said we could go see a movie rated R because it's so scary. I hope we get to."

"Yeah, we hope you get to as well, sweetheart," I say. I feel like a truck just backed over my heart. In self-defense, I change the subject. "Do you have your backpack packed and ready to go to school?"

"Yep."

"What are you talking about in school?"

"Words and numbers," she says, putting a big spoonful of cereal into her mouth.

"What are you doing with words and numbers?"

She crunches for a few moments and then says, "We're spelling the words and subtracting the numbers."

"Sounds interesting," I say.

She shrugs. "I guess so. It's really pretty easy, at least till you get to real big numbers." She takes another bite. "Mrs. James says we're going to learn to write a short story."

"Wow, that's great," Lisa says. "What are you going to write about?"

"About me and Joey and all the stuff we want to do."

Shoot me now.

* * *

Lee looked at the readout from the device and saw the route of Snider's Corvette over the past two hours. First was an address on Ventura Boulevard and then one on Saratoga Street. He put the addresses into an app he had for such purposes and saw that the Ventura Boulevard address was a liquor store. Not much help there. He fed the Saratoga Street address into the app and came up with a self-storage facility. Much better.

Lee gathered up the tools he would need and then headed toward the storage units. The first task was to discover which unit had been visited. He drove to the Saratoga Street address and found a long, wide driveway leading to a gated chain-link fence. There was a keypad on the left in front of the gate for driver access and a small office to the right. The sign out front said "Last Frontier Storage." Lee parked the car in one of two vacant spaces in front of the office and walked inside.

There was a long counter as he entered. A thin-faced woman with large rimmed glasses sat at a desk behind the counter. "Can I help you?" she asked in a voice that suggested more annoyance than desire to help.

Lee advanced his best smile. "Yes, I hope you can. My brother asked me to stop and pay his storage bill for next month because he will be traveling. Can I give you the money?"

"Sure," she replied, now smiling herself. "What garage number?"

Lee paused a moment and then said, "Oh, dear, I don't remember," putting on a concerned expression.

"It's okay," she said, helpfully. "What's his name?"

"Snider. Burt Snider."

She moved a mouse around and looked at the monitor for her computer. "Here it is, Burt Snider." Now Lee knew that he wasn't using an alias for access to whatever he kept here. She paused and then said, "That will be $150."

"Okay," Lee said and handed her the money."

"Let me just print out your receipt." She punched a couple of buttons and a printer whirred to life across the room. She walked over and picked up the document and handed it to Lee. "There you go. You're all set."

Lee smiled and said, "Thank you for your assistance." He glanced at the receipt and did not see what he hoped for.

"Something wrong?" she asked.

"Well, if you could just put the unit number on the document so that my brother's receipt is complete, I would really appreciate it. He's kind of a stickler."

"Sure," she said, grinning. She wrote on the document and then said, "Unit L 117. You're all set."

"Thanks, again, ma'am. You have been most helpful. Maybe I can write a good review of you and your facility online."

"That would be great," she said. "You'll find us at FrontierStorage.com"

"Great, and what's your name?"

"I'm Lilly, manager here."

"Well, Lilly, I will mention just how helpful you were."

"Thank you, Mr. Snider," she said, grinning. "And don't forget to come see us for your storage needs."

"I wouldn't go anywhere else," he said, smiling. "Bye now."

Lee walked out to his car and waited. It took about ten minutes before another car drove up to the gate. The driver entered his access code on the keypad and the gate swung open laterally. The driver moved through the gate and Lee followed closely. There were rows of storage garages with building letters identifying each. Lee drove straight ahead until he found building L and then turned right,

* * *

Lee looked around and saw no one in the area. He lifted the garage door, and an alarm sounded. It was a repetitious beep that was not very loud. He walked into the unit and found that there were two large, four-drawer file cabinets. He grinned widely and began with the top drawer of the cabinet on the left. He found a series of tools suitable to the trade. Printing and engraving equipment, files containing exemplars of driver's licenses by state, and various credit cards. Impressive. In the second drawer was more of the same. In the third, he found what he was looking for. There was a file that contained names; none of them said Jerry Anders, and none of them contained any familiar name. He began to think that he had hit a dead end, but a sudden thought gave him hope. Maybe the names he saw on the file tabs were the new names, the newly minted names, rather than the real names of the people who came to him. He began to look through each file. About twenty files in, he found what he was looking for. There was a reference to Jerry Anders in the file. On the tab, the file said Frank Adams, Boise, Idaho. "I got you, you son of a bitch. Here I come, Anders," Lee said aloud. He looked through the remainder of the drawers and saw that Snider had maintained very nice records of about two hundred different set-ups, dating back almost five years. The final drawer was shallow, and he quickly recognized that it had a false bottom. He pulled the tool he needed from his car and pried the false bottom upward until it gave. There he saw several tall stacks of hundreds. He picked them up and examined them. There was about $12,000. He nodded to himself and then said, "Nice of you to handle the costs of the investigation and some of Joey Winslow's medical expenses, Mr. Snider."

The alarm had stopped, and no one had shown up at the unit. He kept the Frank Adams file, and grabbed about ten others, randomly selected. He affixed the two new padlocks and drove away. He had to wait for someone else to open the gate so that he could exit behind them without being noticed. While he waited, he looked through the file and saw several credit card copies, a copy of Frank's driver's license with a picture of one Jerry Anders on it. After about twenty minutes, he was able to follow another storage customer through the gate without attracting attention. He checked the tracking device readout and saw that Snider's Corvette was at home.

Lee stopped at his office for long enough to make a copy of the Anders file. He left the copy of the Anders file and the originals of all the other files at his office and then drove back to Burt Snider's house with the original Anders file. He was looking forward to this meeting, and he knew it would go better than the last.

Chapter 34

As the day changed color, with blue skies covered by pre-storm clouds, Lee parked a full block from the Snider house. He walked down the sidewalk until he saw that the Corvette was, as the tracking device had told him, parked safely in the driveway. He looked toward the house and saw that no one was looking back at him, either at the front door or at any of the draped windows.

Lee walked next to the car, pulled a cordless nail gun from his jacket pocket and fired two nails into the left front tire of the Corvette, just in case Snider decided a quick getaway was in order. He watched with satisfaction as the tire deflated, and then moved up the driveway to the front porch.

When Lee reached the front door, he knocked and yelled, "UPS delivery."

The front door opened, and the obese man stepped back in surprise.

"May I come in?" Lee asked. Snider said nothing. Lee opened the door and said, "Thanks," as he walked in.

"What the fuck do you want?" Snider said. "Get out of my house."

"Okay, but you'll want to talk to me first."

"I don't want to talk to you, you son of a bitch. Get out."

Lee raised his palms and said, "I'm trying to be nice here. I have information that you will want to know." Snider seethed silently, while Lee continued. "I told you before that I was only after Anders, at least at first. You remember that?" Silence. "You made a bad decision, so I thought I should give you a little more information. So here we are."

"Get the fuck out of my house."

"Mr. Snider, you're not listening well. Now, I need you to tell me where Mr. Anders is living."

"I am not telling you shit."

Lee smiled and pulled the file from inside his jacket. "Recognize this?"

In an instant, the man turned red and then white. Lee thought he would pass out. "Where did you get that?"

"I see that the file is familiar to you." Snider grabbed at the file, and Lee jerked it away. "Now that is just rude," he said. "I'll leave now if you would like."

"What do you want?" Snider asked in a low voice, as if it was hard to push the words out.

"I am willing to sell you this file."

"How much?"

"No money. All I need for it is the name of the city where Jerry Anders, or should I say Frank Adams, relocated. You give me that, I give you the file, and I walk out of here. You'll have to agree that it's a pretty good deal really. But," Lee added dramatically, "if the file isn't that important to you, I understand, and I will be on my way."

"I don't know where he went, man."

"Bullshit."

"I have no idea."

"I'm disappointed, Mr. Snider. We were making such great strides, too."

Snider sat down on the couch and put both hands over his mouth thoughtfully. He stole a glance at the cushion beside him. Lee raced toward him as he pulled a gun from underneath the adjacent cushion. Lee hit Snider in the face, and the crack was audible. Blood poured from the bridge of his nose, and he grabbed the wound with both hands, allowing Lee to pick up the gun. Snider was moving back and forth and groaning audibly as he held his nose.

"You're going to need something to clean this up right away or the blood will stain your furniture," Lee said. "I don't care what they say on infomercials, it's difficult to get blood out of fabric." He shook his head. "See you, Mr. Snider. You can't say I didn't give you a chance to come out of this okay." Lee walked toward the door carrying the gun in one hand and the file in the other.

In nasal tones that sounded like he had suddenly acquired a bad cold, Snider said, "Okay, okay. I'll tell you, but you can't say where you got it, man. That has to be part of the deal, or I never get another case."

"A case? Is that what you call making counterfeit docs for assholes like this? I'll be darned." He watched Snider, who was still holding his nose with both hands as he looked at Lee expectantly. "Yeah, that is part of the deal. I won't say where I learned his whereabouts."

"He went to Vegas. I can't guarantee he stayed there, but that was where he was going."

Lee nodded and then threw the file down on the coffee table. "All yours," he said, smiling. "See how easy that was?" His expression grew stern as he looked at Snider. "Two more things you should know. If you lied to me, or if you attempt to contact this asshole in any way—phone, fax, e-mail, carrier pigeon, semaphore, or a guy who gave you both great blow jobs in the joint—any contact at all, I will be back here to bust up the rest of your face and take your ass to the cops. You got that, Mr. Snider." Snider nodded but said nothing. Lee walked out and down the driveway. He looked at the Corvette and yelled back toward the house, "Looks like you have a flat tire."

* * *

"Frank Adams is a pretty common name," the voice on the phone offered.

Lee responded as he drove. "I know Frank Adams is a common name, but, wait, there's more. I also have a fake Social Security number—probably used to be real but belongs to a dead guy, and a fake Idaho driver license. If the guy is using any of these numbers, we find him, right?"

"It's gonna take some time. We have to dig through the big employers, casinos, apartment owners, and the like. You got anything else?"

"Well, the guy used to be a degenerate gambler, and he had twenty grand when he disappeared. He's also likely to work in a low-profile job when the money is gone, and as far as I know, he doesn't have any specific industry training. My guess is that he would look for something in construction, maintenance, gardening, or repair. Some gig that doesn't have too many people looking at his face because it has been on TV across the country."

"Well, I guess that helps."

"You guess? Come on, there has to be some work left for you guys to do."

"All right, give me forty-eight hours."

"I need it sooner. Get it done in twenty-four, and I'll pay double." Lee smiled, feeling generous with Burt Snider's money.

"Okay, we're on it."

* * *

It was the first time we walked up the stairs together. Lisa held my hand as we sat in the nautical living room and waited. Within two minutes, Pat enters from his door and holds out a hand to Lisa. He smiles and says, "Lisa, I can truthfully say that I have heard a lot about you, and all of it is good."

"Thanks," Lisa says, and shakes Pat's hand. "I'm here because Scott says that you have been helpful to him."

"Thanks for squeezing us in this afternoon, Pat," I offer.

Pat says, "I'm glad you came." He reflects and then says, "Lisa, I understand that you have seen my colleague, Alexandra Sawyer."

"Yes, a couple of times."

"Was that helpful?" he asks.

"I think it was. She is a very compassionate woman."

He smiles. "I think so, too. And Scott tells me that you have close friends that provide support as well?"

"I have a great support group. I have three friends who are very close to me. Two that I've been close to since college and one since junior high. They have been there when I needed to talk." She looks over at me. "And Scott has helped me too. We've been holding each other up through all this."

"That's good. That's what really counts." He stops and takes in the distressed expressions we aren't hiding. "So something is happening right now we should discuss. Please, tell me."

I draw a breath and then say, "The doctors are telling us that it is time to take Joey off the life support system. That he is not going to improve and that we need to let him go." I am tearing up even before I finish this sentence. Lisa squeezes my hand with one of hers and pushes her own tears away with the other.

"I am so sorry," Pat says. "That is awful. What did you tell the doctors?"

"We said no," Lisa says. "We told him that we can't let them pull our baby off the machines that are keeping him alive."

"And you've been talking about it and thinking about it since then," Pat says, not as a question but as a statement of fact.

"Yes," Lisa offers. "We have discussed almost nothing else."

"Of course," Pat says and waits for her to continue.

"We are fighting this so hard," she says. "Fighting and praying and talking and crying."

"And you still don't know what you should do." Another statement.

"Yes. We are feeling trapped in an impossible situation."

"Do you believe that it would be best for Joey if you let him go?" Pat asks softly.

The room goes quiet. Lisa and I look at each other and then I say, "Yes, that is part of what we believe. That maybe we are doing something wrong keeping him here if there is no hope. That maybe we need to let him move on."

"Lisa, how about you?"

Lisa nods and then starts crying hard. She sobs hard until she can hardly get a breath. I take her in my arms and hold her. After a time, she manages to say, "I should never outlive my baby."

"You are right, of course," Pat replies. "No parent should have to outlive their child. It is the worst kind of situation."

Lisa nods through tears and whispers, "We just don't know what to do. Can you help us?"

It occurs to me that Pat seldom shows his own emotion, but now he wears an expression that is part pain and part concern. He is quiet a moment and then says, "I cannot tell you what to do about this, but I can tell you a couple of things that may help. First of all, Joey loves you. He loves you now and forever and that will never be taken away from you." He pauses and lets that settle as we both battle tears. "The other thing you need to know is that none of this is your fault. You didn't do this. A deranged guy did this to all of you." He takes a breath and adds, "Parents often blame themselves for what others do to their children. They believe it was part of their job to prevent anything bad. Truth is we're just not that powerful. The world has bad things in it that are well beyond our control." We listen intently as he adds, "The point of all this is that you have to forgive yourself for any fault you assign yourselves. You don't deserve to be blamed, and often people know that on an intellectual level, but emotionally they haven't reached that conclusion. So forgive yourself for fault you ascribe to yourselves. Forgive yourselves and love each other, Joey, and Katy. Whatever you decide to do, Joey will be with you forever."

I say, "We told the doctors that we couldn't authorize taking him off life support. Ever since, we have been consumed by that decision." I draw a deep breath, looking for words that get caught in my throat. And then I try again. "That decision isn't feeling right to us, and it is haunting us."

"Lisa?" Pat asks. "Do you feel the same?"

She nods. "It doesn't feel like we're protecting our son anymore. It feels like we may be doing something bad for him because we can't stand to lose him."

"It sounds like you may have found the right answer," he says. "And you are thinking the right way—about what is best for your son. I know we all want to hold our family members as long as we can, and sometimes because we are unable to let go, we can hold on too long. I think your heart tells you what is right. As long as you remember that you are making the best decision you can based upon the best medical information available. You are doing what you feel is right for your son. Never let go of that."

There are a few moments of silence while we digest this, and then Lisa says, "When they first put Joey into the coma, I had no doubt that he would be back within days or a couple of weeks. As the weeks went by, I held tight to that belief. Then it was months, and now it is longer than any medically induced coma the doctors had ever known to be successful. But it is only in the last few days that I have allowed myself to even contemplate the decision we are now asked to make. I've always known this was possible intellectually, but emotionally I just refused to believe it. Now we face a Sophie's choice of the worst kind, and it seems like there is no good decision. We are trying to avoid doing something that makes things worse now that we know that nothing can make things better."

"You are great parents," Pat said. "Joey is a lucky boy."

In that nautical living room, we hold hands and say a prayer for Joey. Then we thank Pat for listening and helping us. When we walk from that room, we have decided to follow the advice of the doctors and let our son go. Our hearts hurt, and the world feels merciless, but we know what we must do.

* * *

Lee went to his office and spent a few hours on other assignments needing his attention. Late in the afternoon, he went home to pack a bag and pick up the files he got from Snider's self-storage garage. After he had assembled what he needed, he dialed the phone.

"Yes, Mr. Henry, what now?"

"Now we meet at the same coffee shop. This time you guys are buying, and I want a large coffee. How about two hours from now?"

"You have something good?" agent Sandoval asked.

"I think you'll like it, yeah."

"Can you give me anything more?"

"All in good time. Although I understand your elevated anticipation levels. Tom Petty tells me that the waiting is the hardest part."

"I'm glad you amuse yourself, Mr. Henry."

"See you soon," Lee said and hung up.

Chapter 35

August 31, 2016

We make an appointment to see Dr. Mitchell and drive to the hospital. As soon as we arrive, we are escorted into his office and directed to his two visitor chairs. Five minutes later he appears at the door in his trademark blue operating gear, peeling the blue hat from his head.

He walks in extending a hand and says, "So sorry for the delay." He walks around his desk to his chair and sits; then he waits for one of us to speak.

"We are going to follow your advice, Dr. Mitchell," I say in a pained voice.

He looks at Lisa, and she nods. "I know how hard this is," he replies. "I am so sorry it couldn't have been different."

We nod but do not find any other words.

"Do you want to spend some time with him?"

We both nod. "I need a medical team assembled, so unless you tell me so, I will schedule the team for 7:00 p.m., about four hours from now, unless you tell me that does not work for you."

We look at each other, and Lisa says, "Yes, okay."

"We want to stay with him tonight, until the time comes," I add.

"Of course," Dr. Mitchell says. "That is just fine."

We walk to Joey's room for what we now know will be our last visit. My heart is beating rapidly, and I am sure that my pulse and BP are off the charts. We hold hands and walk into the room, looking at the feeding tubes and breathing equipment swarming around our baby. It somehow looks different. The machines and equipment appear more massive, intrusive, and inhuman. I know that Joey would not want to live like this forever, even if that was possible. I walk over and take his hand. I kiss him on the forehead and tell him how much I love him, how proud I am to be his dad, and how he will be with me always. I talk to him about the times we spent together, the funny comments, the hikes, the ballgames, and the fun we had every day. I tell him how much I respect the way he cares about family and his friends. I tell him that I learned so much from him and that he helped make me a better person. I tell him that he did a great job on this earth bringing love and compassion to us and to everyone he knew. I tell him that I will miss him endlessly, and I will never forget him. Then I lean against the wall and cry while Lisa has her final visit with our brave boy.

* * *

As he drove, Lee hit a single button and waited.

"Yeah."

"Anything yet?"

"Nothing yet. We're going through all the employers we can ID to see if anyone with the Social Security number was hired, but this is a big job."

"Keep at it. Don't forget that double payment I promised," Lee said and hung up.

Lee parked the car and walked into Matthew's Coffee House at 6:00 p.m., carrying the files that used to belong to Burt Snider. Sandoval and Edmonds were seated at their usual booth. They had a coffee cup in front of each of them and a third waited for him.

Lee sat down and said, "Good evening, agent Sandoval, agent Edmonds."

"Mr. Henry," Edmonds said.

Lee looked at his coffee and said, "This looks great." He took a sip and put the cup down. The agents looked at him expectantly. "Turns out we were right," he said. "Mr. Snider is our man."

"How did we establish that?" Sandoval asked.

"We found some evidence. Here is the file on Jerry Anders, who is now one Frank Adams from Boise, Idaho." He dropped the file on the table in front of them.

They both reviewed the file and then asked, "Did he give this to you?"

Lee left the question unanswered. "Can you get the word out on Frank Adams? There is a Social Security number and an Idaho DL with a picture of our man on it in there also."

"Did Mr. Snider share with you where Mr. Anders or Adams might be?"

"He initially moved to Las Vegas, but Snider doesn't know that he stayed there."

"How did you get him to share this information with you?"

Another question Lee chose not to answer. Instead, Lee said, "Here are ten other files from Mr. Snider's collection—some other folks that he has serviced in the not too distant past. All of this should give you PC for a warrant. And to focus the warrant a little bit, you want to go beyond his charming little home to his self-storage garage. It's called Last Frontier Storage on Saratoga Street. You want garage number L 117. There are numerous other files like that stack in front of you in the two file cabinets in that storage garage."

Sandoval furrowed her brow. "What did you do to this guy?"

"He's fine. We had a very nice conversation, and I encouraged him to see things from my perspective." They were both looking at him when he put the cup down. "What?" he asked.

"What are we going to walk into when we approach this guy with a warrant?"

Lee shrugged. "Probably not too much. I mean, how can he resist you guys with a search warrant?" Lee stood and said. "Thanks for the coffee. I have to go." He paused and then added, "Oh, one more thing.

Here are the keys for both locks on L 117. Makes your access easier."
He dropped the keys on the table and said, "See you later."

"He turned these keys over to you?" Edmonds asked.

Lee said, "Not exactly," and then walked out of the coffee house
while Sandoval and Edmonds stared at the keys and the files on the
table. Then they regarded each other with a grin and began to dig
through the files.

* * *

At 7:00 p.m., we stand in Joey's room watching what looks like an
entire surgical team. Dr. Mitchell walks over to us and says, "Do we
proceed now?"

I nod as my heart sinks. He looks to Lisa, who nods with closed eyes.

Dr. Mitchell turns and walks back to the bed. He says, "We begin."
In some mysterious but predefined order, we see hoses and tubes removed one at a time, alarms shut down, fluids taken from hangers, and
machines turned off. It is all done within five minutes. Dr. Mitchell says
to the room, "7:08 p.m.," and a nurse notates a chart. He walks over to
us and says, "Now is your time to be with your son," as our chairs are
placed next to the bed.

We walk over to our son and kiss him. We tell him how much we
love him, and then we sit by him, touching his arm, taking his hand,
and talking to him whenever we are able to find words. We share everything we can while we wait for the inevitable loss that will haunt
us forever.

Nurses check on Joey, and on us, at least every hour all through
the night. At 7:00 a.m., we are still awake, and Joey is still alive and
breathing on his own in a room that is quietly free of machine noises,
alarms, and beeps. We are exhausted, but neither of us will leave, fearing that we will miss the last moment of Joey's life. The hospital brings
us bagels and coffee for breakfast, and we occasionally walk around
the small room to stretch.

At noon, Dr. Mitchell appears. He examines Joey and looks at Lisa
and me, waiting expectantly. "He's doing it all himself," he says. "His

pulse is strong, and blood pressure isn't too low. I'll be back at 3:00 p.m. to check on you."

At 3:00 p.m., nothing has changed. Joey is still hanging on. Dr. Mitchell walks in at 3:10 and examines Joey. He looks at us and nods. "Pulse and BP are still strong." He reflects a moment and then says, "It may be time to make another decision. I can give him some IV fluids to keep him hydrated if you would like."

"We want to," I say, and Lisa agrees.

"I don't want to get your hopes up too high," Dr. Mitchell says. "Sometimes it can be a couple of days before the patient lets go."

"We understand," I say. "But give him what it takes not to starve him while we wait."

"You have to sign additional forms for that, okay?

"Yeah, more than okay."

Within twenty minutes, we sign forms and two drips are set up. We agree to take turns with a two-hour nap and a shower. Lisa leaves to take her turn, not at all sure that she will be able to do any sleeping, while I talk to Joey about the weather, beautiful places we need to visit, and the Walters case and its upcoming trial. I talk of anything and everything. Every half hour, nurses buzz around him, take his vitals, and give me a smile or a satisfied nod.

At five thirty, Lisa walks in wearing clean clothes. She still looks tired. "How is he?" she asks.

"The same. Still hanging on."

Lisa hands me a Starbucks coffee and a roast beef sandwich. "Thank you," I say. "Were you able to sleep?"

"Not for a second. I was totally consumed with getting back. But the shower felt good."

"I'm going to run and do the same, okay?"

"Sure. Take some time for a nap if you can."

"I'm sure I won't be able to sleep," I say. "I'm already anxious about getting back, and I haven't even left yet."

* * *

"You look familiar. Where have I seen you before?" a man walking between the casino and the restroom stops to ask Jerry.

"I don't think I know you, but I do have the kind of face that everyone says they recognize."

"Did you go to school in Boston?"

"No, grew up in Idaho," Jerry says.

"Hmm. I could have sworn ..." he lets his words trail off. "Oh well, have a good day, man."

Jerry took a deep breath. This was the third similar conversation with a stranger since the ads starting running seeking the public's help in locating him. It was just a matter of time until someone could place him. Did he wait until faced with that recognition before leaving, or did he go now? He told himself that there was really no choice. Tomorrow was payday. He would collect his check and then drive for North Carolina. He had heard Charlotte was a nice city, and big enough to allow him to be swallowed up in the sea of humanity. Tonight he would pack the car, and tomorrow he was gone by lunchtime. He felt better just having made the decision. He checked his watch. Two more hours in his shift and in this job. He walked outside to take a cigarette break and reflect. He desperately wanted to hear Vickie's voice again. He would give her a call when he made it to Charlotte. Maybe she could be made to understand that he had no choice. Maybe she could even forgive him. Then his thoughts strayed to Joey Winslow once again. He wondered if the kid was still alive.

* * *

August 31, 2016

We are back in the news. The media is buzzing about the little boy who had been taken off life support after eight months and is still hanging on. We have no idea how they got that information. Articles in newspapers and online picture Jerry Anders and address the kidnapping. This inspires articles about the Walters case and the fact that Jerry

Anders demanded its dismissal to help his brother-in-law and Consolidated Energy CEO Michael Constantine. They address the dismissal of the case that Anders forced, the stipulation to reinstate the case, and the fact that trial is now only a couple of months away. Pictures of Joey go viral on the Internet, with captions about the little boy who hangs on.

Just before noon, Dr. Mitchell examines Joey. He looks at us and says, "He is still strong, but I want to do some more testing. Is that okay?"

We nod. "What are you thinking?" I ask.

"Too early to say just yet. I will set up some imaging."

Dr. Mitchell disappeared, and within twenty minutes a technician appeared and told us that they were ready to run some tests. Joey was wheeled from the room, and we were told that Dr. Mitchell would be with us in an hour. We walked to the hospital cafeteria with some combination of fear and renewed hope.

"You doing okay?" I ask Lisa as we walk down the hospital corridor, following the green line to where coffee awaits.

"I think so," she says. "This can't be bad, right?

I nod, but I have no idea what to make of all this.

* * *

"Team two in place?" Sandoval said softly into her phone.

"Roger."

"Team three in place?"

"Roger," another voice said.

Sandoval nodded to Edmonds, and they took positions on either side of the front door and pounded hard. "This is the FBI, Mr. Snider. Open the door." Silence. "Open the door, Mr. Snider." No response.

Sandoval gave a nod, and two officers hit the front door with a battering ram. As they did, Sandoval's phone crackled to life. "He's trying to get out through a bathroom window. We have him," Dan Ortiz of team two said.

As Sandoval and Edmonds stepped through the broken front door, Ortiz and his team brought Snider back inside through the back door.

"Mr. Snider?" Silence. "Mr. Snider, we have a warrant for your arrest. We have a second warrant to search your residence and your storage unit." She attempted to hand him the warrants, but he did not take them. She spoke into her phone. "Okay, team three, we have him. Hit the storage unit."

"That son of a bitch," Snider mumbled.

Sandoval knew he was referring to Lee Henry and wanted to smile, but she didn't. Instead she said, "Mr. Snider, you are under arrest for wire fraud, mail fraud, money laundering, and counterfeiting of credit cards. You have the right to remain silent. You have the right to be represented by counsel. If you cannot afford an attorney, one will be appointed for you. If you waive your right to remain silent, anything you say can and will be used against you in a court of law. Do you understand these rights?" Silence. "Do you understand these rights? Use your words."

"I want an attorney."

"Good for you; I knew you could do it. You can call your attorney after we book you."

* * *

Lee sat down on the plane and waited for takeoff. He dialed, and the phone rang.

On the second ring, he heard, "Don't have anything yet."

"Time is tight. There is a whole new wave of media surrounding this son of a bitch. It might be enough to make him fly."

"We're working it as fast as possible."

"All right. Just so you know, I'm giving the name, DL, and Social to the FBI so they can start working it through their files as well. See if you can get there first. I'll call you when I land in Vegas. It should be within the hour."

"Got it. We'll stay on it until we get a hit."

Lee sat down in his seat and dialed agent Becky Sandoval.

"Hello, Mr. Henry."

"You got anything on the whereabouts of Frank Adams?"

"We are going through all fourteen persons known as Frank Adams identified as living or working in the greater Las Vegas area. I think that so far they have narrowed the list by half."

"And when you get to the likely guy, you will let me know?"

"I can't do that, Mr. Henry. I'm not permitted to give our official information."

"Agent Sandoval, I got you this far, remember? I am not going to interfere with your investigation. Your local agents will go make the bust. I just want to backstop this project."

"You'll step back, and let our agents go get him?"

"Yes."

"Without getting in the way?"

"Yes."

Sandoval was quiet for a moment and then said, "Okay, but no one knows this but you and me, understood?"

"Understood."

* * *

Dr. Mitchell walks into Joey's room a half hour after Joey was returned. He wears a grin and shakes his head. "Well, I have some news." We stare at him not wanting to delay the news by interjecting words. "The swelling around Joey's brain has been reduced by about 50 percent. The charts show his vitals are stronger as the anesthesia slowly begins to fade."

"He's going to make it?" I ask, holding my breath.

He looks from me to Lisa and says, "We can't be sure, but we have just seen amazing and unexpected improvement. I'd like to have your permission to give him low levels of anesthetic and reduce those levels slowly. We have to see if he can come out of the coma after all this time."

"Yes, yes, of course," Lisa yells excitedly.

"We can't get too far ahead of ourselves, however. First, we don't know that he will come out of the coma, and second, we don't know how his brain has been affected by the long-term swelling and whether there will be permanent damage."

"We understand," I say, taking Lisa's hand.

She nods and says, "As long as he comes back to us, we can deal with anything else."

Dr. Mitchell nods. "I have to say that this is pretty amazing. I've never seen anything like this." As much as he wants to control our excitement, he is grinning again. As he walks away, it occurs to me that I have never seen him smile before.

Chapter 36

September 2, 2016

As soon as the plane touched down at McCarren Airport in Las Vegas, Lee could see that he had a voice mail message from agent Sandoval. He grabbed his carry-on from the overhead and walked briskly off the plane and into the terminal toward the rental car shuttle.

He played the voice mail as he walked. "Mr. Henry, I got your message. We are still running Frank Adams and the Social and driver's license you gave us through our computers. I have alerted our Las Vegas office, and Carl Timmons is working the matter. I will get back to you when we have the guy identified." There was a pause, and then she added, "We picked up Snider and his identity treasure trove. Thanks for the anonymous tip."

When he picked up his Toyota Camry rental car, Lee raced from the lot. He dialed a number and waited. As always, it was answered on the second ring. "Yeah, we're still working on it."

"Okay. The FBI is on it too. See if you can get there first. After all, I gave you guys a head start. I'm here in Vegas and ready to chase whatever you find."

"We'll call you as soon as we get it."

Lee drove toward the strip not sure of what his next step would be.

* * *

Jerry was getting frustrated. His plan was to be gone by noon. He walked into the office operating manager's at Maggie's Casino for the third time that day. "Are the checks in yet?"

Supervisor Jason Lyons said, "No, Frank, not yet. I told you I'd buzz you when they arrived."

Jerry checked his watch. It was just after 4:00 p.m. This was his third attempt to pick up his check.

"You need some money for an appointment or something?" the manager asked.

"No, I'm okay. I just want to get some bills paid."

The manager nodded. "Are you off work now?"

"Not until four thirty."

"All right, check back then." As he spoke, his phone rang, and he checked the readout. "Hang on," he said, "this is going to be about the checks."

"Hello." Silence. "I see." More silence. "Yeah, that's fine, thanks."

He hung up and smiled at Jerry. "Checks are being messengered over from the payroll people, Frank. They should be here in twenty minutes. Stop by when your shift is over, and I should have your check in hand."

"Okay, thanks," Jerry said as he walked out of the office. He hadn't planned on working all day that day, but no problem. He reminded himself that the car was all packed to go, so another twenty minutes wouldn't matter.

* * *

Lee's phone rang. "Yeah?"

"We have him." I'm sending you a company picture and address. Check your phone in about one minute."

"Nice work. I'll be looking for it." As he hung up, there was a ding. Lee looked at the phone, and there was a picture of Jerry Anders. He now had black hair and a close-cropped wraparound beard, the goatee portion bushy, but the deep-set eyes and facial structure were unmistakable. Under the picture, it said "Frank Adams employment photo."

He was a maintenance guy at a casino called Maggie's. Lee put the address in his phone and raced toward the destination. He checked his watch. It was 4:45 p.m.

Lee pushed a button and waited for the second ring. "Did you get it?" a voice asked.

"I got it. Great work. Please get a copy over to agent Carl Timmons at the FBI office in Las Vegas right away."

"You got it, man."

"You earned your double your money."

"We're that good, man. The invoice is being e-mailed to you as we speak."

When he hung up, Lee pulled a number for Maggie's Casino and dialed.

"Maggie's" a well-worn-sounding female voice said.

"Maintenance Department, please."

"One moment."

A series of clicks and then a voice said, "Maintenance, this is Jason Lyons."

"Hi, Jason. Let me talk to Frank Adams, will you?"

"Sorry, he just left for the day."

"Can I talk to your manager?"

"I am the department supervisor."

"Are you going to be there for the next twenty minutes?"

"Yeah, why?"

"I'm an investigator, Jason, and I need to get to Adams."

"Something wrong?"

"He is a suspected kidnapper who is on the run. Now what's his address?"

"I can't give out his contact info. I can call him and have him call you if you would like."

"Are you kidding? The guy is on the run from the law."

"Look, mister, I don't know who you are, and Adams is expected back at work in the morning."

"I'll be there in a few minutes, and so will the FBI. You can tell them his address if you won't share it with me. Do not call him. You got that, Mr. Lyons?"

"Yeah, I have it."

When Lee got to Maggie's Casino, there were three unmarked and a black and white at the door. Another came racing up as Lee ran into the casino and looked around for some clue as to which way to go. One of the casino's directional arrows pointed toward the offices, so he ran in that direction. In the distance, he saw a narrow hallway filled with police.

A uniformed officer stopped him as he approached. "What do you need?"

"I'm an investigator. I turned over Anders's ID to the FBI."

The officer was unimpressed. "And?" he said.

A voice came from down the hall. "Let him in."

As Lee walked past the myriad of officers, a man with short brown hair and dark-rimmed glasses that rested on a large nose walked into the hall and extended a hand. "I'm Carl Timmons. And this is my partner, Margo Barnes. A well-dressed and beautiful black-haired woman with perfect olive skin extended a hand that Lee shook. He apparently looked at her a little too long. Timmons chuckled and said, "Yep, Margo has that effect on people."

"Sorry," Lee said, returning to the world.

"So you're him," Timmons said, smirking.

"Him?" Lee asked.

"Yeah, you're the investigator that Sandoval says is a pain in the ass and a smartass, but, what did she say? Has the soul of a great cop."

Lee grinned and said, "What have we got?"

Timmons replied, "Our man is gone for the day. Expected back at 7:30 a.m."

"Are we betting he shows?" Lee asked.

"Meaning what?"

"Meaning if he gets the scent of this," Lee said, waving an arm toward the cops crowding the hallway, "he is long gone."

"I agree. Now that we know we have the right guy, we are setting up a three-mile containment, which is under way right now, and some of us are headed over to Adams's apartment."

"I'll stay back, but I want to follow. I need to know that we have this guy."

"Fair enough. Let's go."

Timmons and Barnes led Lee and four other agents out to cars scattered around Maggie's, and they pulled out of the lot and raced down the street. Lee followed the last of the three FBI cars as they hurled through traffic, making a sudden left and then two consecutive rights, almost without slowing down. They skidded to a halt double-parked in front of an apartment building, and the officers raced inside. Lee walked around the outside, getting his bearings and looking for anything unusual. Two minutes later, Timmons emerged and said, "The unit is empty. Clothing and bathroom stuff is gone. My guess is that the son of a bitch caught wind of us and ran. Now we just have to figure out which way he went."

Lee ran his hands through his hair. "Dammit," he said, "we have to be right behind him. We have to figure out which way he went in case your containment measures weren't in place before he ran for it. He could have an hour jump on us. An hour and a half if he was already packed when he went to work today and left right from Maggie's."

Timmons nodded. "That is actually quite possible. The maintenance manager said that he came by three times this afternoon to pick up his check. It arrived, and he grabbed it at 4:30 p.m. Could be that he planned on exiting as soon as the paycheck hit."

"So what now?"

"Now we notify police agencies in all directions within five hundred miles that Adams could be coming their way. We know who he is, but we don't know what he's driving. I have people checking all area rental car outlets and car lots to see if Adams rented or bought something in the past two months. We are also checking stolen vehicle reports to see what has disappeared in the last few days. I've also got teams knocking on the doors of neighbors to see when they last saw Adams."

Lee nodded, feeling frustrated. The son of a bitch did it again. He's got the road just before the net came down. Lee said to Timmons, "I suggest you find out whether he cashed the check yet. If so, where and what time so that we know exactly how much of a lead he has on us."

Timmons nodded and reached for his phone.

Agent Barnes approached them. She was talking on the phone. "Yes, in the same radius. Get the picture of Anders and the name Frank Adams out to every gas station, minimarket, and coffee shop. He's likely to stop at one of them." She hangs up and looks at me. "You did some nice work here, Mr. Henry. I understand you are a friend of the victims' parents."

"Yes, they are good people."

She nods. "And they've got a good friend. We'll do everything we can to see that this guy doesn't get past us."

* * *

Jerry stopped for gas for the car. He walked into the minimart and picked up a bag of chips and a soda. Then he went to the register and paid for the food and the gas. The car was from one of those rent-a-wreck places and looked it. Ten years old and full of dings, but the small gray Ford ran well enough. Jerry rented it for the entire week, so he had six more days before they expected it to be returned. Ample time to dump it along the way and get something else.

He made his way back to Interstate 40 and continued eastbound. He would find a hotel in Kingman, Arizona for the night and continue on toward Charlotte in the morning. No one would even know he was gone until he didn't show up for work tomorrow morning, and he was contemplating calling Maggie's Casino and telling his boss that he would be out sick for another day. He felt the relief of the road to some new beginning. Jerry felt good until the moment he saw the red flashing lights behind him. His heart sank. For a moment he thought about making a run for it, but he knew that never worked out. Slowly, he moved to the side of the highway and stopped. He could feel the blood coursing through his veins as the officer appeared at the passenger side window with his hand over the gun in his holster.

"Evening, sir," the officer said politely. "Let me see your driver's license and registration."

Jerry handed him his Frank Adams Idaho driver's license. "This is a rental car, but I'm sure they must have something about its registration in the glove box." Jerry found and handed him the document.

"Just a moment, sir," the officer said and made his way back to his car. Jerry sat, his heart pounding, for three minutes. As the officer returned he could feel himself sweating.

The officer handed him the documents. "You have a rear taillight that is out, Mr. Adams. Seeing as this is a rental car, I'm going to let you go with a warning. Make sure you tell the rental car company to get it fixed, okay?"

"Yes, sir. Thank you for your courtesy."

The officer said, "Drive safely," and walked from the window.

Jerry took off slowly and carefully. As he drove away, he saw the Nevada Highway Patrol officer who had stopped him make a U-turn across the grass median and head back in the other direction.

* * *

The police checkpoints reported in every fifteen minutes. The police captain provided updates to the FBI every time these reports were received. Four reports from each of twelve checkpoints around the city, and nothing on Frank Adams. Lee sat in an FBI conference room listening to the last report. It had been over an hour, and it seemed more and more likely that he had made it through the police dragnet and was safely on the other side. But where? Lee stared at an area map that consumed most of one wall in the conference room. Without knowing where Anders was headed, there were just too many alternatives.

"I hear that you figured out that Adams was really Jerry Anders," agent Barnes said. "Nice piece of work."

"Thanks," Lee said, "But not too damned helpful if he manages to disappear and become someone else before we can track him."

"Want some coffee?"

Lee nodded. "Yeah, make it a double."

She laughed. "So what do you do when you're not chasing Jerry Anders across the country?"

"I chase other people." He poured coffee and then sat down beside her. "What do you do when you're not working, Margo?" He paused. "Can I call you Margo?"

"If I can call you Lee." He nodded, and she continued, "I like hiking, tennis, reading books, and I'd go to the beach if Nevada wasn't landlocked. I grew up in Lincoln City, Oregon, and I love the coast."

"Been there, and I agree. Great spot. So how did you wind up in Vegas?"

"Joined the FBI, and there wasn't enough federal crime on the Oregon coast to keep me there."

Timmons walked into the room. "We got something. A Nevada Highway Patrolman stopped Anders an hour ago for a busted tail. He let Anders go with a warning. Then fifteen minutes ago he saw the all-points on Anders and recognized him. He says Anders is driving a ten-year-old Ford and gave us the tags."

"Where did he stop Anders?" Lee asked.

"That's the good news. He was stopped eastbound on Interstate 40, so now we know which way he's going. My guess is that he stays in Kingman, Arizona for the night." He grinned. "You people ready to go?"

"I hope you're right," Lee said. "Just in case you're not, we should have air support to see if he's headed forever east on 40 or diverting through Needles and into California."

"We're on the same wavelength, Lee. I just arranged for two choppers to conduct a search. With night gear, they will be able to spot the car if it's still rolling."

Six agents and Lee raced out to the parking lot and ran toward different vehicles. Timmons told Lee, "I'm sorry, man, but I'm not allowed to let you ride along. I would if I could."

"No problem," Lee said. "I have a car. I'll follow as long as we go fast enough."

* * *

Jerry saw the signs for available hotels coming up as he approached Kingman. He followed the sign, turning right from Interstate 40 onto Historic Route 66. The gold half-sun on the sign was illuminated, and the Day's Inn looked like a safe haven. He pulled up in front of the hotel office and went in to register.

"Yes, sir," a man in his sixties said, "need a room?"

"I do. A comfortable one where I can get some rest. I'm a little road weary."

"You're in luck. Take number 8. Nice queen-size bed, and a little away from the street. Make you a deal on it tonight for fifty-two dollars."

"That will be fine," Jerry said, handing the man three twenties. The man gave him change and a key, and then said, "Enjoy your stay with us."

Jerry said, "Thanks," and moved out of the lobby as quickly as possible.

Jerry parked in front of Room 8 and then put his suitcase and his duffle inside the room. He was exhausted, but he was also starving. He remembered seeing a Denny's as he exited Interstate 40. It was close enough to walk back to without difficulty. After making sure the door was securely fastened, he looked around him and saw that surrounding businesses were closed, and the area was quiet. He took a deep breath as he looked up at the stars that filled the night sky.

When he arrived at the Denny's, Jerry grabbed a seat and positioned himself so that he looked toward the door. A little caution was always in order. There was an old couple in the corner and an obese teenager on a stool at the counter. The place was otherwise empty.

"Evenin'," a woman in her twenties said. She wore a long pink flowered apron and her hair was up in a bun. "What's it gonna be?"

Jerry smiled and said, "I'll have a beer and a patty melt," he said.

"What kind of beer?"

"Got a Corona?"

"Yep."

"I'll take that."

"Okay, right back," the woman said and walked away.

Jerry saw a jukebox across the room. He went over to it and read the music menu. He dropped a dollar in the jukebox and pushed letters and numbers to play some Beatles and "Hotel California" from the Eagles. He sat down and felt relaxed for the first time in as long as he could remember. Life was definitely getting better already. He thought about becoming someone else in Charlotte, so that anyone who connected the dots between Jerry Anders and Frank Adams wouldn't find him. He would have to make a new connection in Charlotte—someone who could build him a new ID for a fair price.

The Beatles sang about "sitting on a cornflake, waiting for the van to come." The lyrics were drug-induced and nonsensical, but "I Am the Walrus" was somehow still a great song. There was something about the originality of so many of the great Beatle songs. They were all compelling and often unusual, but Lennon and McCartney could write music like no others.

Jerry picked up a local newspaper and read about a council meeting that got out of control, the new homes that were being built in the area, and the cost of living raise for city employees. His patty melt was greasy but good. He ate his way through it as he read about the local water shortage the community experienced. Imagine that, Jerry thought to himself, a water shortage in the desert. Who'd have guessed it? Don Henley and the Eagles sang about "stabbing it with their steely knives, but they just can't kill the beast," and Jerry ordered a second beer and finished it along with his sandwich as he read the sports page.

The waitress returned, snapping her gum before she spoke, "Anything else?"

"No, that's it."

"Okay, here's the check. You pay at the register."

Jerry read the classifieds. He wasn't going to stay here, but it was interesting to see what kind of work was available. A couple of banks needed tellers, a restaurant needed a cook, a couple of retail stores wanted part-time salespeople, and a repair shop needed a mechanic.

As he paid the check and left a tip, the Eagles sang "You can check out anytime you choose, but you can never leave." The words struck him as ominous, and the nervousness he carried with him was instantly back.

* * *

The four cars flew along Interstate 40 at almost a hundred miles per hour. Timmons and Barnes led the parade with a red light atop their unmarked car. Two other FBI cars followed, and Lee rode sweep. They moved around cars on the road like they were standing still. About forty-five minutes into the journey, Lee's phone rang.

"Yeah."

"Lee, it's Margo Barnes."

"I recognize the voice," he said, thinking that he sounded rather obviously flirtatious.

"We just got word that the choppers found his car. He's in Kingman at the Day's Inn."

"That is great," Lee said.

"We're about twenty minutes out. We turn left from 40 onto Route 66, and the hotel is about a block down. Our man is parked in front of Room 8."

"Thanks for the update," Lee said. "I appreciate you keeping me in the loop."

"We're going to push it a little harder. I wanted you to know where we're headed in case your rental car can't keep up."

"I'll be there as quickly as I can. Thanks."

"Good-bye, Lee." With that, he watched as the three cars in front of him accelerated to 120 miles per hour. He pushed the rental Toyota hard, but slowly the distance between him and the FBI cars ahead increased. The road was flat and straight, so he kept them in view even when they were two and three miles ahead. They just kept getting smaller. Soon they would disappear entirely.

Twenty minutes later, Lee turned off Interstate 40 and flew down Route 66. He could see the Day's Inn, and the FBI cars all surrounding Room 8. A couple of the officers were walking around the hotel. He could see a couple of others knocking on other doors. He knew in an instant that they had missed Anders.

* * *

Jerry stepped out of the diner and looked toward the Day's Inn. He froze in his tracks. There were three cars parked all around his and blocking his movement. The place was abuzz with activity as people he was sure were plainclothes cops moved around the building. How in the world did they find him? Maybe it was the Highway Patrol cop that had stopped him.

He couldn't go back to his room. His clothes and most of his remaining money had to be left behind. He was glad he put about fifteen hundred in cash in his wallet. In a few minutes they would be over at the diner as they expanded their search. Thinking of nothing else he could do, Jerry walked the opposite direction along Route 66. He had no idea where to go, but he knew he needed to get as far away as he could as fast as he could.

Jerry decided it would be too risky to hitchhike on Interstate 40. There was Highway Patrol as well as the group back at the Day's Inn, who would know that he was on foot and probably looking for a ride out of town. Jerry stayed on Route 66, walking for about an hour and a half. He tried to get a ride, but the few cars on the road didn't stop.

He was a good distance from where he started and figured he would be safe to sleep for a few hours. He would get back on the road before the sun rose. As he walked, he saw an Orchard Inn. It looked perfect. He checked in and paid fifty-three dollars in cash. The woman behind the counter told him he could park near Room 22 and gave him the key.

Inside the small room, Jerry dialed for an automated wake-up call at 5:00 a.m. He was exhausted. He laid down on the bed without undressing and was asleep in minutes.

* * *

The hotel conference room became a middle of the night command center. Calls were made to surrounding businesses, hotels, restaurants, and bars. Physical description was given and inquiries were made about whether Frank Adams had been near each contact. FBI agents, city police, and Highway Patrol went in every direction, searching Interstate 40 and its off-ramps and Route 66 and cross streets for miles. They monitored taxis and truck drivers in the area to see if any hitchhiker had been picked up. They set up immediate alerts in the event of any car theft anywhere along the Interstate 40 corridor. The choppers watched it all from overhead.

Police officers were assigned to drive about sixty miles farther on to Needles, California, and with the help of local police, they began searching that city. Officers also searched nearby residential areas by going door to door with a picture of Frank Adams. They searched nearby wilderness areas on foot.

Lee was among those searching all along Route 66. He drove around each business, searching on foot behind businesses when it appeared there might be somewhere to hide. He checked in to the command post for updates every half hour. It was now 1:20 a.m., and the search involved over two hundred officers. None of them found any trace of Anders. At 1:30 a.m. and again at 2:00 a.m. Lee checked in, but there was nothing. The man had disappeared once again.

Lee continued searching but found no trace. At two thirty, Lee called in again, feeling discouraged. From the headquarters at the Day's Inn, he was told, "We have a hit; get back here quickly."

Chapter 37

There had been no wake-up call yet, but Jerry suddenly jumped up in bed, wide awake. He checked his watch. It was only 3:10 a.m., but he felt like the walls were closing in. He had to leave now.

He washed his face and made his way to the door. Maybe he could hitch a ride with an eastbound trucker. When he opened the door, his world came crashing down. Cops were lined up across the hotel. Floodlights hit him, and someone with a megaphone told him to step out slowly.

Jerry hesitated for a single moment and then jumped back inside and slammed the door. He sat on the bed and listened.

"Jerry Anders, this is the FBI. Come out with your hands raised. There is nowhere for you to go. The hotel is surrounded."

He looked around the room, realizing that there was no way out. This was the end of his run, and he was going to be taken into custody. He sat on the bed and stared at the wall shaking his head. He just couldn't go back to prison. This time it would be twenty-five years or more. He could not survive it. He didn't want to survive it.

He saw a metal flashlight on the end table next to the bed and made a decision in an instant. He picked it up and stuffed it into his right pant pocket, so that only the handle was visible. He thought about Vickie and how he would miss her. He thought about the Winslow kid, and one more time hoped that he was going to make it. Then he walked to the door and yelled, "I'm coming out."

Jerry opened the door and walked outside.

"Raise your hands," a voice yelled. He did not move his arms. "Raise your hands now!" the voice yelled louder.

Jerry reached for the flashlight and pulled it from his pocket and ran at the officers twenty feet away. He lifted the flashlight and pointed it at the line of cops as he raced forward. There were screams, and then three sudden bursts of gunfire filled the night air. In an instant, Jerry fell to the ground.

* * *

At noon, I am sitting beside Joey reading. Lisa walks into the room holding a cup of coffee in each hand and glances over at Joey. Her eyes open wide, and her expression is of stunned disbelief. I look at Joey, and his eyes are open.

"Joey. Hi, son," I say. No response.

Lisa puts the coffee down and takes his hand. "Hi, Joey. Mom is here." No response.

We watch as Joey seems to look to the right, then to the left, and then straight up at the ceiling. He does not seem to see us or know that we are there. Then he closes his eyes, and he is gone from us again.

Lisa is crying. "Joey, can you hear me. Please come back." No sign of contact.

"Joe, can you hear me buddy?" I say softly. "Mom and Dad are right here." No response. He has gone somewhere far away again—somewhere that we can't reach.

We hold each other for a time, both of us fearing the worst. He was here and couldn't make contact with us. Is that all there will ever be? Have we lost him?

Dr. Mitchell is summoned and arrives in ten minutes. We tell him what happened, and then he examines Joey.

After a time, he looks at us and says, "I can't see any change. There is really no way to account for those kinds of occurrences, except we know that sometimes patients unconsciously open their eyes and engage in a variety of movements involuntarily."

"So does this tell us anything?" I ask in desperation.

"Not really. It could be the beginning of something more. It might just be disassociated bodily movement."

Dr. Mitchell says, "I'm sorry I can't give you more. I'll check back later."

He walks from the room to leave Lisa and me nursing new wounds. We had come so close to what we have been waiting for all these months, and it may be nothing. We stand watching our son for the longest time, but there is no more movement. I have a sinking feeling in the pit of my stomach. There are no words to say how harrowing it is to come that close to a miracle and have it turn out to be a false alarm.

I pick up Katy from school at 2:00 p.m. As we walk into the hospital room at 2:20, I look at Lisa to gauge her expression. She just shakes her head. Katy runs over to the bed to show Joey the drawing of an elephant seal she made at school today. She is accustomed to the way it is. She tells him all about elephant seals: their long excursions to mate and their extended beach stays for birth of their young. She never expects a response. Then she finds a spot on the floor, sits down, and pulls out her homework. It is all a normal part of her day.

At just after 4:00 p.m., Katy is looking at my iPad to see pictures of the Great Wall of China, her latest fascination. Lisa and I sit by Joey's bed. Lisa reviews a real estate contract, and I make notes about what preparation is needed on the Walters case, which goes to trial in a few weeks.

"Daddy," Katy says with furrowed brow, "why did they need to build a wall this big in the first place?"

"Good question, sweetie. As I recall, they wanted to keep enemies away, so that no one could attack their empire."

"They had empires?" she asks. "Like Star Wars?"

"Oh my God," Lisa yells, and we look at her. She stands and walks to the bed. We turn to see Joey with open eyes again. He appears to be looking around.

"Joey," Lisa says. He silently looks around. "Joey," she says one more time.

He appears to be looking at us, but we can't tell if he sees us. There is a quiet moment, and then Joey squints and says, "Where are we anyway?"

We throw our arms around him. "Joey, can you hear me?" I ask.

"Sure," he says with a raspy voice.

"You can hear me?" I ask again, not yet believing.

"Yeah," he says.

"How are you?" I ask, thinking that is a rather inept question as I ask.

"What's this stuff sticking into me?"

"You had a fall, Joey. The doctors have been fixing you up."

"Hi, Joey; I missed you," Katy says. "Want to see some cool pictures of the Great Wall of China?"

"Yeah. Let me see."

Lisa summons the nurse, who comes in quickly and stares like she isn't prepared for the occasion. "Hi, young man."

"Hi," Joey says. "How come I'm here?"

Lisa is crying, and I am pushing back tears. The nurse looks at Joey, and she too begins to cry. She looks at us with a wide grin. "If this isn't a miracle, I don't know what is," she says softly. "You hungry, Joey?"

"Yeah."

"All right, let me see what I'm allowed to give you." She walks out of the room.

In two minutes she appears with ice cream that Joey consumes in record time. In ten minutes, Dr. Mitchell is in the room. He nods to us, a big smile on his face, and then goes over to Joey. "How are you, young man?"

"I'm okay. I have kind of a headache, and I'm still hungry."

"Do you know who these folks are?" Dr. Mitchell asks.

Joey gives him an "Is this a joke?" look and then says, "Of course. They are my mom and dad."

"Who is this person here?" Dr. Mitchell asks, pointing to Katy.

Joey gives him another strange look and says, "Don't you know my sister?"

Dr. Mitchell smiles and says, "Oh yeah. I guess I do remember her." He nods approval and then says, "Joey, do you remember where you were right before you came here?"

Joey reflects a moment and then says, "Me and Katy were trapped in some big building, and we couldn't get out."

Dr. Mitchell's face is alight. "This is amazing. More tests in twenty minutes, okay?"

We nod. As he walks out, we go over to Joey and hug him again, and again, and until we are beginning to annoy him. And we all know that this is a miracle.

* * *

After they take Joey for more testing, I check my phone and see that I have a voice mail message from Lee Henry. I hit the button and Lee's voice says, "We got him, Scott. I'm with the FBI, and we nailed him in Kingman, Arizona. Call me back when you can."

I play the message on speaker so Lisa can hear it. "Oh my God," she says, staring back at me. "They got Jerry Anders. After all this time, they got him."

I hit a button, and I get Lee's voice mail message. "You have my number, so you must have something to say to me." Then the beep.

"Lee, this is Scott. We got your message, great news. We have some of our own as well. Joey is awake. Call me."

I look at Lisa, and she is smiling widely. She comes over to me and gives me a kiss. "I almost don't want to let myself believe we have him back," she says. "Just in case something goes wrong."

I nod. "It is incredible, but I feel like we are walking on eggshells. Like it could all somehow disappear, and our son is gone again."

We both pull Katy into our hug. She says, "I'm glad Joey is back from wherever he went." She pauses and adds, "Do you think he saw heaven?"

"I don't know, sweetheart. You'll have to ask him."

I turn on the TV and see news coverage of the capture in Kingman. The anchor says, "Fugitive Jerry Anders was shot last night in
Kingman, Arizona. The FBI surrounded the motel where Anders was
staying. At about 3:00 a.m., when Anders saw that he was surrounded,
it appears that he attempted suicide by police. He was shot in the right
shoulder but will survive to face trial. Apparently, Anders has spent
the last several months working at a Las Vegas casino under the name
Frank Adams. Law enforcement found him and chased him to Kingman, where last night's showdown took place. This is Michael Ortiz,
for Channel 4 News."

My phone rings. "Hello."

Lee says, "Your message is great, Scott. Damn, that is the best news
of all."

"We still can't believe it. He's awake, and he seems to be unimpaired.
Still holding our breath." I take a moment and then say, "Thank you
for everything, Lee."

"It's my job." He took a moment and added. "And you're my friends."

"When are you back in town?"

"I'll be back tomorrow."

"I'll buy the coffee," I say. "Call me when you're back."

"You're on. See you tomorrow."

It was five minutes later that Joey returned to the room with
Dr. Mitchell right behind him, still grinning. "Brain swelling is less
than 10 percent of what it was. We will do a little more testing, but it
looks like he made it through all of this with no significant residual."
He looked at Lisa and me and added, "I can't tell you the exact odds
on this recovery, but it's fair to say that you guys won the lottery."

* * *

I hug Lee in the middle of the coffee shop where we meet. It was like
brothers who hadn't seen each other for years. And that's how I feel
about him. "You were amazing, Lee. I am in your debt forever, my
friend."

He shrugs. "Anytime, my friend. You have been there for me as well. When I was starting my fledging business, you were the guy who kept tossing me assignments. It's what friends do for each other." He adds, "I am just so glad that Joey is okay."

His compassionate expression slowly turns to a grin. "What?" I ask.

"Well, I guess I benefited from the trip to Vegas, too."

"Yeah, how?"

"I got a date with a gorgeous FBI agent."

"Really?"

"Yeah. Believe it or not, I'm going back to Vegas Saturday to take her out."

"Wow. You must really like her."

"I think I do. She mentioned that we had a 'geographically undesirable' issue that might be a problem. I told her that we should take it date by date. I know this is crazy, but this woman is really something. I'm already thinking about weekends together, and I don't even know if she likes me that much."

"I get it," I say. "I still feel that way about Lisa. After all these years, I still react when she walks into the room."

We finish our coffee, and Lee says, "Will you walk out to the car with me?"

"Sure," I say.

We walk to his car, and he opens the trunk and hands me a cloth shopping bag. I look inside and see bundled cash. "What is this?" I ask.

"You're a lawyer. I know you've seen money from time to time." He grins. "This is the balance after my out-of-pocket expenses of chasing Anders were deducted."

"Balance from what?"

"Call it contributions to Joey's medical bills from a compassionate, creative artist who desperately wanted to lend a hand."

* * *

September 17, 2016

Joey is released from the hospital, and we get to take him home today. All of his tests are good. No brain injury, no memory deficits—just pure miracle.

When we get home, the kids go upstairs to play, and Lisa and I are left alone in the living room. I put my arms around her and kiss her.

"Wow," she says. "What did I do to earn that?"

"It's a long list, but in a nutshell, you gave me those two characters upstairs, and you and they are the essence of my life. I am grateful."

"Me too," she says. "We made it through some dark times, and I believe that we were given a miracle."

From upstairs we hear, "Give that back. That's mine."

"Get out of my room," is the response.

"You are a butthead."

And with that conversation, we know our family is back. We laugh, and then I kiss my lovely wife again.

October 13, 2016

When Jerry Anders was patched up and returned to Los Angeles, the media filled the courtroom where his arraignment was to occur. There were other reporters in a courtroom down the hall, where the proceeding was being televised to accommodate all of the demand.

"Next case is the People v. Gerald Anders," Judge Robert Hughes announced.

"Good morning, Your Honor. Brad Segar for the people."

"Yes, Your Honor," Kathy Carter of the Public Defender's Office for Mr. Anders."

"Read the charges, please."

The courtroom clerk stood and read, "Kidnapping, two counts; false imprisonment, two counts; and extortion; two counts assault and battery."

Jerry stood next to Kathy Carter without movement or expression. The judge regarded him briefly and then said, "How does your client plead, Ms. Carter?"

"Not guilty, Your Honor."

"As to the defendant's request for bail, it is denied. There is no doubt that Mr. Anders is a flight risk."

Judge Hughes looked at the clerk and then at his computer monitor. "Okay, the preliminary hearing for December 8, 2016. See you all then."

Jerry was escorted away while flashes went off all around him. Reporters scribbled notes, and photographers positioned for clear pictures. Jerry never turned around to see that Vickie sat in the back of the courtroom, watching her brother without expression. She fought for him so many times, but there had to be limits, and he had reached those limits when he endangered Katy and Joey Winslow. If he was to spend the rest of his days in prison, she would come to terms with that. If their parents were watching her, they would see how hard she tried to help her brother.

Chapter 38

November 15, 2016

It took a full day to select the twelve citizens who would serve as the jury in the case of Kevin Walters v. Consolidated Energy. Our jury consists of a social worker, a newspaper editor, a small-business owner, a city engineer, a homemaker, a retail store employee, a receiving dock supervisor, a painter, an investment adviser, a tech industry programmer, and two retired workers, one from the hospitality industry and the other from the financial industry. We have five women and seven men.

Juries are, in every sense, our neighbors. They are the people walking around CVS and Costco and filling their cars at the gas station. They are the people who sell you insurance and the people who buy the car you are selling. They are a cross-section of every type of background, culture, and employment history, with one exception. No one employed in the industry involved in the case will be allowed to remain on the jury. They must decide the matter based upon the evidence and law they get in court, not their preconceived notions of the way an industry works. Otherwise, different jurors would be deciding a case based upon different facts—facts that would not be admissible in court for good reason.

So, in arriving at an agreed jury, Harris and I asked endless questions about preconceived notions about the parties and the industry, about philosophies that they hold that would make it hard for them to be fair to our respective clients, and about anything, other than the evidence and the law that they are about to hear, that will influence their verdict in our case. It is a system that I have endless faith in, and it is a system that works because most people take the obligation to serve as a conscientious juror very seriously.

Kevin Walters sits next to me at the counsel table. Michael Constantine is here for opening statements and sits next to Bob Harris. As we begin the second day of this trial, the court reporter occupies space between us and the judge.

"Please stand," the bailiff instructs, and everyone in the packed courtroom does. "Department 39 of the Superior Court for the County of Los Angeles is now in session, the Honorable Roy Carswell presiding."

Carswell enters from chambers and walks to the bench. He glances at his computer, then to each of the parties at the counsel tables. Seeing that we are all in our assigned places, Judge Carswell looks over at the jury. "Ladies and gentlemen, you are about to hear opening statements in this case. The opening statements of the parties are not evidence, but they are the opportunities of both parties to tell you what they believe the evidence will show you." He looks at me. "Mr. Winslow, are you ready to proceed?"

"Yes, Your Honor." I stand and move to the open area next to the witness stand, from which I can look directly at the jurors and move around as I speak. "May it please the court, counsel, ladies and gentlemen of the jury. As you know, I am Scott Winslow, and I represent Mr. Walters. Good morning to each of you, and congratulations on having made it through the jury selection process." I become more serious and say, "You have been told that this is a whistle-blower case. Let me tell you more about what the evidence will show you. Kevin Walters served the defendant, Consolidated Energy, for in excess of twenty-seven years. He worked his way up through the ranks to become a senior vice president, reporting directly to Michael Constantine, the president and CEO. He successfully performed in that role for the last seven years of his twenty-seven-year career.

"You will hear from a number of witnesses that Mr. Walters was good at his job and that he cared greatly about the company. He also cared about protecting the safety of the employees who worked in the mines. You will see that Kevin had eight different positions during his career, six of which involved mine safety, and he was vigilant about watching out for safety issues and protecting workers. During his years in all of these positions, he received compliments, commendations, salary increases, and bonuses. He also received seven promotions and continued to move up in the organization, all the way up to senior vice president, reporting directly to the president and CEO, Michael Constantine."

I let that settle for a moment and then continued. "In 2015 and 2016, Kevin raised concerns about a number of safety issues in a mine, including S&S conditions. S&S are conditions that pose an immediate threat of serious injury or illness to workers. The conditions he complained about include serious ventilation issues, inadequate safety equipment, failing substructure, and inadequate tunnel maintenance. Those are conditions that seriously threatened the safety of workers. Mr. Walters's demand for action to correct some of these conditions was overruled by Mr. Constantine, who thought that it would cost too much. Some of these same issues that Mr. Walters raised became S&S violations, for which the company was cited. Then there was an explosion that killed one and injured three, and Mr. Walters was fired for making complaints about safety conditions that the company did not want to hear.

"You will hear Mr. Walters testify about each of the specific issues he raised concerns about. You will hear other managers testify that they are aware that Mr. Walters was concerned about and raised these issues. And you will hear Mr. Constantine tell you that he doesn't remember whether Mr. Walters raised those issues. And you, ladies and gentlemen, are the judges of who is providing more credible information.

"A couple of important things you should know. The company is going to try to tell you that Mr. Walters's performance in the last year was the reason he was fired. Question that long and hard because the evidence will show you otherwise. Mr. Walters received an energy association award three months before his termination. The energy association award was presented to him by Mr. Constantine in front of many other energy industry companies and employees. Some of them will be here to tell you what they heard. At the time of that award, Mr. Constantine told the crowd that Mr. Walters did great work and that Consolidated was lucky to have him. This was three months before he was fired, purportedly for poor performance over the last twelve months.

"Two months before he was terminated, Mr. Constantine complimented Mr. Walters on his work. That happened in front of some of his colleagues. Two of them will appear to tell you what they heard.

"You will also learn that the company gave bonuses based on performance and that Mr. Walters received a big bonus shortly before his termination. His performance-based bonus was larger than that received by Mr. Clayton or Mr. Peters, the two executives of equal rank to Mr. Walters, and, of course, they were not fired or disciplined. In fact, each of them considered their bonuses to be a reflection of good performance.

"We told you at the outset that you are to decide this case based upon the facts presented to you and the instructions of law you receive from the court. The other thing that you can use and that you are not required to leave at the door is your common sense. When you hear the company say that Mr. Walters was fired for unsatisfactory performance during the last year, your common sense will tell you otherwise.

"But this is only part of the story. We are seeking punitive damages in this case because the company acted with fraud and malice. They acted to endanger, rather than protect, employees, and then they acted to cover it up. You will learn that one of the director-level executives at Consolidated hired a covert operations organization to force the county representatives to alter the records to eliminate violations of record where the explosion occurred. The person hired by the company then blackmailed the county manager responsible for keeping the county records. He was threatened with the ruination of his career based on false accusations if he didn't alter records. They gave the county employee a choice of going to jail based on false charges they had created or altering records for Consolidated Energy and receiving $50,000 to retire far away. You will hear deposition testimony from that county employee about all of this. You will hear that the records were changed by the county employee as Consolidated required because he was blackmailed by the third party—the third party that Consolidated Energy hired to get the records changed. And you know what else? This won't be denied by Consolidated Energy. They are going to tell you that this happened. Then they are going to tell you when they found out who did it, they fired this executive."

The jurors seem fully captivated and appropriately shocked. They all watch me, awaiting what comes next. "We say to you that they ultimately sacrificed one executive, but that makes no difference. The company acted to endanger its workers in order to save money. The company fired Mr. Walters for demanding action to correct problems. The company then hired someone to force the county to change the records to cover up the fact that they failed to make corrections of known conditions. One worker died and others were injured as a result of the conditions that they did not want to spend money to correct."

I walk a little while this information settles, and then I look back at the jury. "The cover-up came about because of a culture that allowed dangerous conditions to exist if they were expensive to correct. That one person was fired doesn't change what they did. That doesn't change what they didn't do—failing to promptly correct life-threatening conditions. And it doesn't change anything for Mr. Walters, a twenty-seven-year executive with an incredible track record who wanted nothing more than to protect the safety of the company workers whose service he valued."

I look at the jury and see that I still have them enrapt. Harris and Constantine can see, too. Twelve sets of eyes are glued on me. "When you dedicate twenty-seven years to a company, your self-image and self-worth comes from the work that you do. It's part of your identity that you have done so well with this company. It was part of Mr. Walters's identity that he spent his career trying to protect workers in dangerous occupations. And on a single day, all of that was taken from Mr. Walters. We are going to ask you to award him damages for the anxiety, humiliation, depression, and emotional injury he has suffered as a result of the loss of his career.

"He has also suffered significant and ongoing financial losses that should never have happened. You will hear the testimony of Dr. Graham Johnston, an economist who will compute those total economic losses for you.

"Finally, we will ask you for punitive damages in an amount sufficient to punish Consolidated Energy for their malicious and fraudulent conduct. They fired an admittedly dedicated, career-long employee for attempting to protect workers. We believe that you will find this conduct to be malice. They attempted to cover up their knowledge of serious safety violations that they elected not to fix. Why? Money. Money valued over human life. We think you will find that this lack of regard for human life and lack of regard for those attempting to protect human life is malice.

"This case is about accountability for corporate behavior that endangered the lives of workers. When you operate a business that is inherently dangerous, you have a responsibility to employees to protect them in every possible way. When that responsibility is disregarded, and the danger is ignored to save money, and when they then attempt to cover up what they have done, they need to be held accountable. And you are the only ones who can hold them accountable. We will ask you for punitive damages in an amount that sends a strong message to the company that none of this conduct is okay, and they will not get away with sacrificing worker safety—that which should be their first and foremost consideration.

"Thank you for your attention this morning, ladies and gentlemen. And thank you for the careful consideration that I know you will give the evidence in this matter. I look forward to having the opportunity to speak with you again after you have heard all of the evidence and before the matter is given to you by the court for a fair and appropriate verdict."

On the way back to my seat, I look at Lisa, who sits in the back of the courtroom. She gives me a nod and a smile. I glance at Bob Harris, who looks appropriately concerned. When I sit down, Kevin pats me on the shoulder and whispers, "Thank you."

We take our noon recess, and Lee is waiting at the door of the courtroom to talk to me. "Hi, Lee. Do we have a problem with one of our witnesses?"

He grins. "No, to the contrary. I received a message that Carl Miller will make himself available to testify if you want him here in person."

I look at him curiously. "He will get arrested if he shows up here."

Lee nods. "Yep. He doesn't care. I think it is some combination of wanting to stand up against the people who forced him out of his career and wanting to assist us because we helped him when he was in trouble."

"Wow," I say, "that's incredible. I don't want to call him unless we really have to though. He's a good guy, and I don't want him to wake up in jail when this is all over. Get a message to him that we really appreciate what he is doing, but we won't call him unless it is an emergency."

"Shall do," Lee says. "By the way, I got all of the witness subpoenas served. I gave Donna the signed agreements from each to come when they are called rather than sitting here for a week or two. I think all is in order." He pauses and adds. "Great opening, by the way. Jurors were going with you."

"Thanks, Lee. You have been unbelievable through all of this. I owe you so much."

"No way," he says. "Just friends being friends."

As Lee walks away, Bob Harris comes over to me. He says, "We need to talk. I have some additional authority to get the case settled."

"Sure," I say. "Let's take a walk down the hall."

As I walk down the courthouse corridor with Harris until we are away from jurors, I am content. I don't know if we will be able to settle this case, but either way, it will be fine. I will give my faith to this jury. Even if Kevin does not settle or win this action, he is starting his safety monitoring company, Protective Environmental Services, for the benefit of the mining industry. I suspect that a settlement or verdict in this case will assist him in getting the business going, and I can't think of anyone who deserves it more.

As for me, I have my family back. Joey is healthy, getting good grades, and playing baseball with no residual from his months of coma. Katy is in charge of, well, everything. And Lisa is gorgeous and brilliant and still the girl of my dreams. And I am doing what I love.

We stop at the end of the hall. "So," Harris says, "here's what we are prepared to do ..."

About the Author

David P. Warren is an experienced trial attorney, advocate, and negotiator with many years of experience focusing on employment litigation. He has handled numerous cases through trial and appeal and represented many whistle-blowers. That experience placed him at the center of litigation focused on proving that employees were fired for raising concerns about safety issues or because they reported fraudulent or unlawful conduct of their employers.

David draws on his extensive experience to bring you *The Whistle-Blower Onslaught*, the story of an energy industry executive alleging he was fired for complaining of uncorrected conditions in coal mines, which resulted in disaster, and the perils resulting from the lawsuit that follows. David P. Warren has written two previous novels, *Altering Destiny* and *Sealing Fate*.

David P. Warren has a passion for storytelling and for characters with human frailties that face situations and obstacles beyond their control. His novels present characters you will feel you know, as you accompany them through fast-paced journeys with many unforeseen surprises.